FALSE LIGHTS

K.J. WHITTAKER is the Carnegie-
nominated author of six YA novels
published by Walker Books under the
name Katy Moran. She lives
in Shropshire.

K.J. WHITTAKER

FALSE LIGHTS

HEAD
ZEUS

First published in the UK in 2017 by Head of Zeus, Ltd.

9 7 5 3 1 2 4 6 8

A catalogue record for this book is available from
the British Library.

ISBN (HB): 9781786695345
ISBN (XTPB): 9781786695352
ISBN (E): 9781786695338

For Suki Kate Bwalya Bell, with love

On 18 June 1815, Napoleon Bonaparte won a narrow victory at the battle of Waterloo. Europe was immediately catapulted into uncharted territory.

Bonaparte left the Duke of Wellington's defeated army in Brussels and marched his own troops to Ostend. Those who survived the two-day ordeal forcibly boarded English transport ships waiting for Wellington's men.

Sailing past the English blockade under false colours, Bonaparte landed five thousand men in Folkestone. With the navy in tatters, many thousands more were soon to land in Cornwall where – after generations of brutal oppression by the English – the Cornish had little choice but to let them pass unchallenged. Promised sovereignty, it did not take the Cornish long to realise they had been betrayed.

By Christmas, the king and the prince regent were both dead, and Bonaparte had placed his younger brother, Jérôme, on the throne of England.

Imprisoned in the Tower of London, the Duke of Wellington remained there for more than a year.

In March 1817, he disappeared.

PART ONE

Isles of Scilly,
Cornwall, 1817

I

Hester killed her first man at Castle Bryher. It happened
after she ran down Shipman Head and scrambled home
across rocks laid bare by the retreating tide, a pair of grouse in
one hand and the pistol at her waist. Tall and built on generous
lines, she slithered across heaps of bladderwrack, ran swift-
footed up barnacle-crusted steps of granite and clattered into
the stillroom on the ground floor of the tower, her light brown
cheeks flushed with the effort. Spirals of hair sprang free of a
frayed green linen headscarf knotted at a rakish angle, and the
wide hem of her oldest muslin gown was sodden, scattering
sand across flagstones swept only that morning. Papa always
said the stillroom had been used for centuries as an armoury
but the curving walls were now neatly whitewashed and hung
with copper pans kept at a liquid shine by Hester's housekeeper, Catlin.

Sitting at a vast scrubbed table littered with neat heaps of
gathered herbs and stacks of bowls, Hester glanced up from the
cleaning of her gun just as Catlin herself came in. Those long-
dead Royalist soldiers had left behind more than their initials
scratched into the ceiling joists: once or twice in a generation,

a child like Catlin Rescorla would still be born to an island family with hair the rust-red of last year's heather and the dark, expressive eyes of the Stuart kings. She eyed the two dead birds and the oil-smeared cloth, looking every inch as warlike as her long-dead mainland ancestors must have done.

Hester was instantly contrite. 'I'm sorry, Cat. I'll clean up.'

Catlin wiped pale, freckled hands on her apron with brisk impatience. 'Miss, why couldn't you have stripped the piece down in the gunroom where it belongs?' She sat down and bent her head over the pestle and mortar, grinding dried geranium petals.

'Because then I would have been on my own,' Hester replied. They both spoke in Cornish, a habit ploughed so deep that English would have seemed unnatural.

Catlin didn't look up from her pestle but the set of her shoulders softened. Strands of dark red hair curled loose around her face, escaping the black bombazine cap she'd worn since the news came that Tom had died at the battle of Waterloo. Silence stretched between them, making a mockery of long-ago nights falling asleep beneath the same ancient crewel-work coverlet, whispering of seal-maids and the souls of drowned sailors.

'I don't know what you mean by it, anyway,' Catlin said at last, without looking up from the task of pouring a stream of whale oil into her bowl. 'You ought to know better than to be crawling up Shipman Head with a pistol. What's got into you?'

Hester stared down at her hands, her fingers grimy with gunpowder and oil. 'Papa has written to Mr Williams again.' It was her duty to marry well, but in truth she'd been relieved when Buonaparte's escape from his island prison and the outbreak of war put an end to negotiations with the Sierra Leonean tea merchant. Now, eighteen months after the defeat and the Occupation, Papa had decided it was time to secure her future.

Catlin shrugged, unsympathetic. 'Mr Williams seemed a kindly enough man to judge from that letter you got, and he's black like yourself, and well educated, and he's got money, too. Your papa says he's built a fine house in Freetown with coconut palms in the garden, whatever they might be. Africa's a long way, but what would you rather – some English nobleman with nothing in the bank and all his friends sneering at you? Such a husband would think he'd made you a gift of his title even as he got his soft hands on all your fortune, miss.'

'Do you really think I want some minor squire to get his hands on everything my father worked for?' Hester demanded. Despite Papa's naval honours and a veneer of respectability acquired in the eyes of those in power, the colour of his skin had barred his entry to the halls of the Exchange. This had not prevented him instructing a broker with Abolitionist leanings to make a series of spectacular investments. Prize money earned capturing French ships had given birth to the sort of fortune that led mothers of marriageable sons from Penzance to St Austell into appallingly transparent attempts to conceal their disgust at Hester's lineage. The notion of marriage into any such family, or even to kindly Mr Williams of Sierra Leone, was insupportable. 'Listen, Cat – no wife has time to paint, let alone to shoot grouse. I'd rather be single forever. It's hardly as if I should be destitute.' Hester was immediately sorry, knowing that Catlin would have given anything to be a wife rather than a widow.

Catlin shook her head, funnelling the geranium oil into one green glass bottle after another. Silence reigned again, and for so long that Hester was almost glad to hear heavy footfalls in the passageway. Wiping her hands on the skirts of her gown, she stepped round the table to meet the trespasser in Catlin's undisputed domain. The door flew open with such force that Hester put out her arms to stop it. It was no ordinary islander but Papa himself, collapsing against the doorframe and bleeding from his mouth. He clutched at his belly, his white shirt blooming crimson. He dropped to his knees, trying to speak.

Catlin ran to him but Hester flew backwards, taking up her reassembled pistol.

'*Nne*—' Papa choked, falling to his knees, thick dark blood seeping from one corner of his mouth. Catlin screamed. '*Nne m o!*' Papa cried again, his meaning unintelligible to Hester. Scrabbling at the table, her fingers closed around a cartridge and with a swift jerk she bit off the end and tasted the bitter burn of gunpowder before forcing the live cartridge down the barrel of her gun. As she lit the powder, four white French soldiers surged in, a rush of filthy blue jackets, old sweat and foul breath. Hester fired, and the first man she had ever killed dropped to the flagstones at her feet, leaving heaped grey brain matter seeping from the shattered remains of his skull.

2

Hester huddled at the stern of a stolen oyster-boat, spray-drenched and rigid with disbelieving grief. God alone knew where the soldiers meant to take her. Why had they come? Papa had feared the French would garrison Scilly as the Parliamentarians had done hundreds of years ago. Acting under Wellington's final orders in 1815, Admiral Comey had destroyed Star Castle on St Mary's as what was left of the navy limped across the Atlantic, leaving Castle Bryher as the obvious target. And so now they had come and Papa was dead. At least if these men meant to kill her too, surely they would have done it by now? After twelve hours at sea the violent shivering had settled, but every time Hester closed her eyes she saw her father's blood in a dark shiny puddle on the flagstones and the French soldier's brains splattered up the whitewashed wall. If Catlin were still alive, she would be furious about the mess. Hester couldn't begin to comprehend that Catlin might also be dead, for surely Papa could not really be gone. Disjointed memories flickered through her mind like moths seeking candlelight. In the days before Papa's naval duties were confined to manning Castle Bryher, whenever he came home on leave she would run away from her lessons with Cousin Jane and tease him into playing at Trafalgar. Assembling the island children, Papa would re-enact his finest hour in the great hall, or sometimes up on Shipman Head Down. *You shall be the* Belle, *Hettie, moving up to attack the* Scipion. *We gave them a time of it! Catlin, you are the* Victory. *Move up to fire your guns at the* Mont Blanc, *and now have at poor Levillegris. That's the trick, Jacca, the poor man went down honourably.* And then in her mind she saw Papa again; she'd cradled his head in her lap as he died. *Bang, bang, you're dead. Now get up.* He could not get up; he would never get up. She'd left him dead, his sightless eyes staring up at her. *Nne* – what had he meant by that? *Nne m o!* What had he been trying to tell her? They were not words in English, Cornish or French, but some other language from his own unspoken past; in not understanding her own father's last words, Hester felt torn from her sense of self, just as she had been forced from her home – she was no longer Miss Harewood of Castle Bryher, but a rootless, unprotected creature.

The youngest soldier had the tiller – just some *seigneur*'s son learning at speed that there was more to sailing than it had appeared when his papa's manservant crewed the day-yacht. Spittle flecked his downy chin as he shouted panicked orders that no one had the skill or inclination to obey. Hester could have done better herself – far better. Stationed on a remote archipelago with a long history of harassment by Dutch pirates, Captain John Harewood had made sure his daughter knew how to sail a small craft, but it was best her captors had no notion of it. Numb, Hester dug her fingertips into the flesh of her arms, forcing herself to stay awake, not knowing how she would bear having no notion what had happened to Catlin, to her entire household.

The mist lifted a little as they neared the mainland, and Buonaparte's ships loomed across Mount's Bay like a string of sinister dark pearls. No English or Cornish ship could sail beyond the stranglehold of the blockade, and neither could trade be done. Buonaparte must be such a vengeful man: not content with winning a war, he clearly meant to grind the British Isles into starved submission. Beyond the blockade, the mainland was gloomy with fog, green and purple moorland just visible behind the port of Marazion, a cluster of slate-roofed cottages glittering with lamplight visible only in snatches when one of the ships manoeuvred.

Hester watched Marazion swing away to the east – if the French had hoped to make landfall in the shelter of Mount's Bay they would be disappointed. The wind was blowing from an odd quarter and they were still much too far west. These useless French soldiers had no hope of navigating the wild, rock-strewn waters around Gwennap Head. Futile rage swept through her, and then disbelief. How could Papa have left her alone to face this? How could he really be gone? She'd barely begun on his portrait: most of it was just red chalk; her paint brushes were still drying by the sink in the scullery. It had been so very hard to get him to sit quietly indoors to be sketched. Now he would never move again save the slow sinking of his flesh into earth, into bone. He'd always hated so much to be still. Hester sat and watched rain and spray dripping from the sails and realised that not only were the soldiers arguing again, their voices sharp with exhaustion, but that she was now the topic of disagreement.

The oldest soldier spoke first, his hard gaze slithering from Hester to the rest of the men. 'You must be out of your mind, Dubois. Ney said to take her straight to headquarters. If you want to risk poking a finger in that kind of wasp's nest, be my guest. You know what Ney's like, expecting orders obeyed to the last letter at the best of times. For the love of Christ, he's got the Duke of Wellington.'

Hester stared firmly at the billowing mainsail. Please God she'd banished any hint of understanding from her expression. Wellington himself was on Bryher. Casting a quick glance at her captors, it was clear they hadn't the smallest suspicion that after eleven years of Cousin Jane's careful tuition, she spoke fluent French. She fought a crazed desire to laugh, thinking how provident it was that poor, genteel Jane hadn't lived to see her charge taken as an unchaperoned prisoner into the company of four strange men.

'Look,' snapped one of the other soldiers – Dubois, she supposed – 'are you really suggesting we let that lazy rat's bastard at the garrison just sit back and take all the glory? De Mornay's the one who'll either guillotine the slut or send her up to London so that King Jérôme and Joséphine can watch someone else do it, not us. It's Harewood's brat. They'll want to make him pay for Trafalgar. She's worth making an example of.'

'Hasn't Ney done that already? We left Harewood dead.' The *seigneur*'s son at the tiller spoke right over Hester's head.

'Aye, as she left Boisson.' When Dubois glanced at Hester his face was blank, an expression she recognised and which sent fresh tendrils of fear creeping down her spine. Nobody on Bryher ever looked at her so – as though she were less than human, a creature with no soul – but on the mainland it happened often. Papa had always quickened his step when they passed such people, hurrying Hester away with one arm round her shoulders. Dubois shrugged. 'Think about it. We can take the little bitch to de Mornay at the garrison and get nothing for our pains, or we can earn ourselves a pretty penny in Bristol.'

They meant to sell her. It was hard to breathe, as though someone with long, cruel fingers had their hands round her neck, crushing her windpipe. Hester forced herself to watch raindrops dripping from the mainsail, silvered by the early evening light. She must not allow them to realise she had understood.

'Well,' said the *seigneur*'s son, breaking a long, considering silence, 'how much do you think we'd get?'

'More than we've got between us as it is. There's plenty of black-market slave-traders in Bristol if you know where to look.'

The other soldier nodded. 'He's right. We can just say she died or drowned herself. Who's going to care?'

Hester repressed a wild urge to call out to Papa for help, knowing now that she must escape or die trying, that she must conserve what remained of her strength. The wind rose again, and dark clouds crept across the sky from the east. Was that small bay Lamorna Cove? Even if these men could be trusted to reach the great stone quay at the western reach of the bay without drowning them all, where might she be safe? The moment she set foot on land, every last scrap of sand, earth and moorland belonged to the Earl of Lamorna. There was a new earl, too – that scandalous boy who had sailed with Papa on the *Belle* and then left the navy to join Wellington's staff in Spain. Hester forced herself to steady her breathing as she weighed up the options: before Buonaparte had escaped his island prison and set Europe alight with another war, Papa had gone to London on naval business, and she'd spent the winter of '14 at Nansmornow, the ancient seat of the Earls of Lamorna. She'd never met the new earl – Papa knew him, of course, but he'd run away to sea at such a young age, afterwards joining the army, that she had never chanced to meet him at Nansmornow. The Lamornas were allies – of a sort. For so many reasons, Hester preferred not to recollect those frostbitten mornings, the sidelong glances of the Lamorna servants, ice on the windowpanes, and the Lamornas' friends – women in fussy silk gowns not quite daring to meet her eye, or staring when they thought she did not attend. Lord Lamorna – Mark – had died not long after Waterloo, they said, of a fever contracted as he searched the battlefield for the corpse of his estranged eldest son. But by the grace of God, that son had survived what should have been mortal wounds and was now the earl, a little-known quantity. Hester had seen his name in *The Times* in the weeks after Waterloo: he was the messenger who had failed to reach Wellington with news that the allies had changed sides. *Typical Wellington,* Papa had said, frowning down at the newspaper. *Always first to lay the blame at someone else's door. Shabby of him to let it get out that it was Crowlas who didn't reach him, poor lad.* Lady Lamorna herself would be in London at this season, the great house Nansmornow cloaked in dust-sheets, but in any case the Lamorna estates were far too close to what Hester had left behind. The French would look for her at Nansmornow, surely. Even if by some miracle she escaped these soldiers, Papa's manumission papers and the codicil confirming her own freedom were locked in his desk in the library on the top floor of the tower at Castle Bryher. Papa had never once left home without them. *The Abolitionists might refuse as much sugar in their tea as they like,* Papa used to say. *The whole economy is bound up in the iniquity of it.* The truth was, she could be kidnapped by anyone from Land's End to the Highlands, disappearing without trace into a slave trade that had diminished, but survived underground. Hester pressed her hands to her face in a useless attempt to smooth away rising panic: the men simply ignored her.

The bright cluster of lights was now no more than half a mile away, and Hester realised she was looking at the little row of fishermen's cottages above Lamorna Cove. Dead ahead, the water was black, ruffled: there was going to be the hugest gust, and no one save herself gave the smallest sign of having noticed the danger. Hester watched the young rifleman grip the tiller with his cold-reddened fingers insultingly close to her face. If he didn't turn into the wind they'd go over. It happened so fast, a movement more natural than breathing: Hester snatched the tiller, forcing it hard over, smashing them away from the wind instead of into it as the gust hit the sails. The mainsail bulged horribly just as the young lieutenant turned on her. He was too late: the wind was everywhere, and in a blur of spray the oyster-boat heeled over and Hester cried out at the shock of the cold water. She screamed and went under; a slew of silver-grey bubbles spewed from her mouth and nose. *Swim.* She remembered Papa holding her by the waist, teaching her how to kick in the shallow waters of Rushy Bay. The sodden gown swirled around her legs, dragging her down. In her mind, she heard Papa's voice. *Swim, take courage.*

Hester gasped, her face streaming. She clutched the rudder as it bobbed and floated. The upturned hull was just yards away but there was no sign of the French, any of them. She heard a man crying out, hidden by the bulk of a wave that crashed over her own head a heartbeat later, his cries punctuated by silence as he went under for longer and longer each time. They deserved to drown. Gasping, Hester wrenched herself around, muttering a prayer as she clutched at the floating rudder; nothing but shouldering waves everywhere she looked, grey and cold, and she must not get cold, she must not give up.

The silence was enormous, as if everyone in the whole world had drowned save her. Hester swallowed a salty mouthful of seawater. She clung to the rudder, watching those lights at the water's edge. Surely someone at Lamorna would help her? Half a mile. No more than half a mile. She could swim half a mile. She wouldn't let the sea beat her. She could not.

3

Come on, come on, come on. Waiting in darkness for the explosion, the Honourable Kitto Helford pressed himself against the wall of the quay house at the top of Fore Street. Newlyn after the last bells was a ghost town. At this time, there was no crowd to be lost in, only the rain and the night and the blasted fucking Occupation. It was so unnaturally quiet: Kitto felt watched at every moment, but it was hardly as if he didn't have a guilty conscience. Seawater swirled about his ankles, inches above the cobblestones, aching cold against his skin. It was birdwitted to have attacked on a spring tide with a full moon hanging against the night like a huge silver penny and seawater washing up into the streets of the town, and he should have told Harry Simmens as much. Kitto was starting to think that maybe Harry didn't have the ear of the Cornish resistance after all. In truth, it was rather difficult to imagine Mr Gloyne, who ran An Gostel as well as the circulating library in Penzance, looking on tonight's work with any degree of approval. In fact, Kitto had last seen Mr Gloyne engaged in a very unwarlike game of chess with his brother at Nansmornow. Well, Crow could go to the devil and take any coward with him who refused to fight the French. Harry had given him half a meat pie when he'd eaten nothing for days. A ticket to the guillotine in exchange for not even a whole meat pie. The night cracked wide open, ringing with the dull thud of an explosion that Kitto felt through the soles of his boots. The sky turned a filthy shade of orange. Above the din of granite smashing against cobblestones he heard breaking glass and men shouting – and the thin, far-off wail of a child. It ought to give the French something to write home about, a damned enormous hole blown in the seaward wall of their garrison. Seawater foamed about his shins as he sprinted alone down Fore Street. Mount's Bay lay to his left like black glass. There was no wind, and a sprinkling of lights bled gold across the still waters: cabin lamps lit by bored French blockade-ship captains screwing the girls of Newlyn, Penzance and Marazion. The fishermen might be forced into idleness, but their daughters, wives and sisters were hard at work instead. The frigates loomed like ghost ships, their sails white in the moonlight. There was only one penalty for breaching the blockade: a hail of grapeshot. Doubtless there was only one lesson for blowing a hole in the French garrison, too, taught by Madame Guillotine.

Fore Street was too near the garrison. There were men shouting in French, louder all the time. Even being out past the last bells was enough for a trip to Bodmin Assizes. He'd die there of gaol-fever before the French ever sliced the head from his shoulders. He had to get away into the open moorland between Newlyn and Paul. After nearly thirteen years of Papa letting him do much as he pleased, Kitto knew every last gorse bush from Lamorna to Penzance, and up on the moor the bastards would have no chance with him. He scrambled up a steep, twisting alley, leaving the bay behind him but not the thunder of heavy footfalls or the shouting. They were on his scent.

Kitto surged uphill, his lungs burning. Why in Christ's name had he ever thought that throwing in his lot with An Gostel was a good idea? Freedom for Cornwall, yes, but he'd be no use to the rebellion dead or on a convict ship. The French were catching up: he had to hide. The houses crammed along the alley had shuttered their windows – no one wanted to draw the eyes of a French night-guard. All but one, a single, blessed oblong of brassy lamplight. The Star and Crown. Its doors were barred for the night, but now he saw John Jenkins passing up kegs of brandy and ale from the cellar trapdoor open to the street, his daughter reaching down from the taproom window to take each one, her fingers bright with gold rings.

Hearing heavy footfalls around the corner, Kitto reached out, snatching the nearest of the kegs, holding it tight against his chest like a life-raft, the reek of brandy raking the back of his throat: better to be transported for stealing than to die on the scaffold for insurrection. The soldiers were now more than a few paces behind him. At a cry from the girl, John Jenkins turned, looking from Kitto to the keg in his arms and then at four infuriated French soldiers in sweat-stained blue jackets backing Kitto hard up against the whitewashed stone bulk of the Star, one pushing him against the wall so it hurt to breathe.

'My lord?' Jenkins was very still in the moonlight, watching him, his fleshy face slack with shock.

There was no answer, nothing to say. He'd never see home again. He'd never reach Nansmornow, never taste those cakes of Nessa's that he'd dreamed of ever since he fled Lamorna House and left London behind.

'Now then,' the guard said, in French. The fingers digging into his throat stank of raw onions, and the guard smiled. 'And what exactly do we have here?'

4

To Arkwright's mind it was all wrong. In the Star, every bastard in the place stared at the pair of them, Boney's blue-jackets included. They all looked away too damned quick before taking their hats off to Crow. Even one of the Frenchies tipped his old-style tricorn but that didn't mean shit. Arkwright had been in enough tight corners to smell rot, and my lord Crow had picked up the scent, too, not that anyone who didn't know him might tell. My fucking lord. Christ. It was nine o'clock in the morning, and every man in the tavern wound up with the promise of bloodletting, just like a pack of hounds kennelled before the chase. It was the French that had done it, sitting at the best table, the one before the fire: Arkwright had spent long enough working in Crow's stables to know the Cornish called Lieutenant de Mornay *ankenedhel*, the monster. A small man with yellow, ratty teeth, de Mornay ruled Cornwall from the garrison at Borlaze with a bloody fist, all right; he sat as judge to decide the fate of men who had once belonged to Crow himself. Now here they were, both men in the same tavern, the deposed lord and the interloper. It felt as though the air was about to shatter like glass. Arkwright watched Crow leaning on the bar in his long black coat, cool as you please, not watching, just waiting. If it were down to Arkwright, they'd go straight to Nansmornow to look for the boy. But when was it ever down to Arkwright? Thirty years a soldier, twenty-five a spy, and Crow wasn't the first arrogant young aristocrat he'd had to take orders from, and nor would he be the last – first Lord Crowlas, now the Earl of pissing Lamorna. Grant would be wondering what the hell they were up to, sitting on his arse in that Belgravia mansion, but Grant could fuck himself for a start and never mind the young Helford brat: coming back to Cornwall meant he could speak to Nessa. It was time: he should've done it before they left for London. She'd be in the old nursery, doing the family's sewing, mending collars and sheets with those stitches so small you couldn't see them, such clever fingers she had. He pictured her looking up at him, smiling. *What are you doing up here, Joe Arkwright?* Jenny wouldn't have wanted him to be a single man forever.

'Brandy, Jenkins,' Crow said, high in the instep as ever. Arkwright prayed to a God he had never really believed in that there would be no trouble. They didn't need this. Not now.

Jenkins wiped two glasses with a folded cloth; then he wiped the bar itself before setting out the glasses and pouring from a tin decanter. Nervy. His hand shook and brandy splashed the bar. Arkwright surveyed the taproom: weatherbeaten lads in oiled sheepskin surtouts staring out of the window at the blockade running along Mount's Bay. Bloody hell. Bloody Cornish. You couldn't trust any of them. Word was the local guerrilla forces had blasted a hole in the French garrison only last night, that some stupid fucker had been arrested – probably hanged already. Fire-setters, dealers in gunpowder. Where did they think it'd get them, aside from Bodmin gaol and the scaffold? The two Frenchies were hard at hazard at the best table, near the fire, and Lieutenant de Mornay with his pockets to let, to judge by the look on his face. Crow sighed; he leaned across to take the decanter from Jenkins, pouring two neat glasses, pushing one along the bar. Arkwright took it, drinking. Brandy burned the back of his gullet: the good stuff. Something was getting through the blockade, then, thanks to the Gentlemen of the free trade, even if half Cornwall starved because no one could fish. Some of the Cornish had their uses.

Jenkins cleared his throat. 'I wonder, my lord, if you might attend my mother, sir? She hasn't got long, and said as she hoped she might get your blessing before she passes. I didn't think it would be possible, sir, at this time of year, when your lordship would be in London as a matter of course, but as you're here?'

Crow knocked back his brandy, and poured another. 'It would be my pleasure. She was always very kind when I was a boy. Wait here, Arkwright. Have another drink.'

Arkwright watched him follow Jenkins through a door behind the bar, to the manner born. *Noblesse oblige* seemed to come more natural than the other virtues. Nothing to remark on, unless you knew like every man in the tavern save the French that Jenkins's mother had been dead fifteen years. Arkwright pushed away the glass. Crow drank too much, like the young fool he was. Arkwright had seen it all before. No one could drink as much as that and hold his mind together, not after seeing what they had seen, doing what they had done.

Crow stepped back into the taproom. There was something up. Arkwright knew that look: blank, dead-eyed. It usually ended badly. Jenkins poured another glass of brandy, but instead of tossing it straight back, Crow leaned against the fireplace, closer to the blue-jackets than anyone else dared get. Idiot. Fucking idiot.

'We're here to look for thy gallows-bait brother: what are you buggering about in this shit-hole for?' Arkwright spoke

K.J. WHITTAKER

in a back-alley dialect of Portuguese that would have been unintelligible to any respectable citizen of that nation. 'What in the name of the devil's cunt are you doing?'

Crow smiled, replying in the same tongue, but with all the fluid, archaic grace of the deposed Portuguese king. 'Is that my gold in your pocket or not, old friend?' He turned to the French soldiers, speaking now in French. 'Hazard tonight? Do you know what, gentlemen, I've a fancy to play. Might I presume to join your table? Lieutenant de Mornay, is it not?'

Arkwright drew up a bar stool. It was going to be a long night.

5

Seven miles from Newlyn, the ancient hall of Borlaze crouched in a dripping, leafy valley as remote as it was beautiful. Dark and dry, the cellar was still home to the remnants of the late Sir John Pendarves's legendary collection of claret – and now Kitto, who was reduced to staring at shadows as he waited to meet a shameful death. Led through the parkland with his wrists bound, he'd seen the leathery remains of Sir John and his wife hanging in separate iron cages from an oak tree in the grounds. No one dared cut them down, and next it would be his turn. In the morning he'd be driven down the lane in an open cart: the French would take him all the way to Bodmin, to the scaffold in the market square where jumbled old houses collapsed forwards on to cobbles hidden beneath generations of horseshit and sullen crowds gathered to watch the executions. No one sold saffron cakes before a killing nowadays. The thought of it turned Kitto's bowels to water – and all because Crow had made him so angry he couldn't stop walking. Not only Crow. He remembered the green silk of their stepmother's gown puddling on the floor in the drawing-room, emerald-bright in the light of dawn, Louisa's fingers trailing on the rug as she arched her back, Crow's head between her pale, slender legs. He'd backed out of the drawing-room before either of them noticed his presence, and had not stopped walking for almost a month. Pa had been dead less than two years: it was a betrayal, and the truth was Kitto would rather die than live beneath the same roof as Crow and Louisa again. Now that he was about to get what he wanted, he wished he'd been a little less rash. He heard footfalls in the stone-flagged passage outside: the French. It was time to stand up and meet them on his feet. The door opened, and a guardsman he'd not seen before leaned in the doorway.

'It's your time, thief. He's come for you.'

The late Lady Pendarves's drawing-room windows were swathed in brocade curtains that made it seem as though twilight had come hours early even though it was only late morning. The walls were papered with hand-painted swallows frozen against a shade of green like a ripening bruise, and for what felt like two thousand years he shared the long, dark drawing-room with a pair of silent French infantrymen, their stained and worn blue jackets bright in the gloom. As if from a long distance off he heard the doors opening, rusted hinges groaning. The militiamen admitted no blue-jacketed French lieutenant but Crow himself – tall and hollow-cheeked, his greatcoat splashed with mud and boots thick with dust. Kitto had last seen his brother in London a month ago; how in Christ's name had he come to be back in Cornwall? Pure cold shock robbed him of all speech, mingled with a sense of relief so acute that it ballooned into overwhelming shame.

True to form, Crow offered no explanation. His gaze travelled around the respectable drawing-room, resting on the two guards and finally settling on Kitto himself. 'Well, this is quite the Cheltenham fucking tragedy.' He spoke in hard-edged, savage Cornish. 'Do you have any idea how long I had to play their flyblown whoremaster of a lieutenant at hazard before I won enough to ruin him? Get up. We're leaving.'

There was little point in wondering how Crow had known to come. Crow always knew. Stunned into silence, Kitto followed him from the drawing-room, half expecting the soldiers not to allow it, to be taken back to his prison, but they only stood at ease, watching with disinterest.

The entrance hall passed in a blur of waxed floorboards and light shafting in through mullioned windows. Crow walked on with swift, violent speed, the tails of his black greatcoat flapping. Another two French soldiers stood guard at the front door, one idly picking at the faded silk wall-dressing with his jack-knife. Crow walked past them and down the sandstone steps and Kitto stopped, unable to go further without saying his piece. The overgrown parkland spread out before them, mid-morning sunlight catching the seed-heads of grass left long unscythed.

'I'm not coming with you.' Had he really walked south-west through the tail end of winter, rain-drenched, hungry and frostbitten, only for Crow to march him back up to London like a common vagrant?

'Indeed, are you not?' Crow paused as they neared his hatchet-faced groom, Arkwright, who held two geldings in the shade of the chestnut tree with a military efficiency that made Kitto ache with envious longing. 'Doubtless you'd prefer execution' – Crow spoke with his black brows arched high, looking so extraordinarily like their father that Kitto had to turn away – 'but until your twenty-first birthday you will do exactly as I ask, a prospect I find just as exhausting and unsatisfactory as you appear to.'

Kitto replied in an undertone. 'Only because you're so irredeemably bloody about everything.' It was the least of all he wanted to say. He looked up and saw a flicker of scorn distort Arkwright's passive features, and was instantly ashamed of his cowardice. Why could he not just tell Crow the truth? *I saw you with our stepmother.*

'Now listen to me. Cornish independence is the least of our concerns, *boya* do you understand?' With the Cornish endearment on his lips, Crow sounded almost gentle. 'Who do you think you are, An Gof or Baron Audley? It'll go the same way as it did in 1497, and you'll end with your head rotting on a pike for everyone on London Bridge to gawp at.'

'And what must I do instead?' Kitto almost shouted. 'Nothing?' His stomach lurched: he'd gone far beyond what was permissible or even wise.

Crow's eyes took on a cold, unpleasant light – greyer and more forbidding than the Helford River in February. His expression otherwise froze with incredulous disbelief that anyone under his authority might address him in such a fashion. 'What must you do, indeed?' He spoke with deceptive lightness. 'I strongly advise that you leave such questions for your elders and betters to decide. But you will listen to what I have to say to you on that head at Nansmornow, not here.'

Kitto thought better of remarking how very much he was looking forward to that particular interview.

Crow stood back to let him mount up. 'You're starting to make me sorry I took you as my winnings instead of ten thousand ducats. I would be so grateful,' he went on with devastating courtesy, 'if you could possibly avoid arrest between here and London. I find my nerves quite shattered by the experience.'

Kitto's relief that he really wasn't going to face the guillotine or the gallows after all was swiftly followed by the chilly realisation that Crow was always at his most dangerous when he became sarcastic.

6

Crow galloped hard along the clifftop from Borlaze to Lamorna, restraining the desire to halt the horse and clout his brother into the following week. Louisa had been right about Kitto; he'd been left far too much with the servants. The boy had spoken pure Cornish before ever he mastered English; now he was setting fucking gunpowder for An Gostel, or for some idiot claiming allegiance to them. An Gostel had more sense. The blame for this lay at the door of a dead man. A barrel-fevered liberal to the last, Papa might have started out believing that children were *tabulae rasae,* innocent minds to be moulded by rational discussion, not born to have the sin beaten from them. He had ended rarely bothering to exert himself on behalf of either of his legitimate offspring, in any respect, and happy to let Roza scrub in the laundry-room of his own house. Crow knew very well that he'd done little better once he'd taken their father's place. Kitto was beyond hope, but as for Roza, their half-sister, no blood of his would spend her life in service: there would be a decent marriage for her, and she should have her own hearth to tend and her own children to care for, not someone else's.

The moors tumbled away inland, disappearing into a stubborn grey mist that had drawn as low as the heather. Land fell away to the sea below, and creamy surf crashed against rock, against flat wet sand. Crow didn't even have to look across at Arkwright to sense his unspoken disapproval, and Kitto exuded sullen fury in the saddle behind him. Crow vowed to school that mutinous expression from his face before long. He and Arkwright were meant to be planning a string of attacks on Buonaparte's so-called imperial fucking post-roads and the mint at Faversham, not chasing down the length of the country for an errant child. How was he supposed to function? Crow knew he was nowhere near a battlefield, but surrendered to the familiar rush of violent emotion that in the past he only felt on going into action. The urge to fight or to flee now might overpower him anywhere from a tavern to a crowded drawing-room with no clear path to the door, and so it was now.

'Crow!' Kitto spoke with such sharp urgency that he reined in.

'What?' He turned in the saddle to face his brother and instead saw a dead rifleman looking back at him, his jaw nothing but bare white bone and half his face bloodied and blackened by the cannon blast that had killed him. Crow stared at the black embroidered frogging on the rifleman's dark green jacket, the three rows of pale buttons: every detail stood out with terrifying clarity.

'Crow?' The rifleman had gone, and in his place Kitto stared at him as though the head had just been blown clear from his shoulders. He slid from the saddle, running to the cliff-edge. 'There's someone drowned on the beach.'

'For Christ's sake.' With great effort, Crow forced himself to breathe steadily, to remember that he was in Cornwall, not Spain or France, and dismounted, following his brother to a cliff-edge fringed with seagrass tossing in the wind. Kitto was right. Down where sand met the black, seaweed-covered rocks littering Lamorna Cove, a sodden heap of pale cloth lay in the shallows: an unmistakably human form. It was all they needed, but this was his land, and whoever had washed up dead on it was now his concern, adding to the limitless weight of responsibilities already borne. 'Arkwright, let's get down there.'

'She's moving, milord.'

Only Arkwright could readily obey an order and still make one feel like some idiot of a subaltern. Shoving past him, Crow ran the rest of the way, skidding down the steep, root-strewn path that led to the beach. By the time he reached the girl she had struggled to her feet, perhaps at the sound of their voices, most assuredly not dead. She was tall and statuesque, her skin a rich, deep golden-brown. Sodden muslin and linen petticoats clung to the strong curves of her body; the fine curls of her hair had started to dry, to spring away from her shoulders, the colour of wet sand. Staggering against cold waves, she swayed. She could hardly stand, clearly at the limit of her endurance. Frigid water plunged over the top of Crow's boots; he had walked in to meet the girl without thinking of it. Her breasts heaved with the sheer exhausted effort of moving, her skin speckled with goosebumps.

'Let me help you,' he heard himself say. 'Has there been a wreck?' Crow's gaze flickered across the bay but he saw nothing save cresting waves and the looming ships of the blockade. How had this girl survived the sea? How had she not drowned? Was she a servant, a runaway slave, even? The trade might be forbidden on English soil, but not slavery itself. And rogue traders still took on water and supplies at Bristol even though their business was technically forbidden. It was possible. Or perhaps she was just one of the sailmaker's daughters from St Endellion. Whoever she was, she should not have been walking out of the sea. It took every last scrap of resolve to keep his eyes on her face, away from her body.

'I wrecked them. They're dead.' Her chest heaved, breasts straining against her bodice. Each word that fell from her lips was polished and glasslike. This was no sailmaker's daughter. 'They killed my father.'

Crow reached out to steady her, taking her arm. 'Who did? Who was your father?' Without thinking, he watched the beach and the row of cottages above it, searching for any sign of movement. He didn't trust Kitto's captors not to send men after them.

'The French soldiers,' said the girl, as though he was stupid. 'They killed my father.'

'Hester!' Kitto called out, running along the beach towards them. 'What's happened?' He turned to Crow, impatient. 'It's Miss Harewood.'

All Crow could think of was Captain John Harewood passing him a sextant on the deck of the *Belle*, long ago, the cold, bronze weight of it in his hands. The loss was so stunning it was hard to find words. In the end, those he reached for were inadequate, he knew: 'Of course. Your likeness hung in your father's cabin all the years I knew him, but you're very much changed.' And the French really were on Bryher, thirty miles from the mainland. Why?

'I'm sorry, Hester,' Kitto said, 'I'm so very sorry.'

'Get back to the horses and stop being so damnably familiar,' Crow said to him in Cornish. 'Mount up behind Arkwright – she's riding with me. You've a lot to answer for when we get to Nansmornow.'

Kitto departed with an expression that would have driven Crow to swift retribution had his former captain's daughter not been watching with disarming candour. She shuddered again as Crow took off his greatcoat, settling it around her shoulders. They progressed a clutch of halting paces up the beach before her legs gave way. He crouched at her side as she heaved and vomited a mouthful of green bile on to a heap of bladderwrack. Unthinking, he held back her sodden hair; she was rigid with mortification. She couldn't seem to stop shaking: she was in a state of exhaustion, of profound shock. How far had she swum? A girl, swimming. It was next to impossible, but here she was.

'They're hunting me,' she said. 'They mean to sell me.'

'They will not,' Crow said. 'It's going to be perfectly all right.'

Hester Harewood stared at him. 'They thought I couldn't understand, but I did. The newspapers were wrong. The Duke of Wellington isn't in Scotland at all. He's at home. He's on Scilly – Marshal Ney has him prisoner at Castle Bryher. I beg you, Lord Lamorna, but it's nothing to smile about.'

Wellington. He was still alive. A rush of victorious relief was swiftly followed by the realisation that a dispatch *en clair* would be far too risky, and that useless lump of flesh Colquhoun Grant would be unable to break a cipher. Alone, Crow could have ridden hard back to London in just over a week. But he was not alone. He looked down at the shivering Miss Harewood. Drops of seawater clung to her eyelashes, but once again her forthright expression put him forcibly in mind of her father, his first captain and commander. From women his own age, he was used to coy smiles and an averted gaze. Miss Harewood thoroughly unsettled him.

'You're coming back to London with me.' All Crow could do was hope she wouldn't give him any trouble.

She stared at him, incredulous. 'Am I, indeed?'

'Yes.' Crow reached for his hip flask and contented himself with a scalding shot of the 1811 Le Courvoisier, before holding the flask to Miss Harewood's lips. 'Yes, indeed you are.'

Somewhat to his surprise, she didn't protest against the

cognac, but took a swallow and straightened herself to her full height, tall and queenly in a sodden gown, and Crow could not escape the notion that he had met his match.

'Take another drink, my lord,' said Miss Harewood. 'You look as though you need it.'

7

The sky boiled with clouds and silvery droplets clung to the scalloped edges of hedgerow leaves as they rode up out of the woods at Lamorna, nearing the barley fields. Crow led the way, with Hester in the saddle before him. Faced with Arkwright's broad, serge-clad back, Kitto listened to the faint crash of surf away to the east, dreading the return to Nansmornow still more now that Hester Harewood would be there. Even if she didn't actually witness Crow dispensing justice, she would soon know about it; he felt sure that the mortification of her knowing he had been hauled over hot coals was going to be worse than whatever Crow actually planned to do. Kitto knew that his crimes were significant. He'd left London without a word to anyone. He'd blown up a French garrison and, worse, been caught. And now Crow was going to make him suffer for doing what he himself did not dare. On top of it all, Crow was guilty of screwing their father's wife even as he played unquestionable lord and master. It was sickening. Whatever happened, Kitto vowed to give as good as he got: he was fourteen, not four, and though he had no mother to shield him from Crow's ire, neither could he go running to his wet-nurse complaining of the injustice. He pushed away a long-ago memory of sitting on Nessa's lap to shell peas into a bowl, his half-sister Roza laughing as she spooned blackcurrant preserve into his bread-and-milk, tracing the shape of a face. Doubtless they'd both be on Crow's side, anyway: he was lord and master, and they had little choice.

Before they reached the village of Nantewas, Crow reined in and dismounted outside the tavern. 'Miss Harewood, I'll take you to Nansmornow as soon as I've attended to my business here.' Kitto was startled to hear him speak with as much consideration. 'You'll be quite safe with Arkwright.'

'Just as you desire, my lord. I'm absolutely in your debt,' Hester replied with chilly courtesy. 'If you wish me to freeze half to death whilst you conduct your affairs, then so I must.'

For a bare half-moment, Crow paused, then recovered the wry, commanding demeanour that had once made Kitto obey even an unspoken request. 'Forgive my stupidity, Miss Harewood. Please, allow me to assist you – the tapman's wife will find you dry clothes.'

'Whether she likes it or not, I suppose.' Hester took his outstretched hand, ignoring the amused tilt of Crow's mouth – almost a smile – and dismounted with an inelegant flurry; Kitto supposed she'd had little enough practice in the saddle when it was said one could walk the length and breadth of Bryher in less than an hour. Crow steadied her, but merely bowed, and, without appearing to notice Hester's flustered countenance, turned to Kitto. 'Come.' There was little choice.

Inside the Wink, the taproom was heaving but an empty space formed around them, Crow's furious and wholly unexpected presence driving the starved men of Lamorna close to the whitewashed walls. No one could fish beyond the blockades, a boundary respected by neither mackerel nor pilchard. Mr Trewarthen must be as good as giving away his brandy: it was all run by the free-traders, anyhow. Crow stood for a moment in silence, taking note of each face: Will and Eddy Simmens, Tom Gwyn, all four of the Chirk brothers. Everyone. To a man, they stared at Hester, too; Crow followed their gaze with an expression of incredulous fury, and Hester was instantly spared scrutiny as everyone from the Simmenses to the Chirks found somewhere else to look. It was so quiet that Kitto heard Eddy Simmens's belly rumbling. Lantern-jawed Tom Gwyn shifted on his stool, and the muffled scrape of wood against sawdust-scattered flagstones rang out, excruciatingly loud.

'First of all,' Crow said, in Cornish. 'You will all immediately forget that you have seen the child of Captain Harewood here today.' He glanced across at Mr Trewarthen, who was wiping down the counter. 'Jôwan Coth, send for Anne, and have her bring dry clothes for Miss Harewood.'

Hester was conveyed, expressionless, into the back room, leaving a trail of seawater. After a month of separation, Kitto found it extraordinary to witness the speed at which Crow's orders were obeyed. The moment the door had closed behind Hester, Crow turned back to the rest of his men. They were all, without exception, utterly focused on him, whether they were staring down at their shoes like the youngest Simmens or facing him directly, like Tom Gwyn. The men of Lamorna were one with Crow, sensitive to the slightest change in his mood; Kitto wondered why he had never noticed this before, and then realised that it was because there had been a time when he had shared the bond and been part of it. He'd faced Crow's displeasure before, but never for long, always so appalled to fall from his brother's favour that he would have done anything to regain it. But Crow was no hero after all, and Kitto knew it. He might no longer crave his brother's approval, but in truth one felt the cold beyond Crow's inner circle.

Crow's gaze travelled around the taproom, taking in each

man. 'I'm only going to ask this once: where the bloody fuck is Harry Simmens?'

Kitto felt the hairs on the back of his neck rise. How did he always know everything? He said, 'Crow, stop it. Newlyn was nothing to do with Harry.' A lie so blatant that John Chirk visibly winced even as he stared out of the window, and Crow clouted him almost without bothering to turn and look. His ears rang with the pain, blood filled his mouth, and still they all looked away. He wanted to die.

Jôwan Coth came in again – Mr Trewarthen to Kitto, 'It might be that Harry's out the back, your honour. I've not seen him today.' Harry Simmens was eighteen, and had not long married one of the Trewarthen girls. 'Folk are lying low, your honour. The valley's been thick with the French these last few days. Antsy, they've been, ever since the garrison at Newlyn went up in flames.' Mr Trewarthen directed a fleeting glance at Kitto, who swallowed rising nausea. Had his own failed mission led Occupation troops to the rest of the rebels?

With a curt nod, Crow stepped back, allowing Kitto to proceed before him. There was no choice but to go behind the bar and push open the door leading into the house. They hadn't waited long in the neatly swept kitchen-parlour before Mistress Trewarthen herself came in carrying a child he didn't recognise: a grubby-faced girl born long after he'd gone to Eton. She was so thin that her fingers resembled dry sticks. They were swiftly followed by Hester who, with an air of one whose patience had been severely tried, was now clad in brown leather shoes, thick stockings, and a dry gown of bilge-green serge that skimmed her ankles in a way that even Kitto could see was indecent. The distinct sense of want was a shock: Kitto had spent a significant portion of his youth beneath Mistress Trewarthen's well-scrubbed kitchen table with various Trewarthen children, but those shelves in the nook by the fireplace were empty now

– there was no bramble jam to slather on fresh bread, and no fresh hot sardines fried in butter. Mistress Trewarthen's face was slack with lack of food. At the sight of Crow, she dropped into a curtsey. Crow made a slight bow to Hester and, with one look at the child, he dropped a handful of silver crowns on the scrubbed table.

'You will be pleased, I'm sure, to await me outside, Miss Harewood,' Crow said.

Hester gave frosty thanks to Mistress Trewarthen for the clothes, and left them. Kitto knew he was for it the moment she'd gone.

'What do you want with Harry, my lord?' Mrs Trewarthen said with a swift, purse-lipped glance at the door Hester had just closed behind her. 'Grateful as I am for the coin, I'm sure.'

'It's all right, mistress.' Harry followed her in, flicking a relieved but faintly scornful look in Kitto's direction. He'd not said a word. Harry had no right to look at him like that. 'What can I do for you, your honour?'

Crow looked Harry up and down. 'You can do your own damned shit-work, for a start. Feel free to get yourself guillotined, stirring up the French like a wasp's nest, but use my brother again and never mind the French, I'll hang you myself.'

Harry turned to Kitto. 'Nice to see you know how to keep your mouth shut.'

'Shut yours, boy,' Mistress Trewarthen said. 'I don't know what manner of nonsense you've been up to, but ten to one Master Kitto said nothing about it.' She nodded at Crow. 'You know what my lord is like, Harry. He knows everything, and so more fool you.'

'The boy wanted to help us,' Harry said, whining, sly. 'At least he wanted to fight for his own country, his own kinsmen.'

Crow smiled, and Kitto longed to disappear. He knew that look. 'My brother was also starving, I expect, not having the wit to think of taking any money on a journey from London to Cornwall. But of course,' Crow went on, 'for every French life you take, they'll have ten Cornish.'

'The English near crushed us, but the French swore oaths they didn't keep, and we'll make them pay for it.'

'Will you hell, Harry. Be more careful, and use your head. The French aren't going to grant Cornwall to the Cornish no matter what they promised. They're clinging to every mile of British soil. You're on a fool's errand if you think otherwise.' He leaned over to light a cigarillo from the tallow lamp on the windowsill, and went on in Cornish. 'Does anyone actually in An Gostel's command know what you've talked my brother into?'

Harry flushed brick-red, and said no more, and Crow watched him with that cold, steady grey gaze for so long that Kitto knew Harry would be wishing himself dead.

'Doubtless the boy and his friends have windmills in their heads,' Mistress Trewarthen said in Cornish. 'But if you were to lead us, my lord, everyone would follow. The whole of Cornwall would follow you, indeed, and then perhaps there might be a chance of chasing the French into England, where they deserve them. And I would lose no more sons, my lord, because it's two now I've had killed, as you know, one hanged by the English and one shot by the French, and all for free-trading when I don't know how else we're meant to feed ourselves. Word is the soldiers went up to Nansmornow.' She broke off a piece of bread for the little girl, who clutched at it with skeletal fingers.

Crow bowed. 'I was taught never to fight a battle I couldn't win, good mistress.'

Kitto followed him to the door: he could do nothing else. When they reached it, Crow looked over his shoulder. 'The soldiers will be gone soon, don't worry.'

He turned and went outside and mounted up without even

looking at Kitto. Saying nothing to anyone, Crow spurred the mare, ignoring even Hester: he and Arkwright seemed to understand one another with little need for speech, and Kitto knew that whatever they found at Nansmornow, it would be his fault. Wind shifted the great drifts of daffodils on either side of the lane, their bright heads bobbing with incongruous cheer. Leaving the cliffs and the sea behind, they rode up to the west gate of the great house to find the iron gates swinging on their hinges, a window in the lodge-house broken and gaping. Crow dismounted, walking towards a pale shape lying across the carriage drive.

'Gelert!' Kitto ran after Crow and crouched at Gelert's side, running one hand across the old Dalmatian's bony head. Bred to run alongside the carriage for miles, trained to protect, he was dead, half his flank a bloody mess. Someone was here that shouldn't be. Blindsided by grief, Kitto stroked Gelert's ear just how he'd liked it, hoping that the end had been quick. Then, not daring to whistle, Kitto clicked his tongue behind his teeth and Gil came streaking out from the rhododendrons to cower at his side, old Gelert's litter sister.

Crow was the first of them back in the saddle. 'Mount up,' he ordered, glancing back at Arkwright, questioning. Hester had gone very still. Arkwright shrugged and Gil whined, breaking away to trot off along the carriage drive. In wordless agreement, they followed her, and something shifted away to the far left, just at the tail of Kitto's eye. Something not right.

Kitto turned to look, and Crow said, '*Arkwright.*' A warning. They hung from a branch of the tallest, oldest chestnut: three long shapes, twisting a little in the wind; and Kitto felt a queer rushing in his head, sure that the earth would have melted away next time he lifted a foot from the ground. The horses' hooves sounded out like drumbeats, or perhaps it was just that the rest of the world was drained of sound. Three hanged corpses, heads lolling at unnatural angles. Closer now. No. Nessa, hanging there from a tree – his foster-mother, his wet-nurse – wearing her favourite blue-and-white-striped gown. One other swung in a smart blue jacket hanging open to show a naked belly slit from groin to gullet, the gaping wound black with a shifting mass of flies. Old Mr Gwyn, who had been butler since Papa was a boy, bayoneted and strung up. The third body was clad in nothing but a little shift fluttering in the wind, her pale, naked legs bloodstained. The head hung forward, a tangle of black hair. Roza. His half-sister. Mounted behind Arkwright, Kitto felt a great shudder pass through the groom's vast frame, but the man made no sound. With an odd sense of detachment, Kitto recalled that even before they'd left for London, the servants' hall had been hot with gossip. Dour Arkwright had been courting Nessa Carew, bringing her snowdrops. Wild, scattered thoughts chased one another, leading nowhere. Crow would skin him for listening to below-stairs gossip. Roza and Nessa and Mr Gwyn were swinging; they had been hanged; they were dead. Arkwright's bride-to-be was dead because of him. The hem of Nessa's gown had dropped; he pictured her forehead puckering into a frown as she threaded her needle. Roza had been murdered, his own half-sister, and it was his fault. They were all dead and it was all his fault, and Hester had seen it. She sat very still, her gaze following the gentle movement of the hanged corpses as they twisted, shifted by a rising sea-wind. Kitto felt as though he were falling through the earth, plunging past layers of earth and rock.

Crow dismounted in one swift movement. 'Don't go into the house, and wait here till I come back.' He drew his pistol.

Arkwright drew his knife and, guessing with horrified, ice-cold detachment that he meant to cut them all down, Kitto slid from the saddle behind him, while Crow ran up the broad steps to the front door. Without a word, Gil nudged at Kitto's hand with her muzzle, licking his fingers, but even that brought no comfort. He'd as good as killed them all himself the moment he'd lit that gunpowder in Newlyn. This was retribution. Arkwright rode closer, stood up in the stirrups, and reached up to begin sawing at the rope that had strangled Roza. She'd not been given the quick release of a broken neck: her face was so swollen and disfigured with the effects of a slow and agonising death that he couldn't bear to look and yet he must: this was his penance. If he'd not blown up the garrison at Newlyn, Roza would be folding sheets in the laundry-room. Hester's hands shook as she passed Kitto Crow's canteen, and until then Kitto hadn't realised he was even making a sound. His own hand shook so hard that brandy slopped down his wrist.

'Go on.' Hester held the canteen to his lips, and brandy burned his mouth. He handed it back, eyes streaming, and there was the first pistol shot, muffled, from inside the great house. *One, two, three, four.*

8

In the woods, Hester sat up in the dark, breathing hard. Sleep brought only dreams of hanged corpses. When Arkwright cut Roza down, she had landed with a sickening, skin-splitting crunch that echoed in Hester's mind even after a week. Heart racing, she searched the moonlit clearing for Crow. For seven days she'd sat in the saddle before him, breathing in the faint, salty scent of his body, his black-clad arms hemming her in on either side as he held the reins. Crow was so monstrously high-handed with everyone including herself and so frigid in his manner towards Kitto that she'd often itched to slap his face, but she had to pray that she was safe under his protection. One still heard of black men, women and children being taken on the streets and bundled into ships in the old slave ports – Bristol, Liverpool; it was a possibility. The thought of being enslaved sent a wave of fresh horror sliding down Hester's back as she remembered the scar around Papa's neck, the puckered and silvery flesh. She would have a chain around her own neck, an iron collar. She would be stripped, beaten, sold for the best price. Papa had never, ever spoken of his childhood on that Jamaican plantation, or how he had managed to join an English warship. And with the blood of four Frenchmen on his hands Crow was now in just as much danger of being taken prisoner by the French as she was herself. Could she really trust him not to use her as a bargaining chip if they were caught? Either way, now he was gone and Kitto nowhere to be seen either. She was alone in the dark woods with a sleeping Arkwright – habitually dour and silent, the broad-shouldered groom was an even more uncertain proposition than Crow himself.

'*Roza!*' Kitto's voice rang out from somewhere within the tangle of trees, and Hester pulled Crow's coat tighter around her shoulders. She was not the only one dreaming, then. If the rumours were true, Roza had been not only a laundry-maid at Nansmornow – the daughter of Crow and Kitto's murdered nurse – but also their half-sister. Roused into wakefulness with liquid speed, Arkwright crouched by the campfire's heap of glowing embers, shouldering his musket as he whistled to Gil, who returned to his side, meek as a lamb. Arkwright laid a hand on the Dalmatian's haunches, but he didn't look at Hester.

'What's the matter?' she whispered. 'Where are they?'

Arkwright shrugged, shoving life back into the unwilling fire with the heel of his boot. 'Nothing for you to mind, miss.' Gil curled up at his side, her black-dappled coat bright in the moonlight.

Hester got to her feet, letting Crow's coat fall to the ground. 'I'm going after him.'

'Not if you've any sense. His lordship's already gone.'

Kitto's voice rang out again, first calling for Roza, then Nessa. 'Well, he hasn't got very far. Let me by!' She stepped past Arkwright, ignoring his expression of long-suffering forbearance. Stepping away from the fire wearing only her own muslin gown, still stiff and salty with dried seawater, she was breathless with cold, but Crow's greatcoat was far too big and heavy to walk in. The thick woollen abomination lent by that sour-faced woman from the inn at Nantewas would doubtless have been warmer, but in her own clothes Hester felt less like a vagabond hunted by Occupation troops and just a sliver more like Miss Harewood of Castle Bryher. Irritated, she brushed away a recollection of the delightful sense of feeling small for the first time in her life when Crow insisted she wear the greatcoat as they rode: it would not do now. Pushing her way out of the clearing through wet undergrowth that caught at the hem of her gown, she followed the sound of Kitto's voice and saw him, a moonlit figure walking with the slow, eerie pace of the sleepwalker. At almost the same time, a tall shape melted from the dark mass of trees: Crow. How could he move like that, so quietly? Hester watched in horror as he turned Kitto around with one hand on his shoulder, giving him a swift, brisk shake, hissing something at him in Cornish of such a depraved nature that she didn't understand more than half.

'He was sleepwalking! How could you not see that?' Buoyed by her own daring, Hester ran forwards and took hold of Crow's arm. 'Leave him alone – really.' It clearly cost Crow some effort not to remove her hand by force, which sent a shiver of righteous satisfaction through her. Abruptly woken, Kitto stared at them both, breathing hard, his face very white in the moonlight, black hair hanging in his eyes.

'It's all right, Hets,' he said, falling back on an old nickname. 'You'd do better not to cross him.' His voice shook with suppressed emotion. What had gone wrong between them? *It's a crying shame my brother's not here on leave,* Kitto had said at Nansmornow, that Christmas before Waterloo, *he's a right one and game for anything, Hets. He sailed under your father's command, too. You should meet him one day.*

'Is the sermon done?' Crow asked, clearly at the limit of his patience. 'Only I'd prefer not to alert every French raiding party within twenty miles to our presence.'

Arkwright watched in silence as they approached the guttering campfire. Without a word to Crow or Hester, Kitto sat down facing the flames, twining together the fingers of both hands in a failed attempt to stall the trembling. Not knowing where to look, Hester felt a burst of pity and instantly crushed it, remembering how much Kitto had loathed the fuss his stepmother made at Nansmornow when he fell from his horse on Boxing Day. It was an insult to pity someone so proud and so careless of injury. Crow crouched down at his side and reached out, shielding Kitto's hands with his own. '*Drog ew genam.* You bloody young idiot,' he said quietly. *I'm sorry.* The tension drained from Kitto's stance, softening the hard set to his shoulders. Half a moment later, though, he jerked away, rigid again with that suppressed emotion, and Hester sat down on the folds of Crow's coat. She looked away, ashamed of not having done so sooner; it felt wrong to have witnessed such a private moment, puzzling though it was. Aware that Crow had turned away from his brother and was now sitting within arm's reach, she hunched herself into the smallest and warmest position she could manage. In the back of her mind she saw Roza in the frozen laundry-yard at Nansmornow, dark hair braided in neat coils at the back of her head: Crow and Kitto's illegitimate half-sister. What a messy, confusing family the Lamornas were, or had been – not that Roza had ever been granted the protection or privilege offered by their father's name.

Oh, miss, you startled me.

It was just your singing, Roza. It was so pretty. I couldn't resist coming closer.

Just my little piece of nonsense, miss.

Hester pushed away another memory of Roza hanged, her thick black hair caught up in the noose; she'd wished to pull it free, as if that might comfort the poor girl. She waited for the rhythm of Kitto's breathing to slow as he slid back into deep sleep. Arkwright was silent, a dark hump half-illuminated by the flames. The fire burned low, a clot of deep orange flames shuddering in the darkness. She looked away at the precise moment Crow looked across at her. They were so close. It would be easier to trust him with her life if she could divine even the vaguest notion of his intentions. She battled a startling urge to reach out and touch him; two or three times, they had awoken near a stream and he'd crouched at the water's edge to shave himself with a cut-throat razor, stripped to the waist, revealing the extraordinary collection of tattoos on his back, writhing blue-black patterns that ran from shoulder to shoulder, from neck to lower spine. Now, though, his high-boned face was dark with new beard; she had never once seen a gentleman not clean-shaven. But then again, Crow was not a very satisfactory gentleman.

'I'm sure you don't care, but when I stayed with your parents at Nansmornow, Kitto never stopped talking about you. You were a great hero to him then.' Hester watched from the tail of one eye as Crow swiftly concealed an expression of unshielded distress. She had no notion what to make of that. Did this arrogant and unkempt earl care, then, that his young brother had once worshipped him? Papa had told her a little of Crow – and he wasn't unknown to her by reputation either. Then Lord Crowlas, he'd absconded from Eton, stowing away on Papa's *Belle*. After five years at sea under Papa's command, he'd abandoned the navy and joined Wellington's personal staff in Spain. What boy would not revere such a brother – first a runaway sailor, then a soldier in Wellington's own inner circle? 'Surely there's no cause to keep Kitto under such close scrutiny, as though he were no more than five years old?' She spoke without giving herself the chance to think better of it and hurtled on, horrified at the depth of her own daring. 'Why must you treat him as though he were a gazetted criminal?'

Crow tossed a stick into the fire. 'Because he is a gazetted criminal. And don't speak of my parents: you stayed with my father. Louisa is not my mother. She's been dead almost as long as your own.'

'I'm sure I'm extremely sorry.' Hester longed to know what crime Kitto had committed, but fell silent: she didn't trust herself to modulate her voice how one should when addressing a man.

Looking away from her, Crow watched the flames, long legs stretched out before him. 'You know, last week I had to bribe Lieutenant de Mornay not to hang him for insurrection.'

Hester stared at him. Even on Scilly, de Mornay's name was spoken with hushed fear and repulsion. 'Insurrection?'

'He blew a hole in the French garrison at Newlyn. I grow unconscionably wary the moment he's out of my sight, which can only be my failing, you need not tell me.' He had the grace to look away, not to demand an apology or to draw attention to the justice of his apparent severity with even a change of expression. Hester held out her hands to the fire's warmth. There was little choice, then, but to put up with the glacial atmosphere, as well as the discomfort of the journey and the nauseating fear that at any moment they might be overtaken by French troops. Each day had been a matter of hungry survival, hunched in the saddle with Crow's warmth behind her and the rain in her face, of steeling herself to swallow charred rabbit or squirrel meat. Stopping to buy provisions was out of the question: descriptions of Hester herself and almost certainly Crow would by now have circulated around every French garrison from Penzance to London, and along every post-road. Even if they evaded capture, every day brought them closer to London, a bald fact that until now Hester had only looked at sidelong. When they reached it, what was to become of her? She couldn't avoid the question forever. She had no desire to stay with the Lamornas again, to face the stares and whispering of Louisa's patronising friends – those who counted themselves Abolitionists were almost as bad as those who still held African men, women and children as enslaved prisoners on their profitable Jamaican estates.

'Oh, don't look so downcast,' Crow said, surprising her. 'In all honesty, this is a damnable mess we're in, and if the fault is anyone's, it's mine. You might be a managing harpy, but I've never known a woman so uncomplaining.' He blew smoke into the fire, looking sideways at her. Hester stared back. What on earth had he just said? Cousin Jane had taught her that the consequences of challenging a man's opinion were misery and shame at one's pride and effrontery, not his rueful capitulation.

'A managing harpy?'

'Yes. But nevertheless, I can only be grateful to you, Miss Harewood,' Crow went on with devastating charity. 'I've known colonels make more more fuss than you about conditions like this. You would have made an admirable soldier's wife. I promise you'll be a great deal more comfortable as my step-mother's guest.'

Hester looked down at her hands, propelled from shocked gratitude at his surprising generosity of spirit to despair at how little he understood the reality of existence for a girl with brown skin, whether she had aristocratic relatives or not. Those relatives had never acknowledged her and never would; neither did she wish them to. He had no notion what her reception in a grand London townhouse would be like: how could he? Fear swelled in a dark burst of dismayed helplessness, driving her to anger. 'Does Lady Lamorna have no choice over the guests she receives? Am I just to be thrust on her? I'm well provided for – if you must know, I've no need of your charity, and I haven't the smallest desire to be anyone's wife, which is just as well considering I'm completely unchaperoned.'

'Why should Louisa object, when I've decided it?' Crow seemed not even to comprehend that his word might be questioned by his stepmother, a mere woman in his household. 'And whilst it's true that you're unchaperoned, that's a circumstance without the least importance when you consider that no one save ourselves knows anything about it. London's no place for a woman living alone, Miss Harewood, not in these times, even for a woman of your considerable means.'

Hester stared at him, trying to understand what it must be like to have such absolute control over circumstance. 'It's important to me.' The words flew from her lips with far more force than she had intended. 'Honour matters just as much to me, you know, even though I don't have your lily-white skin. And it would have been important to my father.' Papa was gone, truly gone. She was never going to see him again: she hadn't truly known it until this moment, as if under Catlin's care he might have made some sort of miraculous recovery. For all Hester knew, Catlin was dead too. She was to be thrust amongst strangers – aristocratic white people just like her mother's family who were so horrified by her very existence that they had never admitted it, let alone written to her or invited her to visit them, not that she would have wished to. It was the very last thing she or Papa had ever wanted.

Saying no more, Crow shifted towards her and in one instinctive, unquestioned and extraordinary moment she in turn moved nearer to him, drawn in so that she sat against the warmth of his chest as he leaned against an ash tree, one arm drawing the blanket close beneath her chin. Her heart raced; within moments, she felt both uncomfortably hot and cold.

'If it's honour that concerns you, I'll guard yours, Miss Harewood,' Crow said quietly, even as he eroded it by holding her so close. He was so warm, and the reassuring weight of his arm melted away terror when she ought to have recoiled from it: instead she revelled for a moment in a shocking sensation of drunken pleasure, just like that Christmas at Nansmornow when Crow's father had given her a second glass of champagne, and she had never in her life tasted anything more exciting than Mr Evans's mild claret cup. How could she ever have imagined then that Lord Lamorna's long-absent son might hold her like this, with her face pressed against the warmth of his shirt?

'You should go to sleep,' Hester said firmly. 'You must be tired. I'll wake you if anyone comes.' And even though she could no longer see Crow's face, she knew that he smiled. Lulled by the heat of his body against hers, Hester could no longer keep her eyes open. Before sleep came again, dark and warm, she felt the lightest of touches against her forehead, his fingertip glancing off her hair.

'*Vous pouvez dormir maintenant,*' he said quietly, and she wondered why he had chosen to speak in French.

9

Crow sat leaning against the ash tree, ridged bark digging into the spare flesh of his back. Hester lay with her head and shoulders in his lap; sleep had banished all that endearing concern for propriety, and she had curled up like a kit as if to press as much of herself against the warmth of his body as she could. He'd known many women but never one like this. She was so brave, and because of him and Kitto she'd witnessed horror impossible to forget. He was a wanted man. All he could do was take her safely to London, and pray that he struck a deal with Joséphine before the Occupation caught up with him. Christ, why was nothing ever simple? He shifted against the ash, careful not to disturb her. The tree was a solid, necessary presence as he cradled her in his arms, recalling in uncomfortable detail his last encounter with Lieutenant Colonel Colquhoun Grant, now Chief of Intelligence for an army that no longer existed.

They'd been summoned to another meeting at Woollet Hall, the country estate of the former prime minister, Lord Castlereagh, each man present well aware that attendance at such a gathering was enough to send every last one to the guillotine. The business of dining had been bad enough, but at least sawing at boiled mutton had given Crow an excuse not to speak, to ignore the naked fact that – still, nearly two years after the defeat – no one could quite bear to look at him. He'd realised, too late, that Castlereagh was addressing him across the table, half obscured by a silver epergne depicting the rape of Persephone.

... a chance, perhaps, to redeem yourself, Lamorna. Castlereagh had paused, and laughed like a braying donkey. *Never mind Waterloo, when one has a French mother into the bargain—*

Crow had heard his own reply as though someone else spoke. *My mother is long dead, you know. Would you also say that I had a French grandfather, or does that not count against me? The Duc de Montausier was, after all, guillotined the year after I was born: I hardly know whether to lay claim to him or not. All I know was that the Duke of Wellington never had cause to question my loyalty to Britain, regardless of my mother's connections. Mine is scarcely the only family of its kind to have relations in France.*

Thick silence had filled the room, flecks of dust suspended in shafts of sleepy early evening sunlight. Looking down at his plate, Crow had gripped the smooth bone handle of his knife, forcing himself to breathe steadily, not to lose control, always so easy now. He'd looked up, from man to man. Castlereagh, Alvanley, Brooks. Their faces blurred into one. His own generation were gone, lost in the appalling savagery of the days following Waterloo and the invasion itself: Alex Gordon, Percy, Fitz – friends he would never drink or hunt or whore with again, faces he could not bear to recall. He'd failed them all. He was unforgivable.

Come now, Castlereagh had said. *Can you not endure a little good-natured jest? Surely no one could suppose the Saint-Maures have any reason to bear loyalty to an upstart emperor who took advantage of their own sorry circumstances.*

I must beg leave to correct you, sir. Thanks to my father, my mother survived the Terror, but she was the only member of her family to do so. To my knowledge, there are no de la Saint-Maures left to bear loyalty to Buonaparte or to anyone else. My name is, after all, Helford, not Saint-Maure.

He'd leaned back in his seat, watching them all, taking a childish enjoyment in their well-bred discomfort. These men here were his father's friends. In that lost world before war broke out again in '15, he'd ignored their avuncular, well-meant attempts to curb his wildness with all the arrogance bestowed by more than twenty years of doing almost exactly as he pleased. Failing to save his own country was a greater sin indeed than arguing with his father at White's or encouraging friends with lesser fortunes into gaming hells. He had nothing to say. Causing the loss of a battle wasn't even the worst of what he had done, what he still must do.

Alvanley had spoken up, clearing his throat. *Come now, Castlereagh, it's hardly fair to blame the boy for – for what happened at Waterloo.*

And Crow had said, *Why, Alvanley? Why is it not fair to blame me for Waterloo? Let us not split hairs. It's true I failed the duke.* Alvanley had sighed, looking out of the rain-spattered window, embarrassed by his outburst. It was his fault that any of them had come here at all, that this poor gathering was even necessary. Because he had not run fast enough through the mud. Because he had not reached Wellington in time, on the morning that he should have died. Everyone knew that. He'd thought it would be impossible to get used to the shame, but the weight of it was ever present, like a rain-soaked jacket he lacked the courage to remove while the rain still fell. Castlereagh's well-trained servants had by now removed the covers, but the air was still greasy with boiled mutton and the thick, sweet scent of a spinach and nutmeg tart. Grant had faced him across the dining table, well fed, with his patrician nose and that fair hair slicked back, watching him as Castlereagh spoke again.

Come now, Lamorna. I think you know why we're all here. Joséphine has extended the hand of friendship to us – the old guard, as it were. We've every reason to believe Buonaparte now wishes for peace and stability – he's always entrusted this sort of delicate affair to Joséphine.

And the fact, Crow said, *that he divorced her seven years ago is excessively promising, I'm sure.*

Castlereagh ignored him. *Joséphine is installed at Carlton House, and she has invited us to send an envoy to her. Our interests will be represented at the Buonaparte court and, in turn, we will have the opportunity to make our own judgements about the state of affairs there.* He smiled, as if inviting Crow to join him at the opera. *Think of it, if you like, as a continuation of your role in the Corps of Guides.* On Castlereagh's other side, Alvanley silently offered his snuff-box.

Crow shook his head, laughed, and lit a cigarillo from one of the candles. *Once a spy, always a spy?* He knew he was conducting himself with a lamentable lack of form, but didn't care. *And, at the same time, Grant and I have our other tasks to attend to, naturally.*

I think we can all agree that the continued disruption of the Occupation government is essential, Grant interrupted. *Look at Buonaparte's retreat from Russia. Everyone blames it on the winter, but such attacks were essential to the Russians' eventual success. We need bridges destroyed, post-roads attacked, even to upset the distribution of currency.*

Crow breathed out a steady stream of smoke. *Naturally, the ordinary people who pay the price for that will be happy to consider themselves a sacrifice when the reprisals begin in earnest. I'm to befriend and spy on Buonaparte's divorced wife because we hold no other cards, and meanwhile construct a web of partisan warfare. I consider myself flattered you hold me in such high esteem.*

Castlereagh's opera-box smile didn't falter for a moment. *Well, we know Joséphine likes a pretty face. I'd go myself, but—*

Crow had got to his feet as Castlereagh, Grant and the gathered men laughed, those friends of his father's who now despised him. He had managed a bow, even, walking straight out into a courtyard planted long before the war with now-overgrown roses. Raindrops clung to a riot of leaves marred with black spot, and he'd looked up at the flat grey sky. Knowing that he deserved the humiliation made it no easier to bear. Grant, of course, had followed him, the unspoken rebuke clearly marked in the set of his fleshy lips, the arrogant, unchallenged angle to his gaze.

What do they mean me to do? Crow had demanded of Grant. *To be Joséphine's whore?*

If necessary. Do whatever you must. Gain her confidence. Learn whether Jérôme is costive after dining, what he speaks of, whether he suffers with a cold. You and I both know how useful the smallest, most insignificant fact can prove to be. I don't care how you do it. War demands sacrifice, Lord Lamorna.

Crow leaned back against the ash tree once more, holding Hester safe against him as he looked up at the cold, distant sky visible between black branches. With no honour left, what more could he give to this lost cause, when his life was worth so little? All the same, he had been gone too long, and Grant awaited him now in London, and return he must.

'I'm sorry,' Crow whispered into the darkness, wanting to reach out and touch Hester's finely moulded mouth with the tip of one finger. 'I'm sorry for carrying you into this.' She trusted him, though; having her sleep in his arms felt akin to holding something so extremely fragile and precious that he was afraid of breaking it. So he held her and waited. He knew it was coming. He sensed the approach of a waking nightmare with the queer burning shiver that passed repeatedly across the backs of his hands and down each finger. There was nothing he could do. Crow glanced down at Hester, at her mass of fine, light curls escaping from a thick braid tied with a hem torn from her gown. He could hardly bear to look up. He had to; he must, unable to fight the surging sense of alert panic. Sure enough, five French infantrymen walked through the dark clearing. Closer and closer they came, muskets cocked, bayonet-tips catching the moonlight. Crow knew their faces; he'd seen them before. One was an old man with a trailing grey moustache, one not more than a boy, a red birthmark splashed across one side of his face. He couldn't kill that many Frenchmen, not even with Arkwright's help. Why was Arkwright still asleep? Why did he not wake to help? He'd not moved an inch, humped by the fire in his stinking greatcoat. Crow knew he should be shouting at them all to run, but somehow his throat was frozen, his lips would not obey. When he next looked, the soldiers were different: now the old man walked with a charred hole in his midriff and the young boy had no face, only a glistening mass of flesh with dark holes gaping where once his eyes had been. A moment later, the French soldiers were gone, every last one, blinking out of existence.

His father's voice echoed: *I'll ask you this only once, Jack. Why were you shot in the back?*

When Crow looked down at his hands again, he was still holding Hester but they were shaking so much that he was afraid he would wake her. He imagined laying her down on the cold leaf mould, priming his pistol and holding it beneath his jaw, and the sheer release from all this when he fired. She had been right. He couldn't blame Kitto for the murders at Nansmornow. He had failed as his brother's guardian just as he had failed Wellington at Waterloo. If anyone was to blame for Roza's death, for the blood of her maidenhead staining her thighs, for her swollen purple lips and dead eyes bursting from their sockets, when once she had been so beautiful and so innocent, it was he. Crow was not at all sure how much longer he could go on.

10

A week earlier...

In the servants' hall at Castle Bryher, no one spoke. Catlin watched sunlight slant in through high, narrow windows set into the curving wall. Blue curtains twitched in the breeze, hemmed when she and Hester had both been little girls, setting stitches side by side when they'd rather have been collecting shells. Lord, where was she? The captain was dead, laid out on the stillroom table, right where she'd been grinding geranium petals just hours earlier, fit to crown Hester for making all that mess with oil and gunpowder. She felt trapped in a nightmare, watching all this unfold. It was like going through the stores in a hard summer to find all the salted mackerel rotten and the dried apples blooming with mould, the same sick horror and disbelief. The smell of seaweed rotting at low tide blew in, mingled with the scent of the rambling rose that clung against all odds to the wave-splattered walls outside, just as if nothing was any different. One of the Garrett girls was crying, which wouldn't do at all. She'd set the others off.

'Now then, Mary,' Catlin said. 'We must all be Christian

soldiers and do our best. Miss Hester can't be helped with tears, and neither can Master. Jacca, give her your handkerchief. There's nothing to be done but wait for Mr Evans to come back.'

'But why are they on the island, the French? Why did they kill him? What've they done with Miss?'

Catlin stared at the young footman till he flushed. 'That's not our business, Jacca.' She smoothed out her apron at the sound of footfalls in the passage leading to the servants' hall, soothed by the crisp weight of starched linen beneath her fingertips. A hall full of panicking servants would be good for nothing. They all took their lead from her: she must calm herself. Uncle Evans came in, that awful old-fashioned periwig still neatly placed, his bloodstained coat brushed down, as if that'd help. If Tilly put bloodied clothes in the hot copper again only to set the stain, Catlin would give her pepper. It was going to take more than a good cold soak to get that lot out.

'Field Marshal Ney.' Uncle Evans spoke in his colourless way, as though announcing a guest of the master's known to be regularly drunk and a trial to all the servants. The sort with roving hands you had to dodge. The staff were all on their feet, bobbing their heads and curtseying in decent order. That was something to be proud of, even if pride was a mortal sin. Uncle Evans stepped to one side, and a man came in after him in a smart French uniform, the epaulettes of his blue jacket glittering with gilt decorations. A proper long-shanks, he was, with broad, meaty shoulders, rusty whiskers and a great sweep of hair. He was like an old dog fox; she could just see him sniffing for blood on a cold night. He seemed to fill the room, in the fashion of one born to command everything precisely as he wished, but there was that odd twitchiness, too, that you sometimes saw in men who'd gone for a soldier. Would Tom have been like that if he weren't rotting in some French field because of men like this? But she couldn't think about that now. Catlin imagined squeezing the grief in both hands, wringing it out like a dirty dish-clout. *Ney*. The name was familiar, somehow. That's it: she'd read it in those month-old editions of the *Morning News* Hester always sent down from above stairs. Some sort of soldier or general or some such.

'Now then,' the marshal said, in good English, 'my wife always tells me no house can go on at all well with the servants overset. It's been an unfortunate business with your master – a misunderstanding – but I can assure you that everyone is quite safe.'

Quite safe, with the captain dead and Hester gone? It was just the sort of impudence Catlin wouldn't allow in the younger servants. The staff stood like so many rocks, even Jacca Garrett and little Tilly. A misunderstanding? How dared he, this Ney? As though it was all a joke.

'There is a guest,' Marshal Ney went on as if he were now master in the house, with the right to give instruction. 'One guest of the greatest distinction, who must be treated with respect and attended by only the most high-ranking of you.' Catlin kept her eyes down, examining her shoes, the carefully oiled brown leather. 'Who,' he said, 'is Mrs Rescorla?'

She dropped into a neat curtsey. 'I am Mrs Rescorla, sir.' *He died at the hands of your men. My Tom.*

And Marshal Ney smiled.

Catlin climbed the narrow, winding tower steps up to the master's library, the soles of her feet sinking into the stair-rug as she balanced the tray. Savoury steam emerged from a crack between one of the bowls and the plate set on top to keep the heat in Aunt Evans's pickled-asparagus velouté. That Marshal Ney had a cheek. Seven different removes, ordered just as if he owned the place.

I should poison the bastards, Aunt Evans had muttered, sprinkling chopped chives and parsley over the dish of jellied sardines, her reddened knuckles looking so sore in the lamp-light. Catlin would have to make more balm for their hands: Mr Garrett must be killing the hoggets grazing Shipman Head Down in a week or more, and there'd be plenty of sheep-grease. She sensed the French soldiers watching her, scorning her pale and sturdy solidity. They weren't going to knock for her. No, they wanted to watch her wait, to suffer and drop the tray as she tried to rap on the door by herself. She wasn't pretty, had never been pretty, only to Tom, her Tom. But that was a good thing, the stories she'd heard of what French soldiers did to pretty girls. The door swung open from within and Marshal Ney looked down at her, all glittered braiding, leathery tobacco and that shock of coarse, foxy-red hair. There was no click of the key turning a barrel: whoever this prisoner was, they were not locked in.

'Ah, Mrs Rescorla.' Ney smiled, displaying sharp yellow teeth. 'Do come in. I'm sure we can count on your discretion.'

'Of course, sir.' Head down, Catlin walked the well-trodden path from the door to the little table by the north-eastern window where Captain Harewood used to sit with his astrolabe. Once she'd caught him in a rare moment of stillness, watching the sea, just watching and watching, and she'd wondered what he was thinking, what he dreamed of, such a man as he was, with those ridged rings of purplish scar-flesh on his wrists and around his neck, too.

She set down the tray at last, feeling the relief in her shoulders, and turned to face Marshal Ney and the man who was sitting at the master's very own desk, looking at a book. Hester's half-finished portrait of her father had been moved, the easel leaning carelessly against a bookshelf. She'd not got far; most of it was still red chalk. It would never be finished now. Where was she? Catlin felt sick to her stomach and forced herself to stop thinking of Hester, for what could she do? The prisoner didn't look up, not that she'd expect him to, but he was well dressed in a smart blue coat, his hair carefully brushed. Quality. Not a young man but not old either. She bobbed a curtsey and waited to be dismissed. What else could they want? Why had Ney asked for her and not been content with one of the footmen?

Marshal Ney nodded. 'Very well, Mrs Rescorla. You may go now.'

At that moment, the prisoner looked up at last, glancing out of the window at the sea, and Catlin knew him; that great big nose like a wedge of cheese had appeared in sketches in the *Western Morning News* and in those satirical cartoons Miss Hester had sent from London: Arthur Wellesley, the Duke of Wellington. Actually here at Castle Bryher, about to drink Aunt Evans's pickled-asparagus velouté. *The Duke of Wellington.* She sensed the Frenchman Ney watching her. Had the papers not said Wellington was to be sent up to Scotland? She'd read the Pretender-King's decree. *My brother, the most noble Emperor, wishes to spare the life of his Greatest Adversary.* Wellington was lucky, she supposed, not to have been murdered like the regent – the fat old prince guillotined after leading the fight for London itseslf, his father and all of the royal family with the misfortune to still be in England dead of gaol-fever, according to *The Times.* And if you believed that, Catlin thought, you'd believe anything. Sure as death, the Buonapartes had seen to it that those royal throats were cut in prison and dared not admit it. Yet here was Wellington, still alive.

Her mouth felt so dry it was hard to speak. 'If you're sure there is nothing else I can do, sir, then I will leave you now.'

Marshal Ney smiled again, and she didn't like the way he watched her, like a man with a dish of braised meat set before him. 'That will be all, Madame Rescorla. I'm sure you and all your staff will understand the need for discretion. How very important it is that news of your guest's whereabouts must not be repeated away from this island, at any cost. After the most regrettable incident this morning, my men and I would be quite desolated if anyone else on Bryher were hurt. Do we understand one another, madame?'

'Perfectly, sir.' Catlin curtseyed, her heart racing.

The Duke of Wellington turned back to his book.

II

A week had gone by, and Wellington breakfasted early, not long past dawn. Catlin set the tray on the ormolu side-table by the north window, not quite able to put it on the desk where Captain Harewood had always taken his morning beef and ale. Aunt Evans had cried all over the tray of spiced tattie cake as she drew it out of the great black oven. Wellington wouldn't be wanting tattie cake, but the captain had been so partial to it: he had a slice with his meat every morning. They'd buried him as the sun sank behind the church tower: no coffin to be had, only a shroud of Catlin's best sheets from the linen-press, handfuls of hedgerow daffodils tossed into the narrow grave. The grate in the captain's library was still thick with grey ash: it should have been swept neat and fresh, a tidy pile of kindling laid ready to light; no Quality ever saw the remains of last night's fire whilst Catlin held the reins, or not till now – for shame. What right had Wellington to get up so early, upsetting everything? He'd dressed already, in that neat blue jacket and close-cut breeches. His boots were thick with salt-stains from where they had marched him through the surf and up the beach. Jacca ought to have a go at those, she supposed.

Wellington stood at the south-facing window with his back to her, a book in one hand. The shutters and windows were both flung open and the thick linen curtains stirred in a sea-breeze angling in from St Mary's Roads. Catlin could see out across the sound, glittering grey water like a sheet flung out, now studded with foaming white horses as the tide began to turn. What was he looking at? Hester was out there somewhere. Catlin cleared her throat, trying to attract his attention. She was meant to wait until he spoke, of course, but it was washday, and Wellington was the kind that took no more notice of servants than of the chair he sat on. He carried on turning the pages of Captain Harewood's own book with a neat flick of his fingers. She caught sight of a page – sea-maps, a little face of the north wind filling his cheeks and ready to blow, a drawing no bigger than her thumbnail, the single, exotic word *Azores*.

'I am very sorry, sir, that the fire is not yet laid. Would you wish me to do it directly, sir?'

'What?' Wellington turned to face her; he had such chilly blue eyes.

Catlin dropped into a little curtsey, looking down at the floor. It wouldn't do to push him too far or he'd be no use to her at all. 'Would you wish me to light the fire, sir?'

He just turned back to his book without replying. *Would that be a yes then, sir?* Catlin went to the breakfast-tray, laying out the dishes of sliced ham and gooseberry preserve, setting yesterday's bread beside the silver coffee pot. Poor Aunt Evans would be mortified to know a guest on the island had tasted the remains of yesterday's loaf, but if Wellington would get up with the lark, what else could he expect? However, the Quality weren't known to be reasonable with their expectations. Catlin poured the coffee.

'Cream, sir?' *He charged at your command, when you knew there was no hope in it. My Tom.*

Wellington shook his head, still reading, flicking one long, pale finger at her in a gesture of dismissal. Catlin went to kneel in the grate to lay the fire like a young girl just starting out in service. When the morning-sticks were crackling, flames licking the thick coils of dried seaweed, she dared to speak again. She didn't see there was any other choice: if she didn't ask now she never would. She had to know. And in truth she was enjoying his discomfort at how she made her presence felt. He'd closed the book and paced across the room to the north window, watching the sound open out towards the Atlantic beyond the dark teeth of the Scilly Rocks. It was as if he hoped he could read the ocean itself.

'I beg pardon, your grace, but if you could tell me what has happened to my mistress, I should be so grateful, sir.'

'I've no idea.' That cold stare again: like having a pail of cold water dashed clean into her face. For half a breath, Catlin met his gaze with her own before directing it once again to the red Turkey rug at her feet.

How could he not care? Hester might have shot a man but she couldn't even dress herself. 'We are all most anxious about her, sir.'

Wellington was annoyed, by the look of him. Not used to this sort of impertinence and not much he could do about it either. 'Given her father's achievements at Trafalgar, Miss Harewood is a prize for Buonaparte. No doubt he expects his brother Jérôme to make an example of her. It's a pity. You may go.'

Catlin dropped into what was more of a twitch than a curtsey – you'd have scarcely noticed it. If one of the lower servants had done such a thing, she would have boxed her ears. *It's a pity.* As though Hester were a second-rate horse that had to be shot. Every night for the first nine years of Catlin's life they'd slept curled over and around each other like pups in the stable. Together, they'd gathered their skirts and stood at the shoreline, watching the waves foam around their legs. They'd pestered Big Jacca Garrett to bore holes in shells, threading them on to strips of a petticoat worn beyond repair. And now Hester was gone, and the only man who might have done something about it would do nothing.

Catlin would just have to manage everything herself, as usual.

PART TWO

London, 1817

12

Thank Christ they'd fetched up in London without getting hanged, shot or guillotined. To Arkwright's mind it was no thanks to Crow, giving cordite payment to French soldiers. Had the bloody young idiot learned nothing? Not that Arkwright himself was any better. He'd a fine collection of dead women to his name. There was nothing to do now but live with it, to get on with each day as it came, and Arkwright was long-practised at that. He held the two greys at a steady pace along Piccadilly, the coach heeling a touch on the left-hand side as they passed rows of tall, white stuccoed houses, thin lines of candlelight and lamplight glowing behind heavy shutters. One of the horses was going lame and the ancient carriage Arkwright had liberated from the stables of a remote rectory on Bodmin Moor listed so badly to the left it took all his skill and most of his patience to drive in a straight line: just as well they'd not far to go now. He'd be a sight less resty once Crow had gone to Joséphine at Carlton House. Done what he needed to do. Crow sat beside him on the box, eyes half shut as though he were falling asleep. He wasn't. Arkwright watched the lights up ahead, a flaming torch on each side of the road: a checkpoint.

It was like being out on reconnaissance: that same old feeling of walking into a right fucking mess with no way to side-step it. It'd been dark for more than an hour, well past the last bells. Even being out past the curfew was enough to stir up a hornet's nest they could do without.

'I'll deal with it,' Crow said, right quiet. It was eerie to see London like this at night. No Cyprians in their flimsy gowns or hordes of cup-shot young bucks, no beggars, no street-sweepers, just empty streets. London was dead.

Arkwright reined in the greys, bringing the barouche to a neat halt beside the sentry box. Quick as a cat, Crow slid off the box, the pocket of his greatcoat jingling with coin, and thank Christ he was still well blunted after days on the road, even with a young mort not used to roughing it. Not that she'd complained, Miss Harewood, he'd give her that.

'Is your lordship not aware of the penalty for travelling after the last bells?' Arkwright heard the sentry ask, some snotty subaltern who wanted the lights belting out of him. Inside the carriage, Gil let off a volley of barking, quickly stilled from within.

'We were most unfortunately and unavoidably detained,' Crow replied in French so fast and slick that Arkwright sensed the sentry's surprise. Most of the so-called Quality spoke French, but hardly any of them spoke it like a Marseille whoremonger. He'd not learned that from his French mother. Arkwright ignored rising unease.

'Unavoidably, sir?' Coin clinked as the bag changed hands. Glancing sideways, Arkwright watched the sentry, how his eyes flickered right and left, wishing for back-up he didn't have save one other man on the far side of the road who, let's face it, was not going to be much use if both Arkwright and Crow chose to make trouble.

'Unavoidably,' Crow replied, and the balance shifted.

'I'm meant to search the carriage, sir.' The sentry didn't sound snotty now – only young and scared.

'I'm quite sure that you are. You will not, however.'

'But, sir—'

Singing a different tune now, my lad. Arkwright waited. Not a word from within the carriage. Harewood's daughter had her head screwed on right. He heard another lot of jangling as more coin changed hands. Crow had kept some of the blunt in reserve. Now if only he could keep his head. Arkwright wasn't sure how much hope he held out for that.

Hester had lost count of the days since Papa's death, but surely they must be well advanced through March: the moonlit garden in the middle of Berkeley Square was carpeted with daffodils, oddly cheerful beyond the weight of her grief. In the darkness she glimpsed tall houses, some iced white with stucco like so many Twelfth-Night cakes, others handsome red brick. With expert ease, Arkwright turned the carriage, tooling it into a spacious stable-mews. She heard a low hum of voices: their arrival was not to be unobtrusive, then. Crow might have talked them all out of the night-guard's hands, but she must still face his home and his stepmother as an unexpected guest. A spurt of nauseous dread sent her clutching Kitto's hand, forcing herself not to think of how horrified Papa would be at such an undignified arrival in London. How could he really be gone? Tears spilled down her face, as uncontrollable as they were undignified. Kitto gave her fingers a brotherly squeeze, grinning at her as he gamely pretended not to notice. 'Believe me, you can't possibly have a nastier time than I'm about to. You're not the one absent without leave for a month, who got caught blowing up a French garrison.' He spoke with wry courage, but there was such a combative light in his eyes that

Hester was suddenly quite sure that she – and possibly even Crow – hadn't heard the full story behind his defection from London.

Hester wiped her eyes with the back of one hand. 'Surely your brother has already given you a rare trimming? He's not so mean-spirited as to do it again, surely?'

'Actually, I haven't yet had the pleasure.' Kitto's smile vanished. 'He was going to, but he didn't. After Nansmornow, I mean.' He leaned across the seat to look out of the window. He sank back against the seat-cushions and shut his eyes. 'Oh.'

'What's the matter?' Hester smoothed out the skirts of her filthy gown, stroking Gil's ears as the Dalmatian rested her muzzle on the seat. 'It can't be anything like as bad as being stopped by the night-guard: I thought I'd die of fright.'

'No, worse: Louisa's entertaining, by the look of all the extra cattle in here.' Kitto glanced with distaste at a showy chestnut gelding tossing its head in one of the stalls.

'Well, goodness, don't let your brother see that look on your face.' Hester clasped her fingers in her lap; relief at escaping the scrutiny of the night-guard faded at the prospect of Lamorna hospitality. Crow's father's Abolitionist friends had always looked at her with such polite astonishment whenever anyone drew her into conversation, as if they'd half expected some unintelligible language to pour forth from her lips, never quite caring if she overheard the things they said. *She'll be quite the exotic prize for someone, with a fortune like that at her back. It's only a shame about the children—*

Kitto shrugged. 'Stop fretting, Hets. You're setting me on edge now. They'll all be in the drawing-room drinking my brother's champagne – no one'll see you come indoors without a woman.'

'It's not Louisa's guests I'm afraid of. You know how servants talk. It won't be long before everyone in London knows I came all the way from Cornwall with no maid.' Now they were here, and as yet unharmed, the truth of the situation was unavoidable. It was an effort to keep her voice steady. They might have survived a perilous journey without being captured by the French, but it scarcely felt a relief. Was it really so unsafe for a woman to live alone – a woman of means? Because who would receive any girl who had slept beneath the sky in the arms of a man? Papa would have been speechless with horror had he even suspected she might find herself in such a situation. *You will be judged twice as harshly as any white girl. You must be better than all of them.* She would be alone, then – at least she could afford it. And yet if French soldiers rode to the gates of Nansmornow to rape and hang Crow's servants when he was not at home, what might they do to a girl who had killed more than one of their own?

'Oh, be easy – you look sick as a cat,' Kitto said. 'Listen, you should know Crow better by now. Trust me, it'll be as if you came to London escorted by nuns.'

'I'd like to see how he does it.' The carriage door swung open and at Hester's side Kitto swore with quiet, blasphemous precision.

'Been in Cornwall at this season, Lamorna? Damned freakish of you, when the good King Jérôme allows us to have our fun in town. The Season commences, dear boy. One might even forget the damned Occupation.' Hester didn't recognise the voice. In the near distance, unbridled laughter rang out across the stable-yard.

'Oh, don't question him, Burford, you know what he is – he's probably been entertaining one of his lightskirts in royal style.' That was Louisa. Her voice drove a chill through Hester's entire body. 'Darling Jack, what on earth do you mean by coming home at a time like this? We're just on the verge of going in to dinner. Burford and dear George laid a bet that your new greys couldn't be those you won from Mr Whitchurch, so we came out here to look.'

'Don't let me stop you, ma'am.' That was Crow: *Jack*. Louisa spoke his given name with a playful sense of ownership. Frozen in her seat, Hester watched Crow step forward to meet her; Louisa had such a slight, girlish figure that he had to duck down to kiss her. Hester longed to point out that the hem of her oyster-grey silk gown was trailing in the trampled straw, but she couldn't move. She was aware of more people gathering closer to the carriage – they had come, quite naturally, to greet Crow but now here she was, in all her unchaperoned disarray, as good as naked. Why had Arkwright opened the door so soon? What difference would it have made, anyway, by the time the Lamorna servants knew she'd come without a maid of her own? Gossip from below stairs spread just as fast as anything that originated in a drawing-room. Why had they not stopped to engage a maid? Surely even a girl from a post-inn would have done – why had they not thought of such a thing? It was too late now.

In a moment of bottomless silence, Louisa turned to the carriage, her necklet of pearls catching moonlight that glanced from the Grecian folds of her gown. She was never less than elegant, with all the poise of the Persian cats she kept in the drawing-room at Nansmornow, and if she was surprised to see either Hester or Kitto, no one gathered in the stable-yard would have guessed it. 'My dear Miss Harewood, how lovely to see you, darling.' Louisa smiled but – as ever – the Countess of Lamorna was unable to quite meet Hester's eyes. She turned to Kitto. 'Where on earth did your brother get such an abominable lot of firewood for a carriage?'

With a lapse of manners that only renewed the silence and made it yet more excruciating, Kitto looked straight ahead without replying. Crow directed a look of such dizzying ferocity at him that Hester could hardly breathe. A gathered party of at least ten people were staring at them with horror and fascination – at Kitto's stunning act of discourtesy and at Hester herself; the Lamornas' fashionable friends, all watching. Hester longed to look back at them all, defiant, but Papa had taught her well. She must be twice as gracious, twice as accomplished and twice as well-mannered as any young white woman, or she would be seen as less than human before they saw her as a girl. And so she looked down at her own hands, concealing her fury, as though waiting with demure patience for instruction.

Across the stable-yard, someone spoke quite distinctly. 'Captain Harewood's daughter, Lamorna?'

Close by, Hester heard someone speak in an undertone, the face indistinct. 'Overstepping the mark somewhat.' Doubtless she'd met the speaker at one of the endless parties endured that winter at Nansmornow. The Lamornas' guests had smiled at her slightest accomplishment, from playing an aria that a child could manage, to correctly dismembering a pear with an ivory-handled knife and fork.

Crow ignored both remarks with his usual hauteur, but the effect of that could last only moments. Hester twined her fingers together. They thought he'd brought her as a mistress to his own family home. Scalding shame washed through her. Too many had seen. It would be impossible to dress the manner of her arrival in clean linen now. Everywhere she went, she would be stared at but never spoken to. Even a fortune wasn't enough to protect her from such a fall; even a white girl could not have carried this off. She wanted none of Louisa's high-society set, true, but there was no way on God's earth she'd be received now by anyone except by young rich men just like Crow, as an expensive mistress. So this was how it was to fall, to be a woman alone. One's world shrank in a matter of seconds. Possibilities dissolved: even a letter to the kindly Sierra Leonean husband Papa had been courting on her behalf would not save her now. Mr Williams's mercantile friends would soon hear that Miss Harewood had travelled to London in company with two men and a boy, and no female to guard her virtue. What merchant would receive damaged goods? She felt a nauseating sensation of loss: in the space of a few moments, control of her own very self had been snatched away. No longer Miss Harewood of Castle Bryher, it was now the right of strangers to define her. Fallen woman. Exotic prize.

'We've come a long way, Lou,' Crow said. 'You'll forgive us if we must wait till tomorrow to raise a toast. Where is Mrs Halls? Miss Harewood is extremely tired.'

'Raise a toast?' Louisa smiled, but for all the world Hester would not have wanted to be on the receiving end of the look she directed at Crow. Hester wanted to die.

Crow smiled back, stepping away to let Kitto jump down from the carriage and watching him walk away across the yard and in through the stable door. 'Of course, Lou. Didn't you read my letter? I suppose you can't have, or you'd have waited before getting up a party. The French have done nothing for the mail. I've had the most undeserved piece of luck – Miss Harewood is going to marry me.'

Hester, twisting a gathered fistful of her filthy muslin skirt in one hand, couldn't look at Louisa, at any of them. Light-headed, she clutched at her seat with the other.

At last, Louisa spoke. 'Well, then I must congratulate you a thousand times, dearest. Ring for Mowbray and tell him dinner will wait quarter of an hour. Halls will be spitting fire about the soufflés, for all that. But I must see Miss Harewood upstairs, poor darling! My girl, I've never seen anyone look so knocked-up – what a journey you must have had.'

Hester couldn't get out of the carriage. She sat still clinging to the seat, letting Louisa's talk of mustard foot-baths flow over her, hardly even listening. It wasn't true, what Crow had said. She wasn't going to marry him and face a lifetime of excruciating silences and sideways looks from his aristocratic friends and family. She couldn't walk across the stable-yard with all those people watching her as though she were a leopard or a dragon, no more than some astonishing creature from a faraway land.

She would simply not allow this to be true.

13

Arkwright always liked to settle the horses himself. They'd not done badly for an ill-matched pair of screws swindled from a tavern. Rubbing down the gelding with a handful of straw, he felt a rush of tension shudder through one ribby flank as he sensed the boy's arrival: Christ, more threepenny tragedies. Kitto came in alone and sat on the floor outside the stall of his brother's favourite mare, forehead resting against his knees. Clear as day, he knew Crow and her upstairs were screwing. It was why he'd run, then. Crow and Lady fucking Lamorna made no effort to hide that spunk-stained linen, after all. And the bloody fool couldn't see what was wrong with the lad either – his own kin – although it was right before his own eyes. Arkwright glanced at the boy, hunched on the cobbles, still as a stone. Crow had been bad since Waterloo, blue-devilled and not able to leave the battlefield, not in his mind, anyway. Sooner or later, there'd be trouble because of it. More trouble even than a month-long trip to fucking Cornwall when they were meant to be harassing the Occupation, upsetting post-roads, the mail, the lot of it. And it'd all had to be left. Without him and Crow, there weren't men enough that knew the work as it should be done. Arkwright took a brush from the hook on the wall and started working over the gelding now he'd cooled down a bit. In the morning, he'd send Jim round to fetch the farrier. Arkwright knew it was daft, but sometimes he spoke to the horses, in his mind and aloud. *Two hundred miles or more, we've come, lad,* he told the gelding. *We'll have you well shod, even if the French soldiers do come for his lordship and me and the lass.* Crow had best not delay getting to Carlton House: he'd some bargaining to lay out unless he wanted to end on the guillotine, the girl too. And, of course, Arkwright had business of his own to attend to, with his own people. He worked over the gelding's skinny quarters, watching how the nap of his coat darkened at the brush-stroke. He'd a sick feeling that Castle was making ready to stir up trouble among the men even before they'd left London, weeks back. If they'd done anything stupid, it'd have been in the news-sheets – Jim and the servants here would know if the English revolutionaries had been setting gunpowder or killing the French. There was a chance some good might come out of this shit-heap of an Occupation – fair treatment for all, equality, like the French were meant to have before Buonaparte came along and set himself up as emperor when they'd only just got rid of the fucking king. But it wasn't going to happen if Arkwright's associates let the horse bolt right out of the gate as An Gostel had done at Newlyn – a clutch of idiot lads who called themselves An Gostel, at least. No, he'd have to keep an eye on Castle.

'Mr Arkwright, sir? Will I do that for you? Mrs Halls says you must be fair starved. There's vittles inside.' The new stable-lad wasn't much to look at, skinny and unremarkable with a mess of thin brown hair and that odd set to the eyes bairns had when the mam had been gin-soaked in pregnancy.

'Good lad, Jim.' Arkwright laid a hand on his shoulder. Petey would've been about that age now. He swallowed a surge of nausea, spew rising right up his throat. *Don't think about that, about him.* Jim was staring at the open door like a trapped rat at a terrier, his face rigid, and Crow came in. Jim froze, not fool enough to risk a move that might draw the master's ire on to his own head. Clever lad, he was learning how to deal with the so-called fucking Quality; Crow was a man born to have his every word obeyed without question, more was the pity.

'On your feet.' Speaking in fierce, hard Cornish, Crow rounded on his brother who was still crouching on the cobbles. Kitto got up slowly, never taking his eyes from Crow's face, in the way only a fool would do when a man was that close to reaching for a horsewhip. 'When Louisa speaks to you, reply and with courtesy. What the devil do you mean by it? I don't know what kind of ill-bred tragedy you want to enact, and I care still less, but if I hear or see such as that again I'll bring you out here and you'll feel that fucking whip across your back. And this time you stay in London, do you hear me?'

'I don't care.' The boy's mouth twisted. 'I wish Papa had never married her.' He was greeting, his filthy face tear-streaked. 'Why did he have to die?' Kitto slammed his fist into the stable door with such force that the mare shied and Jim mouthed silent blasphemies, caught alongside Arkwright in the servants' trap of having witnessed a scene and not being able to move till it was over. The mare backed up into a corner, showing the whites of her eyes, and Arkwright prayed to a God he'd not believed in for years that she hadn't hurt herself.

'Oh, God give me strength.' Crow just stood, levelling that nasty cold grey stare of his at the boy, and Arkwright couldn't tell if it was Kitto he despaired of or just her ladyship's guests, who had taken it upon themselves to come out to the stables in all their dinner gear and now trooped right in, filling the place with their loud voices and witless laughter. Arkwright wasn't sure how long he could stand to be among these people, if he could even bear it for as long as was needed.

14

Kitto fought ballooning panic as Louisa's guests filled the stable with loud talk and laughter; they crowded closer, calling greetings to Crow, and their breath stank of champagne and clove pastilles. As if the outburst had never happened, Crow just turned away and leaned on the stall-gate to talk over the conformation of his mare with Lord Burford and a thin-faced woman in a garnet-red gown. No one looked at Kitto or spoke to him. He didn't care about offending Louisa, but the shame of venting his grief about Papa was rendered more acute at being cut by his father's old friends, and a scalding flush spread across his face and down his neck. Not a word was spoken about Hester's unexpected presence at Lamorna House, or indeed his own. Without asking Crow's leave he turned and pushed past Burford and Maria Sefton; outside, the stable-yard seemed to spin around him. He ran in through the scullery, passing the kitchens and the harsh, familiar scent of soft soap mingled with the odour of onions cooked in butter and boiled lobster. It was so unmistakably the scent of home – of London, anyway – that he felt crushing despair. How could he have travelled so far, alone and friendless, only to end just where he had begun? In the front hall, he passed servants and lingering dinner-guests all staring at him, and found his way to Papa's library, shutting the door behind him. He'd left here one morning with little but a dream of finding a use for his life with the Cornish rebellion, and all it had led to was the deaths of those he loved. The memory of Roza and Nessa's hanged corpses rose up in his mind and he could smell sickly sweet rotting human remains again, and choked on the stink of shit, stale blood and putrefaction. It was his fault. He couldn't begin to forget. He sat on the green velvet chaise, heavy with loss and shame so acute that he gave way to panic: he could see no way to go on.

'Papa, don't leave me here.' Kitto pressed his hands to his face, longing to look again and find his father sitting at the desk as he had always done, but of course he was still alone. Swiping away tears, he stared at the two-hundred-year-old map of Cornwall and the Sabrinian Sea that hung on the wall above the chaise. A shoal of mermaids flexed tails shaded a delicate green; he'd once imagined setting the carmine-red sails of that galleon in pursuit of sea-serpents. He remembered his infant conviction that Jack, away at sea, traded pearls with mermaids just such as those. He covered his face with his hands again and one moment his arms and legs felt numb, like sacks of wheat, and the next he ached. He wished he could strip away the years; he recalled the faint scent of starch, brandy and Arabic snuff as Papa had carried him into a post-inn beneath a cold winter sky, and the extraordinary stink of London on his first visit – sewage and spices and coal-smoke. He remembered the flickering silk of a courtesan's satin gown here in this very library, and a round-faced woman in Grecian sandals with gilded toenails pressing clove-oil-scented lips to his cheek. Once, there had been a time when Papa opened a letter over breakfast at Nansmornow, pressing his lips tight together as he read. He had never forgiven Crow for going to sea, for doing just exactly as he pleased even though Papa himself had always done just exactly as he pleased. And Kitto had waited all that night for the sound of hoofbeats on the long carriage drive, and when he heard them at last, he'd dressed in a hurry and gone out before dawn broke, dew-spattered spiderwebs silvering the grass, all because his brother had lived through the battle of Vitoria, because Crow was coming home, for no more than a week. And when Kitto met him riding through the parkland on a strange chestnut mare, still dressed in his filthy, stained scarlet officers' regimentals, Crow had slid from the saddle and walked at his side. Four years later, Kitto was so mortified by the tears he'd just shed in Crow's presence that his stomach turned at the thought of facing him again. He would just have to meet him as a man: Crow would see that he wasn't the only one to show the world all that cool-headed poise.

Kitto watched the brass doorknob twist: it was the only thing in the room to move. Bookcases reached to the high ceiling; watercolours in gilded frames waited in motionless silence against walls painted the same gold-tinged blue as the sky in an old Italian painting. Crow came in, closing the door. Kitto caught sight of his brother's expression before Crow noticed him, like a dog-fox at the end of a chase: savage and exhausted, a killer run to earth. Waterloo had changed him. Out of habit Kitto got to his feet and was then dismayed that by doing so he'd proved himself Crow's subordinate instead of his equal. He didn't know what to do with his hands. Crow just walked over to Papa's old desk with all his usual composure and poured himself a glass of brandy; candlelight caught the lead-glass decanter as he tipped it.

'Well?' he said. 'You went away without leave, you caused God only knows what chaos with An Gostel, and you seem quite unable to keep civilised company. What am I to do?'

Kitto was so ashamed, and wanted so badly to ask for forgiveness, but he couldn't forget Louisa lying on the drawing-room chaise with the skirts of her gown all around her waist, and Crow kneeling before her with his head between her thighs. Papa had filled the house with rakes, whores and concubines for most of Kitto's life, and it was nothing he hadn't seen before, but Crow and Louisa were a pair of traitors; they'd betrayed Papa. And yet without Crow there was no one else. He'd always been able to fix everything: the wheel of a broken toy chariot, a tangled mackerel line, and even once a perversely brutal schoolmaster whom, returning on leave from Spain and descending on Eton with almost God-like glorious fury, Crow had threatened to choke if he should think of even looking at Kitto again. And yet he could not fix this situation – indeed, he had created it.

'Will I have the privilege of your answer?' Crow said. 'Or indeed any form of explanation at all?'

With an equally confusing and distressing urge to protect Crow from facing his own dishonour, Kitto would rather have thrown himself out of the window than tell what he knew, what he'd seen. 'I suppose one could say I learned from the best.' He forced himself to speak with a degree of calm he was far from feeling. 'You ran away from school when you were younger than I am now, and you joined the navy without Papa's leave, too.'

Crow leaned back against the desk. 'Another cross to bear,' he said, and Kitto knew he meant Waterloo, and how he'd been wounded before he got to Wellington with the dispatch that might have saved the battle. For half a moment, Kitto saw Roza and Nessa hanging again, this time from the gold-embossed library ceiling, their corpses swinging gently before dissolving into shadows cast by the chandelier. Tomorrow morning when he woke in his own bed they would still be dead, and Papa too, and the day after that, forever until he died, too. Instead of apologising, all he'd done was blame his own brother. He wanted to say that he hadn't meant it, that he wished Roza and Nessa and Mr Gwyn were not dead, that he was sorry, but he couldn't find the words. Crow just poured himself another drink and glanced at the door without bothering to conceal his disdain, a wordless dismissal that was so painful and shaming Kitto would rather have been hit.

'Is this it?' Kitto said, before he could stop himself, and trying to pretend he hadn't noticed Crow's expression of incredulous contempt at his effrontery. 'General Allanby has sixty thousand men still in the Americas. Why doesn't anyone do anything? Why can't you do something? We can't live like this forever, French soldiers going all over the countryside and killing whoever they please. People are starving. You saw how it was.'

'Children starved to death in this country long before Buonaparte landed.'

'At least there was a kind of justice! We should fight back,' Kitto almost shouted, and stood with one hand on the doorknob, breathing hard, acutely aware that his brother had not the patience for his word to be questioned in this way.

Crow watched him in silence, reaching in the desk drawer for a cigarillo that he lit at one of the tall white candles burning beside a heap of books. 'Justice?' he said at last. 'Was it? Men, women and children put in chains and sold across the ocean, children hanged for stealing bread? All nations and all governments are iniquitous, this one more so than others. Or maybe it only seems so because this time we're getting the sharp end of it. The world's an evil place: you might as well forget any notions of fighting for truth, bravery or justice.'

Kitto stared back at him, but it was as if he'd already obeyed and gone; Crow just sat down, exhaling cigarillo-smoke as he broke the red wax seal on a letter from a pile by the inkstand. He'd opened the door and was walking out when he heard Crow speak again.

'*Christophe.*'

Kitto stood still, trying to get the better of a rising sense of unease on hearing the French form of his name. French was Crow's mother tongue. She had not just given birth to him and then bled to death. She and Crow had actually known one another, and Crow used French not only when servants were present, but when he was so deeply moved that neither English nor Cornish would suffice. So this was it.

'*Écoute-moi,*' Crow went on in French. 'From now on you will stand absolutely clear of any form of rebellion, whether English or Cornish. Am I comprehensively understood?'

'Yes,' Kitto said. 'Yes, I understand.' He knew only that his brother was a coward and a traitor to their father, but that even so he still longed for his forgiveness and approval.

15

Lamorna House was a whirl of light, colour and the blunt, harsh speech of Crow's London servants. The scent of hyacinths was dizzying, but Hester took the staircase with a steady tread, one hand resting on Louisa's arm as she led her upstairs. The countess moved with her usual casual grace, just as though there was nothing for anyone to remark on. Hester was conscious of a door opening before her and the swish of a maidservant's starched petticoats, and Louisa led her into a bedchamber to a silk-covered ottoman beneath a pair of tall windows hung with white brocade curtains, bright in the candlelight.

'Sleep well, darling – you must be so fatigued.' Louisa bent forwards to kiss her, but the sweetness of her tone and the action itself were completely belied by the imperfectly concealed expression of horror in her eyes. The room was full of servants: no matter how much Hester had to say, all she could do was wish her goodnight. Louisa went out into the hallway, allowing one of the maids to push the door shut behind them. When she'd gone the room felt empty, despite the three strangers unlacing the sweat-stained gown and petticoats. They helped her into a bath before a glowing fireplace, doubtless hardly able to wait till they could escape and gossip about her arrival.

Soaked, scrubbed and wrapped in a starched towel that smelt of pressed lavender, Hester was eased into a nightgown foaming at the neck and cuffs with broderie anglaise; then she was led to the canopied bed. Minutes later, she sat back against a mound of pillows to receive a supper-tray and ate turtle soup garnished with cream and parsley, boiled greens, sliced ham, buttered potatoes, jarred lampreys spread on to a slice of toast and a spoonful of syllabub with orange water stirred into it and candied rose-petals sprinkled on top. After so many days of charred rabbit meat it was a feast – even if the syllabub was so laced with slave-traded sugar that it burned her mouth. To blunt the taste, she drank two glasses of Rhenish wine and a cup of hot milk.

When the servants had gone, Hester plunged her feet down between crisp, chilly sheets towards the hot brick. Her heart thundered with fury that snatched away any relief she might have felt at such comfort after so many days of rain and hunger. She blew out her candle and lay watching moonlight puddling on the floor between the brocade curtains. How had Crow dared? He'd changed the course of her life forever, all on his own whim, without even consulting her. In her mind, she heard Papa's voice again, so close as if he were standing behind her. *With money enough and pretty manners, the high ton may well accept you, especially with your mother's blood, but even to those who count themselves Abolitionists you'll always be a pet. We'll find you an African husband, one day, my dear – you shan't need to be among them much.* Dear God, but what if she did encounter Mama's family here in London? Cousin Jane had not really been family at all but Mama's dearest friend throughout otherwise lonely years in the sort of genteel boarding school where aristocratic families sequestered inconvenient female relations when they knew not what else to do with them. But in London, it was more than possible that she might meet real cousins, aunts and uncles, even. Hester had no memory of her mother, only the childhood invention of a forgiving presence conjured up on the occasions she had displeased Papa and Cousin Jane: Papa only rarely, Cousin Jane with great regularity. Mama would have understood that she'd meant no harm by obscuring the first two pages of her chapbook with a sketch of a flatfish washed up on the beach; Mama would not have chastised her for choking on a dry and indigestible slice of seed-cake when calling on Cousin Jane's elderly and impoverished great-aunt in Plymouth. In reality, Hester had little notion of what Mama had really been like, or what she might have thought of such youthful crimes, because Papa had so rarely spoken of her. She supposed the memories were too painful, his grief too sharp. The thought of finally meeting Mama's family made her heart lurch as though a great fish twisted in her chest. They had refused to acknowledge her: she wanted no part of them, but couldn't deny a perverse longing to see the shadow of Mama's features, even on the faces of those she held in justifiable dislike and contempt. They were part of who she was – without facing them, how could she know herself? She thought of how openly Louisa's friends had stared at her: here in London, she was no longer simply the captain's daughter but at best an outlandish oddity. And if Crow had his way, she would be something quite other. Hester folded back the heavy coverlet and went to the window in her bare feet, the borrowed nightgown not quite long enough to cover her ankles. Sinking down on to the low windowsill, she sat and looked at the moonlit, iron-railed garden flanked on all sides by elegant townhouses. She'd never wanted a husband at all. And now this – Crow had simply assumed she would marry him, of all people, and with sugar bought at the cost of African lives still served at his table. She pushed away a memory of drifting to sleep sheltered in Crow's arms, that surprising rush of joy at his touch. And yet to live as his wife would be so humiliating. Her own mother's parents had never so much as written a letter on her birthday. She didn't want such people to welcome her: most likely they still owned slaves in the West Indies. Even as a captive of the French soldiers, Hester had never felt so helpless. Louisa had been so horrified, perhaps not at her presence, but certainly at Crow's announcement. At home, the whispering song of the sea was the last thing Hester heard every night; here, she heard a faint strain of laughter drifting from some other part of the house and a church bell ringing the hour beyond the square. Was not London meant to be noisy? It was so uneasily silent under the curfew. And yet, as Hester watched the square, she saw a familiar figure emerge on to the moonlit street from somewhere within the bowels of Lamorna House itself. It was Arkwright. He walked away down the street, the collar of his greatcoat turned up against a night breeze. Without looking back, he walked half the length of the square and melted away down an alley between two houses. Either Arkwright had money enough to pay off the night-guard just as Crow had done only a few hours earlier, or he had something to hide in the darkness. Hester knew better than to suppose servants had no secrets. If Arkwright could look after his own destiny, then so would she, by whatever small means possible. She must find out what had become of Catlin – of everyone on Bryher. Crossing the moonlit rug on her bare feet, she went to the escritoire beneath the furthest window and, sitting down beside a sweep of curtain, she opened the lid and took out paper, ink and a pen. She must take affairs into her own hands. Somehow, she must contrive not to be the pawn in this game, but the queen.

16

In the laundry-room at Lamorna House, shadows leaped up walls beaded with moisture and flakes of damp whitewash littered the flagstones. Maggie would have to sweep once her work here was done: it wasn't she who had left the place in such a godless mess but since when had such considerations made any sort of difference? Even just a few paces from the fire, it was so bone-cold that she breathed out wet little clouds, and the air was thick with the roast-mutton stench from one of the tallow lamps set out beside the ironing table. Taking a moment to warm herself, Maggie spread out her skirts and sat by the hearth. She waited for the iron to heat through, trying not to think of those heavy folds of still-damp frilled linen waiting in the basket. She ought to get up and see if she couldn't at least trim the nearest lamp – it might smoke a bit less then – but that would take time she didn't have and she'd rather go squint-eyed ironing in the gloom than risk smirching clean washing. It wasn't even Maggie's job to be down in the laundry-room at this time of night, or at any time, really, but she had always known to quell and conceal her anger at such injustices, aware that worse might easily find their way to her feet. After years of doing double the work of a white woman, Maggie was finally an upper maid in a respectable household. Well, reputable if not respectable, at least. Fashionable, certainly. Maggie had seen Lady Lamorna's sheets of a morning, crusted with a man's seed, and her widowed two years since. Either way, that new young laundry-maid had come into the house bringing influenza with her, and was confined to her pallet. Someone must iron her ladyship's small-linens. Maggie frowned at the flames in the grate. The extra work should have all been dealt out and managed by mid-day; it was slovenly to have washing still not ironed and folded by a Thursday night. But Mrs Halls knew who might be leaned on to pick up the pieces at the last minute, that was the trouble.

With a muttered prayer, Maggie wrapped her hand in a rag and snatched the iron from the fire with a poker. She set it on the hearth to cool a little by the brass firedog, which was pitted with spots of tarnish and wanted polishing, idly wondering what the racket upstairs had all been about. Not long since, there'd been muffled commotion from the stable-yard of the sort that heralded more bodies to fetch and carry for: her ladyship and all those guests trooping outside into the stable-yard, of all places, laughing and talking in their loud, sharp voices about some horse or other, and then a racket of carriage wheels and heavy footfalls that drifted across from the stable-mews to the narrow laundry-yard just outside. From the sudden hush that had preceded more noise, like a breath drawn in and held, Maggie wagered his lordship was back at last, and that Master Kitto had come with him. So at least there was someone in the house likely to endure a worse evening than her. What can have possessed the child to disappear without leave for weeks at a time? Once, long ago and newly christened, Maggie herself had fled from a house like this. But she'd run as a slave bought as a pet to fetch and carry, not a cosseted child of the family.

Living in terror of capture, she'd frozen and starved, saved only by a chance encounter. No, Maggie had reason to be sure that living on the streets, alone and friendless, was anything but a harmless escapade. Perhaps to a spoiled white child like Master Kitto it was just an adventure. Maggie pressed the cooling iron into damp linen, idly wondering if the boy had discovered that his brother was tupping their stepmother. There'd be trouble if that ever got out. Maggie felt almost sorry for the child, because he must be miserable and now he would be punished, but she couldn't quite push away the queasy realisation that if his lordship was back, then so must be Mr Arkwright. All she could do was pray that Mr Arkwright and his friend Mr Wedderburn would have no more of those little requests that were like to see her hanged, if she were not careful.

Goffering the frill of a fine linen shift with the hot tip of the iron, Maggie heard the muffled chiming of the grandfather clock above stairs; it had struck eleven, and she must be up again before five to get the bedroom fires lit. With brisk, long-practised strokes Maggie pressed, spread and folded, stopping again to set another iron to heat. She would be here all night at this rate, with the taste of the pickled brawn they'd had for the fourth night in a row lingering in the back of her mouth with the stale milkiness of a four-day-old tapioca pudding. She longed to scrub her teeth and crawl between her own smooth sheets. There'd been an ugly mood in the hall at dinner, and one of the young footmen banished in shame from the table by Mr Mowbray himself for complaining of the skin of greenish mould on his slice of brawn. Mrs Halls never went to do the marketing now without the protection of the heftier footmen, one of whom had returned last time with a poached eye. There was little enough food to be had. It was the fault of the Frenchies, with the roads being so bad, and the Occupation army having the best of everything. At last, Maggie folded the last shift, having carefully hung the rest to air from a rack before the fire. They were still a little damp, but spread across the back of that spindly chair in her ladyship's dressing-room, one might be set before the hearth there and it would be dry by morning, close at hand. Maggie would retain her status as a most obliging person.

With two folded shifts in her basket, in case that stuck-up Mrs Mowbray or her ladyship were to drop or otherwise dirty one, Maggie climbed the back stairs. Unable to hold both the laundry-basket and a candle, she felt her way in the inky darkness, closing her fingers around the rough hemp rope bolted to the wall for a bannister. Reaching the first floor, she paused for breath and was blinded by candlelight blazing through a door flung open from family quarters. Mr Mowbray himself stood there, butler and tinpot king of the servants' hall, his great bald head shining in the light of the taper he held in a silver dish. Sinking into a deep curtsey, Maggie caught sight of floorboards waxed to a shine, and the edge of a Turkey rug that had doubtless cost double what she'd earned since the day she'd taken her own freedom twenty-five years before. With sinking dread, Maggie realised Mowbray wore an expression of startled harassment that meant he was about to find a use for her. She was now surely another hour from her bed, and there'd be no more than four hours' rest till she must get up again.

'Good lord, Maggie, you startled me, not but what it isn't harder to make you out against the dark.' Mowbray smirked as though he'd let fall the sort of witticism that would be repeated in drawing-rooms across London. 'However, you're just the person. His lordship, as you may apprehend, has returned with his fiancée.' Mowbray paused, as if for a moment the twin faculties of speech and thought had deserted him. 'The – young person is at present retired in the rose guest-chamber. You will oblige me by going to fetch her supper-tray.'

Maggie stared down at the mucky hem of her gown, wishing that she might place both her hands on Mowbray's chest at the top of the stairs and give him a good shove. She'd give a lot to see him fall down two flights of polished oak. A fiancée: well. Not a word had been breathed of the young earl taking one of the lures held out to him by all the fashionable mamas in London. His lordship's fortune and his title were enough to tempt, no matter that they might all say behind his back that Waterloo was lost for his failing, and that he was too wild, still, for marriage to be other than mortification to any wife. One of the more enterprising boot-boys had been reprimanded just after Christmas for running a betting ring on the chances of the earl being snared before the year was out. Well, here was a scandal.

'Do you attend, Maggie? This is no time to be daydreaming.' Mowbray's tone was querulous but severe, and Maggie dropped into another deep curtsey, whispered something obliging and incoherent, and hurried up the stairs clutching her basket. Stepping out into the bright warmth of a landing leading to the family bedchambers, she trod across parquet waxed and polished to a glow, and let herself in to her ladyship's dressing-room. Her ladyship must have not long gone to bed for Mrs Mowbray, her personal maid, was still setting an evening gown of grey satin on a hanger hooked over the walnut armoire. Maggie bobbed a curtsey and spread the two fresh-ironed shifts to air on the back of a gilded cane-chair drawn close to the fire. Not a word of thanks did she get, nor expect, and a swift glance at the evening gown confirmed Maggie's suspicion that the hem would be filthy with muck from the stable-yard. Doubtless her ladyship felt herself most terribly unconventional for trooping out into all that horseshit with her guests.

Maggie carefully lifted the chair, edging it a little closer to the flames, and set the brass fire screen to ensure no spark flew out and burned them all in their beds. The door to her ladyship's chamber was ajar, and she had no desire to be accused of waking her. Just as she set down the screen, a suppressed but still-audible sob drifted into the dressing-room from her ladyship's bedchamber, quickly stifled. A great, hollow silence followed. Maggie dared not look up to meet Mrs Mowbray's eyes. The air seemed to thicken, hard to breathe. And so the soon-to-be-Dowager Countess of Lamorna lay weeping in her bed the night her stepson had brought home this mysterious fiancée. *Three of us within twenty feet of one another,* Maggie thought. *We know she's weeping, and she knows that we know.*

Backing out of the room, Maggie went down the corridor towards the rose-pink guest-chamber, supposing that she was meant to be all full of rational pleasure that his lordship was to marry, and not a little unholy joy at seeing a mistress notoriously high in the instep taken down a peg or two. Lady Lamorna would be only the dowager now, not the countess – her power diminished. But a bridal meant more work, that was all. Maggie hadn't forgotten the chaos wrought at her ladyship's marriage to the late earl. At least the dead lord's whores had not expected their flimmery unchristian gowns to be washed and nor had they thrown balls, with enough extra toil to make the younger servants weep with exhaustion. Maggie's hand closed around the doorknob, smooth brass cool to the touch. No, despite all the bother of it, she couldn't quite suppress a surge of curiosity at Mowbray's purse-lipped announcement. The *young person.* What on earth was that supposed to mean, if not someone the butler considered entirely unsuitable for the task ahead of her? And a task it would be, marriage to such an ungovernable young lord.

Holding her breath, Maggie turned the doorknob without a sound and pushed open the door, stepping into a room that had made her gasp when she first came to work at the house, so pretty as it was. The long white curtains seemed to glow in the moonlight, and Maggie saw a neatly folded letter lying on the escritoire, turned face down. She could see the supper-tray from here, resting on the bedside table. The four-poster's occupant had fallen asleep before drawing the bed-curtains, and with a silent tread Maggie crossed the room, unable to resist a look at the unsuitable young person about to supplant her ladyship as mistress of the house. She lay on her side, turned towards Maggie, who stood for a moment in uncomprehending shock, unable to make sense of what she saw. A mass of curls sprang away from the pillow, gently rising and falling as the girl breathed, her skin a less deep brown than Maggie's own. A well-shaped hand lay against the linen sheet, fingers curled upwards like a child's. Long lashes brushed a high, sculpted cheekbone. She was so beautiful, her features unmistakably African. Never, ever had Maggie thought to see a black person – a person like her – lying asleep in a four-poster bed, between fine linen sheets, with the rose-pink counterpane carelessly tangled about her legs. Maggie's mind raced. The girl was light enough to be mixed, with one white parent and one black. Indeed, there was only one person she could possibly be, to be actually lying here now. The child of Captain John Harewood and the Duke of Albemarle's granddaughter. No, wait – the old duke was dead. This girl's mother, had she lived, would be a niece of the new duke, which made this child great-niece to a man who had been one of the most powerful aristocrats in the land before the French came.

Dear God, Maggie thought. *Dear sweet Lord*. The girl shifted in her sleep, and Maggie took up the tray, holding her breath lest she rattle the cup against a dish and wake the child. Edging out through the half-open door, she bent to set the tray down on the carpet so that she might turn the doorknob in silence. Unease swept through her as she became aware of a male presence – the scent of tobacco-smoke and a dry, sharp cologne, the unmistakable sense of tight-coiled strength. Freezing even as she crouched to set down the tray, Maggie saw his lordship himself step out of the shadows, holding a candle in a pewter dish. Smiling, he reached across and closed the bedchamber door for her with practised discretion. Slowly, Maggie stood up, still holding the tray, and bobbed a curtsey. He was a good-looking young man, if you liked that sort of thing, dressed to go out in a close-cut blue jacket, trim breeches and boots polished to a shine, snowy white linen at his throat, his face all hard angles and sooty-lashed grey eyes hollow with exhaustion. He said nothing, of course; she had not expected him to, but she watched him walk to the top of the stairs without looking back, and wondered if he had even the smallest notion what he was letting this girl in for, if she were really to be his wife.

17

Crow leaned back in the chair opposite Grant, sinking into the faded red leather upholstery. White's was almost empty. There were constant rumours the French would close it, but they hadn't yet. Unlike those who frequented only taverns and gin-hells, the patrons here could afford to pay off the night-guard after the last bells. Crow watched his commander with concealed dislike that he knew to be mutual: not only had he been a favourite of Wellington, who barely tolerated Grant, but till the defeat, he'd been chasing the man up the ranks harder every year since Vitoria. Tall and well fed, with an air of settled superiority and that thick blond hair swept back à la Brutus, Grant had gained his position by name alone. Thanks to years of Arkwright's silent disdain, Crow was only too aware that he himself was no better. After a particularly wild and scandalous shore leave from the *Belle*, Papa had taken the extraordinary step of bestirring himself, and a single letter from Lord Castlereagh to Wellington had attached him, aged twenty, to the duke's personal staff. Once there, he'd earned some merit, but Grant's elevation was utterly unwarranted and due only to his name and influential connections: the man was both pompous and incompetent, and yet Crow must obey his commands. To all appearance, anyway. He was so deprived of sleep that shadows flickered where there were none; he was unable to relax his guard even for a moment. He shut his eyes briefly and saw naked corpses lying in the mud, tumbling black feathers and dead men stripped of their clothes by battlefield thieves. He was a wanted man, and every moment he spared for Grant left Hester in danger, too. Crow knew he must tell his commander the whole before he heard it elsewhere – Kitto's arrest, the murders at Nansmornow, and the lives that he himself had taken in exchange for those of his own people. Grant listened in silence. He said nothing for so long that Crow was hot with reluctant shame, which did nothing for his temper.

When Grant spoke at last, it was with obvious and irritating forbearance. 'Were you seen bringing the Harewood girl to London?'

'No, but I must get to Carlton House. Her life's in danger until I speak to Joséphine.' Crow shut his eyes again, exhaustion rolling over him once more. He'd never spent much time thinking about marriage, supposing when it crossed his mind at all that any proposal would be made, naturally, in the far distant future and met by some suitable, well-reared female with a maidenly blush. Hester's expression of undisguised horror had been something of a surprise.

'And what, precisely,' Grant asked, 'do you mean to do at Carlton House – as a man now wanted for the killing of four French soldiers? Your own life is also in danger, I might add, as I have no doubt you're already aware.'

'They killed my own servants, and my kin,' Crow said lightly. 'What would you have me do? Let it happen without recourse?'

'I'd ask you to remember, Jack, that now is not the time

for such gross dereliction of duty. Your reputation is scarcely unsullied as it is. Are we to let the Occupation go unchallenged while you disappear for a month to chase after your delinquent brother? There is work to be done. And I might add that I still have no very clear notion of how you found yourself riding half the length of the country in company with Captain John Harewood's daughter.' Grant uttered Harewood's naval title with a distinct edge of sarcasm.

Crow leaned back in his chair, smiling even as he thought how very much he loathed the man. 'Well, sir, and had I not, we'd still be wishing to believe that Wellington had been taken to the Hebrides, just as Jérôme Buonaparte said in his writ.' Till the day he died, he would not call the man king.

'What do you mean?' Having dismissed the maître d', Grant poured more claret.

'I've found him. Or rather Miss Harewood did. He's on Scilly – Bryher, to be exact. He was brought there by French troops, and her father killed. Miss Harewood was herself taken prisoner, but escaped.'

'Into your company, I suppose?' Grant lifted his glass up to the light with a critical expression. 'I really must have a word in old George's ear about this claret. Damnable stuff. And you believe every word Miss Harewood told you, I trust? After so many years in the Corps, I'd have thought better of you. Fourth-class information.'

'I believe her. She has no reason to lie, no possible allegiance to the French. If Miss Harewood says that Wellington's on Bryher, that's where he is. It's as good as any a place for Buonaparte to have sent him. Scilly is a damn sight cleverer spot for an exile than Elba was.'

'Well then, I'm glad you place so much faith in the word of Miss Harewood. Blacks are like children and criminals – they lie and cheat whenever they think it might profit them to do so, or when they believe doing so might save them punishment. You have brought Miss Harewood to London: perhaps that's all she wanted.'

Crow stifled his fury. 'It was the last thing Miss Harewood wanted. If you speak again in such terms of a woman under my protection, I must ask you for satisfaction.'

'Oh, hold your water, Jack. You can't call me out. Well, then let's hope that Miss Harewood is telling the truth, and that holding this particular card will save your skin.' Grant drank his claret. 'You'll gratify me with your presence at eight o'clock tomorrow morning, if you're not executed first. There is the issue of the post-roads, and then Faversham.'

Crow stared at Grant, stunned at his carelessness. He knew what Grant was referring to: destabilising His Imperial Majesty's highways by setting explosives at every main bridge on the great post-roads leading north, south, east and west from the city, London's jugular veins. What kind of a fool was the man to refer to it at White's, and then to allude to plans for the mint at Faversham, even indirectly? Wellington would be spitting fire if he knew that Castlereagh and the rest of the English rebels had reinstated Grant's position as head of intelligence. Crow preferred not to think of what Wellington would say if he knew of his own involvement. He closed his eyes for a moment, wishing he could expunge the memory of Wellington's visit to his bedside in Brussels when he'd lain in that rented house on the Rue de la Loi, dying – or so everyone had thought at the time. *Not but what I'm not glad to see you alive, my boy, but it was a damnable shame you did not reach me. A damnable shame indeed. Well, I have had to tender my resignation. It will save them the trouble of cashiering me, at least.*

'I will attend you tomorrow, sir, of course.'

Grant was unable to resist claiming the final word. 'In future,

I beg you will not conduct the affairs of our country as you might a game of hazard. You've been in London just hours and already your name is on everyone's lips. If I were you, I should scotch those rumours about actually marrying the Harewood chit before they gain any credence.'

Crow watched Grant over the rim of his glass. He was the Earl of Lamorna: Grant had no right to question him on this score and they both knew it.

Grant sighed. 'Is it true? Tell me it's not true, for the Lord's sake.'

'You forget yourself: the only man with the right to question whom I choose to marry is dead.' Crow stood up, pushing back his chair. 'I'm going to Carlton House.' The sooner he saw Joséphine, the better.

Crow walked out into the street, the cold air a shock after the firelit warmth of White's. He wished he might one day have the satisfaction of hitting Grant as hard as he deserved. Good Christ, what had he thrust Hester into? She hadn't even formally accepted him but they both knew that because of his lack of foresight she had little choice. And Grant was hardly the only man who would believe her less capable of reasoned thought even than other women simply because she had brown skin.

He leaned back against the wall, closing his eyes as he remembered finding that servant coming out of Hester's bedchamber, and the horrified look she had not managed to quite conceal. What was her name? Mary? Maggie? Before this evening, Crow couldn't recall her appearing anything other than placid, almost expressionless, not that he should have had any earthly reason to notice her. But he hadn't spent five years chasing other men's secrets without learning the difference between the face people showed to the world and their true, hidden thoughts. That woman knew what he had proposed and she was afraid for Hester. Yet it *was* done: his own improvidence had led Hester to ruin unless he extended his protection to the fullest possible extent. If she allowed it, he would shield her both with his name and with physical force, if necessary, and God help her. No one could say he'd excelled himself as Kitto's guardian. The boy was ripe for the gallows, a fact which ignited unquenchable panic in Crow, but it was only fair that Kitto knew about Hester. His room had been moonlit, the curtains not shut, Kitto himself lying face down on his bed, still dressed, not moving. By rights, a boy of that stamp should be away at sea or in his own old regiment. And yet there was no navy, and there was no army. Crow had known he was still awake: without fail, Kitto slept on his back.

I want you to know, Crow had said, *that I'm going to marry Miss Harewood.*

Kitto had neither moved nor replied. Crow could have demanded both, but what was the use? How was he to protect them all – Louisa included, he supposed – when the likelihood of surviving his next mission was so slight? The silence on St James's Street made it seem he was the only man on earth, and as though the stars above were watching and questioning his every move. He felt breathless, his mouth dry, strangely elated, as though he were out on reconnaissance with enemy sharpshooters ready to fire at him; at the same time, he had to force himself not to run. This quarter of London had once been raucous after nightfall, and the eerie quiet was unsettling. The moon was behind a cloud, and Jérôme's curfew forbade the lighting of torches in the street. Stopping to lean against the wall of a shuttered house, Crow raked the hair back from his eyes, breathing in the throat-scorching scent of gunpowder, mud and shit. It was long after nightfall, but still he heard the wet-washing flap of innumerable wingbeats and the harsh call of crows, seagulls and even of common starlings: carrion birds all when there was so much rotting meat to be had; he could hear bursts of musket-fire now even though night blanketed London with that thick pall of unnatural quiet. Once more, his past leaked into his present, an unstoppable flood of memory.

Gunfire raged, punctuated by the screams of wounded men, and Crow crouched in the mud, in air thick with smoke, behind the red-brick garden wall of the Château d'Hougoumont, waiting. He stared down at his right hand, spreading powder-blackened fingers, stiff from running with his musket ready to fire. His horse had been shot under him by French artillery, and he stared with a sense of detachment at her grey-dappled corpse, just yards away, at the mess of tangled purple-grey intestines. He had to rest, even if only for a moment. He still wore the gilded dress jacket he'd shrugged himself into the night of the Duchess of Richmond's ball: he'd scarcely slept for more than an hour at a time in the days since, criss-crossing corpse-littered fields of trampled rye, bearing communications between Wellington and his generals. Now his task was different: he must instead intercept communications. He'd been following the Belgian for hours, but the boy had melted into the smoke and confusion of the battlefield. Everything depended on Crow finding him. On the other side of the garden wall – just yards away, but unseen and unknown – a man died, screaming for his mother in guttural French. Hougoumont was hotting up again, then. Just a few miles from the village of Waterloo, the château had once been an ancient fortified farmhouse with orchards, rose-beds and calf-high yew hedges arranged in an intricate parterre, the dwelling and its outbuildings all mellow red brick in the evening sun. Now, the walled château protected Wellington's right flank, and the roses were trampled into mud, blood and shit from the torn-open bowels of dying soldiers, men of Crow's own regiment charged with holding it against the French. Crow had been here himself just weeks ago at the height of the Season, a guest in the garden behind the very wall that was now his only shelter in the height of battle. Then, he'd attended a champagne picnic arranged by Louisa. He had walked with the Belgian farmer's daughter through her mother's carefully weeded rose garden, bestowing a kiss on her hand and earning a rebuke from his father about trifling with the wrong sort of girl. But today's dawn had seen him return to Hougoumont: he'd found Arkwright in that same garden with the rest of the Coldstreamers readying for almost certain death, the yew hedges of the parterre already trampled and Arkwright cheerfully ignoring Lieutenant Colonel Macdonell's orders to scrape firing-holes into the wall with his bayonet. *Fucking stupid idea,* Arkwright had said, as soon as Macdonell's broad-shouldered back was turned. *The fucking French are going to throw everything they've got at this place. I'll keep the pointy end sharp, if it's all the same to you.*

Hours later, Hougoumont was now a charnel house, home to the dead and the dying – if Macdonell and the Coldstream Guards corralled within those pretty red-brick walls didn't manage to hold the great gates of Hougoumont against the French troops, Buonaparte would likely emerge from this appalling fucking mess as the winner. Buonaparte had already stolen a march on the duke: moving undetected across the border from France into Belgium, he'd attacked with bloody fury at Quatre-Bras and at Ligny. With loyal, dependable Prince Blücher dead on the field, General von Gneisenau had taken control of Prussian high command, retreating with what remained of the Prussian troops, and Wellington's mightiest ally was now fallen. Crow himself must discover who among the allies might follow Gneisenau's lead. With the Prussians licking their wounds away to the east, would Wellington's Dutch–Belgian troops now take fright and run or, worse, defect to the French? After all, some of those very soldiers had fought in a

French army not eighteen months ago. Crow braced himself against the wall. And if he, Brevet Lieutenant Colonel Lord Crowlas, did not intercept the undersized Belgian soldier he had been tracking through no-man's-land for mile after bullet-peppered mile, no one would know what the Dutch–Belgians intended until it was too late; if General Chasse actually betrayed Wellington, the odds would be stacked so heavily in favour of Buonaparte that anything other than total French victory was impossible to contemplate. Swearing softly to himself, Crow leaned back once more against sun-warmed red brick, listening to the roar of battle within the walls of Hougoumont as Macdonell and his men fought to hold the great gates against an assault that increased in fury with every hour. So many chances, like so many shining coins tossed up into the air.

The Belgian child-soldier had left General Chasse hours ago now; Crow had lost all comprehension of how long he had been trailing the boy, picking his way across the no-man's-land between French lines and the reverse slope of sodden, trampled rye concealing the weight of Wellington's army. The air was heavy with the brimstone reek of musket-fire. It was quite simple: he had to take what he needed from the Belgian and report back to Wellington. To do it, he'd have to leave the cover of the garden wall and make for the shelter of the old drovers' road that ran across the scrubby, boggy field rolling away before him to the north, half concealed by trees. Even if he found the child and got what was needed from him, that concealed route alone would only take him to the bottom of Wellington's ridge of farmland. *Just a small matter, then,* Crow told himself, *of running uphill across an open battlefield.* He even smiled: you had to see the humour in it. *One thing at a time.* He couldn't stay here forever; the Earl of Lamorna's son couldn't be found dead hiding behind a garden wall. And, at that moment, drawn away by a sullen breath of wind, the sulphurous white smoke thinned enough for Crow to see clear across the field: a flash of blue among those beech trees lining the ancient track. The Dutch–Belgians wore blue, and so did the French. Was that his prey – Chasse's messenger boy – or simply French troops stealing forwards? That familiar alert, prickling sensation rushed through his body. With swift, sure movements, Crow shouldered his musket; if he had to kill the boy, it must be at close quarters.

He got up and ran, musket-fire whipping past. Hurling himself across tussocks of muddy grass, hearing nothing but his own breathing, he reached the safety of the beech trees, stumbling and slipping down a root-twisted bank to the ancient, sunken track. He crouched down by a tree and waited. The guards had been running ammunition along the drovers' road all day in the savage attempt to hold Hougoumont, but it was quiet now, and sunlight lanced through tendrils of smoke, a lattice of tender new beech leaves. If Crow didn't get this right, all the heroism and sacrifice within Hougoumont itself would be for nothing, the battle lost. And then, with a curdled mixture of joy and terror, he sensed the presence of another just moments before he heard panicked breathing. Cobbles jutted up through the soles of his boots and his feet throbbed. Hardly daring to breathe, Crow turned his head to the left. That was it: there. A slight figure in a blue jacket and black shako. Crow got up and ran closer. Not far now. Ten paces. Five. The figure skittered away. There he was again, no more than eleven or twelve years old, really just a child. Too young to be in this mess. *Don't think about that. Jesus fucking Christ.* At his back, Crow could hear the French now, too, moving up the track in pursuit of him, the rumbling of French artillery away in the woods to the west of the chateau. He'd been seen.

'*Allez*, redcoat!'

Propelled forwards at the cries of the French soldiers now hunting him just as he hunted, Crow slammed into his target, pinning him against a tree. The boy let out a gasp, as though all the living breath had left his body at once.

'Where is it?' Crow hissed in Flemish. He could still hear the French skirmishing in the woods behind him. The drovers' road wouldn't hide him forever, and he could hear French soldiers, swearing and crashing through beech saplings and last year's thick, rust-red bracken, closer all the time. There was no time. 'I know you've got it. The message from General Chasse. Is he going to retreat, or change sides?'

The boy's eyes stretched in terror. 'I don't know. I got nothing.'

'I know you're lying. I've followed you: you've been behind French lines, too.' Crow leaned in, closer. 'Just give me the message and I won't kill you.'

The boy's breath stank of sour milk. 'I got nothing.'

The French were closer all the time. He could hear them talking now, musket-balls slamming into trees all around him, so much white smoke he could scarcely breathe, scarcely see. *Fuck, fuck, fuck.* 'Come on. Listen. If you don't tell me where it is you know I'll kill you.' *Be friendly, encouraging. Come on; come on.* The boy shook his head, his forehead glossy with sweat. *You idiot. You bloody little idiot.* White-hot pain slammed into the back of Crow's arm, burning, but he wasn't on fire, he'd been shot. Breathing in hard and fast, he leaned on the tree trunk, resting on his good elbow, his face now just bare inches from the boy's own. 'Last chance. Don't make me do this. I don't want to fucking do this.'

The boy shook his head, and another musket-ball slammed into the chestnut to their left, and Crow drew his cutlass and cut the boy's throat from ear to ear, just like all those times he'd killed pigs in the mountains in Spain, but the boy didn't scream, he simply died with his grey eyes wide open and dropped to the ground like a sack of wheat, and Crow got down on his knees and his hands were everywhere, in the boy's pockets, drawing out a crumpled letter, but it wouldn't be that, surely it was too obvious: he tore open the letter regardless, scanning the first line, *Dear Maman*— Shit. He ran the other hand down the boy's breeches and there it was, something small and hard in one pocket. A musket canister, but the boy had no musket. The truth was he'd killed an unarmed child. Crow's good hand shook as he held the canister, pushing off the top and digging in his fingers. And there, rolled up inside the cartridge-wadding, was another curl of paper. Scrabbling with shaking fingers, Crow unrolled the *chiffre*, glancing at the first lines, scrawled in French. *We inform your* 98702 8035 *to the aid of* 3498 *on this day* 18*th June* 79798— Jesus Christ. Half of the message was *en clair*. They hadn't bothered to code the entire dispatch; 98702? Crow's stomach turned to water. And 3498: J. B. *Jérôme Bonaparte. On this day, we will come to the aid of Jérôme Bonaparte.* Gneisenau and his Prussians had already deserted. Now General Chasse's Dutch–Belgians had changed sides, pledging their assistance to Buonaparte's brother. What if Chasse meant to throw the full weight of twenty thousand men at the far reaches of Wellington's right flank? Would the men hold formation once they knew they'd been betrayed?

'There he is! Get the bastard!' And the French were behind him: they'd seen him. Crow hurled himself to his feet, pain pulsing through his body; the sticky heat of his own blood spread beneath his jacket. Stumbling, he ran. Dropping to his knees, Crow reached the end of the drovers' road as it skirted behind the château, the roar of the French artillery louder every moment as the guns were dragged up behind him, shaking the beech leaves above; the clamour of the battle at Hougoumont rose up at his right hand, the cries of dying men, smoke so thick he was going to die here without ever seeing the sky again, the pounding of musket-fire, the clash of hand-to-hand fighting with bayonet and sword. He could see the ridge now, Wellington's reverse slope rising away from Hougoumont's walled orchard. Gneisenau had deserted and Chasse had switched sides: the only choice now was to retreat. Wellington had to know. Crow had to reach him. Just a little battlefield to run across first. He laughed, feeling separate from his own body, as though he were hovering above, watching himself crouching in the mud. Crow got to his feet and as he ran, he heard someone cry *cavalry*, and the word filled his mind even as he sprinted, and the air burst with the thunder of iron-shod hooves pounding hardened mud. A great, staggering force knocked him on to his hands and knees, spitting blood. He felt a horrifying rush of liquid down his back, beneath his shirt. Burning now, Crow looked up to see a horse rearing above him, a French cuirassier's arm raised high above his head, and the heavy sword glinting in the washed-out afternoon light.

Crow stood alone in the silence of a moonlit St James's Street. This was London, and Waterloo almost two years in the past, but he could still smell musket-smoke mingled with his own blood and shit. Walking in the quiet and the cold, Crow knew he must keep walking, he must force away memories of crows and seagulls circling above him as he lay for a week among the dead and the dying, that French soldier near him screaming as the birds descended to peck at his eyes, his tongue, his lips and nose. Crow managed a handful of paces before he leaned against the shuttered front window of the wine merchant and spewed on to the paving slabs. London was silent at night because he had not run fast enough through the mud, because he'd failed to reach Wellington. He should have died at Waterloo with Alex Gordon and Fitz and the rest of his friends, bleeding into that mud as they had done, shot in the back as he ran, trampled by horses even as he forced himself to his feet and staggered, bleeding, closer to Wellington with every step. He should not have survived. And still there would be no rest, and there was no choice but to go on; he couldn't blow out his brains and finally curl into the darkness he'd craved for so long, because he was needed. They wouldn't let him go. Wiping his mouth with the back of his hand, loathing himself, he remembered Hester curled up in his lap in the woods at night, with those curls so light to the touch: delicate, perfect spirals springing from a braid tied with a rag torn from her gown. If it hadn't been for her, he would have turned the pistol on himself that night. Lying there in the dark heart of the forest, she had trusted him absolutely. Now he'd not only broken her trust but endangered her life. For her – and for her father's memory – he would go on. But every time Hester smiled at him Crow saw in his mind's eye how she would look at him when she learned that he had murdered a child.

18

Crow leaned back on the gilded chaise, staring at the portrait of Prince George and his sisters that hung above the fireplace. He'd been here before, when this was the regent's own study. He remembered Prince George drinking brandy with Papa in the drawing-room at Nansmornow, idly toying with the breasts of the naked whore in his lap; he remembered lying in his sickbed in Brussels and Louisa coming in with news of the execution. *He's dead*, she'd said, her face tear-streaked. He had wanted to die, too. He had longed for bloodied, pus-filled wounds left by musket-ball, sword and the iron-shod hooves of Buonaparte's cavalry mounts to carry him away into silence, but instead infection had at last receded, fever sinking away as flesh and bone healed. All of this was his fault: the defeat, the invasion, everything.

Joséphine hadn't troubled to replace the paintings since taking up residence in her new quarters: she had the damnedest sense of humour. As a discarded wife, Crow supposed she had little else; the Buonapartes had consigned her to England like an embarrassing great-aunt who needed to be sequestered at a lacklustre country château. So far she had fallen, then, not unlike himself. But Castlereagh was right: Buonaparte had always entrusted her with the smooth running of a court – even one he valued so little as Jérôme's, and if there was anyone likely to be of use to the resistance at the Occupation headquarters headed by Buonaparte's objectionable brother, it was Joséphine. Crow heard her come in but didn't turn his head to look, only listened to the faint shush of her silk slippers against marble. She wore attar of roses again, and it was like standing in the knot garden at Nansmornow and breathing in their scent at night, and he wondered if he'd ever see Nansmornow again or if in the morning he'd be standing on the scaffold at St James's where Prince George had been guillotined for leading the desperate and bloody defence of London. Standing behind him, Joséphine let her hands fall on his shoulders without a word, and he felt the soft warmth of them through his jacket.

'Oh, Lord Lamorna,' Joséphine said. 'You've been impossible.'

He made no answer but only leaned his head back to rest on the upholstered chaise where he'd once seen George screw a girl without spilling a drop of claret, still debating with Alvanley and Brummell the relative merits of Scottish snuff versus Arabic. Crow felt the light touch of Joséphine's fingertips in his hair, then tracing a gentle line along each of his eyebrows. Dear sweet Jesus Christ. She came to sit beside him; well over fifty, she was lithe and trim, favouring the clinging classical gowns that it was said had earned her a place at the zenith of Republican Paris, and he remembered Maman shaking her head over a news-sheet in the drawing-room at Nansmornow. *Joséphine should never have married that upstart Buonaparte. Such a kind woman, but she's not intelligent – even at Versailles she never had a serious thought in her head. She hasn't a hope of holding her own against such a scheming family.*

'For a start' – when Joséphine spoke French, she still had the barest hint of a Creole accent – 'how in the devil's name did you get in, Jack?'

She pronounced his name as his mother had done, *Jacques*, and he told her the truth; it was hardly as if he'd choose the same way another time. 'Straight up the steps and in through the side door on Curzon Street, I'm afraid.'

Joséphine sighed. 'My dear former brother-in-law is far too busy throwing banquets for himself to bother with simple strategy, then.' She reached across, smoothing the hair from Crow's brow with a motherly gesture. 'Four men? Four of my dear Bonaparte's men, quite dead? Shot at close range?'

'I left none alive to tell. What did Jérôme's men do to my people to make them say?' This time the fault would be his alone, not Kitto's.

'Frightened men and women don't need much persuasion. They never have. Now what am I to do with you? Jérôme and the Imperial Council want to see you hanged. Not even guillotined. Hanged.'

'They raped my sister, then hanged her with her mother and my butler. Is that reason enough for you?'

Joséphine sighed, tucking a loose strand of grey-streaked hair behind one ear. 'I expect she was too pretty for her own good, just like you. You must get used to the fact that you may no longer do just as you please.'

'I owe my people their safety. They look to me for it.'

'You're even prettier when you're cross.' Joséphine laughed, covering her mouth with one hand. 'Is it true that your brother dynamited one of Jérôme's garrisons? I didn't know you had a brother, far less one with criminal tendencies.'

'He's extremely sorry for it, if that helps.' Crow kept his tone light. If the war had not been lost, and Cornwall not starving under the weight of a brutal Occupation army, he'd have laughed to buy Kitto out of some lazy Cornish magistrate's cellar.

'If it happens again, you know he'll be hanged higher than the White Tower.' Joséphine watched him, her eyes always so expressive – hazel one moment, glowing gold when she turned towards the candlelight. She meant every word. 'Do you not realise that the English Republicans look to King Jérôme now, Jack? Such an execution as your brother's would be perfection: it would keep them quiet without really changing anything, which is exactly what the Bonapartes want at this moment. So keep a close watch on your brother if you value his life. In the meantime, what are we going to do with you?'

'You are going to listen to me.' He smiled, and his every shred of flesh wormed with tension. If news of Kitto's insurrection had reached the capital already, Jérôme's spies clearly knew their work. He almost felt sorry for Lieutenant de Mornay, who must have had some explaining to do when it was discovered he'd released the boy. 'You know, the imperial post-roads will be targeted by English rebel forces, starting with West Malden in Essex. Do with that as you will.'

She smiled. 'Oh, now that's very good. You are a darling, Jack. With Bonaparte in Russia, and married again, I'm quite sure that it's no exaggeration to say that these little snippets of information you bring are all that has prevented me being poisoned or smothered: Jérôme certainly has no other use for me – you know as well as I how jealous he is that I'm the one Bonaparte trusts to hold court. Never think I'm not extraordinarily grateful.'

'I wish I could say that it is my pleasure.' Crow got up as if to leave. 'One more thing: I have Hester Harewood at Lamorna House.'

She leaned back a little, watching him. 'Captain John Harewood's little mulatto daughter? The Duke of Albemarle's legitimate great-niece – the entire affair so delightfully amusing and for the Albemarles so very embarrassing. Who was Miss

Harewood's mother again? Now yes, I remember the scandal of *her* parents' marriage – it was talked of even in Paris. Old Beau Albemarle's dissolute youngest son running off with an Irish nobody, although I don't doubt she was a diamond of the first water, and both dead within two years. And so their daughter was doubtless eventually marooned in some select seminary, only to marry Captain John Harewood – and now you are in possession of *their* daughter. Such a profusion of extraordinary marriages and children.' And Joséphine smiled. 'Now there's a prize. Miss Harewood's father humiliated my dear former husband at Trafalgar, you know. What are you going to do with her? Are you going to be sensible? Or foolish?'

Crow sighed. More than anything, he wished he didn't have to do this, that he could just ride home and go to sleep. 'I had three letters sent when I reached London, each now in the care of a man even I would trust with my life. If any harm comes to Miss Harewood, those letters will be passed on, and by the following morning every man in England who reads *The Times*, the *Morning News* or the *Chronicle* will know where Wellington is held prisoner.'

Joséphine raised her eyebrows. 'You care for her, then? But Scilly is an island, and have you not noticed the army of Occupation, or the blockade?'

Crow refused with sheer force of will to break into a sweat. 'Perhaps it's a risk you're willing to take. Will Jérôme treat you with any more kindness or respect if Wellington's whereabouts becomes common knowledge? The free trade is alive and well in the Scillies – it wouldn't take such a very great deal for Wellington to be spirited away from his prison. And Jérôme strikes me as the kind of man who punishes those closest to him when he is afraid.' Ashamed of the cruelty he was inflicting, he watched the flicker of fear pass across her face. Her debts, he knew, were as mountainous as ever: she couldn't afford to lose the Buonapartes' grudgingly granted protection. With casual cruelty, her beloved Malmaison had long since been given to Buonaparte's new wife, the Empress Marie-Louise. Without the reluctant sponsorship of her ex-husband's family, she'd be destitute.

'Very well,' said Joséphine, 'although you must understand that I can't ensure Miss Harewood's protection myself. I shall have to apply to his highness, but I'll do my best.'

'I realise he's not an intelligent man,' Crow said, with deceptive lightness, 'but he'd be very foolish indeed not to listen to you on that score.'

She smiled at him. 'One day, I'm very much afraid that you're going to get yourself into serious trouble.'

'But not today,' Crow said. Yet Joséphine was right: no man played a game such as this for long.

19

When Lord Lamorna had gone, Joséphine went to the dead English prince's marble-inlaid desk and took out the miniatures of her son and daughter. She closed her eyes, running a forefinger over the rough surface of the painted ivory, trying to believe that it was really Hortense's cheek she touched, her finger brushed by her daughter's thick, honey-brown hair – so like her father's. Even after so long, it saddened Joséphine to think of Alexandre, and so she pushed him from her mind. She was good at forgetting, and suppressed a little spurt of unwomanly irritation, for Crow had made her remember dear Eugène at the same age, and she ached to see her son, his darling smile always touched with that endearing shyness. In the thirty-eight years since she'd left the tropical waters of her island home and come to this damp and unsatisfactory continent, Joséphine had known so many young men just like Crow. Beautiful, brave, gnawed at by the sacrifices duty demanded of those called to greatness. Poor boy, and so handsome, too – she supposed he must more closely resemble his father, for she saw little in his face of Claire de la Saint-Maure, beautiful though poor Claire had been. Joséphine remembered her at

Versailles all those years ago – a shy creature in hooped white satin, disastrously tall, towering above the other girls, the image of demure submission, all the while plotting to run away with her English lord. Her son was playing a dangerous game, too, coming to Carlton House with tales of English rebels. He was unlikely to survive such a double game for long – a pity. Idly, she wondered at the motivation for his treachery to the English: losses at cards, a hidden crime? Could it even be that Saint-Maure blood in his veins? Surely no relic of the Ducs de Montausier had reason to love the Bonapartes, rising as they had from the ashes of the Terror, but one never knew. Perhaps a Cornish earldom was not enough and he wanted his family's French dukedom back. Napoleon was terrible for handing out noble ranks as if they were twists of barley sugar at a children's party. One might rise from ruin and penury clinging to the coat-tails of the most unexpected people. After all, who would have thought a dirty, unkempt little Corsican soldier might one day be emperor. No, the danger Crow placed himself in cast a light on the precariousness of her own position. Her former husband's siblings had spent the better part of twenty years whispering behind her back; to say that Jérôme and his sisters had enjoyed the divorce and her downfall would be the greatest imaginable understatement. And now here she was, a virtual prisoner in England, languishing under Jérôme's so-called protection. Joséphine knew quite well that if Jérôme or his spying servants realised how she depended on those portraits of Hortense and Eugène hidden in the desk there was a good chance that they too would one day disappear, lost to her just like everything else. She put the miniatures back in poor Prince George's desk drawer, concealing them both beneath a stack of writing paper. She smoothed the snowy white folds of her muslin gown about her legs, tugging the cashmere shawl closer about her shoulders. It was ridiculous, really, to wear white at her age, but – surprisingly for a man capable of such savagery – Napoleon had always been rather floored by the sight of a woman in virginal muslin. Jérôme grudged her even his protection, and so naturally did not keep her appraised of his imperial brother's movements, and there was no reason to suppose that Napoleon was anywhere other the snowy wastes of the forested Russian wastelands beyond St Petersburg, but what if he did come to England? Yes, there was the second marriage to that humourless cheese-faced Austrian tartar, and yes there was the son he had abandoned her to conceive. But Joséphine knew that despite everything she still had power over him. If by chance Napoleon did come to this miserable rain-soaked island to gloat over the conquest of his mightiest adversary, if he only chanced to see her in white muslin, she knew he would not be able to resist her. After the divorce, had he not wept as they walked together in the gardens at Malmaison? She remembered the scent from her rose-bushes, the sharp notes of the north-wind-loving Rose of Dijon mingling with the softer, rounder quality of scent produced by the loose, shabby blooms of the Slater's Crimson China. Memory was such a cruel mistress, offering only shadows of what had once been hers to touch, to love, to hold as her own.

She looked out of the window at the quiet street below. Young Lord Lamorna was the enemy, for all that he betrayed his own people, but she hoped he had got safely away past Jérôme's guards. What was she to do with the weighty knowledge that this young English lord with the blood of the *Ancien Régime* in his veins had discovered the whereabouts of Wellington, the great enemy? She smiled, remembering the martial light in the boy's eyes when she had asked, so casually, what he meant to do with Captain John Harewood's daughter. Miss Harewood would be a valued prisoner, the treasured only child of one who had distinguished himself at the battle of Trafalgar, her former husband's greatest humiliation at English hands. But Joséphine was entirely sure that Crow had meant every word when he said that he would announce Wellington's whereabouts to the world if so much as a breath of harm neared Hester Harewood. It wouldn't do for the English to know where their beloved hero Wellington was held prisoner: no, she could see how dangerous that might be, and that Jérôme would be forced to agree with her. He had no choice but to guarantee the safety of this Miss Harewood. But whilst Wellington was so heavily guarded, by Marshal Ney, no less, Lord Lamorna himself could do nothing with the prize piece of information that had tumbled into his lap. She thought again of the blazing heat in the boy's expression when he spoke of Harewood's daughter and smiled to herself. It was always so heartbreaking and yet so amusing to see a wild and arrogant young man brought to his knees by a woman for the first time.

20

In the dawn light, Crow stood at the foot of his stepmother's bed, looking at the shining dark mess of her hair tangled on the pillow. Louisa woke and sat up; beneath the sheets she wore nothing at all. He pulled off his shirt and – letting her watch him; she'd always liked to look at him – he climbed into bed and knelt at her feet, leaning forwards to kiss her; he owed her this, at least; and he needed her. He had scarcely slept in four weeks, he must have pleasure and the release, and he could never really sleep without a woman in his bed: only then could he be sure he was nowhere near a battlefield.

'I'm sorry,' he said, his hands in her hair. He knew he deserved no forgiveness, springing a new bride on an old lover was the shabbiest behaviour, and the very least of all his crimes, but Louisa kissed him back anyway. It had never been love with her; she had always just wanted him in her bed.

'Don't say a word,' Louisa said. Her lips brushed his neck. 'Not now.'

But a flash of anger rose from nowhere, as so often happened, and he pulled away, looking down at her: 'You were very close to Burford when I got back.'

She laughed. 'You're just too much. Are you jealous? And you're incredibly drunk. Are you ever not? Darling, I'm too old for such intrigues.'

He smiled, nearly laughing. 'Have mercy, Lou. I'm so tired I can't even think.'

'Oh, Jack.' She pulled away from him a little, looking down. 'Not that tired, I see.'

'And you're not old.' He kissed her neck, those hollows of pale flesh at her collarbone; he kissed her again and drew back the sheet, releasing the buttons at the fall of his breeches. When she moved beneath him, he forgot everything, and that was why he had always done it, and that was why he drank enough that he could forget how every time he lay with Louisa, he betrayed his own father. It was the very least of all he needed to forget. Afterwards, he and Louisa lay side by side, his breeches still unbuttoned, her arm draped across his belly with an air of possession.

She turned on her side to watch him, serious now. 'Listen, I'm old enough to know this little dalliance of ours must end unless I marry. Burford really is in a position to make me an offer; I've been out of mourning for three months, and I've buried two husbands. It would be just my luck to conceive a child after nearly twenty years barren, Jack, and then where would we be? Have you no notion of the risks if I were to fall pregnant with your father two years dead? If I were to accept Burford, we shouldn't be together so often, but it wouldn't matter.'

'You speak so easily of passing another man's child off as poor Burford's.' Crow had never seriously imagined that Louisa might bear a child – married at seventeen, first to Lord Colborne, and then at thirty-three to his own father, she had never been able to conceive, a fact that twenty years ago had cost her tears, he knew. And he knew, too, that her grief and disappointment, however sharp in its infancy, had long since resolved into relief. She had been, in so many ways, the perfect mistress, close at hand and with no risk of producing a bastard he must in all honour be responsible for. He stared up at the bed canopy, thinking of Hester again, knowing that she would not lie at his side, but curled up, pressed close beside him. He imagined how she might respond to his touch, and his belly was hollow with longing and desire. She hadn't wanted to marry at all – he wanted to smile at her outrage at the very notion – but if marry she must, she wouldn't view a faithless husband in the same way a girl bred to this world might equate one with an irritating infestation of moth. Crow had always assumed that when he was married, he might please himself wherever he chose as long as he was discreet. Papa, after all, had not even bothered with discretion. But if Hester accepted his proposal, he knew he must have no other but her – he felt no constraint at the prospect, only a pulse of strong and wholly unexpected relief.

Knowing as ever, Louisa turned towards him again. 'So, this marriage of yours.'

The reckoning had come, as he'd known it must. 'Why would my marriage be any business of yours, my diamond?'

'Oh, don't be so silly. Do you actually think me jealous? Frankly, I'm rather fond of Hester, and I wouldn't be so out of reason cross with you about it if I wasn't. It's a dreadful shame about her poor father, and I quite understand that you felt you had to protect her somehow—' Louisa broke off, watching him intently. Crow was only glad that she, like everyone else present, had believed Captain Harewood killed by French soldiers without so much as a mention of Wellington. Louisa sighed. 'You really do mean to marry her, don't you? I've seen that stubborn look before. Listen, I'll do what I can to shield her from the worst of what people will say – but honestly, Jack, it would have been kinder – and a great deal more usual! – to make Hester your mistress. Between us, we could have set her up very creditably: with those looks and all that money she'd have been the height of fashion amongst your set and probably beyond.' Louisa shrugged, lifting delicate, pearl-white shoulders. 'Do you mean to give up the earldom?'

Crow could almost have laughed at her concern with fashion when so much hung in the balance. 'Why should I do that?'

'Darling. Look at Mr Wells; look at General Dumas; look at the poor queen, even. Honestly, I could even name you half a dozen natural children with a touch of the tar brush, but only cits and mushrooms actually marry their Creole mistresses. It simply isn't done. You're the Earl of Lamorna: there is something due to your name, after all.'

'I find nothing insulting to my name in marriage to the legitimate great-niece of a duke, and the child of a man I respected more than my own father.'

'For goodness' sake, Jack – Georgiana Harewood might have had Albemarle blood, but you must know the history! Her father was just a youngest son who married to disoblige his friends and took an Irish beauty of no family at all. I don't believe Georgiana ever met her father's people more than once or twice in her life. Maria Sefton was at school with her – the girl was never even presented. Hester might be a great-niece of the current duke, but trust me, it means little. I should think Georgiana was destined to be a governess had she not run off with a sea captain – a black sea captain! If there could ever be anything more shocking, it's you giving your name to their daughter.'

'The Albemarles' treatment of their children and their dependants is of little interest to me,' Crow said. 'And neither should it be to you.'

Louisa smiled with the smug air of one about to present a *fait accompli*. 'Very well, but darling, what about your heir?'

Crow fought rising anger. 'If we must have a vulgar discussion about lineage, I'm a Helford of Lamorna, and I need not justify myself to you or anyone else. I tire of this conversation, Louisa.'

'Naturally.' Louisa smiled: he was not only a man but the head of the household, and she surrendered her own opinion to his as convention demanded she must, at least superficially. Crow got up, pulling his shirt over his head, and left her in bed. In her own subtle way, Louisa was no less prejudiced than Grant or indeed the vast majority of society, so-called Abolitionists included.

Outside on the landing, he heard a slight commotion downstairs, a smart knock at the front door and the rattling of the front-door chain. It lacked a quarter to six, the sky not yet light. It was an invasion, the fortress of his home breached in the hours of darkness. He crossed the hallway, conscious of the twin battlefield urges to run and to fight rising uncontrollably as he gained the top of the staircase. A serving-girl stood on a studded leather ottoman stool, struggling with the door-chain. It was so early that even Mowbray was not yet up. Crow ran downstairs and the maidservant fled at the sight of him, gabbling incoherent apologies. Another knock sounded and Crow jerked open the door to reveal Hester on the top step, wearing a gown twenty-five years out of fashion that could only have belonged to his mother, hair loose around her head in a cloud of light golden-brown spirals.

She smiled as though they had just met at a ball. 'Oh, good morning. Would you mind letting me pass? It's very cold for March.'

Crow rounded on her with a fury that took him completely by surprise. 'Where on earth have you been? You cannot—'

'I cannot what?' Hester turned to look at the terrified serving-girl, still huddled by the grandfather clock.

How dared she chastise him for speaking privately before

servants? Crow shoved open the wide double doors that led to the drawing-room, aware of a sudden, startling heat in the air as Hester passed him. Shutting them both in, he turned around to find her watching him with an air of amusement and heard himself almost shout: 'You can't just walk around London on your own. Never do that again, do you understand?' He lit a cigarillo whilst Hester waited with infuriating patience for him to finish, as though she were humouring some forgetful old man at a card-party. Controlling his anger, just, he trusted himself to speak again. 'Listen, London is a dangerous place at the best of times, Miss Harewood. Especially now.'

'I know,' Hester said simply. She shrugged back the moth-eaten travelling cloak that must have last been worn before the French Revolution, and laid one of his father's old duelling pistols on the sideboard. 'Be careful,' she said as Crow reached out to take it, 'it's loaded but not primed. I'm sorry to have taken it from your gunroom without asking, but I was anxious to post my letter home, and I remembered my father telling me that the mail-coach to Penzance always leaves the Royal George at five o'clock. My people have waited long enough to hear news of me, and I must know if they're safe.'

He stared at her. 'You went out with my father's duelling pistol to post a letter to Castle Bryher?' Dear sweet Jesus Christ. If Joséphine kept her promise, Jérôme's hands were tied. Even Jérôme would not risk allowing harm to come to Hester if that meant revealing Wellington's whereabouts. Crow was as sure as he could be that Hester was safe for now, but the French could and did intercept the mail: it was why Grant only ever communicated with him by sending carrier pigeons. 'Tell me you made no mention of Wellington in it?' He didn't wait for a reply. 'Do you have any idea how much danger you're now in? It could be read by anyone. Your safety rests on Wellington's whereabouts being kept utterly secret.'

'Well, then it's a good thing I made not a single mention of his name,' Hester replied, with infuriating patience. 'And even if the French read my letter, they wouldn't make any sense of it. I don't suppose you'd understand, but my housekeeper and I used a cipher when we were little girls. No one will be able to read it except her.'

'A cipher?' Crow was so astonished that he had to suppress a sudden and bewildering urge to smile. If only she knew how readily he did understand. Somehow, she had obliterated his anger: nothing seemed to matter save the fact that she was standing just inches away from him. Hester was tall for a woman, but even she had to tilt her head a little to look up at him.

'Yes, a cipher. I don't know what you should have to say to it either.' She stood there, daring him to contradict her.

'Nothing could be further from my mind.' That was true, at least. Looking at her, there was only one thing on his mind. He finished his cigarillo, regained control of himself, and tossed the end into the fireplace. 'I've been to Carlton House – the French will leave you alone now.'

If she was relieved, she didn't show it. 'The French might let me be, and yet it seems you won't. But you have quite made up your mind to order my life as you please.' Hester dropped into a small, clipped curtsey, and walked out, straight past him. She made no mention of his offer, and Crow stared after her. Had he really proposed marriage to a woman quite so capable of unceremoniously disarming him?

21

Four hours later, at nearly half past ten, Mrs Mowbray laced Hester's stays in frigid silence. Ten minutes earlier, she'd knocked on the door as Hester lay sleeping in the ancient silk lustring gown liberated from the armoire, shattering her slumber with the announcement that his lordship had said that she was to find Miss Harewood more seemly attire at once. Watching herself in the mirror, Hester heard Cat's voice in the back of her mind, disastrously clear: *Do you not think the poor woman hasn't enough to do elsewhere?* At home, she would be watching St Mary's Roads from the tower window of her own bedchamber, sunlight striking off the great shear of water, clouds tossing in the sky above. She pictured the enciphered letter to Catlin lying in a burlap sack. It would be one among hundreds; there was such a long way for her word to travel, along the length of the great western post-road from London to Penzance, then from Penzance harbour across the Cornish sea to the mail-boat moored at Hugh-town on St Mary's, and finally across the water to Bryher. *Please God let Catlin still be alive to read it.* Mrs Mowbray gave the stay-ribbons a firm tug and tied them with expert ease, reaching for the rose-pink

overdress and undergown of white muslin laid across the end
of Hester's bed.

'It's so kind of you,' Hester said, to fill the uncomfortable
silence. 'I'm so grateful for the trouble you've taken.'

Mrs Mowbray lifted the gown above her head, releasing
the caustic but oddly comforting scent of her fresh underarm
sweat, strong lye soap and clove pastilles. Smoothing the
overgown's long, modishly tight sleeves over Hester's arms she
set to work on the row of silk-covered buttons at the back of
the close-fitting bodice. The white muslin underdress spilled
to the carpet at Hester's feet. Hester stared down in horror
at her almost-naked breasts. 'Very much in the current French
mode, I believe,' Mrs Mowbray said repressively. 'The stays
and small-linens belonged to the late countess. You are much
of a size as the present earl's mother was, may God rest her
soul. Her gowns, such as that you put on this morning, miss,
are all quite out of the present style. I might add that it is the
usual custom of ladies in this house to keep to their beds for
most of the morning, otherwise someone would have assisted
you into more suitable attire in the first instance, I'm sure.'
She paused, either to draw breath or to wait for an apology,
but Hester dared not compromise her position by apologising
to a servant. This established, Mrs Mowbray went on with
a barely more conciliatory air. 'This gown, however, was
left behind not a month ago by a cousin of her ladyship's
whose maid, I might venture to say, did not attend to her
mistress's things in the proper fashion.' An expressive silence
communicated Mrs Mowbray's views not only on ladies' maids
who left their mistress's clothes in the laundry-room, but also
unexpected visitors who got out of bed in the early hours of
the morning and scrambled into gowns belonging to the late
mistress of the house, having arrived with no maid at all. Could
there be anything in the world more crushing than a servant

who had been with a family for decades when faced with an unwelcome guest?

Hester briefly closed her eyes, wishing that she might open them and find Cat briskly smoothing out the skirts of one of her comfortable old muslins and little Tilly looking for her shoes, with the warm scent of Mrs Evans's spiced tattie cake rising through the whole castle from the open kitchen door. Instead, she was trapped in a grand London townhouse with this impertinent woman buttoning her into a confection that left her indecently exposed, when she ought to have been wearing black for Papa. Swift and shocking, tears slipped down her cheeks. Mrs Mowbray straightened up and went to tug the skirts neatly over Hester's petticoat. With an indecipherable change of expression, she opened a dresser drawer, took out a folded handkerchief and pressed it into Hester's hand with a squeeze so slight it might have been imagined.

'Not that I should wish to put myself forward, miss, but I might venture to say that I have known his lordship these twenty years or more, and I can quite see that travelling with him must be a very exhausting experience. He was always a most unrestful person, even from a child.'

Hester unfolded the handkerchief and pressed it to her face, stunned at Mrs Mowbray's daring: no one on Bryher would have mentioned Papa in such terms, and certainly not in the hearing of a guest, but Mrs Mowbray had spoken of Crow with real affection. She ignored the realisation that with Crow at her side she would have felt safe hiking up the ashy volcanic slopes of Mount Tambora. 'It's just that my father died – which is how his lordship came to escort me here with no servant of my own – and I ought to be wearing black.' After a year in mourning, would she still feel such raw agony and so naked, like a boiled shrimp squeezed from the shell?

'I'm sure I'm ever so sorry,' Mrs Mowbray went on. 'I expect her ladyship will soon arrange a *modiste* to come and take your measurements.' She lifted a silver hairbrush from the dressing-table, looking at Hester's mass of curls in much the same manner as a surgeon might face a gangrenous leg.

There was quite enough to bear without having her hair pulled out by the roots. Papa had done his best, but even Catlin had never mastered the art of managing it. Hester summoned her blankest expression, disguising an extraordinary longing for home and suppressing the desire to take Mrs Mowbray by the shoulders and shriek into her face that there was nothing wrong with her hair. 'Thank you, I shall go along quite well by myself.'

Kitto was already in the high-ceilinged breakfast-parlour when Hester came in, the scant remains of a large repast on his plate: a white gelatinous ham-rind, a bright smear of jam and a great deal of breadcrumbs. Lost in his own thoughts, he wore a clean shirt; his black hair was damp. Here, he seemed a different person from the feral boy she'd ridden alongside for so long; it was as if she saw him now for the first time: he had the same sooty, heavy-lashed grey eyes as his brother, but given how much Crow resembled their father, she supposed Kitto must look more as their mother had done, with those deep-cut dimples. The forced intimacy of their long journey north seemed distant now: morning light struck off a silver dish of gooseberry preserve and a carriage clock ticked on the mantelpiece with oppressive insistence. The walls had been painted a soothing shade of pale green, but Hester could not have felt less at peace. A liveried footman waiting beside a gilded sideboard glanced at her once, and then took obvious pains to fix his attention on the large glazed ham nestling among crystals of pale yellow fat on a china platter. Above the sideboard hung a huge portrait of the goddess Diana, shocking in its abundance of dimpled, naked white flesh.

'Shirred eggs, miss, if you please?' the footman said, speaking to the wall behind Hester's left shoulder.

Suppressing a sigh, she shook her head; it was so exhausting being in a place like this, where she was unknown, and where everyone stared. 'Coffee only, for the moment, I thank you.'

Kitto looked up with one of his sudden, irrepressible smiles. 'You look bang up to the mark, Hets. Thank God it's you – I always find it so awkward trying to breakfast with everyone Friday-faced as if I were quite on my way to the gallows.'

'Which I don't doubt happens to you quite a lot?' Hester sipped her coffee, pretending not to notice Diana's vast, blue-veined globular breasts, and trying not to feel so appallingly conscious of the low-cut bodice of her gown. Kitto appeared not to pay the slightest heed to her breasts spilling from the inadequate confines of white muslin and pink silk, but if the gossip about the late Earl of Lamorna's courtesans were true, he'd been brought up in the lap of Venus, and a fashionably revealing gown would be nothing new to him.

He grinned. 'Since my stepmother never stops trying to civilise me, then yes, I find myself at outs quite a bit. I hope to God all her hideous satellites are gone.' If he knew that Crow had proposed marriage, he was keeping quiet on that head, for now at least.

'You're in luck – we caused such an upset that Lady Lamorna's guests risked the night-guard. I suppose they're all rich enough to pay them off.' Kitto looked so relieved that Hester smiled. After two weeks in close company with him and Crow, she knew there was an undercurrent of affection beneath suffocating anger and frustration. What, then, had made Kitto run from this place, arriving in Cornwall so half-starved that he laid gunpowder for An Gostel in exchange for food and companionship?

'Well, good – I'm glad of it.' Kitto switched seamlessly into French so that they could speak without fear of sending further ripples of gossip through the servants' hall. 'Louisa's friends are a pack of irrelevant old windsuckers, at any rate. All tonnish parties and pointless damned gossip, as if the war and the Occupation never happened – it makes me sick. Listen, Hets, are you really going to marry my brother?'

'Scarcely for you to say, *boya*.' Crow stood in the doorway, watching them both. Pale with lack of sleep, he was dressed for the day, his face almost as colourless as the drift of starched white linen at his throat. Hester found herself remembering the sight of him shirtless by the river, smooth muscle beneath pale skin, with those black tattoos swirling between his shoulder blades and down his back. He didn't take his eyes from her now, not for a moment. Kitto got up, looking so uncharacteristically confused that Hester had to force herself not to laugh.

Crow let him pass, smiling once he'd gone. He turned to the footman. 'I believe there is something you must urgently attend to in the scullery, Ben.'

The footman jumped as though Crow had fired a pistol by his ear. 'My lord? I don't think so, your honour, leastways I came straight here when Mr Mowbray told me to.'

'Are you questioning me, Ben?'

Rictus-faced with horror, the footman walked straight past him, right out of the room, leaving Hester and Crow quite alone.

'Now that,' said Hester, trying to ignore the painful thudding of her heart, 'was extremely unkind. And you needn't have sent him away: you should know I speak French just as well as your brother.' Less than twelve hours ago, Crow had told what remained of the cream of English society that he was going to marry her. Now they were alone again, and this time she could not walk away. She didn't for a moment think that he would try to prevent her, but the crisis must be faced.

He closed the door, and the air of amused, authoritative reserve left him. He smiled at her, running both hands through his hair. 'Miss Harewood...'

She looked down at the cutlery set out before her, glittering silver knives, forks and spoons with age-yellowed ivory handles. She thought again of Roza's hanged corpse, her ruined face and bloodstained naked legs; she imagined having taken a house of her own, being woken in the night by Occupation soldiers hammering at the door, frightened or disloyal servants unable or unwilling to protect her from the same fate. In one convulsive movement, Hester got to her feet, pushing back the chair. Her coffee cup rattled against the gilded saucer, and she remembered the warmth of Crow's presence, lying in his arms in the wood, the slightest touch of his fingertip on her forehead as she had drifted to sleep.

'I'm sorry,' Crow said. 'It's inexcusable to have sprung such a thing on you. It was the best I could do.'

She watched him across the room, sure the floor would give way beneath her. He was going to change his mind. He hadn't meant it. Wasn't that what she wanted? For him to find another way out, so that she didn't have to marry him and face the ill-concealed disdain of his peers for the rest of her life? And yet what other choice was there?

He crossed the room, so close that if she reached out she might even touch him. 'When it's done,' he said, '*if* it's done, if you don't object, please have your free rein if that's what you want. I shan't stand in your way if there's someone else you prefer: marriage needn't be a closed shop as long as you're discreet. I won't force myself on you; I want you to know that. I don't wish you to be afraid.'

There was something so dishevelled about him; she longed to push that dark hair back from his forehead. If only she could have him alone, and not the world that he lived in. If only

K.J. WHITTAKER

she could have him because he wanted her. 'I'm not afraid of you.'

'Miss Harewood, if you don't like it, I'll find a way out. But I'll be honest. In truth, I wish you did like it.'

She heard the words leave her lips as if they'd been spoken by someone else. 'Despite all the obvious disadvantages, I like it just enough to risk learning if I'll like it more.'

22

Catlin emptied the linen cupboard into her basket: sheets, lappets, cuffs, collars, all of it, even a baby's bonnet that would cap an apple. Hester's: a seven-month child, lucky to survive. Her own baby things would hardly have been kept, but passed around the island's children until they fell apart at the seams and could be patched no longer. Where was she?

Look after them, Catlin. Hester had turned back as the French soldiers dragged her to the door, wearing a brave, defiant expression so recognisable from their childhood that for a moment Catlin couldn't even breathe as she recalled it. *Look after them?* How was Catlin meant to have time to mop Tilly's tears, to soothe Aunt Evans's shredded nerves, to talk Jacca Garrett and the other young men out of their idiotic notions of fighting back? They would all be dead in half an hour. They were trained to polish boots and carry trays, not kill armed men. Look after them, indeed. But Hester had no notion of the practicalities; she never had.

The scent of dried lavender enveloped Catlin as she folded one of Master's fine white shirts, mingling with the day-old-roast-mutton stink of the grease she'd rubbed into her cracked fingers. Her hands always played up after washday. The men below had made so much extra work – they drank and puked on their clothes; they were repulsive. She supposed they had little else to do. One had drunk so much that he even made filth in his own breeches and those had been sent down for her to wash, too, so that she had been forced to scrape crusted shit from the worsted before putting it to soak. And that was without the extra cooking, Marshal Ney ordering dinner as though this were his own house, not a prison, always to be served at the ungodly hour of seven o'clock at night so that no one got to bed till after midnight. Town ways, French ways: she neither knew nor cared. They were not island ways.

She'd left Mary and Tilly in the kitchen to weather Aunt Evans's temper, Mary scattering cloves over a dish of last year's vinegared pears and Tilly frantically plucking a capon, cramming hake into the fish-kettle with the cream and chopped fennel, her hands spangled with scales, fingernails still black with fowl-blood. It wasn't fair on them, not really, but Catlin had taken about as much as she could for one day, and in any case, the linen cupboard was a genuine shame – a tangle of chemises and sheets. Catlin folded and smoothed. She would be damned if the house fell into disorder. She would keep it trimmed tighter than the sails on a mackerel-lugger chasing the shoals, just to spite them all, to show Ney and his nasty men that they didn't scare her.

'Mistress?'

She turned to face Tilly. The girl's apron was smeared with watery fish-blood, her wide brown eyes watchful as a seal's.

'What on earth are you doing up here? Mrs Evans will be having kittens.' Anger boiled up. 'Couldn't you have been more careful with that apron? All that muck'll have to come out, you silly girl.'

Tilly nodded. 'I'm sorry, mistress. We were in that much of a rush. I'll be more careful next time. Mistress?'

Catlin frowned. 'What?' It was hell's breakfast in the kitchen without her to lend a hand: that was the gist of it. Now she'd have to put up with Aunt Evans's pickled-in-salt remarks when they all at last sat down to their own supper: simmered greens, the last of that cold fat beef before the joint went sour. 'What do you want, Tilly? We don't want to keep the men waiting. Like it or not, we need to keep on the right side of them.'

'That's it, mistress. The marshal sent a boy down to the kitchen. He was looking for you, missus. They've sent for you. They want you to bring the dinner, not Mr Evans.'

The crack on Catlin's forefinger split again, leaking blood on to the chemise in her hands. Now that would have to be washed again, too.

'Well, it's not ready yet, is it? Get on, Tilly.' Catlin turned back to her linen. Tilly was just a girl, only ten years old. It wouldn't do to let her see how frightened she was.

'Wait out here, do.' The tray was heavy; Catlin could see a faint reflection of her face in the polished dining-room door. Beside her, Uncle Evans shifted from one foot to the other, another nick in his chin scabbed over. She'd never known her uncle to cut himself with the strop before the master was killed. Now he was all nerves, his hands forever on the quiver. His gaze slid towards the door, fearful.

'It's not right, you going in there alone, Catlin, that's all I'm saying. Soldiers are soldiers.'

Yes, and if they do try anything what could you do about it, anyway?

'They've done nothing amiss since killing the master, Uncle, they'll have finished the first set of removes, and this'll be getting cold.' Catlin's belly twisted as she breathed in the rich, savoury smell issuing from beneath the lid of the fish-kettle: herbs, poached hake, salted, buttered cream. 'Let me get on, will you?'

He frowned. 'Your dame wouldn't have liked it. Your sire, neither. You going in there with all those men. It's not proper.'

'Mother wouldn't have liked us to send in a cold dinner either, Uncle. I'm invisible to them, anyway. They don't see us, do they? No more than the master's guests would ever really see us.'

'I'll wait out here then, if I may.'

'If you wouldn't mind just letting me in, that'd be a start.' Catlin felt the men's eyes on her before Uncle Evans had even closed the door. Ten Frenchmen, all in their regimental blue jackets, with that gilded frogging that was such a finger-splitting bind to wash when they were sent down, fishing out bits of food, the smell of sweat never quite gone no matter how long the cloth was steeped. Most of them weren't even watching her, but Ney was, and the two he was talking to direct at that moment. The youngest one coloured up and looked away, hardly more than a boy – nice-looking, with sandy hair and long eyelashes that brushed his freckled cheekbones when she stood behind him to pass the dish of spiced pears.

Blood pounded in Catlin's ears as she moved around the table, picking up those carefully scoured dishes that had been picked clean of sliced beef in green sauce or roasted fowls or last year's dried beans, boiled, spiced and buttered, and were now in need of scrubbing again: hours, it would take, and the pans would need doing too, and the bucket of sand by the scullery door was close to empty again, and someone must fill it. She would do it herself, just for the chance to escape the castle at low tide and pick her way across the rocks to Kitchen Porth. She'd walk down the beach, watch the tide froth at the shoreline; she longed for a clear head. Away from all her endless jobs just for a moment, she might see her way around what to do about Hester.

She replaced the dirty dishes with the fish-kettles, three of them, lids off, the savoury cream still bubbling. Now it was her job to wait, to watch the men chewing and swallowing, their oily cheeks working away. She must move a sauceboat close to the elbow of the young lieutenant who had taken three slices of baked ham and pass the dish of buttered beans to Marshal Ney: Lord, how they fed, it was never-ending. They drank, oh, how they drank, breathing in Captain Harewood's claret as though it were air and, as they drank, the noise grew till her ears rang with loud voices, with laughter. She couldn't understand a word, not a word, and bright white pain gathered in the small of her back until she wanted to shriek; it shot down her right leg, leaving her toes numb. Tom would never rub her back again, his warm hands against her skin, his questing fingers kneading the knotted flesh. Her back would ache every day until she died.

And then, at last, at last, the dishes were scraped clean, every last smear of parsley sauce, gravy and spiced cream sopped up with bread or crushed into the crust of Aunt Evans's preserved-apple tart, and Catlin was free to gather the dishes, leaning sideways between meaty, blue-jacketed shoulders as first Mother and then poor Mrs Hicks had taught her, long ago, on the odd occasion that she had helped Uncle Evans and the Garrett boys wait at the captain's table. She filled one tray, turning to retreat to the sideboard; she must rearrange the heaped-up crockery so that the dishes didn't slide off and crash to the flagstones. And as she turned, an arm circled her waist, hot and heavy. Without thinking, Catlin stepped away, breathless, and the chatter seemed to grow louder, if anything, as if it meant nothing that a man had just touched her. Ney.

He leered up at her from his chair, the bristles of his moustache slick with oil.

'Are you shy, Mrs Rescorla? I didn't expect that from a pretty young girl with all that red hair. Red is the colour of passion, they say.'

Was that the best he could come up with? 'I wouldn't know about that, sir.' She turned to the sideboard, ready to pick up the tray, and never mind if Aunt Evans's best crockery smashed all to pieces on her way out, but the scrape of his chair against the flagstones was so swift, and he moved so fast: he was too quick for her. His breath was hot and damp on the back of her neck; he took hold of her, his hands all over her body, as though she were a horse he wanted to be sure of before parting with good money for it. His touch burned: she felt sick. Away. Get away. She lurched forwards but he was stronger than her – he wanted to hold her, to keep her for a moment, and so he did, his hands at her waist, her breasts, squeezing her buttocks, before all his men, the shame of it.

Don't say a word. Don't give him an excuse to hurt you. He can do what he likes. Put up with it and get out. She'd grown up with the truth of this. Say nothing, do nothing. Report to Mrs Hicks or Mr Evans and they will have a quiet word with the master, and matters would be arranged, and it would be someone else's job to light the fire in that particular gentleman-guest's room from now on. But Mrs Hicks was three years dead; it was Catlin herself who had charge of the house, and Captain Harewood could hear no grievances lying cold in the lych-yard. And anyway, she sensed Ney would enjoy her fury, that her rage would thicken his desire, which was hot enough as it was. She could feel the swelling of his parts pressing into the small of her back as he pressed his hot hands all over her breasts, pushing aside her linen fichu, padding at her flesh. He turned her to face him again, cupping the side of her face in one of his hands, thick fingers fringed with coarse reddish hair that caught the candlelight.

'There you are,' he said. 'A hot little thing, aren't you, Madame Rescorla? You'll keep till another time, though. I'll look forward to it.'

Catlin dropped into a curtsey and picked up her tray, walking steadily towards the door as Ney's men laughed and jeered. She didn't understand what they were saying but she could guess. Her flesh burned where he had touched her – even if she filled the tin bucket with cold water from the pump and stood by the fire in her room and scrubbed at her skin with an old rag until she could not bear the pain, Catlin knew that she would never feel clean again.

23

Catlin threw a handful of lavender stalks into the fire and turned up the Davy lamp, banishing as much of the dark as she could. The stillroom had felt wrong ever since the master died in it. Catlin could swear his spirit walked, even though they'd laid his body to rest with daffodils scattered on the earth of his grave-mound. But at past two o'clock in the morning, he felt closer than ever. She could smell his tobacco, the faint, fresh scent of the special soap he liked her to make: oil of applemint. A chill settled over her, and Catlin knew she must occupy herself or she'd run from here too afraid to look behind her, and the stillroom would no longer be her very own refuge. She glanced at Hester's letter, unfolded on the table, not only in Cornish but peppered with those silly numbers they used to write in as children. Catlin couldn't remember what they stood for; the only way to unravel it all would be to go into the library whilst Wellington slept and find the old leather folder they'd got it from years ago. And what would Wellington say if he caught her rifling through her dead master's books? He probably didn't even think she could read, although any decent housekeeper had to make sense of receipts and accounts.

If she were forced to explain, he might even demand to see Hester's letter. As if there wasn't plenty to be done without wasting these night hours daydreaming about childhood games, with the French to deal with and a three-day fever raging across the island. Why could Hester never understand that others had their work even if she didn't? Aggie Garrett was already dead, and Catlin remembered the night the child was born, her mother crouching on the cottage hearthstone, warmed by the embers, letting out a strange, high cry that was almost like singing as little Aggie slithered out. And Aggie had gone from sitting among the pebble-lined rows of kale outside the cottage, passing sea-bleached shells from one fat hand to the other, right to threading her first needle, and now she was two days buried, taken by a sickness come with the French soldiers. There was work enough, and at least Hester was alive or had been when she wrote the letter – Catlin had that to cling to, much as she could have crowned her.

Taking her knife, Catlin chopped through the mess of violet flowers on the wooden board, scraping them sideways into the bowl of good oil to steep while she ground the white poppy seeds. Aunt Evans's old rag rug was laid neatly over the stains she couldn't scrub out of the flagstones, but the dark remains of Captain Harewood's blood would take years to fade, sunken quite into the fabric of the stone. Hidden but not forgotten. Who did that Marshal Ney think he was? Catlin had put up with the worst of her master's visitors, with their roving, sweaty hands, sheets stained with their own spunk, pots under the bed full of shit for other people to carry. Uninvited guests were worse still and the French, as Aunt Evans muttered, were turning out worse for Scilly than even the Parliamentarians had been. Catlin hadn't forgotten her lessons: nearly two hundred years ago, young Prince Charles had found safe harbour on St Mary's. If it hadn't been for the Scillonians, those sour-faced Roundheads would still be banning Christmas, not that every island family hadn't paid a blood-price for their rebellion. Catlin looked up from her pestle, letting the thick paste of poppy seeds drop into the bowl of oil, stirring up the warm scent of the violets. English, Dutch or French, mainlanders always made the same mistake: they supposed that in calling such small islands home, islanders had also small hearts and small brains. She wondered how quick they'd learn their lesson this time.

Catlin's gaze ran along the length of the high shelf by the window where all her bottled preparations stayed cool and beyond reach of any trespassing child. Dark ale, egg yolks steeped in wine for acne, chamomile oil, aniseed butter, dried seaweed and, there, in a small green glass jar, poor Miss Jane's oil of foxglove: restorative in small doses to those with a weak heart but any more than a teaspoon and you'd shit till you were dead. Well, then. Catlin got up from the old wooden bench and took another earthenware bowl from by the fire where they were always stacked to keep the heat in case anyone needed broth or warm milk. It was probably best, she decided, that if any more of Ney's soldiers should catch the fever they had their own special remedy for it.

24

Catlin's lamp filled the stairwell with a golden bubble of light which only thickened the darkness. What a sapskull to be jumping at shadows. She and Hester had crept around the castle at night often enough, but that was in the time before, when Mother's sweet, rising-dough warmth had still been a safe harbour when their games were over. Milk-sisters, they'd been then, not mistress and servant. She and Hester had begun together, even if they would end apart. She had to read the letter for Hester's sake, or at least try. She paused outside the door at the top of the tower, listening. Not a sound. With any luck, Wellington would be asleep in the small tower-top bedchamber above Captain Harewood's vast, circular library. The door was never locked: Uncle Evans speculated that this oversight had to do with honour between gentlemen. Buonaparte himself had not been locked up when a prisoner on Elba, after all; they had all read as much in the *Morning News*. And yet Buonaparte had escaped Elba. But a gentleman's word was his bond, and Wellington walked free. At low tide, he'd even been allowed to scrabble across the rocks to explore the rest of Bryher, interfering and causing trouble. He'd sent the Hicks children attending the smouldering kelp pits above the sands at Kitchen Porth running home to their mother like rabbits before a fox when he complained about the stench of the smoke.

Catlin stepped into the library, holding the Davy lamp out before her, praying that Wellington was asleep, and that the draught between the library and the stairs up to his bedchamber had ensured he pushed the draught-stop up close to the bottom of the door, blocking out the light she cast. Stepping from bookshelf to bookshelf, Catlin held up her lamp, reading the spines. Aeschylus, whoever he was, Shakespeare – that name she knew – Plato, Lord Byron, Grammaticus. How on earth was she ever to find where they had left it? Captain Harewood had a maddening habit of never arranging his books in order, always claiming to know where every last book was shelved.

The lamp was burning low by the time she finally traced a finger over the familiar spine between Hester's calf-bound copy of Miss Austen's *Persuasion* and a dusty, evil-smelling edition of Milton's verses. Setting down her lantern, Catlin prised the book from the shelf. She'd done it. Now at last she could go over Hester's letters and be sure of what she'd read. How could Hester remember all those numbers from so long ago? Probably because her head had nothing else to fill it, and Wellington surely wouldn't notice one little book missing. It wasn't stealing, not really. Miss had written, after all. She might just as well have given a direct order for Catlin to search the library for this very book. Catlin tucked it into her apron pocket, and was halfway across the Turkey rug and almost at the stairs' door before she heard the hinges of the door behind her creak, and the library was flooded with flickering light from an upheld candlebra.

'What in the devil's name do you think you're doing?' Each word stumbled into the last, and even from here with her back turned Catlin smelt brandy and sour breath. Wellington was drunk. But, even though he might be six sheets to the wind, she'd be cast off for sneaking around in here uninvited – what possible excuse could there be at gone two o'clock in the morning? She'd be sent away without a character. She'd never get another position on the islands or anywhere else, for that matter. She'd unpick sacks in Penzance poorhouse until her fingers bled or she died of the shame, whichever came first. For the briefest of moments, Catlin squeezed her eyes shut, praying that when she opened them, the room would be in near darkness once more; that she had imagined the voice, the shuddering candlelight.

'I'm waiting, damn it.'

She turned to face him, and fought a wild urge to laugh. There was always gossip in the papers about Wellington and the ladies, and now Catlin herself had joined the ranks of those abandoned females who had seen the Iron Duke in a dressing gown. He was very angry, his lips pressed tight together in a thin line.

'Your grace, I needed a book. I'm very sorry to have disturbed you, sir.'

Wellington stared at her as though she'd asked for a waybill to the moon. 'What? You needed what?'

'A book. From Captain Harewood's library, sir.' *Yes, your grace, I do possess the remarkable ability to read.* His frozen blue gaze darted towards the little brass bell on her master's desk: he was going to ring for Uncle Evans. *Just tell him the truth.* She smoothed down her apron with both hands. 'Miss Hester is alive, sir, and has written to me. As children we used a cipher, your grace, and I couldn't remember the key.'

Wellington held out one hand, a silent order. He wasn't even going to waste speech on her, and Catlin swallowed a flare of anger. She passed him the book, never taking her eyes from his face. She knew she should look at the floor, but somehow couldn't make herself do it.

'How many letters have you exchanged with your mistress since she was taken from Bryher?' His speech still ran together a little, slurred.

'None, sir. I have today received one letter. It was enciphered, sir, but I found myself not able to remember the code we used to use. That's why I came to look for the book.' He didn't look like a man about to show mercy to a housekeeper. He looked disgusted, as though this step up from her God-given duties was revolting, like a leaking boil. He was going to ruin her for this. 'I'm sorry to have come up without your leave, sir, but my first loyalty must be to my mistress. I must know what she says.'

'*Enciphered?*'

'Yes, your grace. A code we used as children – just a game.'

They watched each other like hare and hawk, Wellington in the act of taking up the bell. And then, slowly, as though he couldn't help himself, Wellington flicked open the book instead, rapidly scanning the first few pages. Catlin could remember every line of the introductory chapter. *And let him take a series of numbers, and each of these four numbers shall take place of a word, so that without the key, any dishonest person who may intercept letters might not make sense of their contents.* Why in Mother Mary's name had she been able to remember what was written on the first page but nothing useful?

Wellington frowned. 'This cipher is a French invention. The author's name is French – had you not realised? – and if Ney and his men intercept your correspondence, they'll recognise the cipher and perhaps there is even one among them who knows how to read it. If your mistress hopes to conceal her whereabouts, she would have done better not to write at all.'

Catlin nodded. 'Yes, sir. Except that Miss Hester and I always write to one another in Cornish. She wrote the numbers in Cornish, not as numerals. See.' Her hand shaking, Catlin reached into the pocket of her apron and removed the letter, unfolding it, holding it out to him. Wellington took it as though she'd handed him an arsewipe from the basket kept by his chamber pot, but as he read, his expression changed, and he looked up at Catlin.

'French numeric cipher written in Cornish.' Wellington folded the letter, handing it back to her, laying the book upon Captain Harewood's leather-inlaid desk. His face was impossible to read, itself enciphered. 'The lengths a man is driven to. Well, here is the key, Mrs Rescorla. What does it say?'

Wellington tapped one finger on the unfolded letter, thoughtful. 'So Crowlas has the girl. I should call him Lamorna – his father's dead now, of course. Now what's young Lamorna's game?'

'I've heard such stories, your grace,' Catlin said. 'I shouldn't think his intentions are proper. I fear for my mistress.'

'At least she's not dead,' Wellington remarked.

'If his lordship doesn't behave as he should, she might as well be,' Catlin replied, made bold by the fact that Wellington showed no sign of sending her off.

'Very pert, aren't you, for a housekeeper? What age are you, anyway?'

Catlin wished she hadn't taken out her plaits, by day always coiled, knotted and pinned beneath the black cap. But she hadn't expected to be found, and instead her hair was brushed loose, hanging down her back in waves, the cap neatly folded on her bedside table. An odd, wild sensation of power flooded through her. 'I'm sure you have many more important matters to worry about than to concern yourself with a person like me, sir.'

'You're lucky I'm drunk.' He stared past her again, and Catlin was sure he no longer saw the gloomy, lamp-lit library but some faraway battlefield. The letter from Tom had been splattered with mud, rusty with dried blood along one edge. *My dearest Catlin, if you are reading this then I have fallen, and some kind soul has sent on my very dearest love to you—*

'Poor lad was a week on the battlefield after Waterloo,' Wellington said, and Catlin knew he wasn't really talking to her, not any more. 'His father came to me, but even I couldn't tell the man where to find the boy's body. He was my ADC, you know. Carrying messages. No one knew where to look for him, and the place was a mess. We'd have managed well enough were it not for the Dutch–Belgians at Braine l'Alleud. Only time Grant and young Lamorna ever failed me: I don't know why they didn't know Chasse was going to turn traitor. I wish they'd known. I never did like Colquhoun Grant, mind you. Rather wished the French had finished the job in Paris and simply shot the man when they captured him back in '14. One's got to wonder what he was doing all that time in Paris. Buonaparte was a damn fool to let him escape. If Castlereagh knows what he's about – which I doubt – then he'll send the man packing, if the old fool has any influence left at all.'

Catlin had no idea why Wellington should apparently wish one of his own men dead at the hands of the enemy. She cared still less. 'Why don't *you* escape, your grace?' She smoothed out the folds of her apron, and Wellington stared out of the window at the dark Atlantic. 'There must be a way. With Ney, there's only ten of them, my lord. And together with Bryher and all of us serving in the castle we are more than forty.'

'You're uncommonly warlike for a housekeeper, Mrs Rescorla.' That was the second time he had used her name: the Duke of Wellington had listened; he knew what she was called. 'But the men that came with Ney are cuirassiers – from Buonaparte's own regiment of guards. In the unlikely event I managed to get out of here with the assistance of a houseful of servants, what do you think Ney would do to you? Every last one of you dead, even the children. You can bank on that.' He tapped the letter again with his forefinger. 'I never fought a battle I knew I couldn't win, Mrs Rescorla. Retreat and live to fight another day – that's what carried me from Portugal to Brussels, and if it hadn't been for a pack of traitorous Dutch–Belgians, I wouldn't be sitting here now.'

Was Tom dead for nothing, his life just wasted? 'But what if the French were to die, sir? You'd be free to escape then. There's a nasty fever going through the old town, as we call the village, sir. Children dead already, my lord.' Those hot hands all over her. She would make Ney pay for that.

'Pour me another drink.' Wellington tossed back the brandy, turning Hester's letter over and over in his delicate white hands. 'No, we can't bet on the likelihood of Ney and his men succumbing to a fever, Mrs Rescorla. Fevers don't discriminate.'

'No, sir. Of course.' Catlin swallowed, her throat dry. Must she spell it out? 'But fevers might be made to look discriminating. What if it only appeared that the French were sickening naturally?' Where did he think a poultice for a sick headache came from, or tincture of strawberry leaves for pustules on the skin? 'My remedies, sir. Any remedy can kill, my lord, given the right measure. If the French were to die, sir, just as a killing fever comes to the island, none of them could suspect, and you'd be free to leave: we're already beyond the blockade out here on the islands, sir. The French on the mainland would never know you were gone until it was too late. Retreat to fight another day, my lord.' So that it wouldn't be for nothing. She would do it to punish a man who thought nothing of grabbing hold of a servant as though she were a side of ham; she would do it for Tom, and the baby who would never lie at her side to be fed in the night, for the child who would never need her. She would do it for Hester.

For the longest while, Wellington said nothing. Then at last he opened the captain's desk, taking out a single sheet of paper, a jar of Indian ink, a pen, and her dead master's own little pearl-handled knife to cut the nib.

'Get yourself a chair, Mrs Rescorla. Miss Harewood will be expecting her reply.'

25

It was close to curfew, and the inhabitants of Seven Dials hurried to close their illicit businesses. Snatching down ragged awnings, they loaded black-market barrels of salt pork and illegally distilled gin on to carts, packed alongside sacks of beans and flour. Before long, the jumbled network of narrow, cobbled London streets was empty, waiting for the night-guard. Arkwright walked with steady purpose along an alley swimming with shit and piss tossed from the upper-storey windows of the overhanging houses. The quiet was thick and oppressive, broken only by an incongruous creaking, like a mooring line holding a ship to shore in a gathering wind, and a thin, half-broken wailing from inside one of the houses. Arkwright recognised the insistent cry of a starving child. Soon, it would lose the strength to call out. Even the rubbish in the street had rotted down into the waist-high dandelion weeds springing up between cobbles: there was nothing to add to it, no onion skins or cabbage rinds, there was so little food to be had. The roads into town from the countryside were harried by those desperate enough to risk a noose, armed with whatever they could find: the drovers couldn't get into Smithfield with herds for the slaughter; and few farms had gone unnoticed by a starving Occupation army – barns were raided and burned, root-clamps kicked into a mess of sand, the crop taken. Arkwright had seen this before – they were a step away from Paris in that bitter cold winter of 1794, after the Terror, when grand houses had stood empty with all the windows long since smashed, and every woman who could sold her body, and mothers drowned themselves in the Seine for shame at not feeding their own children. London was dying, and so was England.

Arkwright heard the night-guard beating their drums, still at a distance, a few streets away. His destination wasn't far off. Picking up his pace, he turned down an even smaller alleyway between an abandoned pawnbroker's and a tavern with nailed-shut windows, almost tripping on a hunched shape slumped in the gutter, face down in the shit. *Christ.* Arkwright nudged the ragged heap with his foot. 'Get up, man – the guard are coming.' There was no movement, nothing. He crouched down to shake the drunk awake, but when he rolled the man on to his back, he was faced with a corpse with a mouth stretched wide open, and one eye socket seething with maggots. Wiping his hand idly on his coat, Arkwright went on – the dead held no fear for him, and precious little disgust. The closer he got to his destination, the louder the creaking got. He stopped, listening, alert like a harrier hound before the chase. There was something not right; Arkwright had fought enough battles and killed enough men to hear the terror of recent death screaming back at him from the gloomy quiet. The creaking grew louder still, irregular. Arkwright turned another corner, painfully close to the relative safety of his destination, and saw a long, dark shape hanging from one of the tall iron street-braziers that had once cast light along the alley. Hot spew rushed up Arkwright's throat; he pushed away a memory of Nessa's bloated face, her lips swollen with the effort of strangulation, and the blood on

Roza's naked, stained legs. The rag-clad hanged corpse swung in the gathering dark at the foot of the alleyway, rope creaking at the weight; it was unclear at this distance whether it had been a man or a woman, and he wasn't about to get any closer. Clearly, someone without funds for a pay-off had encountered the night-guard after curfew. They must have hung all day, the inhabitants of Seven Dials too afraid to cut the rope. Hurrying on, Arkwright kept to the shadows and at last rapped three times on a narrow door constructed from innumerable wooden pallets nailed together and fortified with sackcloth. Following the agreed signal, he waited, and then rapped three more times. The door swung open, revealing an underfed girl in the entrance. She wore a satin dress cut for a tantalising glimpse of a woman's dugs, but her ribcage showed through her skin.

'Evening, Gertrude.'

'You again.' Gertrude's breath reeked of gin: cheaper than bread and easier to get. Greasy tallow lamplight illuminated a cheerless parlour, inhabited by a handful of other whores in varying states of undress, including a young lad. The air was sickly with opium-smoke. They were lucky: it'd be a sweeter descent into starvation.

'I know my way, lass.' Arkwright went past Gertrude and up a narrow, twisting flight of stairs that gave out into a dark hallway. A small window with leaded panes admitted dim twilight that puddled on bare floorboards. Arkwright pushed open the second door on the left, letting himself into a plain, neatly swept library with bookshelves lining the walls. A guttering lamp glowed on an old crate used for a desk. Robert Wedderburn looked up from his reading, and Arkwright gave him a grim nod. The revolutionary got to his feet and they clasped hands across the makeshift desk. Wedderburn smiled, wry. Not a tall man, and as dark-skinned as the Harewood girl, he was slight, too. He couldn't have been further from the hulking brute whose so-called likeness appeared in news-sheets printed by the Occupation now and the regent's men before, but in Arkwright's experience the way folk looked bore little relation to what they really were: he'd known plenty of sweet-faced killers. A dyed-in-the-wool rebel, Wedderburn was one of the most dangerous men in England – or her saviour, depending on who a man might ask. The so-called King Jérôme could have had him hunted down and guillotined, but he'd chosen not to. Arkwright was sure he recognised the emperor's hand there – Buonaparte was a man who liked to keep an arsenal of weapons ready for his own choosing.

'I'd offer you refreshment, Arkwright,' Wedderburn said, 'but I'm afraid the cellar is sorely lacking.' Wedderburn had presence. Folk said he was the bastard child of a plantation owner who'd sold the mother when she was still pregnant. You'd think he was gentle, harmless, but Arkwright was damned sure you'd have to be a hard man to escape a Jamaican plantation and survive the English navy. 'You've been gone a while, Arkwright,' Wedderburn added lightly.

Arkwright pulled up a stool and sat down. 'I know. But it's done now. If I must work for his lordship, I can't not follow his orders. Family business, and he trusts me. His brother ran off back down to Cornwall.' He wasn't about to tell Wedderburn about Wellington, and not through any loyalty to Crow. Buonaparte wasn't the only one who liked to keep his powder dry. 'Any news your end?'

Wedderburn frowned. 'Castle still thinks we're not doing enough. Says we should be guillotining the aristocracy.'

'He's twenty-five years behind the times, lad.' The regent had been guillotined, true, along with any other prominent person who refused to surrender and swear allegiance to Buonaparte, and anyone with any sense knew the royal family had no more died of gaol-fever than Arkwright was a lord, but the great purge of the aristocracy that men like Castle dreamed of had never come. Bloodshed on that scale would change nothing. The poor would still suffer and starve, just as they'd done in France after the revolution. All that ever altered, really, were the faces of those at the top. The French had hoped to make life fairer. But men were men, and in exchange for their king in the end they'd got a tyrant in the shape of Buonaparte. Bloody fools. The same would happen on English soil, no question of it, whoever England's Buonaparte might turn out to be.

'All the same,' Wedderburn went on, 'Castle's damned persuasive when he wants to be. He's getting the men worked up – the young jobbernolls among us, at any rate.'

Arkwright had known it would likely come to this. The varnish of civilisation that kept men from killing each other like dogs in the street had worn thinner than Gertrude's threadbare satin gown. 'Fucking town feels like a powder keg,' he said. 'When's the next meeting?'

'It'll be tomorrow, now I know you're back from your travels, Mr Arkwright. Be ready, will you?'

'You know me, man,' Arkwright said. 'I'm always ready.'

26

You'd have to be a halfwit to complain about being promoted to such a position as ladies' maid with two extra shillings a year, but it was just Maggie's luck that Miss Hester must be on her courses. She'd miss her tea now scrubbing blood from her new mistress's underthings, back in the laundry-room again. Annie Jones might mutter about sly, encroaching creatures all she liked, but she could piss into the wind for all Maggie cared. The single time Lady Lamorna had called upon Annie to dress her, when Mrs Mowbray took ill, the skirts of milady's fine satin evening gown looked as if they'd been put through the mangle by a drunk. Maggie dipped her fingertips in the bowl of good sweet almond oil on the dressing-table and teased out the last few tangles and knots in Miss Hester's hair. The oil softened Maggie's own hands so that her dark brown skin shone.

'There, milady. Now you mustn't try to brush your hair dry again, but let me see to it all for you.' Maggie bobbed a curtsey, and Miss Hester smiled. She was quite lovely, with those long lashes and a beautiful generous mouth.

'I promise. Thank you, Maggie. Be at your leisure now – I shan't want you again until it's time to dress for supper.'

Maggie bobbed another curtsey and went out with yesterday's bloodied shift to wash, leaving milady to rest in her bedchamber and bear the cramps as best she could. At your leisure, indeed. Ten minutes later, Maggie was in the laundry-room again, scraping soft-soap from the barrel and stirring it into a bowl of cool water when all the others would be already having their tea in the hall. Hers would be cold and stewed by the time she got it, and all this blood must be got out of the linen before the stain set. She had that hat to trim for the new laundry-maid, too, and, astonishingly, Lady Lamorna's chip straw bonnet to make over. The other maids were forever asking Maggie to dress their hats with whatever little baubles they'd scraped together – a pair of wax cherries bequeathed by a former mistress and carefully kept in a box beneath the bed, a mean halfpenny length of sky-blue ribbon purchased from the door-to-door tinker – but Maggie had never worked on a commission for a someone like Lady Louisa. At this rate, she might save enough to set up as a milliner, and then she'd never have to scrub other people's underthings again.

'Busy again, Mistress Baines?'

Maggie stiffened. Mr Arkwright. She had been waiting for this, dreading it, truth be told. Mistress indeed. He knew as well as anyone she'd never been married. He was buttering her up. 'What do you want this time?'

Arkwright leaned in the doorway. Like all those men who'd been for a soldier he'd that edgy watchfulness to him – he was nothing like as twitchy as the young lord, but enough so that you noticed it. 'Mr Wedderburn was hoping you might do us another favour, Mrs Baines.'

Maggie looked down at her hands in the sink. This was the trouble with taking coin from men like Arkwright. They always came back. Miss Hester's shift broke the water's skin like a great white blister, streaked with soap bubbles. Her mouth felt dry and it was hard to swallow. 'What for and what do you want me to do?'

Arkwright smiled. 'Just listen when her ladyship talks in French. Unless she's got to know you understand?' He held out one hand, uncurling his fingers to reveal the hard, bright glint of a silver crown. Maggie's belly clenched at the sight of it. She had no one to take care of her when her limbs or her sight failed: taken from her mother's arms so long ago, if she still had kin alive God alone knew where on the face of the earth they might be. Cold fear slid down her spine when she thought of dying flea-bitten in some workhouse or St Giles slum. Cash. She needed to swell her savings. Arkwright and his friend Mr Wedderburn were playing with fire, clear as day, but it was a risk worth taking. Anyway, Maggie couldn't see that she had much choice.

'Very well, I'll listen. Anything I learn,' she told Arkwright, 'I'll tell you. But you pay me now.'

Men like him were not to be trusted.

27

Arkwright sat with a jug of porter at the back of the top room at the Carlisle tavern, eyeing the revolutionaries he'd come to meet with little enthusiasm. Ever since Spence died in the winter of '14, the whole libertarian movement had splintered off into factions, and nothing got done. Some might say the French hadn't gone far enough, only guillotining the lords who refused to sign the Decree of Acquiescence. All Arkwright knew was that with the French in power, King George and the Prince Regent dead and the aristocrats kicked out of parliament, all this feckless shower had done was argue among themselves whilst the poor continued to starve. They had gathered around a single bare table sticky with generations of spilled ale unhastily wiped. Wedderburn spoke first, as usual, addressing the gathering of seven men – working men in neckcloths and broadcloth. They were angry men and had reason to be, but Wedderburn spoke with his usual quiet calm.

'Gentlemen, we've waited long enough. This is our opportunity for equality, and we stand in danger of losing our chance.' Wedderburn turned to look at Arkwright with a sardonic tilt to his smile. 'What news from the aristocracy, Mr Arkwright?'

Arkwright allowed his gaze to travel across the faces of the assembled men. They were all listening. They'd waited a long time for this. There was something up with Castle, though, sitting there with his eyelids lowered, suspicious, both hands beneath the tabletop. A thin-shouldered rat of a man, he was, with shifty eyes. Arkwright was watching him. 'Lady Lamorna has tongue enough for two sets of teeth. She's been talking in front of the servants again. In French, mind – thinking they wouldn't understand.' Arkwright blew out a plume of cigarillo-smoke. *Calm yourself.* He knew he wasn't anything like as bad as Crow, but sometimes his hands would shake and quiver as though he were palsied. Wedderburn was all right, but the others didn't trust him, since he lived under the Lamornas' so-called protection. He glanced again at Castle. 'It might be that her ladyship's got a notion her late husband freed all his father's slaves, but it must've passed her by that Mistress Maggie Baines was first sold on Martinique and speaks the better French.'

Wedderburn twisted the pipe between a thumb and one long, elegant forefinger. Folk said that Wedderburn's mother was still enslaved in Jamaica, that he was too poor to buy her freedom. 'Of course it passed by her ladyship. What did Maggie tell you?'

'In good time. With no House of Lords, a lot have stayed in the countryside when they'd normally be sitting in parliament – we knew that already. But if what Maggie Baines said still holds true, Joséphine means to hold court with those who did come to London. With the women – all out in the open, too, at Carlton House. Jérôme – maybe even Buonaparte himself – has instructed her to hold out the hand of friendship.' Arkwright didn't bother keeping the sarcasm out of his voice.

'Then Buonaparte's a traitor!' Tom Barnett thumped the table, slopping ale over the top of his cup, the young fool.

'He promised it'd all change, that it wouldn't be the nobility sitting pretty any more while the rest of us damn well starve. He said they'd have no influence at all.'

'Men like Buonaparte always do what serves them best,' Arkwright said. 'We need to know what he's thinking. The man's not an idiot. You can't conquer half the known world without a canny turn of mind. What he promised us back in '15 makes no difference: he's got choices. On the one hand, too much power in the hands of working men and why should we leave the French sitting pretty in Carlton House? Buonaparte keeps the likes of us down at the bottom and leaves what's left of the gentry with their heads on to do it for him. Or maybe he lies awake of a night fretting that the aristocracy might rise up against him, like King John and his barons. For all we know, he really does want rid of the bastards for good, just like us. And yet look at what he did in France: maybe he'll just make the lot of us into fucking knights, and we'll be too busy counting our gold and our acres to bother him.'

Tom stared down at his pint. 'How are we meant to know what Napoleon Buonaparte's thinking, Mr Arkwright? We're stuck, then.'

A lad at the back got to his feet. 'I say we serve Buonaparte as we should have served our own king. Who's to say we shouldn't burn Carlton House to the ground?'

Wedderburn stared up at the ceiling, leaving it to Arkwright, who looked up and for one sickening moment saw Nessa, Roza and Mr Gwyn swinging from a soot-blackened beam above the fireplace, the hem of Nessa's blue-striped dress all come loose. 'Don't waste my time. Who wants to attack the French, here and now?' Arkwright stared from face to face, wanting to kick that mazey fool into a bloody mess till he stopped talking, stopped breathing, even. 'Try it, and you'll be hanged by morning, choking and shitting yourself on the way to hell.'

Castle turned to Arkwright, his thin face now sharp with anger. 'Know it all, do you? Seems you want to hold us back. Seems you're not loyal to the cause.'

Arkwright sensed the tide of opinion shift against him: the others were even more suspicious now, not that it ever took much – all save Wedderburn, who carefully tapped his pipe against the table edge, tipping ash to the sawdust-scattered floor before grinding it beneath the heel of his boot. Arkwright watched Castle but said nothing. Yes, very interesting that it was always Castle spurring the rest of them on.

Later, when the rest of the men were gone, Arkwright was left alone with Robert Wedderburn. They sat alone at the table, Arkwright smoking a cigarillo. Wedderburn stared across the room at a cheap portrait of the former queen hanging in state above the fireplace.

'Shall I do it, then?' Briefly, Arkwright closed his eyes, weary of the whole worthless game. Kings, princes, emperors and republicans – what did it matter? He'd no true home, no hearth, and now no regiment either. Nessa was dead, and she wasn't the first he'd loved to be lost. Learning men's secrets and killing was all he had left: it gave shape to everything. If he didn't keep on, he'd be just like a dog with nowhere to lie, a sniffing scratching pissing mess.

Wedderburn turned to look at him. 'You best had,' he said. 'Better inform Her Imperial Highness Joséphine or whatever she calls herself these days that her most gracious invitation has been accepted. How kind of her to invite the likes of us as well as the Quality.'

Arkwright walked over to the door and opened it, all the racket and stink of the taproom below rolling up the stairs towards him. 'Brandy?' he said. 'Or blue ruin?' He needed another drink, and more than one.

28

On the afternoon of Hester's wedding day, she sat alone at her dressing-table. The distant sound of the wedding breakfast drifted up from a drawing-room ringing with voices and laughter. The heady scent of narcissi cut from Scillonian bulbs and arrayed in silver bowls all over the house released a flood of memories: her own bare feet dusted with glittering silver sand on the beach at Church Quay; the taste of Mrs Evans's fresh bread. She was married and, even if the French went away, Castle Bryher would never be home again. She was a stranger to herself. It was true that, on Bryher, Hester had often been aware that she looked different to the other island children, but even so she'd simply been Miss Hester the captain's daughter, an islander and Cornish before she was anything else. Here, every sidelong glance from a servant and every impertinent question from Louisa or her friends served as a reminder that she was black, and held in contempt for it. Hester stared down at the narrow gold band on the third finger of her left hand, adorned with an elegant cluster of diamonds. It was, Crow had said, his own mother's ring. This morning, she'd become Hester, Countess of Lamorna. Her papa's final words had been spoken in a language she did not understand, a language from his hidden past: *Nne! Nne m o!* If only she knew what he'd meant, she might know a little more of who she really was beneath the unfamiliar carapace of this new name. Countess of Lamorna. Lady Lamorna. Now that the immediate terror of the journey from Cornwall to London had passed, she was left dizzy at the speed of change, no longer certain who she was, or where home might really be. It was not here, she thought, eyeing the reflection of her bedchamber in the mirror: the soothing rose-pink walls, old paintings in gilded frames, the enormous canopied bed. Downstairs, she was quite sure Crow laboured under no such uncertainty. He was probably still moving among the guests with impossible ease, the portraits of his ancestors looking down at him with shocked disapproval that he cared nothing for. The twenty downstairs might as well have been two hundred. Some were Papa's friends whom Hester knew from visits to the islands: red-faced Admiral Gunning with his kind, chatty wife, Lord Dewsbury, Mr Sancho with his ink-stained fingers; but most had been carefully selected by Louisa and were of extremely high *ton*: Countess Esterházy, Lord Byron, who had eyes only for her bosom. Surely all this was really happening to someone else? More memories rose to the surface of her mind, just like bubbles drifting through the glass of straw-gold champagne Crow had touched to her lips in the barouche on the way home from church. Holding a posy of hellebores and hyacinths dotted with pearls of dew and tied with silver ribbon, she'd seen a barefoot child sweeping the crossing as Arkwright drove along St James's, and the emerald silk of Louisa's gown catching thin morning light. She'd found herself looking at Crow's hands as the curate spoke in an almost empty St George's Chapel; she remembered his lean, strong fingers and the swallow inked into the pale skin on the back of his hand, but not the words they had both spoken. She'd really noticed his eyes for the first time as he looked at her then – that wintery Atlantic grey below those arched brows like flicks of Indian ink. After the ceremony, they'd found themselves alone in the lee of the chapel's vast wooden doors, the curate having followed Louisa and Kitto out into Hanover Square. Crow had turned, taking her hands in his once more. His kiss sent an oddly exhilarating sensation soaring through her as his lips touched hers, his thumb just grazing a spot behind one ear that sent a sweet sensation spreading through her body.

Before the end of the month, I'll have every girl in London regretting her fair ringlets, Louisa had said in the carriage on the way back to Berkeley Square. *You'll be the toast of the Season, darling.* If Papa had not taught her better, Hester would have been tempted to laugh: it was naivety at best, arrogance at worst. Perhaps Louisa had never noticed the puckered scars on Papa's wrists where irons had chafed, or the purplish, silvery impression left on Maggie's neck by a collar she must have worn for decades? Sitting before the mirror in her bedchamber, Hester reached for the bell and rang for Maggie. She could not stay here alone all afternoon. Her time was no longer her own, but her husband's. He would soon expect her.

Maggie came so quickly that Hester suspected she had been waiting nearby, and felt oddly comforted by her tact. Maggie smoothed out her apron. 'Your hair looks very well to me, milady, but I can dress it again if you wish. Or did you ring me for something else?'

Hester smiled at Maggie's reflection. 'Oh, I'm daydreaming. In truth, I needed five minutes without being goggled at by all those people downstairs.'

'I'm not surprised, milady.' Maggie gently drew the pins from Hester's simple coiffure, tipping sweet almond oil into the palm of one hand as she teased out snags and tangles with swift, deft fingertips; one of Hester's earliest memories was of Papa gently

K.J. WHITTAKER

rubbing oil into her scalp, but she still hadn't swallowed the delicious shock of having her hair dressed by a woman who really understood how to cope with such a mass of curls.

Did Louisa really believe she alone had the power to whisk away the stain of at least a hundred years of slavery and oppression by simply making one fashionable? Best not to remind Louisa, then, that Mama's family had declined today's invitation just as they had declined ever to know her. Hester wasn't sure she could bear to go downstairs.

'Tell me again how you met my papa.' Hester longed for his presence, if only as a shared memory.

Maggie paused before she spoke, as if she had been asked to give away her last penny. 'Well, I had run away from the people who kept me, milady. As your papa will have told you, some of the white Abolitionists were good men who wanted to put right an injustice. Even so, most of them thought of us as little better than children.'

'I know that well enough,' Hester said. 'Most of the Lamornas' friends seem astonished that I'm able to speak English. Papa told me once that when Mr Wilberforce arranged a breakfast for all the prominent Africans then in London, he and the others were seated at another end of the table from the white men and women, with a screen set up to separate them.'

'Indeed, milady. It was thought, too, even by the Abolitionists, that we wouldn't be able to shift for ourselves if we were fully liberated, that we wouldn't know how to go on if our masters were forced to pay us an honest wage. So even when the law was changed, slavery was abolished only in name. My master and mistress still expected me to fetch and carry, with nothing said of money, and I came to realise that I would have to take my own freedom. So I left the house one night.' She paused. 'Exning Hall wasn't far from London, but when I got here, I was starving. I had nothing, and without a letter of recommendation I couldn't find even the most menial position. I was a skinny child, not feminine, and so I went to the India Docks to see if I might hide my sex and join the crew of a vessel. The docks were a horribly dangerous place, milady, but I couldn't see another choice. I was lucky: your papa found me trying to steal a cake of tack as his ship was loaded.' Maggie shook her head slightly, smiling. 'He didn't believe I was a boy, not even for a moment, and he took me himself to the African Academy in Clapham, where the sons of African princes and merchants were educated then, and he told Mr Greaves that I would make a very good maid-of-all-work. I was seventeen years old then, and I had worked all my life. That was the first time I was ever paid.'

Hester's mouth was dry. 'I wonder, Maggie, what my father would say if he knew what I have done this morning.'

It was impossible to read the expression on Maggie's face. 'He would want you to be safe, milady, I'm sure.'

Hester looked down at her hands. 'If you knew Papa then, did you ever meet my mother, Maggie? She died three weeks after I was born: I remember nothing of her.' Papa had been happy with Mama, hadn't he? Was there not a chance for her to be happy with Crow?

'No, milady.' There was an edge of finality to Maggie's voice now, as though she'd decided that all these confidences had gone far enough. 'It's such a shame you can't have flowers pinned in your hair. It would look so pretty.'

'It's a very odd thing to do, getting married when one is in full mourning.'

'In these topsy-turvy times, nothing is as usual, milady.'

That much was true: all she could do was pray that Papa would understand that there had been little choice but to accept Crow's proposal. Much as she longed to have nothing to do with these white aristocrats who stared at her as though she were a creature from another world – some with open disgust – she must now live among them for the rest of her life. Then she remembered the shock of pleasure whenever Crow touched her, even in passing. If only she could have him alone, and not the rest of his world.

'Milady? Should I neaten your gown before you go downstairs? It's a little crushed.'

Hester looked up; she had been quite lost in her own thoughts. *Milady.* My lady. She couldn't get used to the sound of it.

'You look very well as you are, Hester.'

As one, Maggie and Hester turned to the door, and Crow himself walked in. It was the first time he had called her anything other than Miss Harewood. He leaned against one of the bed-posts, watching as Maggie shook out the creases in the skirts of Hester's black mourning gown. Even after almost a week in London, it was still a shock to see him clean-shaven and dressed in the first style of elegance, wearing a white cravat stark against a jacket cut close to his form, the black band for Papa tied around his upper arm. She pictured the smooth skin and lean muscle beneath his jacket, his fine shirt. There was always something a little *déshabillé* about her new husband, even dressed for his wedding, his dark hair permanently rumpled.

He smiled, and for a moment looked shockingly young. 'I came to give you something, as a matter of fact.'

Hester felt heat rush to her cheeks. 'You've already given me diamonds – which I can assure you I won't wear for a year.'

'I know – entirely stupid of me. So I got you something else: here.' Crow handed her a long, narrow box of plain silver with a filigreed clasp and Hester took it, lifting the lid. What was she to do with more jewellery that she could not wear in mourning? But when she opened the lid, there were no diamonds winking at her but a set of paintbrushes with pale, oiled ash handles and fine-cut tips.

'Are they the right kind?' Crow asked. 'Do you still paint? Your father was always very proud. He hung your pictures in his cabin on the *Belle*.'

Hester's eyes burned with tears, for her father and for the fact that this spoiled nobleman-soldier she had just married would remember such a thing. 'Not that awful portrait of myself I painted when I was eleven?' She smiled. 'I made him hang it where no one else might chance to see. You're very kind.'

'I'm nothing of the sort,' he said. 'We've not long to endure the company, you know. Will you come downstairs?' He stood beside her chair as she rose, cupping her elbow in one hand, and again his touch sent a burst of pleasure rushing through her. Hester realised the next time they came upstairs together she must go to his bed. He led her to the door as though she were so precious and fragile that he must protect her at any cost. When they reached the doorway he turned her to face him, gently, and with the side of his thumb he smoothed the tears from her face, first beneath the right eye, then the left; and then he closed the door to leave them alone in the hallway and kissed her, again very gently, on the mouth. She caught her breath; he tasted of salt, of champagne, of something indefinable. She kissed him back, parting her lips, and when he returned the kiss, it was not gentle. Hester, her hands in his hair, felt a pulse of joy, and Crow kissed her again, letting out a long sigh, like an exhausted traveller who had at last found shelter.

29

'Darling Hester!' In the morning-room, Louisa cast aside her embroidery-ring, stretching like a cat on the chaise longue. 'You're so obliging that I'm sure you won't mind, but I said we'd be at home to Lady Osborne today. She's my most particular friend – as dear to me as a sister – and she's left so many cards since your wedding, I can't tell you.'

'My mourning should not deprive you of her company, then.' Standing by the window, Hester watched a crested town carriage roll up alongside the house, drawn by a pair of steaming grey horses with dappled flanks. She thought of Crow and flushed, recalling the faint line of black hair that ran south from his belly button. On their wedding night, she'd watched him take off his shirt, terror mingling with unbecoming impatience. Two weeks later, she waited for him to come to her bed with longing, and last night, he had not. He was still almost a stranger: their shared knowledge of one another was expressed only in a language of touch, and when morning came he was always gone, leaving Hester to wake alone and remember that Papa was still dead, and all she had ever known wholly lost. No, she had no desire to discuss the latest fashions with women who could barely be bothered to disguise their curiosity about her. If Louisa must fill the house with her friends, it would be a good morning as any to visit Mr Coutts: she might even feel less naked and vulnerable with banknotes in her possession. *Money is power* – Papa always said so, and he'd made sure that she was left with plenty of it. She rang the bell for Maggie just as Lady Osborne swept in with three of her indistinguishable daughters, a flurry of exquisite Indian muslin and intricately coiled glossy chestnut plaits pinned atop their bobbing heads, fussy crimped curls clustering about their ears that emanated a faint smell of burning. An expensive, subtle scent failed to disguise how long it had been since Lady Osborne had washed beneath her arms. Powerless, Hester got to her feet and, at Louisa's side, was soon surrounded. She had just exchanged curtseys with Lady Osborne's daughters when the oldest Osborne girl reached out and touched Hester's own hair, turned to her sisters, and giggled: it was the sort of careless gesture with which one might stroke a cat. Hester took a step backwards, stunned as if she had been slapped, convulsively clenching and unclenching her fists at her sides. Nobody appeared to notice the imposition: the Osborne girl herself had already gathered with her sisters by the pianoforte to fawn and giggle over a miniature of Crow, leaving Hester standing alone and helpless with fury, wishing that she might just turn and walk out.

Maggie saved her the trouble; she came in wearing a long apron, looking harassed. 'You rang for me, milady?'

'Indeed I did. Please would you ask Mr Arkwright to send around the carriage?'

'Very good, milady.' Maggie dropped a curtsey and retreated towards the door, but not before Louisa had turned to watch. Hester stared after Maggie: had she imagined that swift expression of unease when she spoke Arkwright's name? What possible cause could Maggie have to be wary of Crow's taciturn groom? Hester had scarcely heard him utter more than three words together, but perhaps matters were different in the servants' hall: as she knew too well it was another world, and one into which Catlin had retreated as they grew older together, leaving her friendless.

'Darling, but where are you going?' Louisa spoke from across the room, which instantly fell silent, and Hester found herself scrutinised.

'It's of no great moment,' Hester said, irritated at being forced to air her affairs before Louisa's particular friends. 'I've written to Mr Coutts, that's all. He's expecting me any day now.'

'Mr *who*?' Lady Osborne looked as though she'd opened a barrel of bacon only to find it seething with maggots – not that Hester could suppose the woman had ever done anything so prosaic as inspect her own kitchen stores.

'You can't mean the banker?' Louisa smiled. 'Hester, really?'

Hester flushed, conscious of Maggie hovering in the doorway, waiting for her instruction. Lady Osborne and her daughters watched in such silent astonishment it was as though she had stripped naked before them all. 'Papa – my father—' Stunned by the intrusion, she found herself quite unable to speak. Surely Louisa was well bred enough to possess more tact than this? 'My father left me an independence. I should think there will soon be bills from the dressmaker, at least.'

Louisa stared at her, lips slightly parted, as though she were hungry for something. 'But, my dear girl – such matters need not concern you in the slightest. No dressmaker would have the temerity to dun you in this house, I can assure you. It's not as though you had a gambling debt that must be paid! It's really entirely irrelevant. And Lamorna is not here.'

'I know he is not.' Hester felt hot and constricted in her gown, as though Maggie had laced her stays too tight. No,

Crow had not come to her bed last night, and neither had she seen him at the breakfast-table. It was to be expected that young men would stay out all night: she was foolish to feel so alone because of it.

Louisa smiled at her. 'But surely he cannot have given his permission for you to go to the bank? My dear, it's on the Strand, and I am very sure you ought not to be going to such a place without a man to escort you, and most particularly not with your husband knowing nothing about it.'

The youngest Osborne girl tittered, covering her mouth with both hands.

'I should hate to be thought interfering,' Lady Osborne said, 'but I must own I think it's the sort of thing we women need not concern ourselves with, Lady Lamorna. Surely you would not wish to attract more comment?'

Hester swallowed. *More comment.* Lady Osborne might just as well have admitted that the entire town spoke of nothing but her marriage. With appalling clarity, she saw that despite the obvious injustice Louisa and Lady Osborne were right: she could not, in propriety, visit a bank without her husband's consent. She had known Crow little more than a month, and the realisation that she was actually now subject to his authority took hold with uncomfortable force. He was a man, and men always had the last say, but Papa had earned her uncomplaining compliance by loving her for twenty-two years, and never being unreasonable. She had ridden in Crow's company, night and day, for a scant few weeks. She knew the shape of his mouth when he spent seed, and that he could be both autocratic and impossibly gentle, but little more, and yet she now owed him unquestioning obedience. It was a crushing realisation. She wasn't about to admit as much before Lady Osborne and her staring, giggling daughters. 'I'll take a servant, if it would be thought improper to go alone.'

Louisa passed Lady Osborne a plate of madeleines. 'We must forget that on her Cornish island my dear daughter-in-law led the sort of untrammelled existence that we could only dream of, Lady Osborne, slaves as we are to the whims of our menfolk. No, Hester, you cannot think of going without Lord Lamorna's express permission. Even if he should grant it, which I doubt extremely, it would attract the sort of comment I know you would not like.'

'Indeed,' Lady Osborne said, nibbling a madeleine with a sidelong glance at her daughters, 'we poor women really might as well be slaves – we certainly have as little say in what happens to us.'

Hester curtseyed, suppressing her fury. 'I must confess, my lady, that I should think our luxurious situation here is almost incomprehensibly distant from that of a slave.'

She withdrew without another word; without a doubt, the moment Maggie shut the door behind her she would become the topic of all conversation.

Scent drifted from the narcissi as Hester earthed the bulbs in a china bowl; ensconced in the small ornamental glasshouse attached to the back of the ballroom, she felt an unsettling combination of loneliness and fury curdling with relief at having escaped Louisa's veiled broadside attack. Yet her anger ebbed away as she bedded onion-skin flakes of bulb-casing in dark earth, pressing down the soil with the flat edge of her trowel. She remembered roaming the hothouses at Nansmornow on a frost-crisp winter's morning and overhearing the head gardener telling one of his boys that Crow's father had ordered the seventy-year-old firewalls in the pineapple sheds to be lit and the crowns to be cultivated once more, all so that her ladyship might have green pineapple juice for her complexion.

Louisa's beauty had been her greatest currency: likely she was afraid that age would steal it. Hester herself was now the Countess of Lamorna and Louisa the dowager: her own marriage had forced Louisa, unwilling, into the next generation. Weak spring sunlight was intensified by the glass, enough to warm her shoulders and release the earthy scents of damp soil and greenery. Catlin always said work was the best remedy for any sort of ill humour. Catlin had little choice in the matter, she supposed, but there was truth in it all the same.

A light cough behind her signalled the presence of Mowbray, and she turned to face him. 'Have you everything you need, ma'am? I must say that it is most gratifying to see the glasshouse in use again. The late earl had it commissioned for his first wife. She was most interested in plants and botanical specimens. A French lady she was, but Quality. Not one of your Republicans.'

Hester couldn't help smiling. Mowbray's confidences may not have been quite proper, but the servants at least were beginning to accept her. 'I think that will be all for today, thank you.' It was true that Mowbray's manner had defrosted since learning of her visits to the glasshouse, but she couldn't be quite sure whether his conscientious arrangement of seed deliveries and his procurement of a new watering-can were not just a ruse to keep her from the rest of the house.

Mowbray bowed, nodding at the bowl of narcissi. 'Very pretty, ma'am, if I might make so bold. Where would you like them put?'

'Please don't trouble yourself, Mr Mowbray. I'll find somewhere.' She brushed off her hands on the heavy cotton apron, picked up the sun-warmed bowl and went out past him. How was she to fill the rest of the day? Every time she took up a paintbrush the memory of Papa's unfinished portrait reproached her. If only she might step through that gilded door at the far end of the ballroom and find herself at home in the tower, with the rotten, salty smell of kelp on the beach at low tide. The walls in the ballroom were mirrored on both sides, and Hester saw multitudes of herself reflected, a lone, unrecognisable figure in a black gown and a drab cotton apron, carrying a bowl of bright flowers. She felt a stranger to herself as much as she was a stranger in her own home. She should just be happy that she was under Crow's protection and, thanks to his influence, safe from harassment by Occupation troops. She might have been sitting in a prison cell, or worse. And yet she found herself making for Crow's library, telling herself sternly that of course she was not such a maw-worm as to go seeking him out, but only thought to brighten the room with the arrangement of narcissi. She passed Annie carrying a basket of pressed sheets, ignoring the maid's startled expression as she went to the library door, clasping the brass doorknob, so cool at her touch. Pausing, she leaned back against the door, breathing in the warm, dry scent of beeswax. She might need to seek her husband's permission to go out, or to withdraw her quarterly allowance from the account at Coutts, but surely not to enter a room in her own house? *His* house. Even though Castle Bryher had been granted to her in Papa's will, it now also belonged to Crow, along with all she owned save for the independence Papa had settled solely upon her, and even this she could not, in propriety, withdraw from the bank without Crow's permission. She'd become his, just as much as that favourite mare was his. At least she need not have worried about dancing on Crow's every whim. Her new husband had been out more often than he was at home, and he was not here now, so what did he care if she went to put flowers on his desk?

The library was cool and dark, each wall lined with shelves from floor to ceiling. The scent of narcissi mingled with the smell of old leather emanating from the rows of gold-embossed calfskin-bound volumes, and Hester set the bowl down on the large desk inlaid with green leather. At home on Bryher, the narcissi would be over by now, but here in London they were only just coming into bloom, and she swallowed another nauseous burst of homesickness. In less than a week Crow would be out of London, she knew, attending to business on one of his estates. She had never expected to feel quite so hollow at the prospect of his absence. *This isn't part of the plan,* she told herself. *What an absurd complication. As if he would ever feel so if you were to go away without him, not that you ever could.* In the unforgiving light of day, what did she really know of him, this man who held her life in his hands?

Turning impulsively, she went to the window and stood for a moment to look out over Berkeley Square, scythed grass within the railed-off garden now studded with purple and yellow crocuses. She longed to walk barefoot and alone down Town Beach, watched only by seagulls, listening to nothing but the hiss of creamy surf rushing up the sand. It was too painful to think of: Bryher was hers no longer, occupied by French soldiers and the castle itself legally owned by Crow, absorbed into his vast estates. Even if those soldiers were gone, the Countess of Lamorna could never live in a tower with only her servants to please. She had become someone else entirely, and hardly knew herself. Hester rested her forehead on the cool glass. Out there, she'd find nothing but an endless warren of streets and buildings: there was nowhere earth met sky, and nowhere she could be unwatched. And as she looked out of the window, Arkwright led Crow's new mare around to wait by the front door, and a small thrill of excitement shot through her. He was here. He had come home. As if sensing her gaze, Arkwright looked up with such an expression of blank hatred that Hester took a step backwards. Had he seen her? He couldn't have, surely, not with no lamp lit in the room. Arkwright looked away, and walked the mare up the street, keeping her warm. Either she'd imagined that look of loathing, or Crow had been unreasonable in his demands.

Turning the brass catches, Hester lifted the window, but the washed-clean sky visible above the white houses and treetops of the square was deceptive; the air in London never tasted fresh. And, as she watched, another pigeon tumbled straight from the sky, landing directly on the sill outside her own window, a blur of swift-moving claws and pearl-grey feathers. With one glasslike eye turned towards her, wings spread, it flew past and straight into the gloomy upper reaches of the library, making a wide sweep of the higher shelves before plummeting back down to the window in a blur of speed. Without thinking, Hester reached out and it came to her, warm life throbbing in her own two hands, shivering feathers, scratching claws. She felt the chill of metal and lifted her prize to see a small bronze canister strapped to the pigeon's reptilian leg.

'And what are you doing in my library?'

Hester turned to find Crow watching her from the doorway. She clasped the bird, not trusting herself to speak. The swift pulse of joy she'd felt at the sight of him vanished. He didn't sound angry precisely, but it was by no means an affectionate greeting, and it was galling, coming so hard on the heels of her own realisation at how much she would miss him when he was gone; last night, she had lain awake for hours, waiting, and he had not come. In two steps, he was at her side; in the time it took him to reach her, her chagrin gave way to anger, and she sensed a rush of tension pass through him as he took hold of the pigeon and released it from the open window, never taking his grey eyes from hers. His lashes were very thick and black. *Eyes put in with a sooty finger,* Catlin would say. The bird flew away, hurtling across the open space of the square. She supposed carrier pigeons must get lost all the time. 'Well?' he said. The unfriendliness had quite gone – had she imagined it?

He looked down at her with the smallest hint of a provocative smile, as if it was nothing particularly extraordinary that he could expect her to answer to him on every subject, including which room she should choose to adorn with spring flowers.

'Forgive me,' Hester said, quietly but irrevocably losing hold of her temper, 'I have never been married before. Perhaps you ought to tell me exactly what I might do without having to obtain your consent? Must I ask permission before going about the house? I do wish you would be a little more prescriptive or I don't know how many times I shall go wrong.'

He stared at her for a moment, startled. 'I meant no such thing. Why are you so quick to anger? It's not your business to advise me on my conduct.' Had she not been so angry herself, his own lightning-flash show of temper would have been a treat to watch, lending such animation to those fine grey eyes of his.

'You're very quick to anger yourself!' Was it not enough to have lost not only her home but all sense of her own self, to belong to him, to be so completely at his mercy? They were standing so close together, and she felt the heat of his body. With the desk behind her she could retreat no further, but in truth she really had no wish to. She wasn't afraid of him. 'If you mean to treat me like a child, you'd better think again, Lord Lamorna.'

'Believe me,' Crow said, stepping closer still, so that Hester was now almost sitting on the desk, 'that's the very last way I wish to use you precisely at this moment.'

She breathed in his scent of soap, of tobacco-smoke. 'But you can do whatever you want to with me – I'm quite in your power.'

Watching her, he closed his eyes for a half-moment, those black lashes dark against his pale skin. Bare inches away, he reached out and tucked a flyaway hair behind her ear. 'What makes you think I mean to be so medieval as all that? I should

not have spoken to you as I did, and I'm sincerely sorry—'
He broke off. 'I would not upset you.'

She opened her mouth to speak and could not. Instead, she took hold of the lapel of his jacket, closing the space between them. She had to offer very little force – he kissed her back with such vehemence that for a moment she was afraid of what she had unleashed.

30

The landlord at the St George's Arms in the village of Stepney had long since ordered his nervous tap-girl to close the shutters. Crow could only hope the man was as devoutly anti-French as Grant's sources had assured him, or that he had been well paid for his troubles. Neither would be worth much if Occupation troops asked questions in this place. He wished that he could just ride home, back along the Ratcliffe Highway, through Whitechapel, Shoreditch and Clerkenwell, along Upper Holborn and back to Berkeley Square. He knew he had not quite been able to disguise his panic at seeing Hester alone in the library, and holding a carrier pigeon. She was too close: what if she stumbled on the truth? Extraordinarily, she even knew how to read cipher. And yet even so, he still could not force himself to wish that he'd never married her, that she'd never stumbled into his lamentable protection. Never had a woman spoken to him as Hester did, much less grabbed hold of the lapel of his jacket and kissed him with such inflammatory force. He smiled at the memory, but all he could do was pray that she would be safe when he was dead, because this duty would cost him his life before long. He'd married Hester to protect her, to uphold what remained of his honour, but he hadn't expected that he would always want to see her one last time. He prayed that thinking of her would bring him courage when it was finally his turn to die: he prayed that the desire to make her proud would be stronger than the fear. This time, he would not be shot in the back.

The tavern's upper room was thick with smoke, but Crow knew whom he was looking for. Smith and Lessing had both been Riflemen in the 95th, although not of the officer class: he'd known them both by sight out in the Peninsula for at least two years before Waterloo. Crow hadn't known Masters before the defeat and couldn't be sure of his worth, but he was hardly in a position to be choosy over his choice of volunteers. He spotted them immediately: three hard-eyed men, two in farmhouse-homespun and one in a battered greatcoat. Hunched at the same table, each had that shielded, alert watchfulness of the soldier, instantly recognisable: the two in homespun could not have looked less like field-labourers. Those of Wellington's defeated men who had survived the carnage after Waterloo had taken their time coming home to England, often slipping ashore at night with free-traders; anyone known to have been a soldier in Wellington's army was soon made an example of and hanged at the nearest crossroads, save the aristocracy, of course. After so many years, Buonaparte still nursed a fascination for the upper classes who had sneered at him when he was a young Corsican soldier with a bad accent and no connections. He was also, Crow reflected, still a tactician: attacking the English nobility in its entirety would have been like lancing a boil, a risk too far. It was doubtless why the brazen lie about the royal family dying of gaol-fever had circulated: Crow was willing to bet their deaths had been ordered by Jérôme, and that Buonaparte himself had been furious at the risk of stirring up the populace. Crow joined the three men in silence; they exchanged only swift, curt nods in greeting.

'Listen.' Crow swirled the cheap brandy in his glass. 'We're none of us commissioned, not sworn to serve anyone. We've all got more to lose than perhaps there is to gain. Now's your chance to get out of this if you want to.' He sat back in his chair, watching them. The brandy burned his throat. 'I'll not think less of any man who chooses to walk out of here now. You choose.'

'Fucking stupid idea if you ask me,' Masters said. 'Boney has the post-roads watched pretty close, doesn't he?'

Blowing up the bridge at Malden was a dangerous plan, true. Masters would be a damn sight more reticent if he had the slightest inkling that Joséphine herself knew all about it and that Crow himself had told her.

Crow set down his glass and lit a cigarillo, smoking through a moment of unbearable tension. No matter how you looked at it, he was betraying his own side, putting English soldiers into inexcusable danger. These men had homes, and families who depended on whatever coin or sustenance they could bring in. They'd risked enough even meeting in this place, and they'd done it because their children were hungry. Thanks to him, in less than two weeks, Masters, Smith and Lessing were going to risk even more. Each remained in his place on the bench. They were dead men now to the last, and with the promise of armed combat closer by the day, Crow knew he was close – too close – to the nightmares that haunted his sleep now stalking him by daylight.

Riding home through the empty, silent streets of London, the fear returned, as Crow had been sure it would, and memories took hold with such force that the rain-soaked night retreated, and four years peeled away like sections of the dry, layered skin of an onion. He was in England no more, but in occupied Spain, when the invasion of England had seemed so unlikely. The citadel of Vitoria sat at the top of the largest hill, sleeping behind crumbling walls, quiet and full of dark-eyed girls with the scent of rising bread and rain-wet earth. Arkwright leaned against the wall of the barn, exhaling a pale curl of smoke. 'What're you waiting for, my lord?'

Crow watched him from the tail of one eye. Arkwright waited with calm belligerence, his gaze flickering constantly across the tumbling, moonlit sierra rearing up before them on the far side of the valley. Crow had always suspected that Arkwright loathed him more than he hated the rest of the staff. Small wonder, really. He'd been Scovell's right-hand man in the Corps of Guides since before the siege of Badajoz and a soldier in the British army since before Crow was born. And by an accident of birth it was Crow, not Arkwright, who was now in command. Buonaparte's brother Joseph had sixty thousand men out there somewhere, waiting for Wellington to lead out the whole bloody dance. He'd be waiting the devil of a long time. Wellington never liked to move first. The valley and the mountains beyond waited, too, in the light of the moon. There wasn't a sign of movement, and yet Crow couldn't shake off the feeling that someone was out there, watching.

'There's no time for a rendezvous,' Crow said. 'If you find anything, ride back to Santa María. I'll do likewise.'

Arkwright watched him with a contempt which Crow ignored, along with the barely there salute. He ran the gully's length, dust in his eyes, in his hair. Shouldering his musket, he waited, sheltered by a shallow curve in the ground and the sparse covering of moonlit olive trees. If he got his head shot off without reporting to Wellington, Grant would kill him all over again. Even that'd be better than Arkwright's sarcasm if he cocked this up. There it was again: a half-heard exhalation. Stillness spread through Crow's body. He waited. Again. Scree crunched underfoot: some idiot trying to be quiet but not. Moving in silence, Crow stepped from the shelter of the closest olive tree. He found nothing but a shrine – a cairn of sun-baked stones littered with the dried stalks of the wild rosemary and thyme blanketing the dry, rolling foothills of the sierra.

Crow was close enough now to reach out and touch the nearest of the stones. A gorse root snapped beneath his boot with a crack that rang up to the heavens and out across the parched, moonlit lowlands. *Fuck.* He waited again, scarcely even drawing breath, raking the landscape for the smallest sign of a French sharpshooter who might now have the back of his skull lined up behind the sight-bead of his musket. Nothing. The ragged breathing began again. Crow lifted his own musket, ready to fire, the weight of it still a surprise, stepping behind the cairn.

A girl crouched behind the sun-warmed stones, her face streaked with the red dust of the foothills. Crow found himself looking at the faded pattern of cherries and roses on her gown. She was no older than his half-sister Roza. She looked away, shielding her face with her arms, terrified. Crow was acutely aware that he was filthy, stinking and twice her size.

'Why in hell's name are you sneaking around on the front line?' he demanded in rapid Spanish; even his thoughts flowed in Spanish now. The girl shook her head, wide-eyed with terror. She was carrying information – either for the guerrilla allies or the French themselves. Why else would she be roaming between the French and the English lines in the middle of the night?

'Come on, where is it – what have you got?' Crow inwardly cursed the red jacket and the regimental Coldstream star. He should have worn the brown of Scovell's Guides. He might then have passed for a Spaniard, at least. The girl moved a little, dragging the muslin gown tight across her midriff, and Crow saw for the first time that she was big with child.

Crow drew his bayonet. *Don't think about it. Just do it.* 'Give me what they gave you, or I'll spill your guts here on the stones, understand? Then they'll all starve, won't they – all your family?' The words spilled out in a rush. 'And your baby will be dead before it's even born.'

She let out one sobbing breath. What had happened to the father? He was probably dead: the French had laid waste to Portugal, to Spain, killing with no discrimination. Maybe she'd been raped by a French soldier. Or an English. It happened. Crow heard the trickle of liquid and the smell of hot urine hit him, sickening. The backs of his fingers tingled as he gripped the bayonet. He'd just made a girl no older than his sister piss herself with terror.

'Have it then, and kill me afterwards. The men will hang me now anyway.' Snot and tears streamed down her face. She was shockingly beautiful, with strong black brows and a mouth that he would have kissed if he'd met her in a village one night with everyone so pleased to see English troops and the Rioja flowing. He'd never killed at such close quarters. Never a woman. She drew a cigarillo from somewhere within the folds of her gown, thrusting it at him. Her hand quivered, her eyes fixed on the blade pointing at her ripe belly. *What kind of a soldier is too cowardly to kill?*

His fingers closed around the cigarillo. 'They won't kill you. There's going to be a battle before morning – no one'll know if you delivered this or not. Now run. Run, all right?'

She scurried off into the night, making for the dim cluster of lights marking one of the mountainside villages on the far side of the valley. Now she was gone, Crow's hands shook so hard he dropped the cigarillo. Cursing, he picked it up, breaking it open to unroll a scrap of paper no longer than his little finger. The message was in Spanish, *en clair* – no one had even bothered to encipher it.

His Majesty King Joseph has thirty thousand men – he moves to meet Jourdan.

Crow mourned the dried tobacco leaf spilling from the torn paper and between his fingers, blowing away into the darkness. Napoleon Buonaparte's brother was at this moment marching an entire army behind the British: if King Joseph met with Marshal Jourdan before this news reached Wellington, they'd be cut off from behind, their position impossibly weakened. If Wellington didn't order an attack before dawn, they'd be routed. It was already too late. He ran.

Many hours later, and now seven miles from Vitoria, Crow reined in on the Heights of Puebla with the sun beating against his back as he looked down on the carnage in the valley below. The 91st were holding steady, men crouching in formation, bayonets glittering in the late morning sunlight as the French cavalry made ready to charge them; he had to ride on: he'd just passed on orders to Ponsonby and the 91st, but Wellington was waiting for the report from Lord Hill. Crow had reached Wellington in time – because of him, they'd surprised King Joseph's men; in fact, it looked like a rout. Surrounded by dead and dying men, Crow didn't feel part of a victory.

An infantryman from the regiment stationed behind him turned to speak, his face gunpowder-black and streaked with sweat. 'We've got them on the run, sir.' Before Crow could spur on the mare the man's head was blown clean from his shoulders; the rest of him took an age to topple and fall, his head rolled away, a wide-eyed blur in the dust.

'Who got that?' someone called from the back, but Crow didn't know the soldier's name. What was he doing here in the madness of this battle when death could come just like that? He should turn and ride south, and damn the shame of it.

'Crow, what the devil are you doing?'

Crow turned to face Alex Gordon. His fellow ADC was pale with exhaustion and blackened too with the smoke of spent powder, cut through with trails of perspiration; Crow knew he looked no better but felt so curiously removed from the chaos that it was almost like watching it all happen to someone else. Perhaps being an ADC wasn't the soft job after all but, in the end, worse than fighting and dying shoulder to shoulder with one's own regiment. Criss-crossing the battlefield, carrying orders from Wellington and returning with reports from his commanders: they were all of them nothing but slow-moving targets, never knowing if the next moment was to be their last.

'I'm on my way to Hill. Where are you off to? Picton's made a proper mess of Jourdan's right flank and Wellington says we're not to chase them off.' Crow kept his voice steady. He'd known fear but this was worse – a cold, creeping certainty that if he spurred the mare down across that hellish plain, this time he would be the one to catch a shot; it would be him with both legs removed by a cannonball, or the side-plate of his skull obliterated so that his brain slid out on to the mud-trampled grass like a hardboiled egg peeled at a picnic.

'Convinced yourself there's a musket-ball down there with your name on it, Jack?' Gordon's use of his given name plucked Crow from his frozen state. 'Listen,' Gordon went on. 'Only thing to do is pretend you don't know, old lad. There's nothing else for it, after all. What the devil would you do if you deserted? Get a move on. We're both of us sitting here like a pair of clay pigeons. We've got the French on the run. Ponsonby said King Joey leaped clean from the carriage just before the 95th got to him with all the court treasury left behind – paintings, gold, women, the lot. We'll be across the Pyrenees this time next month, so take heart.'

Gordon was right; he had no choice. Desertion would be worse than death. He was half aware of Gordon calling out to him as he rode away, galloping off towards General Picton's right flank as the Connaught Rangers hassled the French retreat, but his voice was snatched away by the cries of wounded men, even though the thundering of cannon-fire had faded now into sporadic shots as the French retreat gathered pace. It was time to go. The smoke began to lift as Crow galloped across the valley; he was never going to catch up with Hill at this rate. The earth was littered with dead and dying men lying in rutted mud that glittered with gold coins. Gordon had been right as usual: those left alive were looting the French baggage train – it was to be expected. Crow spurred the mare on as women and girls in fine muslin gowns smeared with blood and mud pleaded with him in French and Spanish – *Sir, please help us* – women of the French retinue left to fend for themselves as their one-time protectors retreated in full disorder. He couldn't stop; he had to reach Hill or face Wellington's fury if the order to hold back from the chase was not delivered. There was no use, Wellington claimed, in over-stretching the men – although anyone could see that they were letting almost the entire French army run to fight on another morning. Crow almost crushed the pregnant woman beneath the iron-shod hooves of his mare. He reined in just in time, wheeling away, the breath snatched from his lungs in horror at what he had so nearly done.

The girl lay on her side, one thin, brown arm draped protectively across the ripe swell of her belly. She must be got to safety – he'd have her up in the saddle and take her behind the lines once he'd spoken to Hill; the women in the camp would see to her. He slid from the saddle and crouched at her side – she was motionless; he recognised the cherry-patterned muslin of her gown before he knew her face. It was the messenger girl who'd given him the French *chiffre* in the cold dark before dawn, before the battle, and she was dead. In life, she had been pretty even terrified, with those long dark eyes; in death she was ethereal, such breathtaking beauty, her skin drained of colour, so pale, as if she had been carved from marble by a master. He fought the urge to reach out and touch her face, repelled by his own fascination even as the appalling truth of it settled upon him; she'd looked near her time – perhaps the child still lived, perhaps something could be done, surely one of the camp-followers would be able to nurse the baby if it could be saved? He'd heard of women being cut open to deliver a child, although God only knew what McDonnell and the other surgeons would say if he brought a dead pregnant woman behind the lines when there were men of fighting age to be patched up ready to face death on another day. Fuck them. Fuck them all. He would take her; he would save the child. And for the first time Crow looked down at her lower belly and saw that it was split open to reveal a shining mass. Was that a tiny crooked elbow? Crow got to his feet and immediately vomited into the bloodstained dust, tears spilling down his face, unstoppable, the sting of regurgitated rum on his lips, burning his throat.

Wheeling away, he dropped to his knees once more; how could he go on? They were all nothing but chess pieces in a game played by men far away. And then he felt it: he was being watched. Cold horror washed through him. This was it. The musket-ball with his name inscribed on it, some lone French *tirailleur* getting in one last shot for the emperor: he sensed the creeping hatred. He'd not die with a shot in the back, he'd not have that in the letter home. Getting to his feet, Crow turned, shouldering his own musket, and lighting the flint with subconscious speed he came face to face with Arkwright, who stood holding the mare's reins. It was only Arkwright. He was going crazy, Crow told himself, jumping at shadows, and yet even as he reasoned with himself he knew that Arkwright himself had been watching him with pure, unadulterated hatred. He pushed the thought from his mind. Resentment, yes, but Arkwright had no reason to hate him. He was imagining things.

And in that moment, another shuddering surge of unease pulsed through him. 'Get down on the fucking ground—' Crow threw himself into the dust, dragging Arkwright down beside him, just as a hail of grapeshot slammed into the horse-tramped grass at the precise spot they had been standing.

Together, they lay in the dirt for one bare half-moment before unshouldering their muskets, lighting powder, making ready to fire, to kill or be killed. It would never end, Crow knew.

'They're using us, Arkwright.' He had to speak; the fury of it burst from him and he didn't care if Arkwright really wanted him dead or only thought him crazy: judging by the expression of wordless exhaustion Arkwright sure as Christ didn't care that his life had just been saved. 'Men in London, just like my father. Our lives just don't mean anything to them.'

Arkwright got up and clicked his tongue behind his teeth for the mare, who stepped out from the smoke. It seemed a miracle to Crow that she had not bolted altogether but she came to Arkwright, trusting as a child, letting him take the reins. She shifted, calm in his presence; Arkwright was as good with horses as he was at deciphering codes and learning languages – just as good as Crow himself. 'Only just realised, your honour?' Without waiting for a reply, Arkwright handed Crow the reins, shouldered his own musket and turned away, walking into the pall of smoke from which the mare had emerged, soon lost, leaving Crow with only the cries of the wounded and the dying.

On reaching Berkeley Square, Crow walked through the stable-mews and then the across the laundry-yard between lines of damp washing hanging limp in the cold, grey dawn light. Beneath his jacket and greatcoat, his shirt was sweat-drenched, and not from the exertion of a hard gallop on a cold night. The dogs came for him with cacophonous speed, but he clicked his tongue behind his teeth and they quietened, Gil nuzzling at his hand, the mastiff sniffing at his boots. He stabled the mare himself, rubbing her down, envious that she could sleep now when he could not. He'd paid off the night-guard twice, once on the Ratcliffe Highway and then again outside Mayfair. Doubtless there was a password he could charm from Joséphine's lips, but no one knew better than Crow that such knowledge might kill a man. Or a child.

Walking up the back stairs, he sent servants wheeling from his path, curtseying or bowing as he passed, like a crop of wheat blown by the wind. The reputation of a whoring gamester had proved useful enough: one might come home at dawn any day of the week and never attract comment from one's servants. In these times, even one's most valued retainers couldn't be trusted not to pass on any unusual information to the Occupation. Pushing open the green baize door into the family quarters, he stepped out into the silent hallway. The Turkey rug stretched across waxed and polished floorboards. The shutters had been pulled open and light streamed in, striking off the vast crystal chandelier. An undersized serving-girl in a blue-and-white-striped cotton dress knelt before the great hearth; another crouched on the rug beneath the chandelier, levering dried coins of white candle-wax from the wool. Both froze at the sound of his footfalls.

He went swiftly up the great staircase, straight to Hester's bedchamber. In silence, he opened the door: she was asleep, uncovered, the sheets had slipped away from her. Wearing one of the nightgowns from her new toilette, she lay on her side, her breasts spilling from diaphanous lace-edged linen so fine that it was almost transparent. Had she waited for him, wearing that? He looked down again and lying in Hester's place was the dead pregnant Spanish girl, the sheets black with her blood. *God save me. Enough.* Crow closed his eyes, forcing away the memory. It was so real. Too real. What in Christ's name would happen to Hester when he was not here to protect her? The truth was no man played a game such as his for long. It would all end soon with a bullet, a rope or the guillotine, his part played. He looked down at Hester, herself again, and he ached to wake her: the nightgown promised more than it concealed, and in giving her pleasure he could forget the enormity of his betrayals, and that he lived on borrowed time. He peeled off his jacket and shirt and, still watching his beautiful young wife, to whom he had sworn protection, Crow heard the faint but distinct creak of a floorboard at the far end of the house. He knew precisely where it had come from. *Fuck. Fucking hell.*

Shirtless, he walked swiftly down the corridor to his own bedchamber, ignoring the servant-girl who was meant to be sweeping grates but was instead staring in open-mouthed horror and fascination at his naked torso: doubtless she'd heard of his tattoos. Well, now she'd seen them. He pushed open the door to his own room and found his stepmother standing before the mirror, wearing nothing but a Chinese wrap that his father had given her. Dark green silk skimmed the small of her back and revealed all below, provocation that he would once have dealt with at peremptory speed.

'Louisa.'

She turned to face him, smiling. 'How perfectly horrible of you to keep me waiting like this. You've been married two weeks, darling. There's really no need for this neglect to continue.'

He sat down on the bed, exhaustion rolling over him as he raked his fingers through his hair. 'I'm sorry,' he said. 'Louisa, I really am sorry, but no more.'

She watched him, half-smiling. 'Oh, don't be ridiculous. What difference does it make that you're married? To us?' She was right: what claim had he to any superior morality?

He looked up at her. 'Hester is nothing like my father, for a start. We betrayed him, but, Lou, he knew how to play this game. He played it all his life, and my mother lived with it, with all his whores and mistresses, just as you did. She expected nothing more and neither did you, as I'm sure is true of any other debutante today. But Hester wasn't brought up in this world.'

Louisa raised delicately arched brows: there was a tinny edge to her laughter. 'Well, that much is certainly true. Don't say I didn't warn you.'

'You have Burford waiting on your word,' Crow said. 'You don't need me any more.' He knew her well enough to be quite certain that this had never been more than a game to her. But as she stood before him now, Crow couldn't deny, even to himself, that he precisely understood the expression on her face. To Louisa, their affair might never have been more than a chess match as pleasurable as it had been sinful, but she was not one to tolerate having her favourite plaything taken away.

31

In her customary place at the dead prince's desk, looking out at the quiet street, Joséphine waited for supper to be announced, hunger and apprehension curdling in her belly. Glancing at one of the four clocks lined up on the mantelpiece, she saw that the gong was late tonight. She hadn't really needed so many clocks, but they were so pretty, with their little golden cogs, and she had not been able to resist sending for them. Supper must still be endured. The decades had done nothing to dim Jérôme Bonaparte's chagrin at seeing his brother married to her, and Queen Catharina barbed each evening gathering with those soft, adulatory remarks about the Austrian woman's son, his growth, his extraordinary achievements in calculus, in battledore, in playing his father at chess. Oh, how Catharina's plump lips savoured those two words, *his father*, so well aware of the exquisite pain inflicted. She dreaded facing them both across the dining-room table.

Joséphine glanced at the clocks again. Two told her that it was almost nine o'clock, one that it was five minutes past the hour, the fourth that it was a quarter past. Jérôme and Catharina dined precisely at eight, much later than so many of these unsophisticated English. She'd been invited at the extraordinary hour of five o'clock to dine at the home of Lord Castlereagh, the former prime minister. Napoleon wanted her to charm his former enemies, to tuck a counterpane of social ease over the defeated English aristocracy and their new royal family. The English were softening towards her, she was sure. She would do what Napoleon had never really achieved with his new subjects, and nurse into strength the accord without which any government or court was nothing but a nest of fighting rats, all dead before long. And, surely, in a civilised country, no one save peasants, children or elderly eccentrics dined at five o'clock. No, nobody could say she hadn't tried her best. But why had the gong not sounded? Her belly clenched with real hunger now and she got up and pushed open the door. Moonlight flooded in through tall windows with heavy crimson velvet curtains left undrawn. Polished parquet stretched out on either side; the hallway was of dazzling length. There was no footman, and no lamps had been lit. Joséphine tugged the Indian wrap around her shoulders and trod the length of the hallway, suppressing a childish fear of the dark birthed in a long-ago encounter with a yellow-fanged cane-rat that had scuttled across her bedchamber floor on Martinique. Even now, she still caught the sweet, heady scent of boiling sugar when alone in the dark, as if she had been somehow transported back to the island of her childhood. It was so quiet she heard a soft shushing as the muslin fabric of her gown shifted about her legs. It was as if this part of the palace had been forgotten, deserted. *Your quarters,* she realised, as unease spread cold fingers across her back. Were Jérôme and Catharina simply going to pretend she no longer existed? She didn't see a single servant until she had gone down the stairs, the brash scarlet carpet soft beneath her thin satin slippers. Always fond of pomp, the new king and queen had taken Prince George's suite of state chambers for their own. The footman looked embarrassed as she approached the gilded door, hesitating before he obeyed the command to announce her.

Joséphine blinked in the light; the former prince regent's vast drawing-room was ablaze with candles. Despite the fire, the cold drove through her straight to the bone. This was a room that had been intended for a crowd, and the warmth of jostling bodies, but Jérôme sat alone near the fire. He didn't look up when she came in. There was no sign of the stolid Catharina, who usually retired to her own quarters not long after the removes had been cleared. Joséphine had to go and stand right by her former brother-in-law's chair before he deigned to notice her.

She must be at her most conciliating. 'Jérôme, dear, are you not quite well? If you are feeling low, you should still dine, or the malaise may settle in your lungs, which you are quite a martyr to, I know.'

He looked up, his face always such an unsatisfactory reflection of his brother's, unable to resist a smile. 'We dined two hours ago. How terribly remiss, Joséphine – some footman or other must have neglected to inform you.'

Joséphine watched him a moment, her mouth dry. Not content with her downfall, Jérôme and Catharina were manoeuvring. If they succeeded in confining her to quarters, granting her a status little better than that of Wellington imprisoned on his island, then she would have no chance of reconciling with Napoleon. What's more, she would become irrelevant. She couldn't allow that to happen: in any court, irrelevance was so often fatal. Uninvited, she sat down in the chair opposite her former brother-in-law, revelling for a moment in the fire's warmth. Now was the time to employ the information young Lord Lamorna had so kindly imparted. If she didn't, it would be too late. Joséphine understood for the first time that her position as Jérôme's guest at Carlton House was far more precarious than she had realised. 'My dear sir,' she said, 'I don't suppose you'd find it useful to know of a little rumour that I chanced on?'

Jérôme actually sneered. 'I'm sure listening to aggrieved English aristocrats at those little salons you like to hold will yield vastly useful information.' He picked up a French periodical, flicking through the pages. He didn't even look up at her, much less ring a footman to bring supper, not even a selection of the dishes left to grow cold and congealed after his own doubtless lengthy repast.

Joséphine adjusted her shawl. 'Forgive my impudence, dear. I only thought you might find it useful to know when the English rebels next plan to attack the post-roads. Just a little something that a young person let slip – I'm sure he must be so aggrieved! My dear former husband sounded very upset about that incident in Cornwall, you know.' Napoleon hadn't written to her in almost a year, in fact, but Jérôme didn't need to know that.

It was a fortunate guess. He looked up. He had never quite been able to disguise a lively terror of his imperial brother. 'What?'

Joséphine smiled. 'I find that I'm rather hungry, and that I should enjoy a glass of Rhenish. If you could bear to ring for your footman, Jérôme, I'm sure I'll remember all the details.'

When she had eaten a fricassee of green beans, thick slices of boiled ham, and a dish of syllabub, the new King of England poured himself another glass of wine. 'I think,' Jérôme said, 'that the time has come to teach the English a lesson they won't forget.' It was extraordinary to Joséphine, but he seemed to have no concept that they were his subjects, and she wondered what she had unleashed; to protect herself, she had let loose the wrath of a foolish, self-important man on a conquered people. Joséphine prayed for God and the Mother Mary to forgive her.

32

Hester and Kitto sat at a card-table drawn up to the fire in the morning-room. Rain hammered against the tall windows and trailed like quicksilver down the glass; perhaps it would be enough to stop Louisa's friends coming to gawp at Hester as though she were one of the lions on display at Astley's. Hester peered at Kitto over the top of her hand of cards, her fingers clad in black lace gloves. 'What will it be then – do you twist?' Nothing in her expression gave the slightest hint at what cards she herself might hold or if she had come to dread Louisa's curious morning callers and the constant presence of Lord Burford. In the morning-room, Hester was more demure than a convent-girl, but even so the men Louisa invited flocked about her in such a way that Kitto was glad Crow rarely witnessed it. A few of Louisa's younger friends had begun to copy Hester's simple style of piling her hair up on top of her head, but for the most part, the women and girls rarely spoke to her more than basic good *ton* demanded. And yet she was always so composed, showing the world a face of civil diffidence.

'You ought to play poker, Hets.' Kitto rapidly calculated his own hand. 'No, I shan't stick. Buy a card.' She smiled, watching him draw one from those spread out on the table before him. Kitto grinned, showing his hand.

'A five-card trick? You monster.' Hester sat back in her chair, sipping her tea. Her smile vanished as Mowbray and Ben, one of the footmen, opened the double doors and Louisa walked in with Lord Burford, all rustling silk and that scent she wore. She smiled graciously upon them both, as if bestowing some sort of royal favour; as usual, the expression failed to reach her eyes. Burford was as fat as a fawn and creaked when he moved: Kitto was willing to bet he wore corsets, just as the prince regent had done.

'Your hand, Kits,' Hester went on smoothly, and Kitto swallowed a surge of anger on her behalf. Doubtless Crow was still fucking Louisa, despite the fact that on the rare days he was at home, he rarely left Hester's bed before noon. Hester raised both eyebrows at him and got to her feet, allowing Burford to lower his head over her gloved hand.

'My dear Lady Lamorna.' The baron lingered a little too long over Hester's lace-clad fingers, in Kitto's opinion.

He stood, holding out his hand with unwilling courtesy. 'Good morning, sir.' Burford's palm was warm and slightly damp, and Kitto longed to wipe his hand on his breeches.

'I hope you are attending to your studies, young man, instead of causing more worry to poor Lady Lamorna.' Lord Burford directed a conciliating smirk at Louisa, and Kitto wondered with a curious sense of disgusted detachment why the man's pale blue eyes always looked a little wet, almost as if his eyeballs had been greased.

'Oh, I've learned my lesson, sir,' Kitto said. *And I hope you come up to scratch and marry the bitch before you find out she's been fucking my brother.*

'I don't doubt Lord Lamorna made sure of that – I expect

you were quite unable to sit down.' Burford spoke with an unmistakable leer, and Hester caught Kitto's eye with an expression of such deliberately ill-concealed mirth and horror that he had to look away. The loathsome grub was welcome to Louisa, if she would have him.

'Twist,' he said, sitting down to take another set of cards, just as Mowbray announced Lady Osborne and Lady Sefton. Hester shot him another warning look and got to her feet, curtseying to Louisa's guests. It was as if she'd never married Crow, and Louisa still governed who was admitted to the house. Crow had the last word, as he did on every subject. Had Hester never mentioned her desire for solitude, or had he ruled in favour of Louisa?

'Lady Lamorna, how delightful to see you.' A trace of a smirk lingered on Lady Osborne's lips as she greeted Hester with the full title she now shared with Louisa, red paint seeping into the lines around her mouth. 'I was saying to dear Countess Esterházy last night what a pity it is that you're in mourning – everyone is simply agog to meet you. Not but that Almack's wasn't a sad crush yesterday evening!'

'How kind of you to say so,' Hester said. 'I must admit, I think more of my loss than the inconvenience of not being able to attend subscription balls. Would you like some tea?'

Lady Osborne looked momentarily disconcerted and Louisa got to her feet, smiling as she went to the tea-tray herself. 'Pray, don't trouble yourself, darling Hester.' She looked at Kitto with an arch expression that had him silently counting to twenty. 'You're doing such a wonderful job nursemaiding Kitto – we wouldn't want him to think of running away again!'

The implication was too subtle to comment on, but the sudden silence proved it well understood: Hester was better suited to a nursemaid's role. Lady Osborne sat down, tittering, and Maria Sefton glanced pointedly out of the window at the railed garden. 'How charming the daffodils are at this time of year – they quite lift my spirits!'

'Oh, I couldn't agree more, Lady Sefton,' Hester said, 'although I will own it seems strange to me that they are still out here. At home, they come in December and will have long gone by now.'

Lady Sefton smiled. 'They are late here too this year, after the dreadful winter we had. Now that is interesting – I had no notion the climate was so much warmer in the Scillies. It sounds an extraordinary place.'

'I don't doubt you've sampled Mrs Yarpole's almond biscuits before, Lady Sefton, but you must have one – they're particularly good today.'

'Thank you, my dear.' Maria Sefton accepted the plate. She was one of the few who seemed able to look Hester in the eye, Kitto had noticed.

'I'm sure Kitto is grateful for all *you've* done, dear Louisa, as his stepmama,' Lady Osborne said pointedly, as if he were not even in the room. It was sickening the way people sucked up to her. Maria Sefton didn't because she didn't have to, secure in her position at the very top of the social ladder, but even Kitto knew that although the Osbornes were respectable, they had three unremarkable daughters to dispose of and were not sought after as Lady Sefton and Louisa were. 'Living in *such* circumstances as he did before your marriage to the late earl.'

Louisa smiled as she poured milk into two cups of tea. 'Children ought not to be left too often with servants – I have always said it.' She knew that Roza and Nessa were dead. She knew what it would mean to him to hear them disparaged. If he rose to the bait, Louisa would be quick to whisper sweetly savage reports of his conduct to Crow. Once more, Hester gave him a warning glance over her cards. Crow might go to the devil, but for her sake, he'd keep quiet, dear though it cost him.

'Servants were the very least of it, I believe,' Lady Osborne went on, a brick-red flush seeping up her neck as Maria Sefton and Louisa each turned to her with a frozen smile. Burford stared rigidly out of the window as he stood in attendance by Louisa's chaise.

'Indeed, my dear,' Louisa said. 'But I should say we don't mention my late husband's fondness for ladies of that sort. No doubt they gave poor Kitto a great many sweetmeats, and he is fortunate that his teeth are not quite ruined, and that he never became fat. I do think it dreadful to see a really fat child.' She turned to him with another arch smile. 'No, with so many youthful disadvantages we can't really blame poor Kitto for his conduct, despite all the trouble it has cost my dear son-in-law. At any rate, all is quite forgiven and I'm quite sure he'll strive to be more rational in his behaviour now that dear Lady Lamorna is here to guide him. One does not return to Cornwall alone, Kitto, just because one is in a pet about some obscure issue! But we understand that now, do we not?'

Rage jolted through him; it felt like being kicked in the belly by a horse, and for a moment he was speechless. If he did not reply, Crow would hear of it. He could stand the promised whipping, but such a great part of him still wanted to please his brother – despite everything – that Kitto forced himself to speak. 'Indeed, I would do anything to please my sister,' he said, and Maria Sefton, whom he had known his entire life, crossed the room and laid one hand upon his shoulder.

'Of course you would, you dear boy. And if you have grieved Lord Lamorna, I am sure it is long forgotten.' She squeezed his shoulder, giving Louisa a bland smile. Hester laid down her cards and shot Kitto such a quizzical look that he laughed.

'Royal twenty-one. The game's yours, Hets.' He shuffled the cards, praying that she would never learn the truth about her husband, or why he himself had left London. It was easier, he knew, to believe Crow a hero.

33

Crow came to Hester's bedchamber immediately after supper, wearing such an uncharacteristically shy expression that she couldn't help smiling at him. He was holding a case of polished walnut with silver clasps, and she shook her head. 'What have you done?' she asked. 'You look exactly like a boy caught stealing jam tarts. You'll have to stop giving me presents, you know. I shall become quite spoiled.'

'I know you're more used to going after grouse or stealing my father's duelling pistols, but I should like you to have a weapon of your own.'

Hester flinched as she took the pistol-case, remembering Papa staggering into the stillroom and how moments later she'd shot a man in the head, fragments of skull and brain matter and so much blood.

'I'm sorry,' Crow said instantly. 'I really am sorry, to make you think of it. But if anything ever happens to me, I don't want you to be helpless.'

'Nothing will happen to you,' Hester told him, unnerved by his unspoken fear. Men like Crow were not supposed to be afraid of anything, but only that morning Louisa had looked up from her arrangement of tulips and said, *What is that?* And it had been the intermittent thudding of gunfire all the way from the slums at St Giles – the first time Hester had actually heard the unmistakable clamour of rioting since her arrival in London. 'It will be something to do,' she said to him casually. 'Where does one go in London for target practice?'

To all appearances he was serious. 'Well, I would go to Manton's – he keeps a gallery above the shop – but you can scarcely do that, and the French have banned us from carrying firearms. You wouldn't disturb anyone or risk arrest in the stables, though.' He did smile then. 'Only for God's sake make sure you tell Arkwright before you begin. We'll spend the summer wherever you wish, you know. Cornwall isn't safe but you might choose between Kent, North Yorkshire, Scotland or Bedfordshire. I think you'd like Oakhurst or my stalking lodge in Scotland best – they're both by the sea.'

Hester couldn't help laughing: invested in bonds and shares, her own fortune was invisible, often spoken of but never seen. Crow's riches were tangible: she knew he had funds as impressive as hers, but much of his wealth was held in acres and ancient homesteads. His complete lack of self-consciousness about it was both infuriating and yet oddly endearing, his unshakable sense of self bound up in those fields, in those houses filled with portraits of ancestors who shared his features. 'What an absurd quantity of houses you seem to own.'

'Yes,' he said, gloriously unrepentant, 'and we shall do this in every one of them.' He kissed her then, lifting her on to the bed. When they were together, he was becoming enough to fill her world – the rare tilt of his smile, black hair hanging in his eyes. That night, they made love only once but talked until dawn began to lighten the sky, their limbs entwined, and Hester learned that Crow could talk on any subject except the war: the paintings of Turner, the relative heft of a pistol crafted in Manton's workshop compared against one of Purdey's, the stream running down the Lamorna valley where he had trapped minnows as a boy; and in return he listened to her speak of Bryher, of Catlin and their lost friendship, her sadness at not being able to remember her mother's face, and how she longed to sit on the silver sand at Popplestone Porth and watch the sunset light up an ocean creamed into white peaks where the tide pooled around the Scilly Rocks. For those hours, talking and listening, she felt like Hester Harewood again, that in sketching out the details of her life to him she had made it real once more. And, that night, for the first time in her presence, Crow fell asleep. It happened with endearing simplicity; he had curled his body around hers so that they lay like a pair of silver spoons in a drawer, and she asked if he thought she might ever see Bryher again. He didn't reply, and Hester turned to face him, her heart quickening, and found that his eyes were closed, black lashes brushing pale skin. She sat up and watched him – he wore nothing, his nakedness half concealed by the starched linen sheet. In their lovemaking, she'd followed with one fingertip the curved blue-black line of a tattoo that ran from his breastbone to his navel; he was all muscle and bone, the smooth hard lines of his body so different to the softer hollows and curves of her own. He was beautiful to look at, and she lay there in remorseless glory at her possession of him; as if sensing her movement, he rolled on to his back, so still, and so peaceful. Before she succumbed herself, Hester's last thought was to wonder if everyone looked so trusting when they were asleep.

The noise forced her into a state of wakeful half-panic, snatching the sheets to her chest. Crow was sitting up, staring ahead with an expression of exquisite horror. His black hair was drenched with sweat that streamed down his face. The echo of an animal cry hung in the quiet; the mantelpiece clock ticked with oblivious regularity.

'What's the matter?' she whispered, laying a hand upon his arm. His skin was hot and damp to the touch, almost feverish. 'Crow?'

He tore himself away from her with a sudden jerk and leaned forwards, resting his forehead on knees drawn up to his chest, breathing hard. 'Good Christ, I'm sorry. I'm so sorry.' He swung his legs over the edge of the bed, facing away from her; the dimples at the small of his back made him seem, for once, impossibly vulnerable.

'But you really mustn't apologise. What is it?' Hester knew straight away that she shouldn't have asked, that more than anything he wished she had never seen or heard him cry out like that. He sat for what seemed a long time, facing away from her, shoulders heaving as though he'd run for miles. Then he pulled on his breeches and shirt, thrown aside the night before in a moment that now felt cavernously distant, and left her without another word. When she woke again, not long after dawn, she reached out for him before remembering that he had gone. Had he dreamed of the war? How could he think that she would mind? He trusted her far less than she trusted him, a realisation that made her sit up and stare with blank discomfort at the silver brushes laid out on her dressing-table at the far end of the room. The pistol-case was still resting on her escritoire by the window, early morning light stroking the polished walnut through a crack in the curtains. A maid must have been in while she slept to kindle the fire, but unless she rang the bell it would likely be hours before Maggie came to dress her. Summoning Maggie would mean that she must break her fast, and then not only Maggie but half the household would know where she was going and what she was doing.

Hester dressed as best she could and took the pistol from the velvet-lined case. She sensed by the weight of it that it was still loaded, and slipped down the stairs. Was it really so wrong to want to be alone with her thoughts, to simply be herself, for no more than half an hour?

The stables were quiet, neatly swept cobbles redolent with the scent of warm straw. Unlike his father and much to Kitto's disgust, Crow kept only the mare and one pair of chestnuts in London. Hester made her way to the unoccupied north end of the stable-mews, checking first that Arkwright's boy hadn't begun work in any of the empty stalls. She removed the pistol from its case and was about to heap a pile of gunpowder on to the tray ready for the lighting-flint when she first heard voices. Even so early, she was not to be alone, then. Once more Hester longed for the solitude of Bryher, with Papa safely ensconced in his study and every corner of the island hers to roam. The stables seemed to lurch around her as if she had taken too many glasses of madeira. She sat on the cobbles, leaning back against the smooth wooden partition between two stalls. After all she had endured, was she now some fainting miss so terrified at the thought of encountering strangers in her own husband's stable that she might be sick like a child who had eaten too much syllabub at a Christmas party?

Hester heard footfalls, the cacophony of male presence. The way men breathed and trod – even servants – seemed to say, *I'm here, I make no apology for it.*

'You'd best not come again, Castle – what do you mean by it?' Arkwright's no-nonsense tone was unmistakable.

'I've heard rumours. I wanted to speak to you before Wedderburn. I'm afraid he's a backslider, that he's not got the guts to finish this.' Castle – if that was really this intruder's name – spoke with an unfamiliar northern accent. Arkwright himself was from the north of England, but this Castle sounded different.

'Whatever you've heard, man, this isn't the place to talk.' Arkwright sounded uninterested now, impatient even. They were now closer than ever, and Hester realised with horror that both men must be about to walk right past the stall where she sat huddled against the wall. Gripping her pistol, Hester sat frozen on the cobbles, watching as Arkwright passed by in company with a much shorter man in a dusty, half-flattened, old-fashioned tricorn hat: he seemed almost childlike against Arkwright's bulk. If they turned, if they looked back and saw her, what would they do? What could they do? She had every right to be here; it was Arkwright in the wrong, receiving acquaintances at his master's house. Then why could she not ignore the prickling sensation of cold apprehension between her shoulder blades? *Finish this?* What did Arkwright's guest mean by that?

'Where then, Arkwright? Like I said, I don't trust Wedderburn not to backslide. We need to see the matter through.'

'I'll be at Tattersall's tomorrow. His lordship's minded to buy new horseflesh. If what you say's so urgent, find me at the Golden Fleece. And you'd best be away from here, Castle, before the stable-lad hauls his carcass out of bed. The fewer you're seen by, the better.'

They'd reached the door of the stable-yard that opened out into the cobbled mews behind Lamorna House. Both men stopped, and for a moment Hester was terrified that Arkwright would turn and come back. She'd be face to face with him; there was no chance of moving without making a noise. But after a pause, Arkwright followed Castle outside. When Hester looked down at the pistol she saw that her hands were shaking. It was hard to make them stop.

34

Two days later, Hester sat beside Kitto in the drawing-room, the table before them littered with sheets of foolscap; they worked in easy silence as Louisa reclined on the chaise in a half-dress of teal satin, alternately smiling and frowning at her correspondence. Lost in concentration, Kitto inked Latin names beside his botanical illustrations, and Hester's brush crested waves with white horses as she painted the view south from Samson Hill. It was no use: she couldn't capture the slant of the light. It didn't look real, and she couldn't help wondering if she ought to tell Crow that Arkwright had been receiving acquaintances. It was improper for a servant to do so without permission, but perhaps Crow had granted him leave? Arkwright had served with Crow in the war, so perhaps he wasn't governed by the same rules as other servants, but was allowed a greater degree of autonomy. Why was it that she could never feel quite at ease in the man's presence?

She set down her brush, her gaze drawn to the vast portrait of Kitto's grandfather hanging above the fireplace. The fifth earl glared down at her from horseback, an African groom in an elaborate green silk waistcoat kneeling at his feet. The artist had directed the man's gaze up at the dead earl, as if in awe of his master, and lascivious attention had been lavished on his burnished umber-brown skin, as though he were more polished ornament than a living person. Hester imagined him turning to her with a gaze of horrified disbelief. How had this happened to him? She wondered who he had really been: a coppersmith, a fisherman, even a prince?

'Don't look at my grandfather, Hets,' Kitto advised, glancing up from his work. 'Enough to put anyone off, the godawful old tartar.'

'If you cannot mind your manners, Kitto, then leave the room.' Louisa didn't look up from her letters as she spoke.

'What business is it of yours?'

Hester gave him a sharp kick beneath the table: she didn't doubt Louisa would find a way of laying a trap for him when Crow arrived. Louisa ignored Kitto, glancing up at Hester instead. 'Still nothing from the Albemarles. If your great-aunt and -uncle persist with this discourtesy much longer, darling, I'll have to break with convention and write myself.'

Hester had never heard anyone utter an endearment with more ill-disguised venom. She set down her paintbrush. 'You need not: I've no desire to beg my mother's family to notice me.'

'That doesn't come into it at all,' Louisa said. 'You move in the same circles now. Believe me, you'd find it much worse to encounter them by chance. It really would be odd in me to write first, though – perhaps we can let it rest a little while longer.'

'It's a risk I'm willing to take.' Not for a moment did Hester believe Louisa's solicitude genuine: she was only concerned that an embarrassing encounter might reflect badly on her carefully curated portrayal of the Abolitionists' most fashionable apogee. Hester turned back to her painting, wishing for a moment that she might step through it and be home. It was not her best work, true, but it was something. Since Papa's death and her arrival in London, all other attempts had ended in her walking in frustrated misery from a blank canvas. It was easier to forget the unfinished portrait of Papa, she found, surrounded by the distractions of the drawing-room – Kitto's absorption in his botany, the ticking of a carriage clock on a mantelpiece. She stared at her painting, longing to feel the sand beneath her feet and the sea-grass whipping her bare ankles, and to smell the salty, almost rotten stink of the great ocean rolling away at low tide. She looked down at the brush in her hands, her skin so much darker than Kitto's or Louisa's. She'd written to Catlin three times now and still no reply. *Your servants will be safe: no soldier willingly makes his billet less comfortable,* Crow had said, but there was no way to be certain that the French had left anyone alive on Bryher, servant or not. Hester laid down her brush, fighting rising panic that squeezed the breath from her lungs. Catlin would write soon. She must. Louisa laughed at something in one of her own letters, and Hester could have cheerfully thrown them all out into the street. Why did nothing come for her? All she could do was keep going and pray that Catlin was still alive, that she remembered how to break the cipher. She must arrange flowers, she must read, she must visit the kitchen stores with Mrs Halls and look approvingly over shelf after shelf of dried beans in jars, pickled pears, sides of salted ham and eggs bottled in isinglass. She must ignore the fact that there was no fresh meat to be had, even for the Earl of Lamorna, because the drovers couldn't get their herds into London without being attacked by the hungry. She must instead say the right thing: *Why, Mrs Halls – no one would ever guess there was so little to be found at market!*

And then there was Crow. She'd last seen him sprawled on his back in her bed as the first of dawn's light illuminated a torso like sculpted marble, the pale skin damp with perspiration and inscribed with blue-black tattoos, with the warmth of his spent seed between her legs. She'd heard herself ask, *What happened to you?*

He'd turned on his side to face her, hair falling into his eyes, looking down as he tensed, long, lean muscles moving beneath his tattooed skin. *What do you mean?* He emitted a shielded wariness, and she was conscious of a mild wave of unease at all the possible answers there might be. He thought she was going to ask why he cried out in his sleep, she knew. *These.* She'd run her fingers along the twisted patterns on his chest.

He'd smiled, relaxing. *My tattoos? On my first voyage with your papa, we went to Otaheite. Like a bloody young fool, I had stowed away – did you know that?*

He said you were not broken to the bridle, but that you learned.

They flogged me when I was found. Your father had gone to the flagship to consult with Admiral Gunning, and when he came back, he took one look at me, with my back still bleeding, and said, What in the devil is this? A nobleman's son overly familiar with the novels of Daniel Defoe?

And what did you say? she had asked, horrified that he had been flogged.

Nothing. I was quickly learning what, despite a certain amount of savagery, Eton failed to teach me – the valuable lesson of knowing when to keep my mouth shut. Crow had smiled – the memory of Papa had transformed him – and Hester saw then what he must have looked like as a boy. *Your father let me stay, though. He taught me how to use a sextant and, to return to the point, he called me a damned idiot when I got my tattoos. He said I didn't know what they signified, that it was no different to an Otaheitian wearing a crucifix if they did not believe in our God. He was right: I was a young fool.*

But they are part of me. And his hand had moved down her own naked back, light and teasing.

She had watched herself reach out and touch the silver-edged pockmark just beside his left shoulderblade, and tried to imagine a musket-ball slamming into flesh, the shattering of bone. Her fingertip traced the line of the purple, puckered crevasse that ran from the top of his ribcage, halfway down his torso, dotted with smaller indentures left by the chirugeon's needle and catgut, trying to imagine the moment of impact. She remembered failing to turn the heel of a green woollen stocking in Papa's library as he read aloud from *The Times,* even as Buonaparte's troops advanced on London. It had all seemed so far away from Scilly, even a little irrelevant.

'Lord Crowlas has been recovered from the field of battle after lying among the dead with injuries of such a severe nature that the French thought him among the legions of the slain. It is thought that Lord Crowlas was carrying a dispatch to Wellington that might have saved the battle, had he reached him.'

Wellington down to the brass buttons, Papa had said, with no small amount of distaste. *There's always someone else to blame, and you can bet that he spread that about.*

The candle had guttered and gone out, and Crow had rolled over, putting an end to speculation by kissing her in the dark. She'd never looked for this, for a room to seem empty because he was not there. She'd not expected to feel so hollow, waking on another morning to find that he hadn't come to her bed at all. He didn't trust her with whatever painful secrets he carried: this was no surprise, but only reminded her that she could fall asleep in Crow's arms feeling as though she had known him all her life, when perhaps she didn't really know him at all.

★

In the morning-room, Maggie brought a rush of cool air with her as she came in with a silver tray. 'Will I set out the coffee-pot here or by the fire, milady?' With long-practised tact, she addressed the question specifically neither to Hester nor Louisa, but when her gaze ran across the paintbrushes and sheets of foolscap scattered across the table, Hester was reminded so forcibly of Catlin's expression on seeing her pistol dismantled all over the scrubbed stillroom table that she couldn't reply, not knowing whether she wanted most to laugh or cry.

'Hester?' Louisa looked up from her letter with one of her inscrutable smiles. 'It's you who must decide these things now.'

'His lordship is coming to take coffee with you before he goes out,' Maggie said.

'Oh, by the window then, if you please.' It hadn't taken Hester long to notice how restless Crow was withindoors, especially if he had no clear sight out to the street.

As Maggie crossed the room with the tray Louisa lay down her letters and said, with an air of condescension that made Hester itch, 'Did I tell you, Maria, that I wore the chip-straw bonnet you dressed for me in Hyde Park, and Countess Esterházy asked where I'd come by it? If you could bear to make over my riding-hat, I should be so grateful.'

'Maggie,' Hester said. 'Her name is Maggie, not Maria.'

Louisa turned to Hester, speaking as if Maggie were not still standing by the window. 'I'm not talking about her name but her hats, darling. She really does have an eye for millinery, you know. And it cost me nothing! Everyone ought to have a ladies' maid in the house with a turn for trimming hats – it really was excessively pretty.'

Crow came in before Hester could fathom a response. She looked down at her painting, hoping Kitto and Louisa wouldn't notice how her colour rose in his presence. In those very early hours of the morning, she had not been able to help crying out as he moved inside her. Crow's hands rested on her own shoulders as he came to stand behind her, his thumb brushing the naked skin at the nape of her neck. When she turned to him, he was looking down at the painting and frowning a little. Was he thinking of Wellington on Bryher – still their secret – or was there too much yellow in the grass?

Kitto spoke without looking up from his work. 'No luck at Tattersall's yesterday? Arkwright said there was nothing but bone-shakers. Do you ride into Essex to look at that mare?'

'I do. If she's up to your weight and not touched in the wind, you may have her, *boya*.'

Kitto grinned. 'Thank you, Jack. Might I come with you, then?'

Crow shook his head. 'Not this time.'

Hester didn't miss Kitto's swiftly concealed expression; he looked almost despairing. *Nothing good ever came of an idle boy,* Catlin had always been fond of saying.

'Listen,' Crow said, glancing up from Hester's painting, 'if you come up to the mark, we'll ride out to Oakhurst before the end of the Season. It'll be yours one day, after all.'

'Lord, look at this!' Louisa said. Kitto stopped smiling at the interruption, looking down once again at his work. Louisa held a delicate sheet of paper almost at arm's length to read it – she was long-sighted, Hester had noticed, but too vain for a lorgnette. 'But it's too extraordinary, Jack. Do look.'

Crow turned away from his brother with an air of distraction. 'What is it, ma'am?'

'Only a note from Maria Sefton wanting to know if Hester and I will accept that invitation from Carlton House. Maria says she scarcely knows how to reply, and I can hardly blame her with her sister's poor boys dead at Waterloo. So Joséphine's trying her hand at diplomacy with the Seftons, too. I wonder what she might possibly mean by it.'

'Little more than that, I should think.' Crow glanced at the letter with apparent disinterest. 'Who knows, Lou, if anyone might make the French fashionable again, it's you. Buonaparte was never a fool. The behaviour of his troops in Spain and Portugal nearly cost him the war: no doubt he instructs Joséphine to befriend anyone with the power to alter opinion. The Buonapartes must have some use for her, after all.'

The nib of Kitto's pen broke, splattering black ink across his drawing of an oak-gall. He set down the quill, and Hester thought of Papa bleeding to death on Bryher, and of Roza Carew and her mother dead at Nansmornow. How could Crow sound so dispassionate, so unconcerned?

'Well then, have we your leave to attend, Jack? I ought to reply sooner rather than later, I suppose.' Louisa let Maria Sefton's letter fall to the pile on the rug beside her chaise, already reaching for the next as though the summons from the emperor's divorced wife and the quiet ripple of scandal it had caused was nothing out of the ordinary.

'Is it safe for me to go, I wonder?' Even as Hester spoke, she couldn't deny that there would be a certain grim fascination in facing the Occupation on their own stolen territory. 'I ought not to go out, though, in all my mourning.'

'You'll be perfectly safe,' Crow said. 'But as you wish.' He smiled at her but swiftly looked away, and Hester was uncomfortably sure that he kept something from her.

'Milady, Ben has just come up with a packet for you.' Maggie held out a silver tray, and Hester turned to her, taking the weight of a tissue-wrapped gift.

'What pretty paper,' Louisa said, glancing up from her next letter. 'I wonder who sent it?'

Kitto looked up from his work. 'As long as it's not another

improving chapbook from that ingrate Alice Osborne as though you were quite eleven years old, Hets.'

'Lady Osborne meant it kindly.' Louisa spoke without putting down her letter. 'Kitto, you are not yet fifteen – you ought not to speak badly of your elders. You know how much your papa despised such impertinence.'

'It was the most condescending abomination I've ever seen, and the Osborne woman is inexcusably ignorant,' said Crow as Hester unwrapped layers of gold tissue paper studded with a pattern of tiny gold-leaf petals, relieved that Crow had the sense to change the course of the conversation. Kitto had, for some reason, gone ominously still at the mention of their father, as if struggling to control some powerful emotion that went beyond the simple grief one might expect him to feel. There was an odd, cold heft to the parcel; she folded back the last sheet of paper and polished silver shone at her, inscribed with neat copperplate script. Hester picked up the silver torc, turning it to read: *Property of the Earl of Lamorna*. It was not a torc but a silver collar of the type worn by slaves. Behind her, Maggie drew in a sharp breath and set down the cup she was halfway through pouring for Hester, slopping hot coffee into the saucer.

'Of all the disgusting things to do!' Kitto stood up, pushing back his chair. 'Crow, look.'

Hester herself had nothing to say. First a great heat pulsed through her; the next second she felt cold, as though in a fever. She looked down at the silver collar in her hands, imagining the cold weight of it around her own neck, as indeed the sender must have meant her to do. It was made in two parts, hinged and locked. One would never be able to sleep in any comfort; how had Maggie borne it all those years, long enough for a scar to be left around her throat? Someone had hated her enough to bespeak this from a silversmith, to actually pay for it, a joke among friends perhaps.

'How childish,' Louisa said. 'Probably some silly debutante with a *tendre* for Jack: certainly there are enough of them.'

'I've never heard such rubbish,' Kitto said, with such barely restrained and intimidating anger that for a moment Hester glimpsed his adult self: he would be a match for his brother. 'And never speak to me about my father again.'

'Kitto, don't,' Hester said. The expression of stunned disbelief on Louisa's face made her look like a porcelain doll, her mouth frozen in a small round O. Crow watched him with a cold ferocity that left her breathless.

Kitto made a visible effort to control himself and turned on Louisa, in wild disregard of the expression on his brother's face. 'You did it: you bespoke that thing and had it sent here. You're envious of her. It's pathetic.'

As soon as he spoke, Hester knew he was right. It couldn't have been anyone else, and Louisa had reason enough: no longer Countess of Lamorna, she had been forced to relinquish her position as mistress of the house.

Louisa stood up. 'Of all the ridiculous tales – Jack—'

Crow ignored her and turned to Kitto, speaking to him as if there were no one else in the room. 'That,' he said, 'was a foolish mistake. You will oblige me by leaving the room, if you cannot be civil.'

Kitto slammed the door behind him. Hester watched Crow suppress a flinch at the sound of the door crashing into the frame, and Louisa smiled, shaking her head as if Kitto were a child who had just been banished from the dining-table for impertinence, or for eating with his elbows resting on the cloth. No, if Kitto was right, then Louisa's strategy was to distress and humiliate her, and Hester would not give her the satisfaction of seeing how well she had succeeded in her first objective, nor how well she had failed in the second. She felt no humiliation, only a cold, logical certainty that she would have her revenge.

'Louisa?' Crow said. 'For God's sake, just tell me he's wrong.'

Hester shook her head. 'Of course he's mistaken. How could it be anything to do with Louisa? It's the sort of thing a spiteful child might do, not a grown woman.'

Crow watched her; for the first time, he looked helpless, shaking his head as he looked down at the torc, still lying in its tissue wrapping. 'Hester—'

'It's nothing,' Hester said. 'Think nothing of it. It's just a child's stupid game.'

Louisa shrugged; her face gave away nothing but well-constructed horror and dismay. 'Indeed, it's horrid. Hester, darling, give it to Maggie to take away. So dreadful.'

How could one put a slave collar in Maggie's hands when she herself had been forced to wear such a thing? How could Louisa have so little sensitivity, even towards a servant? Kitto was right. Louisa had done it, even if her part could never be proven.

'Maggie, you need not touch it,' Crow said. 'Hester, give it to me, my love.'

My love. She was inches away from allowing herself to cry. Hester set her wedding gift down on the table and walked out of the morning parlour. If it killed her, she would confront Louisa with her part in this.

35

Crow had chosen a moonless night for the attack. The post-road was barely distinguishable as it stretched across barley-sown fields thick with ridged mud. He had to admit that Buonaparte could still be ingenious – the length and breadth of Britain, the fat little tyrant had ordered trees and vegetation close to the roads to be cut down and burned. There was so little cover, they'd been forced to lay the gunpowder in plain sight, hunched low to the ground by the bridge, and clearly silhouetted against the night sky. The Occupation knew how to look out for moving shadows, and Crow's hair was thick with sweat that trailed in runnels down the back of his neck. It was done, though. With Smith beside him, he held his position in the lee of the ruined barn, watching and waiting. Ancient stone buttresses were just visible as the rutted track bridged the silent river, and his hands were still sticky with residue from the tarred rope they'd used as a fuse. It would be difficult, he knew, to claim innocence if they were caught, smeared in tar to a man. If Jérôme had taken Joséphine's warning seriously, Occupation guardsmen would be in the village of West Malden – that cluster of lights and dark, humped buildings just visible across the fields

– ready to descend. He'd set a trap, and promised Joséphine to deliver the English rebels. And if Crow didn't give the Buonapartes what they were expecting, the flow of information from Joséphine herself would stop. More than anything, Crow needed that trickle of information to continue. It was done: the gunpowder was laid, and all they must do now was wait for the bridge to blow. Above all, Joséphine must continue to trust him. In the back of his mind, he heard Wellington speak: *Sometimes, Jack, a man must make impossible choices in the theatre of war.* Imprisoned on Bryher, Wellington had it easy: he didn't need to make choices for anyone. He didn't need to lie and cheat, to lure English soldiers towards certain death. Crow stared down at his tar-smeared hands as they cradled the loaded musket, his fingers curling around polished walnut and filigreed silver. At his side, Smith was silent. In the deep quiet, he heard a barn owl cry out, and sensed Smith's readiness to move at the slightest noise, his momentary relaxation as the pale shape of the owl soared overhead. Somewhere at the edge of his consciousness, he was aware of wet grass soaking through his jacket and breeches. There was precious little but grass growing: he'd heard stories of people boiling it to feed their children. This part of the country, like most of the south, had seen the worst of the action in the invasion. It was his fault – had he run faster at Waterloo, had he made it past Hougoumont with the news that the Belgians meant to turn on Wellington, so many lives would have been saved. And if he wasn't damned fucking careful, Smith, Masters and Lessing would be sacrificed now.

'What's going on, sir?' Smith spoke with the practised quiet of the experienced soldier. 'That bridge ought to be pretty well alight by now.'

Crow shook his head. 'There's time.' The fuses leading to the gunpowder kegs left under each of the bridge's ancient buttresses had been necessarily long, but he'd been thorough in his own work and checked Smith's. It ought to go up like a beauty. There was nothing to do but wait a while, despite the appalling tension. Kitto was a decent hand at laying gunpowder. Was shielding all this from the boy his worst mistake? He was fourteen. At that age, Crow had been at sea for two years; at Trafalgar, he'd loaded Captain Harewood's guns on the *Belle*. He was already a killer. Yet if Kitto joined him in this lethal game, the House of Lamorna could well end with them both dead: it was simply too dangerous. And when his own time was up, it would be better for Kitto and Hester to have one another. God only knew he needed to find a way of dealing with Louisa, too. Crow had gone to her dressing-room to confront her about the slave collar; she'd stood up to meet him, clutching the back of a gilded Queen Anne chair that had belonged to his mother. *I hope you've given that boy the whipping he deserves. Of all the ridiculous accusations!* He'd leaned in the doorway, watching her. *As it happens, Louisa, I didn't.* Kitto had been devastatingly accurate, and they both knew it: he'd had plenty to say to the young idiot about deepening Hester's distress with the timing of his revelation, but Louisa herself was to blame for the crime itself. Or rather, Crow himself was, for manoeuvring Louisa into a vengeful frame of mind. How in the devil's name was he to get rid of her? Like it or not, she was under his protection too. No immediate solution presented itself, short of forcing Burford to come up to scratch and make an offer. From Louisa's room he'd gone to Hester's and found Maggie with her arms around her mistress, holding Hester as she sobbed. Maggie had looked at him over Hester's shoulder, and before she could rearrange her features into the blank expression of the well-trained servant, he'd seen how much she blamed him.

Maggie dismissed, he'd held Hester in his own arms. *I'm so sorry. Do you want me to send Louisa away?*

Hester had looked up at him, her face tear-stained and angry. *What, and have everyone say that I caused her to be thrown out into the street? You must know that everyone would soon forget the reason why, and that I will always be judged to a far harsher standard than anyone else.* Even now, waiting for the bridge to explode, knowing that French troops were likely waiting to blow him and his men into a bloody grapeshot mess, Crow had never felt so helpless, so absolutely out of his depth, as he had done when Hester wept.

At his side, in the lee of the barn, Smith shook his head again. 'I don't like it, sir. The whole lot should have gone up by now.'

He was right. It was time to get on with the task at hand. They'd waited long enough – too long, even. Digging in his pocket, Crow felt for the cold silver weight of his tinderbox and flint. He'd have to go back and check the fuse, light it again if need be. Across the field, concealed in a small coppice just outside the dark hump of the village, Masters and Lessing were waiting as back-up. Should he give the signal now to abort? The French would find the gunpowder by the bridge, sure enough. Joséphine would remain trusted by the Buonapartes as a useful source of information. He might be a traitor to men under his own command, but this was his chance to get Masters, Lessing and Smith out of here unscathed. 'I'm going to light it again,' Crow said. 'Cover me, but if anything goes wrong, run like fuck, do you understand?'

Grim-faced, Smith nodded, and side by side, low to the ground, they hurled themselves towards the bridge; barley-sown mud clung to Crow's boots and he cursed the rain. As they ran, a crackle of musket-fire sounded from the west, just south of West Malden, where Masters and Lessing were waiting. And in the same moment that Smith dropped like a shot pheasant tumbling from the sky, his life snuffed out in an instant, the darkness was obliterated by the roar of an explosion and the hammering of falling masonry as the bridge exploded. Forcing himself up into a crouch, his teeth gritty with mud, Crow cocked his musket, aimed and fired, again and again and again.

36

Arkwright had not expected to be shown to Joséphine's private quarters. Wedderburn had made all the arrangements: the clever bastard had done his work well. She waited alone, sitting behind a polished desk that he supposed the regent had fucked his Cyprians over when a French invasion had still been something to joke about. *The navy would never let it happen. Even if it all goes to the devil in Belgium, the Russians and Austrians will keep Boney busy enough.* How wrong they'd all been. He felt almost sorry for Joséphine, turned off by Buonaparte and divorced because she'd given him no sons. And now here she was, dependent on Buonaparte's puppet-king of a brother.

'You look surprised, Monsieur Arkwright.' Joséphine smiled. She wasn't a bad-looking woman for her age. Shame about the teeth, but they'd been bad when he'd first met her, and they'd both been younger then. There was no flicker of recognition in her heavy-lashed hazel eyes, but Arkwright remembered that night with vivid clarity – Paris in 1795, in the wake of the Terror: one of Thérésia Tallien's wild supper-parties. A great deal of black-market wine, and everyone bringing their own bread.

Bacchanalian, he supposed you'd call it, the women in gowns you could hardly see, everyone there so fucking relieved not to be dead that they drank until they dropped, men and women down on the floor and fucking like beasts, even in the dining-room. He'd watched as she approached, a lithe figure in clinging white muslin, her hair still shorn for the guillotine. Might I fill your cup, *citoyen*? They'd conversed a little while, sweat sliding down his back for fear that she would see behind the accent he'd perfected after a year in Narbonne. But if Joséphine had known him then for an English spy, she'd kept it to herself.

'I wasn't expecting to be met by you in these quarters,' he told her in French. 'Men such as myself usually aren't received in this way by the Quality.'

Joséphine smiled. 'Well, we might let your aristocrats gather in London for their parties and balls, but really they're power-less, and at any rate I can no longer call myself empress. You and I meet on equal terms. Will you take tea?' She took up the steaming silver pot laid ready on the tray, eyebrows lifted. 'How many languages do you speak with such elegant fluency?'

'Five, your grace, not including English. French, Spanish, Portuguese, Flemish and Rhenish.'

'A crime, Arkwright, that such a learned man should have ended a long career with no rank to speak of. A corporal in the Guides, were you not?'

Arkwright nodded. How much did she know, really, of his career? He knew a little of hers: he knew that during the Revolution – all those years ago now – she had been kept in prison a full five days after her first husband was led to the scaffold, released at the eleventh hour by the death of Robespierre. What did that sort of fear do to a person? 'An injustice, your grace, that wouldn't be permitted now that England is part of the Empire, I'm sure.'

'Of course not. We believe in promoting a man according to

his merit, not the age and ascendancy of his father's noble house. Look at the heights my dear former husband has reached: ruler of all Europe; but no one would have believed it when he first came to Paris. He spoke French with the most appalling accent, you know, his nails were always filthy, and no one would look at him – except me.' Joséphine poured a straw-gold stream of tea into a porcelain cup. 'There are many injustices which are now a thing of the past – I realise that my brother-in-law's Occupation forces commit the sort of regrettable excesses that one expects under a weak, changeable leader, and such a one is his majesty. But even so, we live at the dawn of a more civilised age.' She passed him the cup and saucer, allowing her pale fingers to brush his, work-worn and sun-browned. 'But you have suffered far more over such injustices than I could ever comprehend, I believe. My condolences on the death of your son, Monsieur Arkwright, and the manner in which it came about. So shocking.'

Arkwright willed his hands to remain steady, raising the teacup to his lips. 'My organisation would wish to know, your grace, what our new king and government proposes to do to ensure such a situation never arises again.'

She smiled, sipping her own tea. 'Well, there will always be thievery and consequences. But poor families driven to desperate measures by starvation whilst not half a mile away their so-called lord and protector indulges in luxuries unimaginable to them, I hope will be a thing of the past.'

'They're still where they always were: all the lords, dukes and earls – the aristocracy. Still living in their grand houses whilst poor folk starve.' Arkwright set down his teacup. 'We'd thought that they might all be gone by now, I suppose, or really powerless at least. No one's truly powerless when they've got money and land. We hoped we'd get the equality we were promised. Instead, everyone starves.'

'So dreadful,' Joséphine said, and he could tell she meant it. She'd seen suffering, known not a little of it herself.

'The views of my organisation chime with your own. But the king's troops are severe, and I suppose they've brought about a sort of madness.' It was galling to call Jérôme Buonaparte king of anything. Arkwright directed his gaze at a host of almost identical silver jugs arranged on the desk. He'd heard she spent without being able to stop herself, squandering millions. He'd expected Crow back two days ago, but there had been no word from him. Nothing. Arkwright studied the filigreed handle of the nearest jug, a distortion of his own unremarkable face reflected back at him from the polished silver. He'd always been unmemorable: it was better that way. If Crow were lying dead, bayoneted by Occupation troops in some lonely copse, would that make all this simpler?

Joséphine smiled gently. 'And yet the bloodshed in France all those years ago was extreme and distressing. The last thing we wish for is a population driven distracted by such terror. No, in this more civilised age we must move our chess pieces with a little circumspection – surely you can see that? His esteemed majesty, my brother-in-law, has come to believe that perhaps it might be wise for the English aristocracy to topple after all, but there must be a more precise sense of justice behind it than there was in France.' Joséphine sipped her tea, watching him over the gold-plated rim of her cup. 'I believe,' she said, 'that the Earl of Lamorna has a brother given to rebellion against the Empire. A young man, I'm told, already abandoned to crime and disorder.'

'Happen he does.' Best she'd no idea that her precious Earl of Lamorna might be rotting under some hedge like any one of the starving that had taken to the king's highways.

Joséphine set down her teacup once more. 'Listen, Monsieur Arkwright. All I can say is that the friends of the Earl of

Lamorna's young brother ought to be keeping a very close eye on him indeed. If he commits an atrocity that would lead him straight to the scaffold, King Jérôme will make sure the aristocracy begin to fully understand that they are no longer untouchable. And yet you are an intelligent man: even if there *is* a more precise sense of justice behind the purge of the English aristocracy, such sanguinary affairs have a habit of taking on their own life and spreading, rather like gossip. I understand that I must leave this decision in your own hands.'

Arkwright nodded. 'It would be my pleasure to consider the benefits and disadvantages of such a situation, your grace.'

'You talk of pleasure, Arkwright, and yet I have yet to see you smile.'

'We live in such difficult times, your grace. I don't like to think of a woman surrounded by her enemies as you are.'

Joséphine looked across at him. Yes, she'd been a fine-looking woman. 'How very kind of you to consider it so, Monsieur Arkwright.' She smiled. 'I must admit, I look forward to your visits. Would you believe I have not a single companion here I can really talk to?'

'I believe you were ill served, your grace, coming to live in England. You ought to be settled somewhere safe.'

'I'm not going to deny that I fear for my life,' Joséphine said. 'Believe me, Monsieur Arkwright, it would be a lot easier for my former husband and his family if I were to die at the hands of rebels in this country.'

Arkwright stirred a spoonful of sugar into his tea. It was getting cold, but he was glad he'd waited about. He'd seen real evil: little girls and old women raped after the break of a siege, mothers and fathers closing shutters at midday and speaking in whispers so as not to wake children in the last stages of starvation when the Quality passed by in their carriages, wearing silk and precious stones. No, Joséphine was just terrified enough to offer up a lad of fourteen as a sacrifice if it would save her own skin. He'd seen enough men try to keep secrets to know that she had now dropped all pretence, and was a very frightened woman indeed.

37

At half past eight in the morning, Hester walked down the front steps of Lamorna House. With a black merino cloak buttoned over her mourning gown, she crossed Berkeley Square alone. A brisk wind sent ripples through the purple and yellow tulips carpeting the iron-railed garden in the middle of the square, threatening to tug the hood away from her face. Married, she no longer had need of a chaperone, and although she had long been used to her own company on Bryher, the sense of freedom in London was exhilarating, as was the mild effort required to walk after so many weeks of doing little but drinking tea indoors. She and Louisa circled one another with icy courtesy, Kitto's accusation an unspeakable presence, like a jilted bride standing up to dance at a ball only to find her faithless suitor in the next set. It was a relief to escape the atmosphere of unspoken tension; she was certain now just how much Louisa hated her, and she loathed the woman in return. Every night she must sit opposite the dowager at supper, listening to platitudes of such monumental insincerity that Hester wondered how she kept a straight face. Crow had been gone for almost a week. She'd expected him back after one night, perhaps two. How could it take a week to ride into Essex to look over a new mare? She might have been foolish in believing, even for a moment, that this marriage had been anything other than an appalling mistake, but at least Louisa would soon find out that she had been unwise in her choice of opponent. At the same time, Hester was furious with herself for aching to see Crow; at night, she lay helpless and awake, longing for him to come, for his touch, to be sure that he was safe.

Hester was so preoccupied, she was halfway along Hay Hill before noticing that there were no other people of her class to be seen, only the poor: crossing-sweepers and itinerant beggars haunting the entrances to side-alleys. There was poverty on Bryher, true, but Papa had never allowed it to reach these depths. Hollow-eyed seamen haunted the docks at Hugh-town on St Mary's, and there were beggars in Penzance, but only in London had she seen so many desperate men, women and children at such close quarters. With growing unease, she realised London's poor were easier to ignore when the streets were also populated with maids running errands for their mistresses, well-dressed gentlemen on the way to their clubs, and starched children escorted by governesses in high-necked gowns. Where was everyone? Why were the streets so quiet? *Be careful,* Crow had said, kissing her on the morning of his departure. *Don't go out alone.* It seemed that every other respectable person had followed his advice save her. Trying to ignore rising unease as she hurried along, Hester eventually stopped on Dover Street, tall white houses looming on all sides. It was a mistake. A shoeless man in an ancient, greasy shirt advanced on her, holding out his hand. 'Please, miss,' he said. 'Spare something for an old man, won't you?'

Hester closed her fingers around her reticule, the beaded black satin cold beneath her touch. 'I'm very sorry,' she said.

'I've no money with me.' It was true: she had come out in search of revenge, not to buy gloves or jet earrings. Walking on, she sensed that she was being followed. At the corner of Dover Street and Stafford Street she turned to face a gang of ragged children.

'Please, miss.' Hester looked down into the emaciated face of a little girl with thin straggles of pale brown hair. 'We're so hungry. Haven't you got nothing to spare?'

'I'm sorry.' A quick glance down the street confirmed her suspicion – she was being watched by the two men leaning with apparent disinterest against an iron railing. She was conscious of a fleeting regret that she had not brought her pistol.

'Not even your pretty gloves?' The little girl spoke with a swift look over her shoulder at the watching men.

If the little girl didn't deliver, what would happen to her? Cold sweat slipped down Hester's spine as she peeled off her black lace gloves. 'Here.' She turned and walked on, almost running as the crowd behind her thickened – people appeared as if from nowhere, melting out from between buildings, running or limping towards her down alleyways. They were hungry and desperate with it. By the time she crossed Albemarle Street, she was surrounded by children tugging at the skirts of her cloak. Dry-mouthed, she stopped. She was trapped: she had not the smallest notion of how to help them, or even to get away, and a voice rang sharply down the street.

'Fuck off. All of you, fuck off now.'

Ashamed at her relief as the children scattered, Hester turned to face Kitto, running towards her. He stopped a foot or so away from her, and she saw him now as if for the first time. He was a child, but on a London street he was tall, white and well-dressed enough for this not to matter. *I'm a grown woman of twenty-two,* she thought, *and my word holds less weight than a child's.*

Kitto looked at her, all the cold haughtiness quite gone from his expression. 'Hets, what on earth are you doing? Maggie told me you'd gone out without a word to her. You're lucky I caught up with you – if Crow hears of this he'll be up on his high ropes, and I swear to God you won't like it.'

'Maggie ought to mind her own business, and so I shall tell her. And Crow isn't here, for all that he told us to expect him by Tuesday.' Relieved, irritated and chastened all in equal measure, Hester almost shouted at him. She forced away an image of Crow lying dead in some lonely hedgerow, his sightless grey eyes staring up at the clouds. 'My God, those poor people. I'm sorry. I'm sorry. You won't understand.'

'Well, I shan't cry rope on you, anyhow.' Kitto fell into pace beside her. 'At least let me escort you. What are you doing, anyway? I might help, if you'd only tell me.'

Hester smiled at him. 'I've a little commission to execute on Bond Street, if you would know my every last motivation. There's a jeweller I must visit.'

Kitto turned to her in frank admiration. 'You're going to Storr's?' He grinned. 'You don't mean to let Louisa get away with it after all, do you?'

'No,' Hester said, 'I'm not at all sure that I do.' No, she would never demand that Crow turned his own stepmother out of doors, but she could force Louisa to face the shame of her crime. 'I just hope she did go to Storr's. If she went all the way over to Mr Rundell, there'll be a lot of bother about getting the carriage.'

'You'd have been better off with the carriage either way,' Kitto said, bluntly. 'I don't like this above half. The streets are too quiet.'

With Kitto at her side, Hester paused on the threshold of Bond Street's most fashionable jeweller and silversmith. Bond Street, too, was oddly deserted. When she had come here with Louisa to buy a hat for her wedding, the pavements had flocked with men in tan breeches and close-cut jackets, flurries of women in thin muslin gowns whipping about their ankles in the cold. The pavements had been crowded with the fashionable and the well dressed, all pretending not to stare after them; Louisa had gratified those she graced with her acquaintanceship with smiles and bows. *We shall make you the height of fashion,* Louisa had said. Hester shuddered at the memory. Kitto was right: today, the apparent tranquillity was unsettling. It was as if London had been deserted, or some medieval plague had swept through the city, killing all in its path.

'I don't like it,' Kitto said again. 'Let's get this done and get home. It's too damned quiet – the Occupation must be patrolling somewhere nearby. We don't want to get in their way. Knowing my luck, Crow will be back and he'll want to know where we've been. Best get it over with.'

'Well, you may leave your brother to me when he deigns to grace us with his presence,' Hester said, and pushed open the door, knowing what was likely to happen the moment she did but no less sickened when the expression of the man behind the counter subtly altered as he took in her appearance: the fine-woven, expensive merino of her black cloak, the intricate lace of her veil, and the colour of her skin.

'How might I help you?' Short and pale, with small, child-like hands spread before him on the glass counter-top, Mr Storr spoke with the faintest sneer. 'I'm not at all sure that you have come to the correct establishment, miss. I think Ptolemy here will know where you ought to execute your commissions.' He nodded towards an apron-clad boy with deep brown skin and close-cropped hair standing in a doorway that led away from the shop-floor. Uneasily, Hester wondered if he was paid for his labour. One heard of people still kept as slaves, too afraid of starvation to risk seeking paid employment without a letter of recommendation.

'She's the Countess of Lamorna,' Kitto said. 'And she's certainly come to the right place.'

'There was a commission with my name on it,' Hester said. 'A silver slave collar. You'll tell me who had it made, if you please.'

Storr gave her an oily smile. 'I'm sure your ladyship understands that one's reputation depends on the utmost discretion—'

He was silenced by the muffled but unmistakable peppering of musket-fire from outside, followed by screams. Freezing, Hester found her gaze fixed on Mr Storr's wet-lipped mouth as it hung open.

'That's it,' Kitto said roughly. 'Hets, I knew this was a mistake—'

Hester grabbed his arm; acting on an unnamed instinct, she rushed him behind the glass-topped counter, shoving past Storr. The jeweller's protests were silenced by a deafening explosion. Hester screamed into a shattering of glass. At her side, Mr Storr muttered a Hail Mary as he sat on the floor; his face was blood-streaked, and Hester breathed in the hot, sharp scent of urine. Rubies, sapphires, emeralds and diamonds winked at her amidst the shards of broken glass carpeting the polished oak floorboards.

'Holy Christ!' Kitto laughed, brushing glass and sapphires out of his hair.

'I beg your pardon, ma'am!' Crouching in a heap of scattered pearls, Ptolemy jabbed a finger at a doorway behind the counter. 'This way. Better to get out quickly.'

Hester took hold of Kitto's hand and, half running, half crouching, they followed Ptolemy through the door and into a dim hallway papered with yellowing silk-printed birds of paradise. He led them out into a narrow side-street. 'Run, my lady. You and your friend. The French have been up and down the street all morning. It's my belief the rebels are setting gunpowder wherever they can.'

Hester clasped his hands. 'Thank you – thank you so much. I'd like—'

'There's no time, Hets, come on!' Kitto grabbed her arm, rushing her away down the street; he was surprisingly strong. He would not be a child in anyone's eyes for much longer. The heavy skirts of Hester's gown and cloak caught about her ankles; running was almost impossible, and she stumbled in a dank, cobbled passageway leading to the main thoroughfare of Bond Street. Kitto knelt at her side, and they both froze, watching a steady stream of gaunt, filthy Londoners surge down the street at the end of the alley, followed by at least twenty blue-jacketed Occupation soldiers shouting at the starving rioters to disperse. A woman carrying a cloth-wrapped bundle broke away from the crowd, hurrying down the alleyway towards them.

'Help me!' she cried. 'The baby, oh help me—' Musket-fire cracked out once more and the woman fell face down on the street before them.

At her side, Kitto swore under his breath. 'Run, Hester,' he said. 'Run with me. Now.'

Hester thought only of the child. Mechanically, she recognised that the mother was dead. Her brown eyes stared, blank and unseeing, and a trickle of blood slipped from the corner of her cracked lips, dripping on to the cobbles. Hester felt beneath her body for the cloth-wrapped bundle, but her fingers met only with a limp unresisting leg. Gasping, Hester pulled the baby towards her; still half wrapped in a faded shawl now sticky with warm blood, it couldn't have been more than a few weeks old. The small face was dusty and still, the tuft of soft black hair like swansdown beneath her fingertips.

'He's dead,' Kitto said roughly. 'The shot must have gone

through him. Look – there's so much blood. I'm sorry, Hester, but we can't do anything to help them. Quickly!'

Numb, Hester arranged the tiny corpse on the cobbles beneath the dead woman's cloak; she would want to protect her child. 'We mustn't run. They can't see us here. We must wait till they've passed. We need to hide.' Even as she spoke, musket-fire cracked out above the shouting and, pressing herself back against a damp brick chimney buttress, she watched soldier after soldier run past the end of the alleyway. Rather than fading, the clamour of the riot grew louder: people running in their hundreds, voices raised in fear and panic, shattering glass and the thunder of shot slamming into masonry. She realised with detached horror that she was in London – *London* – and soldiers were firing at will into a crowd of unarmed citizens. This wasn't just an occupation. It was a tyranny. She caught hold of a thread of memory: on a trip to Penzance as a little girl, she'd slipped away from Cousin Jane, leaving her to wait at the draper's for a green silk ribbon to be measured along the counter-top. Once outside, Hester had run down Gun Alley to Fore Street for a sight of the ships in the harbour and come upon a dog-fight: a pack of curs fighting over a stolen lobster-pot that still contained a rotting mackerel tail. Pressing herself against the wall of the chandlery, she'd watched as a riding-officer and a gentleman in a bearskin hat had tried to separate them, ten dogs or more, kicking and swearing into the swirling mass of teeth and bloodied fur. In the end, the riding-officer had simply shot into the melee, reloading all the while and firing until all the dogs were dead. These were poor starving people, not dogs, but there was the same sense of lawlessness, that the usual order of things had been swept quite away. When at last the street grew quiet, Hester ached with the need to relieve herself, hissing at Kitto to turn his back as she did so. He did the same, swearing to himself, and then helped her to her feet; her legs were hot with pain after crouching so long, her feet numb, her toes crushed inside her boots. The sun was now overhead, skeined behind thin cloud: it was gone mid-day. They had been in hiding for more than two hours. Flies hovered above the dead woman and her baby.

'We've got to go,' Kitto said, steadying her. 'God knows what'll follow that, and who's to know but that they won't search the whole place for stragglers. We'll be killed if they find us – please let's go.'

Desperately afraid to leave the shelter of the alleyway, but knowing there was no other choice, she took Kitto's hand, held her skirts and ran with him as best she could, praying that she wouldn't fall again, that they wouldn't be overtaken and arrested. Kitto seemed to know the streets as intimately as she knew the moorland and the beaches at home – he hurried her along without stopping, darting down side-alleys and rushing her past houses with shuttered windows. In one small, fashionable square they passed a shoeless man hanged from an elm tree in the iron-railed garden. He wore only breeches stained with waste forced from his body by the hanging; he had been stripped of his jacket and shirt, anything that might be sold to fend off starvation.

'Don't look, Hets,' Kitto kept saying. 'Just don't look. I'll get you home, I swear to God.'

The streets were beginning to look familiar once more when they heard the harsh breathing of a high-couraged horse and the uneven clatter of iron-shod hooves on paving stones. 'Shit,' Kitto said quietly. Hester turned around to face the horseman, and it was no French cavalry officer but Crow mounted on his grey mare, watching them from the far side of the street. He was utterly still in the saddle, observing them with the poised menace of a cat. But he was here, he would take her safely home, and she could deal with his alarmingly hostile expression then.

He had not been captured by French soldiers. He was safe, and not rotting in the long grass and cow parsley shoots at the side of some forgotten country lane. He said nothing, but only dismounted, walking swiftly towards them. He was unshaven, his face shadowed with several days' blue-black growth; his jacket was streaked with green lichen dust and dark, sticky unnameable filth and his breeches and boots were liberally splashed with mud. No, he was very much alive: dangerous, powerful and wholly uncivilised. Hester was almost overcome by the desire to take hold of his arms and shriek in his face: how dared he be gone so long, how dared he worry her so; she wanted him to hold her as she wept; she wanted to take him to bed. She had never seen him look so angry.

'Oh, Christ,' Kitto said, but Hester was breathless with indignation. How did Crow have the nerve to look so angry when he was the one who had been gone for so long?

'You will have the goodness to mount,' Crow said to Hester when he reached them, and that was it: nothing but a peremptory command. The mare was far too big for her to mount alone, and when he handed her up into the saddle she was dizzy and breathless at his touch. Her body betrayed her, responding with delicious heat to his nearness even as she suppressed a high, wild fury at his high-handedness, and the sheer unfairness of it. Refusing to demean herself by laying down a challenge to her husband in the open street, she allowed him to lead the mare without remarking that she was perfectly well able to ride a distance of a hundred feet without assistance. Kitto followed her lead and said nothing, walking in silence alongside his brother. The street was quiet, with no sign of Occupation troops, but as they rounded the corner into Berkeley Square Hester gripped the reins so hard that the oiled leather cut into her palms, praying that they'd meet no troops. She was in no mood to watch Crow kill more French soldiers, and she had no reason, either, to suppose he was in any temper to hold fire.

Arkwright came out into the street from the stable-mews, with Jim the stable-boy at his heels. Hester watched a speaking look pass between Arkwright and Crow, but neither said a word. She saw Jim cast a single, sympathetic look at Kitto, but Crow said nothing to his brother or to her until they were inside the house, servants scattering from their path as they went from the stable-yard through the scullery, up the narrow stairs and into the entrance hall, all Turkish rugs and glowing floorboards, in contrast to the white-washed sobriety of the servants' quarters. Then, and only then, did Crow turn on them both.

'What,' he said savagely, 'in the name of Christ were you both doing out there in the middle of that fucking appalling mess?' He turned on Kitto. 'You at least ought to know better. Did I not clearly instruct all of you to keep off the streets when I was gone?'

Hester was so stunned at the language he dared use in her presence, and so light-headed with fury, that for a moment she had to fight to catch her breath. 'It's not his fault. You need not be quite so high in the instep. Am I your servant that I must listen to your instruction?'

'You are not my servant.' Crow brought one hand down on to the top of the japanned cabinet with a resounding slap. 'You are my wife.'

Hester stared at him, floored by memories of her father. Men of course expected their wishes to be respected, their instructions to be followed, but unlike Crow, Papa had not made her feel like a thwarted child since the day she'd ceased to actually be one. Kitto, with a keen instinct for self-preservation, had slipped back into the servants' quarters, but in any case she saw no one save her husband. Standing before her, he was white-faced with exhaustion and rage, and she wondered how it was possible to feel such a wild soaring hatred for the person whom she could watch for hours as he slept. Turning his back on her, he went upstairs, but if he thought he would have the last word in such a Gothic style, he was sorely mistaken. Gathering up her dusty skirts, Hester ran up the stairs after him, pushing open his bedchamber door before it slammed shut. Hoby, Crow's valet, paused in the act of helping him out of his filthy jacket.

'Leave us, if you please,' Hester demanded.

Hoby shot an enquiring, terrified glance at Crow, who merely nodded, tossing the jacket on the floor. Pausing only to snatch it up, the valet departed with undignified speed. He closed the door and only then did Hester turn on her husband, facing him as they stood beside the bed. His eyes were dark with anger and another quite different emotion that left Hester breathless again. 'If anything happened to you,' Crow said, never taking his eyes from her, 'God knows, I would never forgive myself.'

Hester fought for words. 'I thought you were dead. I thought you were never coming back.'

He stood before her and they embraced at last, her face pressed against his mud-splattered shirt; he cupped the back of her head with one hand, his thumb grazing the delicate skin behind her ear.

'Dare I ask,' he said, 'why your hair is full of all these tiny emeralds?'

38

Kitto sat at the escritoire by the window in his bedchamber, carefully inking and labelling the interior parts of a tulip spread out on a sheet of blotting paper, the glossy, yellow-streaked crimson petals wilting and darkening as he worked. He looked up and stared out of the window at the coppered roof of the ballroom abutting the back of the house, the small garden behind, rooftops and houses beyond, a forest of smoking chimney-pots, a clear blue sky arching above, clouds of starlings tossed and buffeted by the wind. To look at it, no one would have guessed that blood had been spilled on the streets of London today. There would be a reckoning for his part in it, however small. It was typical of Crow to let him stew. The sky had begun to darken when Mowbray knocked.

'You're to come to his lordship's library at once, Master Kitto.'

'On an empty stomach, Mowbray?'

'Mrs Halls will send up a tray directly afterwards, sir.' Mowbray shook his head as he held open the door. 'Not that I suppose you'll have much appetite for it after catching the sharp end of his tongue. I must say that I'm sure I don't know why you can't stay out of hot water for more than five minutes, but he was the same before you, that I will admit, forever brangling with your father, as I don't doubt you recall.'

'Oh, I recall it, all right,' Kitto said, but it was not the same. Papa had always been languorous, moved to chilling criticism only when Crow's excesses led to gossip, or were attributed to a lack of form. Crow, however, had come home from Essex with that air of constant agitation and the strangely absent expression in his eyes, just as he'd looked for so long after Waterloo. He was likely in no case to be reasonable.

He waited in the library, sitting at the desk with a glass of brandy, looking so much like Papa, and yet so catastrophically different as a man, that Kitto could not bring himself to speak, or to understand how Papa could still be dead.

'Will there be anything else, my lord?' Mowbray said, and Kitto wished he would stay.

'I think not, thank you.' The door closed with a quiet click, and Crow turned to him. 'You have exactly half a minute to explain your part in today's events.' He spoke in French, and Kitto felt an unpleasant twisting sensation in his chest.

'I can do no better a job at explaining what happened than Hester has already done, sir.'

'But I don't ask what Hester knew. I ask what you know.'

Kitto hated himself for feeling just a little afraid of his brother. 'I swear to God I had nothing to do with any of it. I followed Hester and went with her to Storr's because I didn't think you'd want her to go out alone. Blame Louisa if you must blame anyone. But someone must do something about the French. Or maybe you don't want to.' He paused, breathing hard. He'd gone too far now to turn back. 'Maybe you want Buonaparte to give you a French duchy. We're the last of the Saint-Maures, after all. Is that what you want – the Montausier title?'

Kitto expected to be back-handed across the room. Crow was more than capable of dealing out such barbarous penalties, however rarely he chose to deploy those tactics, but instead he just looked at him over the rim of his glass, idly swirling the amber-gold brandy. 'Spare me the tragedy,' he said in such chilling accents that Kitto would have preferred to be hit. 'I find that one title and all the responsibility it brings is more than sufficient for my vaulting ambition. I quite agree: someone must do something about the Occupation. But not you. You will promise me now, again, to have no involvement in this rebellion.'

Kitto stared at him, fear giving way to disgust that he was unable to quite conceal. Crow himself meant to do nothing. He meant to let the French truly win. When Papa died, Louisa said people never spoke the truth in a fever. *Shot in the back. Nothing but a coward after all.* But perhaps Papa was right; Crow had never been a hero, just a disgrace to the name of Lamorna. It was time to act, if he would not. For the first time in his life, Kitto swore an oath that he had every intention of breaking as soon as he possibly could, as though Crow's dishonour were infectious. 'All right, then. If you insist. I promise.'

Crow merely nodded, glancing at the door, and Kitto had known he was dismissed. He wished he could say that he'd been only too glad to oblige, but he felt the withdrawal of Crow's approval like a cloak whisked away in the rain. He wished that he still wanted it as much as he needed it.

Early the following morning, before Louisa had the chance to insist with breathtaking hypocrisy that he attended church, Kitto made unobtrusive progress across the silent taproom at the Star and Garter on Bracegirdle Street, letting himself in through the door at the back and into a dank passageway.

It led to a flight of steps. He paused at the bottom, looking up at the darkness. Despite his anger, Kitto still felt a small, cold and distinct fear in the pit of his belly at the thought his brother might ever learn of this betrayal, but a broken promise was a small sacrifice to courage. He pushed away a memory of the dead woman and her baby, the dust caught in its soft black eyelashes. Why did Crow not understand how simple it was? One was either a coward, or one fought back against the Occupation. How could Crow just do nothing but spend half the day in bed with Hester?

Kitto ran up the stairs at the back of the tavern, praying that Harry Simmens hadn't been talking out of his arse back in St Austell when he said where and when An Gostel liked to drink in London. On a dark, narrow landing heavy with the scent of boiled cabbage, he knocked at a heavy door, suppressing another spurt of chilly dread at the thought of Crow finding out that he'd gone to meet the Cornish resistance. *So what?* Kitto told himself furiously. Perhaps he'd be shamed into acting like a man. Kitto knocked again, and this time someone spoke, a voice muffled by the closed door.

'*Piw eus ena?*' *Who is it?* 'And where are you from?'

'From my father's house,' Kitto replied, in Cornish, and the door opened to a slope-roofed room thick with pipe-smoke. The men clustered around the single table looked poor for the most part, worn-out jackets and untrimmed hair; one wore an old-fashioned wig, probably a servant.

'Who the bloody fuck are you?' Pipe-smoke raked Kitto's lungs, and the man leaned in the doorway, glancing past his shoulder, suspicious. 'Think you took a wrong turn, sir.'

'Kick him out, Mr Pendeen. What do you wait for?' Laughter drifted from the table and Kitto felt shameful heat spread across his face. Why hadn't he thought to change his clothes? There must have been something in the servants' quarters less likely to give him away than a linen shirt so fine and so white that it lit up the gloom.

He spoke in Cornish again. 'Harry Simmens sent me.' It wasn't true, but what choice did he have? 'I can help you. I know how to lay gunpowder.' Had they heard about Newlyn? He hoped not. Nessa, Roza and Mr Gwyn were dead because of him. It didn't matter if he died making the French pay for that. It was no more than he deserved.

Mr Pendeen leaned above Kitto's head, closing the door behind him, as he stood by the table, not invited to sit. 'I want to help,' he heard himself say. 'I'm as Cornish as you are. The French promised our freedom, didn't they? Isn't it time we made them pay for all their lies? They think they've got away with it, but they've not.'

Mr Pendeen laughed, and so did four of the others. The remaining three only watched. The oldest of the gathered men was dressed in respectable, old-fashioned clothes. He tapped tobacco into the bowl of his clay pipe, tamping it with the edge of his thumb. 'A Cornish boy in London. Where are you from? Mousehole lad, are you? Marazion? One of the farms up by Hawk's Tor? How do you know Harry Simmens? It occurs to me that Harry Simmens ought to mind his tongue.'

'Come on, Mr Trewarthen. What's it to do with us? We can't have him in here, whatever way you cut it. Some mine-owner's son – he'll be no more than trouble.'

'Roseland. I come from Roseland.' It wasn't a lie: Crow's lands marched with the Roseland peninsula but nothing would help him now there was a Trewarthen in the room. They knew everyone and always had.

Mr Trewarthen sighed. 'Mine-owner's son? That and more.' He turned to the others. 'He's a Helford of Lamorna – bastard or not I don't know. They all look the same.'

Mr Pendeen looked him up and down. Coils of blue-grey

smoke drifted from his nostrils. 'Now look, little lord, if you put the sort of price on your own skin that I put on mine you'll get out of here and not come back.'

'Think about it,' said one of the others. 'We'll have to take him home. After what Lamorna said.'

Crow had been here first, then. He would always be there first. Slow, cold dread slid through Kitto's body from head to toe. He would have to do this alone. He knew, too, that having broken his word, he would not be able to go home. Crow would find the letter he'd left, and he would read it. He couldn't go back.

39

Crow woke, bewildered with sleep of such deep and peaceful darkness that for a moment he could only sprawl in Hester's bed with her head resting on his chest as she slept naked beside him. He stared up at the bed-canopy, closing his eyes again in sheer relief; for a day or so, he'd escaped the sleepless state that made his skin itch and his thoughts skitter like spiders, sharpening the ever-present sense of danger that could only otherwise be dulled with claret, brandy or rum. Even as Hester lay soundly asleep with her hair tickling his chin, Crow knew this luxury was a risk he could ill afford to take. It was almost impossible to sleep except in the arms of a woman – only then could he be sure he was nowhere near a battlefield – but if the nightmares came, Hester would hear him call out again. The shame was immense, only deepening when he thought of Smith tumbling into the mud at his side, the back of his skull obliterated by a musket-ball. He might as well have pulled the trigger himself. *Bad luck – we lost Smith,* he'd said to Lessing and Masters when they had met in the mean little stretch of woodland north of West Malden, mud-splattered, still breathing hard from the chase. *Damned shame. He was a good man.* Worse still had been the visit to Smith's young widow; riding long past dawn, he'd found the woman hanging out wet bedlinen in the garden of the small cottage, a grubby-faced child clinging to her skirts. *But it's washday,* she'd said, unnecessarily. *Oh, I wish I hadn't done the sheets, I shall never feel close to him now, sir.* Only then did her tears come. Crow loathed himself: he couldn't play this game for much longer. The prospect of leaving Hester forever filled him with grief so vast and aching that he had to push the thought away, knowing that duty came first. Before too long, he must make provision for all those who depended on him. To judge by the slant of the light filtered through pale, heavy curtains, morning had given way to afternoon. He heard soft footfalls in the hallway beyond and pulled up the sheet, reluctantly concealing Hester's nakedness as well as his own: he could look at her for hours, and there was so little time left. The brass doorknob turned with a click, and Maggie stepped in.

'Excuse me, your lordship, but there's a man waiting for you downstairs.' In deference to Hester, Maggie spoke in an undertone, and Crow knew that Hester had found another willing protector, at least.

He stretched, gently easing Hester's head from his chest. 'Thank you, Maggie. Tell Mowbray to have him shown into the library.'

She frowned. 'He's not the sort of person, milord, I venture to suggest, that would ordinarily be received there.'

In his dressing-room, Crow hauled on his boots and tied his cravat with military precision; he'd neither the time nor the inclination to wait for Hoby. He'd ignored Maggie's stricture, sending orders for Mowbray to escort the visitor immediately to the library, and went there to find a man of late middle age in neat but unfashionable clothes looking out of the large window as if he'd have much preferred to be on the other side of it. At a glance, George Trewarthen was unremarkable, but Crow knew perfectly well that he led Cornish opposition in London. It would only take a whisper here and there to lead the man to the guillotine.

'Your honour.' Trewarthen bowed.

Crow wished he'd not left his cigarillo-case in his dressing-room. He spoke in Cornish. 'I needn't ask what troubles you.'

Trewarthen replied in English, a set-down. 'Indeed not, your honour. You asked me to send word if the boy – your brother – came to offer his assistance to An Gostel. I dared not put such a matter in writing, and so have come myself. The offer was made.'

'Then I thank you for telling me.' It was a clear dismissal, but still Trewarthen waited. Crow raised his eyebrows, questioning. He knew what was to come.

'My lord,' said Trewarthen, switching to Cornish, 'we accepted no help from the boy, but it's your right. If ever you—'

'Brother,' Crow said, 'if it was a battle we could win, I'd fight it. The French lied to you with false promises of freedom. They've been just as brutal as the English. My own kin at Nansmornow paid the price for rebellion.' He held the man's gaze. 'Now isn't the time, Mr Trewarthen. Have you ever been to war? I can't lead the Cornish to victory like a king from a story.'

For what seemed a long while, they faced each other in silence. Bowing, Mr Trewarthen went out, leaving Crow to wonder how many ways it was possible to fail those who relied upon him. Pouring himself a measure of brandy, he drank it, unable to dampen the rising heat of his anger. Kitto had broken his word. Was not one traitor in the family enough? Crow thrust back his chair: holy God, when he found that boy, he'd make him sorry. He shoved open the door to the morning-room and found Louisa ensconced on the chaise by the window between

Tessa Esterházy and the Duchess of Rutland. If they knew what she'd done to Hester, would they be so happy to fawn all over her? Many would agree with the sentiment, even those who claimed to be Abolitionists, but no one would condone the lack of finesse. He'd gone to sea at twelve to escape this insincerity, this hypocrisy.

'Where is my brother?'

Crow didn't miss the steely edge to Louisa's smile, or the countess raising her eyebrows at Rutland's wife in silent censure of his discourtesy. 'I haven't the smallest notion, darling.'

Crow ran upstairs, his fury swelling by the moment; he should have gone to the stables to get a crop. Some lessons could only be learned one way, only truly recalled by blood, by bone. Fuck it, Kitto would just have to take his beating in the yard – let him be dragged through the house in full view of all the servants; the stubborn little bastard deserved it. Crow cornered Mowbray outside the drawing-room, but the butler only shook his head.

'Master Kitto hasn't been seen this morning at all, your honour. Perhaps he's unwell – it's not like him to keep to his bed so late in the day.'

'He'll be damned sight worse when I find him.' Crow took the stairs at a run, slamming open the door to his brother's bedchamber only to find it empty, and a folded letter left on the faded blue Indian counterpane that he remembered from his own childhood. His mother always used to come upstairs to bid him goodnight before going out to a ball. He saw her now: she leaned over to kiss him, wearing cobalt silk and that particular French eau de toilette: the grassy, lemony scent of verbena mixed with something indefinable. Crow broke the letter's seal; when he had read the contents, he sat down on the bed, holding his head in his hands. With shattering clarity, he remembered the curate talking to his father as Maman lay on her deathbed at Nansmornow. *My lady might find peace if she were only easier in her mind about Jack and the infant. She wishes not to leave them. She wishes to be sure that they will be safe.*

40

Joséphine set her daughter's letter down on the side-table beside her chaise, massaging her temples. Darkness had long since fallen and the room was rosy with candlelight, but Hortense's letter shattered the sense of warmth, of safety.

And I fear, Maman, that Louis's moods grow worse even as he sees the rest of the Bonaparte brothers elevated to far greater heights than he himself is allowed to attain – may the entire abominable Bonaparte family go to the Devil! God save my soul for saying so, but after the way we have all been so ill used by them, after our loyalty to your former husband – to my stepfather, who was always so fond of me! – it is what I truly think. May God keep you, Maman, for I cannot but fear for you, living under the protection of those who have loathed us since they first knew us.

Yes, Hortense's missive made for uneasy reading. Daughter of a discarded empress and married to a Bonaparte brother who loathed her, the dear child's situation had been rendered more precarious still at the death of poor little Napoléon Louis Charles. Hortense had lost not only her child, but her position as mother to the emperor's intended heir. And now that Austrian woman had spawned, Hortense's surviving children bore only the slenderest chance of succession – but it had still been a chance, and it had shielded her from the most spiteful excesses of her own Napoleon's siblings. Joséphine had no desire for her grandchildren to be emperors, but Hortense's plaintive note made her long for the opportunity to comfort her daughter, exiled with her spiteful, incompetent husband to a remote French duchy. She longed to smooth Hortense's thick, honey-brown hair from her brow, to hear the low music of her voice. But she was not fool enough to believe that permission for such a visit would ever be granted. Napoleon, after all, had made his intentions clear. She was to do the impossible and establish a court here in England. A small smile played about her lips. Once, it had been thought impossible to establish a court for an ill-formed, underbred Corsican soldier with greasy hair, an ill-fitting army uniform and filth in his fingernails, and yet she had done it. Napoleon had never known how to talk to people, how to charm them. Always, he had relied upon her. She had succeeded. Perhaps that was one of the reasons why she'd come to love him so much: he needed her. He always had. Clearly, the Austrian woman was not up to the task of winning over the English, and that was why she had been allowed to take Malmaison for her own, leaving his first wife – his most loyal wife – with this most delicate task. Widely loathed and blamed for the deaths of the royal family, Jérôme and Catharina were certainly of no use.

'Your majesty.' She looked up to find Crow standing before her. He bowed. How nice it was to see a well-brought-up young man who knew his manners, even if he would insist on calling at such unconventional hours.

'You move so very quietly, my dear Lord Lamorna. How did you get in this time?'

He smiled, looking very young. 'Through the window in your bedchamber, ma'am. I'm very sorry.'

She couldn't help smiling back. 'It's been a long time since a man climbed in through my window, you may be sure of that. Now, sit down and tell me what in the world you mean by visiting me at this hour? Carlton House is a dangerous place for an uninvited Englishman, particularly at night. Have you no news for me?'

Crow shrugged. 'I was hoping that it would be my turn, ma'am. I gave you what was needed, did I not?'

'I suppose you did. Jérôme was grateful enough for news of the attack on the post-road.' Joséphine watched him, her mouth dry. Could she really take this step? Doing so, she would be an avowed traitor to the Bonaparte family. She loved Napoleon. He still loved her, she knew. And yet that had not stopped him abandoning her for the breeding-sow he had thought so essential to his rising star, or failing to extend his protection to her children. 'Very well,' she went on. 'What you need to understand about the Bonapartes, Lord Lamorna, is that none of them really understand what they are doing, lifting the lid from society in this way, putting down riots with musket-fire and killing innocent citizens in the street. The Bonapartes were not imprisoned in Paris during the Terror. They have no real concept – no real, informed understanding – of what happens when the established order of a country is turned upside down: thousands upon thousands die, Lord Lamorna, as you have reason to understand – your own grandfather among them. You think England is oppressed now, but the scale of slaughter can and will be far greater. Don't you comprehend the significance of what happened in France, how so very close we all are to seeing the same tragedy and terror unfold on your grey little island? The executions will not end with the aristocracy. Why should it be any different?'

He watched her carefully. 'Much as I can only grieve for how my mother's family suffered, and how she herself suffered on their behalf, I understand that although the Revolution started with reasonable justification, it grew into a monster.'

Did he really understand, though? This rich young English nobleman with the blood of the Saint-Maures in his veins? He'd survived battles, true, but that was not the same as watching innocent people led to the guillotine in their thousands, murdered one after another as if their lives meant nothing, like pigs and cows slaughtered to be salted and packed into barrels for the winter. He can't have been old enough to remember his French grandfather. 'The justified anger of the starving poor was stolen from them, do you understand?' Joséphine went on. 'It was simply used by men hungry for power to further their own positions. Thousands upon thousands will die here in England, just as they did in France all those years ago. The streets will run with blood.'

'And so what do you mean to do about it? Nothing?' He watched her so closely she felt he might almost see her most secret thoughts, her hidden fears.

Too horrified by the memory to articulate it, even now, Joséphine remembered the night in prison when, quite sure that her name would be on tomorrow's list of those to be called to the guillotine, she and a coterie of equally terrified friends had, quite calmly and with no former discussion, cut off their own hair, shearing it down to their skulls as though they had been children with lice. Anything to save the indignity of having one's hair hacked off on the scaffold. The same desperate sense of determination rose up in her once more, even now, so many years later, only this time she held a much more valuable hand of cards. This time, she had choices. She had influence. She was conscious of a moment's sickening regret at what she had told Arkwright about Lord Lamorna's young brother.

And Arkwright was not the only one she had told. What choice had there been? She'd no friend or protector here at Carlton House. She had only the currency of favours granted and hoped for in return, which was why she'd also whispered to Mr Castle as well as Mr Arkwright that the young Lamorna boy might spark full revolution. In doing so, she'd given the Spencean English revolutionaries the weapon they needed. And revolutions, as she knew to her cost, never stopped with justice for the poor. She felt as though she were playing chess with mortal lives, considering her next move. Mother Mary, what had she done?

'Listen, Lord Lamorna,' Joséphine said. 'The little Bonaparte kingling currently snoring in his bed downstairs means to bring England to her knees. I must own I've never been certain of your loyalties, but if you mean to stop him, now is the time.'

41

Hester sat at Louisa's side on a chaise longue upholstered in a pale oyster-grey silk: Joséphine must have refurbished Carlton House since taking possession of the Prince Regent's former home: there was now no trace of his reputed love for chinoiserie and elaborate gilding, and all was now drawn from the palette of a late summer sky, soft greys and pinks with touches of gold. The reception chamber was cavernous but thinly populated: Joséphine had been circumspect in the choice of her guests, and yet Hester still felt the heat of people watching her when they thought she was not looking. She wouldn't have put it past Louisa to render her discomfort even more acute by allowing news of the slave collar to spread – without, of course, mentioning her own part in it. Kitto had been missing all yesterday, and Crow in a silent, shocking temper, out of the house for most of that time. She felt as though she were crossing a river in spate wearing a blindfold, never sure whether her next step would lead to a fall, perhaps even to drowning.

'Well, here we are – no one can fault Joséphine's taste, at least.' Louisa leaned closer on the chaise, so close that Hester breathed in her scent, and it was like standing in the bluebell wood at Annet's

Point on a hot day in May. 'Poor woman. Imagine being rejected like that – it must have been so humiliating to watch Buonaparte take a new wife. One can't help but feel a little sorry for her.'

Hester forced a polite smile. Louisa would be a sight less sanguine if she knew how close she was to seeing her own reputation tarnished beyond repair. The *ton* might disapprove of Hester herself all they wished, but they were hypocritical enough – she was quite certain – that when Louisa's spite became common knowledge, her precious pile of invitation cards would dwindle. She was a woman, after all, born to present a face of charming amiability. Louisa would be a lot less brazenly sanguine if she knew of the letter that Maggie had brought up with Hester's breakfast-tray that morning, a thin sheet of cheap paper, hastily folded and sealed, tucked between her plate of bread and butter and cup of chocolate.

DEAR LADY LAMORNA,

I hope you will forgive my presumption in writing to you, and my earnest wish that you and your companion reached safety on that Dreadful morning. In the hope that you did, I wish to convey Information that I believe will be of interest, although I am afraid it will also cause Distress. The commission of which you made Enquiries was indeed paid for by the Dowager Countess of Lamorna. I am sorry to bear what must be news that can only bring pain, but hope that in doing so you might be better able to guard yourself from further Malice. I am sorry also for the length of time it has taken me to write – it took many hours to restore my employer's premises, and the Dowager Countess's name was only found after searching through the private paperwork of Mr Storr. I believe some effort was expended in attempting to conceal from General Knowledge who paid for this particular Commission.

Yours,

PTOLEMY STORR

Hester smiled as she remembered it, and instantly thought of Kitto, praying that he was safe. There would be a time and a place to confront Louisa with proof of her vitriol. She tried not to shudder as Louisa laid one hand on her arm. 'Oh, Lord, Hester – Mrs Piozzi is advancing on us. She'll be most abominably curious about you, but she's so old I can't give her a set-down; we must bear with her, I'm afraid.'

Hester tensed as an elderly white lady bore down upon them, wrapped in a voluminous and very ugly tasselled shawl. She sat next to Louisa, leaving the much larger space next to Hester cold, vast and empty.

'What a crush Joséphine has here this morning, Louisa darling!' She turned to Hester. 'Do you know, my dear, I've been observing you since I came in, and I must say your English is so good that listening to you no one would ever suspect you were not English yourself. Where exactly in the Colonies were you born? The West Indies? You will have something in common with our French hostess, then. I believe she herself was born on Martinique or some such place.'

Hester smiled, knowing it wouldn't serve to bring Mrs Piozzi's own ignorance to her attention. 'I'm not quite sure that you will have heard of the place where I was born, ma'am.'

Louisa's forefinger hooked tight around the handle of her teacup. 'Don't look now, but Joséphine is coming.'

'I don't know how she dared invite us to this reception,' Mrs Piozzi remarked, 'considering what so many of us lost at Waterloo. So degrading, to be paraded before her curtseying like a schoolgirl.'

'I've not encountered the like since I was presented at Court,' Louisa replied in an undertone, and an uneasy silence fell. Hester still couldn't quite believe that the regent and so many of his family were dead. Her fingers curled tight around her fan of dyed black chicken-skin as Joséphine approached them.

Protocol demanded they must wait until she spoke first before saying another word. They waited in tense silence, and Hester breathed in Joséphine's rose-oil scent, noticing that the dusk-pink lace gown worn over a cream satin slip was embroidered with bees, Buonaparte's own symbol. She was not even his wife, cast aside for another woman because she could not give the emperor a son. Hester looked up, surprised to find Joséphine taking Louisa's gloved hand with the over-eager haste of a social outcast.

'How lovely to meet you, Lady Lamorna.' Joséphine turned to Hester, speaking in a low, melodious voice with an intriguing accent – French, but something else, also. 'And this must be the new Countess of Lamorna.'

Hester dropped into a curtsey, bowing her head. She had come prepared to loathe Joséphine on sight, but saw only how old she was, and how disarmingly kind she looked, and how, despite the inadequate fire sulking at one end of the great hall, Joséphine's gown was dark with sweat beneath the arms. She was still very beautiful. Hester watched as Louisa engaged the empress in desultory chat about the unseasonably cold spring and, as Joséphine moved away, smiling mechanically, Hester found that any hatred had been replaced by despondent pity.

Louisa raised both eyebrows at Mrs Piozzi. 'I feel rather sorry for her. It's as though she's committed some sort of awful solecism and no one wants to talk to her, but we all must.'

Mrs Piozzi smirked, casting a quick, knowing look at Hester, as though she must surely have been on the receiving end of similar treatment. 'But look – Margaret has just come in. In that case, I'll leave you now. I expect she'd love to have a cose with you both.'

'Margaret?' Louisa smiled. 'I wasn't expecting the Donningtons – I thought they hadn't come to town at all. I wish I'd had the sense to stay at Nansmornow. I don't know why we're all pretending that this charade is no different to any other season.'

Mrs Piozzi had already heaved her bulk from the chaise, for which Hester could only be thankful. 'Not the Donningtons, dear – Margaret Albemarle. She's just come in with one of the girls.'

At Hester's side, Louisa went still, and Hester found that it was impossible either to draw breath or to look away from the door: she was to face her mother's kindred at last. The Duchess of Albemarle was just an old lady like any other – an old white woman like foolish Mrs Piozzi, with pale skin that sagged beneath her eyes and below her chin, her head wrapped in a turban of marbled green silk. She had gone to sit on a duck-egg-blue silk chaise on the far side of the drawing-room, staring, milk-pale hands pressed together in her lap: a great-aunt by marriage, but a stranger. This was the woman who had refused to know her, even to write. Everyone near Hester stared, too, by turn delighted at the scandal of such a meeting or horrified by it, even as Her Grace of Albemarle lifted her lorgnette and stared openly at Hester across the enormous space. She beckoned.

Louisa stood up. 'Come on. We can't ignore that, I'm afraid.'

'But—' Even in her horror, Hester knew that she would attract far more attention, and far more comment, by ignoring her great-aunt's summons. The room spun around her as she crossed it at Louisa's side, a whirl of gilded mirrors and bright gowns. Clearly, Louisa wasn't able to resist the prospect of a ringside seat. At breathtaking speed, Hester found herself standing before the duchess. The entire room fell silent, conversation trailing off as the scandal of it rippled irrevocably from one gathered knot of people to another. Hester knew she should do something, that everyone was watching. She executed a slight curtsey, but instead of acknowledging the courtesy the duchess only raised the brass lorgnette again and looked at Hester through it with a gaze that swept her from head to foot.

'You, I trust, will wait on me tomorrow at Albemarle House.' That was it, the words spoken with a dry, accustomed air of command that brooked no argument. A summons had been issued: clearly, Mama's family expected nothing more than unquestioned obedience from her. In a distant corner of the drawing-room, someone let out a stifled laugh. And at that moment the drawing-room that had seemed so airy and beautiful when she walked into it that morning was now ugly, the walls closing in.

42

Before Louisa could say a word, Hester pushed through the crowd. All that mattered was that she got outside with no one to watch her any more, no one to whisper. Chilly air flooded her lungs as she stepped out into a whitewashed passageway; one of the servants must have left a door open, and in her haste she'd stepped into a network of rooms and passageways quite alien to her: the servants' quarters. There had to be a way out. She could not go back into that drawing-room to be stared at, she would tolerate no more whispering from Mrs Piozzi or those clutches of dimpled, dough-armed debutante girls. A hand closed roughly about her arm; she was pushed against the wall.

'What do you think you're doing?' The liveried footman sneered as he looked her up and down. The back of his hand was cross-hatched with reddish brown hairs as though the legs of some monstrous insect were protruding from his pale skin.

For a moment, Hester was unable to speak: to be handled so for only the second time in her life brought back the day French soldiers had killed her father. 'Take your hand from my arm and direct someone to show me the way out to my carriage, or you'll be sorry the sooner.'

'*Show me the way to my carriage?*' The footman mimicked her speech. 'You're no more a guest of her upstairs, you poxy blackamoor slut, than I'm a Dutchman. Lightskirt or thief more likely. Out with you.'

Hester was sure he would have enjoyed a struggle: determined not to oblige, she walked at his side, loathing the hot sensation of his thick fingers grasping her upper arm, nauseous with anger. A laundry-maid in a grubby apron watched with insolent fascination as they went through a steam-filled washroom, the flagstones still slick with grease-tainted water.

'You're lucky we've none of us time to call the Watch. She upstairs keeps us busy enough.' The footman pushed his face closer to hers with each word; his breath stank of stale cheese and Hester fought the urge to retch. He shoved her out of an open door into a yard hung with damp linen of every description: boil-washed chemises, aprons, sheets; the air knifed her face. Hester walked past a laundry-girl hollow-eyed with exhaustion as she pegged out a row of muslin clouts. Joséphine must be past fifty, but even if she no longer bled, her army of servants suffered every month.

'Where do the carriages wait?' Hester demanded, forcing her voice to remain steady.

'Go down the side-alley, missus.'

Hester hardly noticed her surroundings. Half-running down an alleyway flanked with stacked barrels, she pushed her way past the two men in filthy leather aprons who were heaving one of the barrels towards an open cellar door.

'What d'you think you're doing?' demanded one, turning to her in indignation: heaven forbid a white man should be pushed by anybody.

'Leave it, she's none of our concern.'

Hester glanced at the second of the wine merchant's lackeys and immediately knew his face. She was looking at the slight, narrow-shouldered man she'd seen with Arkwright in the stable-yard at Lamorna House: Mr Castle. Did his gaze linger on her for a moment? She must just get away, as far from this place as possible. Hurrying on, Hester found herself in the carriage-crowded confusion of Pall Mall. Clouds studded a bright blue sky: for such a cold day the light was stark, glinting from gilded crests adorning the row of elegant vehicles waiting in the road. Arkwright was walking the horses up and down when Hester reached Louisa's carriage. Without a word, he led the two chestnut geldings back down the street towards her and stood holding the pair of them as he reached to open the door, handing her up into the carriage. It was only when Hester sank into the deep, upholstered cushions that she noticed her black satin slippers were so sodden they were coming apart at the seams.

Louisa did not keep her waiting long. Hardly had Hester sat down than she settled herself on the carriage seat opposite and passed over a lace-edged handkerchief. 'You really must attend the Albemarles tomorrow; we can't have this sort of low-bred family muddle in the house – I don't know what on earth Margaret thinks she's about, stirring up a hornet's nest by appearing like that only to cause a scene. She must have known it would have everyone talking – and you gave her every satisfaction by falling for it, like the greenest debutante in the world.'

'Believe it or not,' Hester said, controlling her anger with some considerable effort, 'I actually don't care what you think.' The time for manoeuvre had long gone: she was ready to fire the first shots, and intended to leave the field victorious.

Louisa started, shocked, but continued with smooth confidence, as if Hester hadn't even spoken. 'Margaret Albemarle is idiotic to enact such dramatics, but she won't risk her granddaughters' chances of marriage. Not with their father's habit of losing at dice, anyway. If what I hear is true, they must want to dispatch those girls before the end of May. This must all be wrapped up in clean linen without delay. Which, I might add, is precisely what should have been done when your mother ran off to Cornwall all those years ago, and then your poor father wouldn't have spent the last twenty-three years marooned on an island, and you with him.'

'My father adored Bryher. And he loved Mama.'

'I doubt that extremely.' Louisa's face hardened as she spoke and, not for the first time, Hester wondered what she had done to earn such dislike. 'It was hardly a love story, darling. Georgiana threw herself at your father in the most embarrassing way. He was rather sensible about it and left London immediately. But Georgiana followed him to Cornwall alone, before her friends could do anything about it.'

Hester itched to slap the self-satisfied smile from Louisa's face; she refused to show how very much it hurt to hear the story of her own beginning reduced to the spoilt tantrum of a young girl simply denied what she wanted. 'Unfortunately for everyone except the islanders and myself, my father loved Bryher. We were very happy there.'

'It was an exile, all the same. A punishment. You would have been safely married long before now had the Albemarles not chosen to enact such a ridiculous Cheltenham tragedy over the whole affair. God knows, they had scarcely bothered with Georgiana much before.'

Safely married, and not to Crow. Surely that could not be it? Surely Louisa could not be jealous of her in that respect? Hester smiled. 'Do you want everyone to know that you commissioned that slave collar, that you had my name inscribed on it at Storr's? Or would you just prefer to find somewhere else to live? I wouldn't leave it too long, if I were you.'

Louisa stared at her, and for the first time her mask fell, and Hester saw all the hatred in her face, the pretty eyes narrowed into malevolent slits, the pretty mouth budded into the pout of a spoiled child. She could go to the devil.

43

Grant's butler left a silver tray on the table between them. Sunlight struck the lead-crystal decanter and the two glasses, spilling diamonds of light on to polished wood. Crow ached for brandy but knew his hand would shake if he poured. The long velvet curtains at the window smelled faintly of dust, as though they had not been taken out and beaten for many years. A brass vase of tulips spilled glossy crimson petals like bright tarnished rubies against the gloom of the heavy oak bookshelves behind. The street outside was quiet save for a pair of liveried footmen loading strapped leather trunks into a large carriage. One slipped and stumbled, and stood leaning against the crested carriage to straighten his wig. The Hunstforths were leaving London, then. They were not the first of the *ton* to flee in stunned silence, and they would not be the last. Even in Belgravia, people were afraid now, and Kitto was out there somewhere, uncontrollable.

Grant poured the brandy and handed him a glass. 'It seems very unfortunate to me, Jack,' he said, with light ease, 'that French troops happened to be nearby when you took the bridge at West Malden.'

Jesus Christ. He didn't need Grant to start suspecting him – not on top of everything else. Crow felt the brandy set his throat alight, momentarily stilling the surges of alert half-panic that had not left him since he found Kitto's bedchamber empty. *You're in Belgravia, not on a fucking battlefield.* Telling himself so made little difference; flesh and bone betrayed him nonetheless. 'Hardly surprising, I should say, sir. Buonaparte can hardly be said to have been remiss on that front: every post-road is patrolled.' Grant made a vague, noncommittal sound, a half-burned log settled behind the grate with a bright burst of sparks, and Crow wondered if he would be able to force his hands to be steady long enough to light a cigarillo. On balance, no. 'We were lucky only to lose Smith.' Crow pushed away a memory of Smith's widow's face crumpling, her bitten-down nails and reddened fingertips as she fumbled for a washing-peg, trying not to let the clean sheet fall, the child clinging to her skirts. *Dear Christ. Dear fucking Christ.* 'It was a bad business, all the same. It's going to get worse. Joséphine told me that Jérôme means to come down hard on the rioters – on us all.'

'The man's an idiot,' Grant said, crossing and uncrossing his legs. 'I can't imagine for a moment that Buonaparte has given him leave to set this place alight, with most of his troops in Russia. Still, it's to our benefit. It's about time we moved on Faversham then, isn't it?'

'When do you wish to begin?' Crow knew he sounded cool enough, but a wave of panic shuddered through him like a choleric belly cramp, leaving a bloody, metallic taste in his mouth. Kitto was still nowhere to be found: London had wholly absorbed him. Even Arkwright had not been able to track him down. He could be anywhere. Joséphine's words rang in his mind. *He'll be hanged higher than the White Tower.* And now Grant had decided it was time for the next attack, and he must leave London altogether.

'Let's meet at Oakhurst, it's near enough to Faversham.' Grant stretched out the long, fleshy fingers of one hand to inspect his carefully pared nails. 'Where would be the best place – at the house?'

Not at Oakhurst. Without knowing precisely why, Crow recoiled at the notion of inviting Grant to cross the threshold of a house belonging to him, of watching the man warm those fleshy hands at a hearth below the portrait of his grandmother as a little girl. 'There's a gamekeeper's cottage lying empty at the edge of the wood by Green Lane. We'll meet there.'

Grant watched him a moment. 'Very well. Make sure Arkwright is ready, too. We'll need him, this time, with Masters and Lessing deployed in Sussex.'

With casual ease that cost him some considerable effort, Crow at last drew a cigarillo from the silver case in his breast pocket and reached for a brass-inlaid quartz tinderbox on the table. Kitto would be looking for trouble; Crow had seen it in his face after the last bout of rioting, loathing him for apparently doing nothing to avenge such atrocity. What manner of fairy-tale hero had the bloody young fool thought him? How it was to fall from such a pedestal. And now, in consequence, Kitto was setting himself up to fall foul of the Occupation. He'd already offered his services to An Gostel: what would he do next? No, Crow would hunt the streets of London and find that boy, and the devil might take his eyes. He felt an utter lack of control, as if he were a child clinging to the mane of a bolting horse. The battlefield thirst for decisive, bloody action soared through him, and the stuffy quiet of Grant's library was broken by the thin tap-tapping of liquid dripping on to polished floorboards. *No, no, no—* Crow lit his cigarillo and finished the brandy, feeling the tell-tale shivering sensation passing across the backs of his hands. Sure enough, in a dark corner of Grant's library, a young Belgian soldier now stood with his throat laid open from ear to ear. Blood gushed from the wound, unstoppable, pooling on the waxed floorboards at his feet.

'Jack?' Grant was staring at him. 'Do you not attend me?'

'I'm sorry. I suppose you'll send a bird when you want to move?' Crow managed – just – to keep his voice steady, to look at Grant's well-fed face instead of the Belgian child-soldier whose throat he had cut. Dripping blood struck polished oak floorboard with the relentless tap-tapping of rainfall breaching a leaking roof in some Spanish bivouac.

'It seems wisest,' Grant went on. 'I'll go ahead. If the Occupation are patrolling at night with that much tenacity, we need to be sure they've had a decent look around and gone on somewhere else by the time we move. When it's clear, I'll send word, and you follow with Arkwright.'

'It's only thirty miles – we'll be with you a day after I hear.' Crow lit his cigarillo. When the pall of smoke dispersed, the dead soldier had gone, thank Christ. 'If there was but a way to get Wellington off Scilly. I can't stand knowing he is there without being able to lift a finger to do anything about it.'

Grant dealt him a satirical smile. 'What, with the Iron Duke at our backs we might just finish the job at hand and force Jérôme Buonaparte into the sea? Jack, Wellington is under heavy guard in an island fortress. How many soldiers did your wife estimate she left there?'

'No more than ten or so, she thought.' Grant was right, for all that Crow longed to wipe the self-satisfied smirk from his face. It was simply impossible to get close enough to overpower Wellington's captors without being seen. The duke would likely get his throat cut. No, there was no choice but to play a longer game, to pray that there was something left to save when all was done.

44

Crow left Grant's Belgravia mansion long before the last bells. Tension rippled through him. Arkwright should have sourced the gunpowder already: they had only to wait for Grant's word. *Only.* How long did that give him to find Kitto? Reaching Berkeley Square, one glance at Mowbray's hang-dog expression told him the boy still had not come home, and that Arkwright hadn't found him either. He let a footman take his coat, cast off his gloves in the hallway, dropping them on to the side-table, and went straight up to the library, unlocking the door. He must do the impossible. Kitto must be discovered before word came from Grant. The simple fact was that he likely needed to be in two places at once. The waiting before a battle or a skirmish had always given him a burning sense of excitement, not knowing if he would come out of it or not. Some men wanted to be alone; others wanted to drink; others dropped into a sleep of cold black exhaustion, depending on how far they had marched. In the back of Crow's mind, he saw men of his own regiment at the Château d'Hougoumont, none of them knowing if they'd see another morning; MacConnell and Jones sharing a canteen, Robbie Cooper smacking firing-holes in the garden wall with his bayonet. All gone. Before facing death, Crow had always needed a woman. Now it was not just any woman he wanted, but one woman. There was time, surely, before he must go out again in search of Kitto. If he didn't relieve a little of the tension he would not be able to move, to speak. Hester was sitting in her bed when he let himself in, turning the pages of a book. Her hair spread out in a halo of light curls gilded by the candlelight; her nightgown was unlaced at the bosom, showing the brown curve of her breasts.

'Have you found Kitto?' She didn't look up from her reading, but her obvious worry swelled his own.

'Not yet. He'll be damned sorry when I do.' He untied his cravat, letting it fall to the floor in a heap of starched white muslin.

'What are you doing?' She still didn't look up. To all appearances, she appeared perfectly calm, but she was fretting with a corner of the sheet.

This was going to be more complicated than it had first appeared: what was the matter with her? It was more than concern for Kitto: she was angry with him. 'Distracting you. And myself. What are you doing in bed so early?' He knew the answer to that already: she was avoiding Louisa, and that was another mess he must unravel. The weight of responsibility crushed the air from his lungs.

She didn't smile, but she did look at him now. 'Why is the library locked?'

'Because I don't want you or anyone else to go in.' Arch dissemblers themselves, were not women always disarmed by honesty?

'Interesting.' Hester looked down at her novel, turning another page. 'When we married, I had no idea I was contracting myself to an ogre from a fairy tale. I thought that perhaps you might trust me to go into your library and read a book.'

'Trust me, Hester – I never do anything without good reason.'

'I might trust you if I were granted the same respect. Now, if you wouldn't mind leaving me in peace, I'm trying to read.'

How dared she speak to him in such a way: who did she think she was? Too angry to ask what was the matter with her, he turned to the door. 'Of course, but you'd do well to remember that I may order my own house however I please.'

'Oh no, I never do forget that.' She got up, then, pushing back the coverlet and sheets, walking right up to him, so insolent and so close that he wanted her more than ever. The worst of it was she was right. He should have explained as much as he was able, and yet if he were ever caught, they would look for accomplices. 'And you'd do well to remember,' Hester went on, 'that I was used to ordering my own father's house just as I pleased. I don't take well to being treated like a child.'

'Then your father was a fool to give you the helm so young: you've forgotten your place.' He regretted his words the moment they were out, knowing they would infuriate rather than chasten her; he was furious at the realisation he was so much in the wrong, but without the least idea of what he could have done instead.

She stepped away. 'Leave me alone.' Her eyes were bright with tears. He'd made her cry. The shame was as bad as it had been after the ruin of Waterloo. He couldn't move, couldn't speak. 'Go!' Hester spoke with quiet, scalding anger. He turned, leaving her standing alone by the bed.

Crow leaned on the wall outside Hester's bedchamber, pushing the hair back from his face. It was still so early. Even though she'd gone to bed, there was still much of the evening left to endure. If he left her a few hours, perhaps her fury would recede. She might even forgive him. She might allow him to push that unlaced nightgown down over her shoulders and free the warm weight of her breasts. Inside her, he could forget that this might be the last time, that when Grant summoned him, he'd likely die, and without knowing where Kitto had gone, or what he was doing, or if he was even safe. The need for a drink overwhelmed him. There would be brandy and port still laid out – he need not even ring for it and face Mowbray's expression of professional indifference. Forcing himself not to run down the stairs, Crow walked straight past his footman and pushed open the double doors that led into the drawing-room to find that he was not alone. Louisa and Burford stood by the fire: he was clasping her hands with his doughy white fingers. Despite an intense sensation of relief, to actually see her with another man sent a surprising burst of rage soaring through him. Judging by Louisa's amused expression and Burford's look of slight alarm – those wet, pale blue eyes nearly starting from their sockets – Crow failed to entirely conceal his outrage.

'How wonderful,' Louisa said, gazing up at Burford. 'You can be the first to wish us happy, Jack.'

Crow went straight to the sideboard and poured a measure of brandy, the first – that night – of many. At least she would be gone. At least he no longer had to look at her, knowing the malice concealed by her pale, pretty exterior, her face a constant reminder of one of the worst sins he had committed in a career so rich with dishonour. 'My dear stepmama,' he said, 'I couldn't be more delighted.'

45

Having left Louisa and Burford to their arrangements, Crow took to the streets: he knew it wouldn't be long before Grant summoned him and Arkwright to Kent. He searched taverns frequented by An Gostel and those haunted by the English revolutionaries, but no one had seen or heard of Kitto. Crow had spent long enough reading men's faces to sense a lie: his brother really had not been seen by anyone he spoke to. The boy had just melted into the vastness of London. A night's enquiry was fruitless, and he reached Mrs Dawnay's establishment in the hours before dawn, where a footman begged to relieve him of his coat before showing him up a glossy oak staircase to the upper apartments. At least Louisa would be out of the way, married to Burford: at least he did not have to think about her, and what he had done. Mrs Dawnay's saloon was furnished in the first style of fashion, the walls painted a soothing shade of dove grey, a pattern of fleur-de-lys on the intricately embossed ceiling picked out in gold leaf that glittered in light cast by candle-flames shivering along the branches of two large lead-glass chandeliers. Shown in by another footman, Crow was greeted by an old acquaintance.

'Exquisite hat, Meg.' He took the glass of champagne she poured. She wore nothing else, her tawny hair pinned up beneath a military-style shako overlaid with gold braid.

'You're very kind, my lord.' Meg smiled. One of her side-teeth was missing. 'Madam desired me to wait for Captain Gronow – how charming to find you instead. I'm surprised to see you here, so newly married.'

'It wasn't my intention, I'll be honest.' Crow sank down on to a chaise beneath a handsome window draped with folds of rose-pink velvet. He couldn't go on. It happened like this at times: the sleeplessness would creep up on him, and he must give in to the returning dreams. He had slept last night in Hester's arms, but there had been too many weeks and months preceding it in which he'd known so little rest that shadows crawled at the edge of his vision. Yes, with Louisa gone, there would at least be one less person to think about. Burford had informed him the marriage would take place with no loss of time, celebrated at his family seat in Pembrokeshire. Until that time, Louisa would be a guest of his mother. Kitto would be happy enough, if the bloody young idiot ever came home.

Meg sat down beside him, draping one leg over his. The soft fair hairs on her thigh caught the candlelight as she edged closer. 'Does the African countess not please you, my lord? So soon?'

'She's from Cornwall, Meg. And it's more that I don't please her.'

With one swift, expert movement, Meg shifted herself on to his lap, facing him, naked, enveloping him in her scent of oil of violets and other men's stale spunk. 'Perhaps I might please you instead?' Meg was good at her trade, her smile would have seemed real to a young idiot down from Oxford with funds enough to afford the superior services of Mrs Dawnay's girls.

He drained his glass of champagne, leaning back in the

chaise. 'How did you get here, Meg? Really. Where did you live before this?'

She reached over, pushing back his hair. 'I was promised to an officer in an army regiment, if you must know. Every girl in Halam wanted his attention, but I was the one who had it. He was excessively handsome, just like you.' Meg leaned forwards now, closer still, whispering in his ear. 'But after he fucked me, my lord, my officer found that there was another lady who pleased him more. So he went away to Belgium with his regiment, and I chose not to stay in Nottinghamshire to have cabbage skins and insults thrown at me after church by all the goodwives who were wet between the legs imagining themselves in my place no more than a week before.'

Crow shut his eyes. Unprotected, Hester might have ended up here, in a place like this, with men like him paying for her attentions.

'What's wrong?' Meg said. 'Listen, why don't I call Mrs D. and get her to fetch the new girl. She's dark, if that's what you prefer these days.'

Crow shook his head. 'Meg, don't get me a girl. I don't want one now. Get me drunk.'

46

Kitto kept to the darkness, and in Shoreditch there was plenty of it. There were no torches flaring in this part of London. Narrow, scrimping houses lurched over an alley split lengthways by a long slick of green-tinged shit, the gutter dammed by the balding, swollen corpse of a dog. It had taken him most of the evening to ask the right sort of question in the wrong sort of tavern and he'd risked his neck and wasted half the night before finally gaining admittance to the meeting-room above a Methodist chapel off the Ratcliffe Highway, only to find it full of highwaymen and pickpockets who had now found the Lord. But to one of these reformed criminals a purse of half-crowns had proved more attractive than Jesus or even common sense. Crow would thank him for stealing the money to pay for gunpowder when the French were defeated.

The Carlisle was at the tail-end of a narrow alleyway, and it was late. Even if Kitto at last found the men he was looking for, he'd be lucky to get home before dawn. Running anywhere near an establishment like the Carlisle would draw too much attention and so he walked, copying the habits of those few locals brave or desperate enough to risk meeting with the night-guard: fast and with purpose, head down. He longed to feel the reassuring weight of the leather pouch hanging at his belt, but that would have been dangerous, too. He felt the heat of the forge paces away, but the smithy next door to the Carlisle tavern was deserted except for a barefoot child, skirts tucked up into her sash as she made a half-hearted attempt at sweeping the cobbled yard by the inadequate light of a cloud-skeined moon. Cabbage-scented steam boiled from an overlooking window, mingling with the scent of piss and dung. The child looked Kitto up and down and stopped sweeping, leaning on her broom.

'What do you want?' She had to shout above the clamour from the tavern.

'I'm looking for Mr Castle. Is he here? He drinks in the Carlisle.'

The child watched him, quick-eyed. 'Maybe. Maybe not.'

Kitto dug into the pockets of his waistcoat as if he were searching everywhere for a single coin. She didn't need to know what was in the bag. He held out a penny, lifting it just out of reach of her hands. Her fingers were thin and dry as rabbit-bones picked clean on the high moor above Lamorna.

'Bring him out here first, then you'll get your coin.'

'Get yourself fucked, my sweet lord. Your kind can't be trusted.' She spat on the cobbles and went off into the back entrance of the tavern, gaping windows nailed across with boards, half the roof-tiles gone, and Kitto stared after her, waiting. For all her bravado, she was desperate enough to risk being cheated.

Castle appeared in his shirtsleeves with a pipe between his teeth, carrying a rag-wrapped bundle. 'And what can I do for you, my good sir?'

'You know why I'm here.' Kitto nodded at the bundle, forcing himself not to cough. Castle's tobacco stank as if it was cut with dried dung. 'I've got the money, like you said. It took me long enough to find you.'

'I'm a hard man to find, it's true.' Castle's narrow, blackened fingers curled around the roll of banknotes, and Kitto watched as the man counted, mouthing the numbers.

'Hold steady, my good sir. You're no less likely to cheat me as any other.'

'Just get on with it.'

At last, at long last, Castle was satisfied, and Kitto took the rag-wrapped package – a terrifying weight when he thought back to Newlyn. This would have taken the whole of Fore Street with it straight to oblivion, never mind the guardhouse. Even so, such was the vast size of Carlton House that, without help, he couldn't carry enough gunpowder to more than rattle the glasses on Joséphine's supper-table. But it would be enough to spread a fire beneath that bastard Jérôme's stolen palace. A fire that would grow and grow when it reached the coal-cellar, a fire that would be hungry enough to consume Jérôme and all his guards. He would make Napoleon Buonaparte pay for Nessa and Roza's lives. He would make the French pay for all that they had done, and that included the mess they had made of Crow.

Kitto turned from the narrow darkness of Pike Lane and on to Lord Street, which wasn't much lighter, still overhung with a jumble of narrow, ancient buildings that all seemed to have reached varying stages of decay, their collapse arrested by boards unevenly nailed across unshuttered windows and plain, rotting straw heaped atop thatch no one had the funds to replace. He was being watched; he sensed that cold sensation spreading between his shoulder blades, sliding down the back of his neck. Castle? It wouldn't be the first time someone trading in this quarter of Whitechapel had the very illicit goods they had just bought stolen back from them, Kitto knew.

Damn it. He walked directly south towards the white spire of the Church of St John, just visible in a gap between two houses. The trick was to look as though he belonged. But if Castle had sent a man after him, even looking like a local would be of no use. Only a few more paces and he'd be back out on Whitechapel Lane. It was too quiet here, that was the trouble. Kitto quickened his pace, ducking down Creeping Lane, silent and moonlit.

'Funny sort of place to come visiting.'

Kitto looked up. Arkwright stood right in front of him. 'No you don't, lad.' He reached out and grabbed a handful of Kitto's shirt, twisting it with one elegant, expert flick of the wrist. Quick as a fish, Kitto went to slide out of it, but Arkwright was quicker, and had him by the arm. The newspaper-wrapped packet of gunpowder landed on the street between them, beside a curl of white, mud-splattered cabbage leaf. 'Well, what've we got here, then?'

'Nothing!'

'Is that right?' Arkwright bent to pick it up, and with all his strength Kitto forced up a knee, aiming at his face, but Arkwright moved too fast and stood up, weighing the packet in his spare hand. 'Let's take it home then, shall we? A little bit of nothing never troubled anyone, did it?'

47

Catlin breathed through her mouth as she went into the great hall. The smell was like a living thing – the vomit and shit of men in a confined space. Eight out of ten French soldiers lay humped on the polished parquet as if they had simply collapsed where they stood. At least they weren't in the beds, no mattresses ruined, all the doors locked, the keys safe at her belt, a reassuring weight. Hester's mother, Mistress Georgiana, looked down on them all from her portrait above the great marble fireplace. Her blonde ringlets were frosted with white powder. Aunt Evans said the captain had commissioned the painting from a London artist on a reducing diet who'd stayed three months, and would eat nothing but potatoes and vinegar.

What would you say, my fine lady, if you knew I was passing on messages from the Duke of Wellington to your only child? What would you say if you knew your servants had become killers? Catlin laid her pan of broth down on the sideboard, herb-scented steam drifting from a crack between the lid and the dish. Pearl barley, garden greens, mutton-bone stock, handfuls of sage, chervil and thyme. And tincture of foxglove. Not quite enough to kill. Not yet.

Bowls. She needed mugs or bowls. She wouldn't nurse them all, oh no. They'd have to see to themselves. Tom, poor Tom. There had been no one to nurse him, dying in the mud all alone. Catlin turned back to the door, opening her mouth in a silent scream when a hand tugged at the hem of her gown. He'd crawled along the floor, clothes stained with his own waste. A rush of nausea burned Catlin's throat. He wasn't much more than a boy, lank pale brown hair hanging in his eyes. He had looked away as Ney put his hands all over her body; no one had told him to stop, because she did not matter.

'Mademoiselle,' he whispered, 'please help me. Please bring water.'

Catlin drew away her skirts, smoothing her apron with both hands. Her fault. He was dying – so young – and it was her fault, her choice. She'd go to hell for this. She was a killer. A murderess. *No. You're a soldier. You're acting on the orders of Wellington himself.* But they had to be got off Bryher. First the French, then Wellington. There was no other way. Quickening her step, Catlin reached the door. *Mother Mary—*

'*Maman, oh Maman—*'

He was calling for his mother. Cups. Bowls. Water. They were all going to die. Gripping the Davy lamp, Catlin trod carefully around the great hall in search of the pitcher she'd brought in that morning, her heart clenching as the yellow glow illuminated a dead face, eyes open, dried blood at the corner of his mouth, congealing in a thick bristle of brown whiskers. He would never see home again, she'd made sure of that. But perhaps he'd been the first to drive his bayonet into Captain Harewood's belly. Perhaps he deserved it. She walked on – the lamp held out before her lent long, shuddering shadows to the chairs still gathered around a leather-inlaid card table – and found the pewter jug resting on the mantelpiece. Five dead at the first count, lying in their own filth, one curled over on his side like a child. She crouched by him to make sure, glimpsing a letter crumpled in his outstretched fingers: childish, unformed handwriting; the word *Papa*. He had been a father. She'd killed the father of a little child.

Tom would never know what they'd missed, what she'd lost, and what she'd now never have. *Because of the French. But not these men. These men might have been a hundred miles from Tom at Quatre Bras. These men were just as scared as he had been.* She was going to hell for this. She'd burn. She went back to the young one and knelt at his side. A boy. Just a boy. She'd killed a boy, too. His lips were stained with blood, his eyes closed, bronze-gold lashes brushing his cheekbone. She reached for his wrist. A pulse: a faint, fluttering pulse. Not dead. Not yet. His lips formed a word, a single word.

Water.

'Here.' She crouched at his side with the jug. If he knew what she'd done, would he still open his eyes and look at her like that – trusting and grateful, so ashamed of his own dirt? 'You must sit up a little. I'll help you.'

He turned his face to one side, his lips moving, flaked with dry skin, a silent plea. Catlin drew his head and shoulders on to her lap. She would have to boil-wash the apron and her gown: the old one of Hester's she'd made over to fit and always loved, the sprigged muslin now sodden with stale sick. She held the jug to his mouth, tipping it awkwardly. He drank. His eyelashes fluttered like the wings of a moth trapped against a windowpane.

'Don't leave,' he said. 'Please don't leave me. I want to go home. Please, I just want to go home.'

He was dying and it was her fault. The least she could do was stay at his side so that he wasn't alone, and his last sight would be of a girl he thought was kind. She'd do this so Wellington might fight another day; so that Tom wouldn't have died for nothing. Tom had never even known about the baby growing inside her – just a fluttering coil of flesh no bigger than a robin's egg that had died before she even began to swell with the pregnancy. She would fetch water. Clean water, this time. Catlin stepped out into the stone-flagged corridor, breathing hard as she closed the door behind her. He was so young, just a boy no older than twenty. And there was life in him. He wasn't going to die, not if she didn't want him to. What difference would it make if just one French soldier boy remained? What could he do, after all, against the whole island?

'Mrs Rescorla.' Catlin looked up; Ney backed her up to the wall, tall, heavy. He stank of stale tobacco, sour breath. 'What a ministering angel you are, madame. Tending to the needs of my men with such diligent care.' He spoke without a smile.

Catlin flattened herself against the wall, cold hard stone touching her body. Anything to escape him: even just an inch further away.

'Your men brought this sickness, sir. I only do what I can to stop it killing any more of my own people.'

'But it's so kind of you to tend my soldiers in their hour of need.' Ney smiled now. He'd been drinking. She could smell the brandy on his breath, Captain Harewood's brandy. 'How much you must hate us, and yet still the broth, the water, the risk of infection. You must have enough to do, with such a house as this to look after, and so many extra inhabitants.'

Thief. Killer. Thief. He'd killed Hester's father and ruined Hester for good. Concubines and whores: that was all she'd ever heard of the Earls of Lamorna, and the young one as bad as his father had been. Even if the earl never laid a hand on Hester, being in his company was enough to finish her, and it was Ney's fault. 'I only do my duty as a Christian, sir.'

Ney reached out, tracing a line down Catlin's left cheek with the tip of one rough, hardened finger. 'Then what a very good

Christian girl you are, Madame Rescorla. And now I think there's something else you might help me with.'

'You must forgive me, sir. I've so much to do in the kitchen. I must wash these pots.' Blood pounded in Catlin's ears; every shred of flesh in her body urged her to run. Ney's fingers closed around her wrist. Slowly, he lifted her hand, raising it above her head, pushing it against the wall. 'I must go.' Her voice cracked as she spoke, knowing that he would not let her go. His face was less than a finger's width from her own; his body pressed against hers, hard. The vinegary smell of his sweat turned her stomach and she fought the urge to be sick herself; she turned her face away, but there was nowhere else to go.

48

Ney pushed Catlin to the floor with such force that her head cracked against the flagstones. Bright hot pain exploded across the back of her skull and down her neck. His hands were all over her, his stale, breath hot in her face; he scrabbled at the skirts of her gown, snatching at her petticoats.

'I've waited for this. I'm not in the habit of waiting.' His spittle-wet lips parted in a snarl; she glimpsed his grey teeth and she screamed, and his thick, soft palm slammed against her mouth, covering her nose, and she couldn't breathe. 'Isn't it strange, Madame Rescorla, that I'm the only one of my men still alive? Who hasn't succumbed to this fever? I'm the only one who hasn't touched the broth you so kindly brought. Isn't that just so unaccountable?'

He knew what she'd done. He was going to break her. He was going to kill her, even though the Duke of Wellington was in the same house, one of the most powerful men on God's earth. She was facing this alone. Ney grabbed at her fichu, tearing the starched muslin away, jerking at her bodice. She couldn't breathe – spots of light danced before her eyes;

shadows fell where there should be none. Wrenching her head to the side, she snatched a breath, half choking on her own spittle.

'You weren't clever enough, Madame Rescorla, and you'll hang for this. All that pretty hair, just blowing in the wind as you swing. What a shame. I've sent for more men, and you'll go to the mainland. You'll go all the way to Bodmin Assizes. That's a long way, isn't it? A long way to think about how you're going to hang, you murdering little bitch. But that's not to say I won't take my pleasure before you go.'

And Catlin tried to scream, managing only an airless gasp, because one moment Ney's bristling, sweaty face loomed before hers, and the next it was gone, his head smashed into a mess of brain matter and shattered purple flesh. His hand fell away from her mouth and she rolled sideways, hot blood on her face, in her eyes, in her mouth. On her hands and knees, gasping for breath, Catlin looked up and saw Wellington in the doorway, lowering Hester's pistol. Smoke coiled from the tip of the barrel. He came to her, holding out one hand. Flinching away, she got to her feet alone.

'I'm sorry you were so troubled, Mrs Rescorla.' As though he were talking about a nasty bout of stomach-fever. She couldn't stop shaking. She leaned against the wall. *Don't look. Don't look at the floor. At what's left of him—*

'He knew.' Catlin gasped for breath, scrubbing blood and the memory of the dead man's heavy, damp touch away from her mouth. 'He knew what I've done. He's sent for more men. He said they're going to hang me, he said—'

'Nonsense.' Wellington spoke with crisp, arrogant authority, but at least he didn't try to touch her again. He seemed now to understand that the very idea of being touched was unbearable. 'No one is going to hang you, Mrs Rescorla.'

'But the French—'

'They'll be dealt with.' Wellington glanced at the door to the great hall. 'Are they all dead?'

And Catlin thought of the amber-eyed young boy, the boy who had looked away the first time Ney put his hands on her. Less than an hour ago, he'd still been alive, his breathing stronger and more regular with each moment that passed. 'Yes, your grace. All dead.'

Wellington nodded. 'Very well. Call Mr Evans. He'd better have this mess cleared up.'

49

Catlin crouched at the boy's side. Leaving Uncle Evans and the Garrett boys to dispose of Ney's corpse, Wellington had retreated to his library. Catlin caught herself: not his library, the captain's. Wellington seemed almost to belong here now. He'd saved her life. The sick boy watched her spill the bundle of clothes from her apron, dirty washing taken from the heaps piling up in the laundry-room.

'What's your name?' Catlin asked. She needed to know that he wasn't just a faceless French soldier. Jacca's breeches and waistcoat would fit him, so would Uncle Evans's shirt and jacket.

'Bleiz. Bleiz Lozac'h. They are all dead, aren't they?' The boy's voice was stronger now. Like Ney, had he guessed that the broth and the jugs of water were what was killing them all, not the three-day fever?

Catlin nodded. 'You said your father was a fisherman, that you come from a place like this. Can you sail?'

Bleiz forced himself to sit up. 'Of course.'

'And can I trust you? You must never tell. We just want to be left alone. We want to be safe.'

He nodded, and Catlin pointed at the pile of clothes with her toe. 'Then get dressed. You must leave. You must go tonight, before it's too late.'

'But where? I can't sail alone to France from here. I do not know—'

'You must go to the big island across the channel to the east – Trescaw. Tomorrow we'll have a spring tide, and you can walk right across at noon. Hide, then steal a boat and sail up the sound to St Mary's. You'll be able to get a passage back to the mainland from there. That's the best I can do for now.'

Bleiz smiled at her. He didn't know that she'd killed his friends, his companions. 'It is something, madame. Thank you.'

Catlin backed out of the door. Then she turned and ran.

50

Maggie's belly clenched as she breathed in the chocolate-scented steam curling from the silver jug. It was hours now since her slice of pudding, and sour that had been, too. It was going to be a long day with the whole household turned upside down. But the sooner that nasty wench Lady Louisa was gone off to be married to her gullible white lord, the better it would be. Perhaps then Master Kitto might come home: where had he gone this time? Was he close by, watching the house, waiting?

Lady Hester was sitting at the escritoire by the window, dressed to go out. 'You seem a little preoccupied, Maggie. I'm sorry to ask for more chocolate. I can't seem to get enough of it.'

'I'm sorry, milady. I mean nothing by it. It's only that the house is all turned upside down.'

'Poor Mrs Mowbray,' Lady Hester said. 'She must have been up since dawn, packing valises. The carriage leaves for Burford Court this evening, doesn't it?'

Maggie nodded warily. There was no time to be lost in more ways than one: every last laundry-maid knew that Lady Louisa had not bled in two months. Best Lady Hester never knew of that, though. 'I've finished altering that bonnet for you, milady. Would it please you to see it now? I only left it on the table at the top of the stairs.'

'Oh, I'd love to see my hat if you've finished it!' Lady Hester smiled with genuine pleasure. 'You are astonishing, Maggie – I don't know how you find the time, not with all your other duties.' The smile vanished just as suddenly as it had appeared. 'If I must attend my great-aunt, I might as well look dashing. I don't know whether to call it an invitation or a summons, but I'm determined the Albemarles shouldn't think I'm afraid of them.'

'I'm sure you're not, milady, and you shall look very elegant.' Maggie stepped out on to the landing, hurrying to fetch the hatbox before sharp-eyed Annie Jones 'cleared it away to help Mrs Halls'. His lordship's eyes never left Lady Hester when they were together. He might have fallen in love, but it seemed that the novelty of his new bride had worn off already. Once again, he wasn't yet home when by rights he should have been sitting down to his breakfast. Old habits died hard, that much was clear. It was difficult to see how such a marriage would cause Lady Hester anything other than pain, even with Lady Louisa gone, and the child's bravery was painful to witness.

Maggie paused as she lifted the hatbox from a polished walnut table with those inlaid mother-of-pearl flowers that had always been so awkward to clean in the days when she was just an upper-maid. There was an eerie stillness about the hallway in this part of the house when usually Annie would have been carrying hot water up to Master Kitto's room, and Hoby making his way up the stairs with a carefully pressed pile of cravats for his lordship to crumple and drop on the floor at the least sign of a wrinkle in the wrong place. Where were they all? So doubtless his lordship had come home drunk again, and everyone with any sense had rushed to keep out of his way. Maggie hurried back to Lady Hester's room. His lordship wasn't the kind with wandering hands – at least not among the servants, unlike his father – but she'd rather not be the first to meet him if he was drunk.

'The black lace is perfect,' Hester said. 'You've a talent for this, Maggie – Louisa was right about one thing: you should set up as a milliner.'

John Harewood had sheltered her from the realities of life, that much was clear. 'It would be very difficult, my lady. It would take a great deal of funds to set up alone, the premises—'

Their eyes met as the sudden crack of the front door slamming shut echoed up the stairs. Maggie had known it would only be a matter of time. A drunk was a drunk, and no new bride could cure one as easily as all that. His lordship was coming up the stairs, cursing but steady on his feet.

'Lock us in, Maggie,' Lady Hester said. 'My husband will be mortified if I see him in such an odious condition.'

Maggie knew she hadn't been quick enough. His lordship had gained the top of the stairs and seen her at the door.

'Better luck next time,' he said, and Maggie tried her best not to think of him as a bad man. For one thing, he'd made sure she'd not lost her position when Annie complained about the 'fuss' she made at night, crying out in her dreams. Instead, he'd seen her moved to share a garret with young Betty instead, who'd been the better part deaf since measles swept through the household. He was a good man in his way, his lordship, but he was also now a very drunk man. And now Maggie supposed he would want to rut his wife, who was watching him take off his gloves with a look of blank despair.

'Might I ring for Mr Hoby to assist your lordship?' Maggie said. Anything to get him out of here. His eyes were glassy, not fixing on either of them. One after the other, he dropped the gloves nearly a foot away from the dressing-table where she supposed he meant to leave them.

'What are you suggesting, Maggie? That I'm not able to walk without help? I've walked a very long way in my time, you know. A very long way. The length of Spain and France, and then a little more.' His lordship laughed. His cravat was missing, his shirt unlaced at the throat, revealing those unchristian tattoos that went all over his chest. 'I'm not that drunk, not really. I'll be in the library if my dear wife has nothing to say to me this morning. Bring me some brandy and some spirit of vervain, would you? I find I can't seem to sleep. What the devil is that noise below stairs?'

'I will endeavour to discover the source as soon as possible, milord.' Anything not to be in the room with him and that blank look in his eyes, quite empty of natural feeling as though there were a piece of him missing. There was a bright clash of glass smashing against a tiled floor and his lordship pushed past Maggie on his way out. Following him, she stood at the top of the stairs and watched as Arkwright came into the hall with Master Kitto. Gone the best part of two days, he was filthy, his good cambric shirt mired with the Lord knew what and all for some poor soul in the laundry-room to scrub out.

His lordship leaned against the stair-post, watching them. 'Well?'

'Christ's sake.' Arkwright looked his master up and down like a man at the limit of his patience. Maggie had every sympathy. Being in service was so often just like clearing up after a lot of grubby children. Arkwright turned to Master Kitto. 'Tell him what you've been shopping for.'

His lordship now seemed chillingly sober, although he couldn't be. 'Show me.' He held out one hand, waiting, and Arkwright handed him a packet wrapped in old newspaper. He lifted it, testing the weight, looking down at Master Kitto.

When he spoke, it was in that savage tongue they'd learned from their wet-nurse, so Mrs Halls said. Maggie couldn't make sense of a single word, but the boy flinched at each one. He replied in the same language: a furious, unmannerly stream of what was clearly nothing polite, and Maggie sensed the presence of someone standing behind her. She turned to see Lady Hester watching them, her lips parted in shock. Surely she couldn't understand what they were saying?

'Maggie,' she said briskly. 'I'm going out.'

Maggie couldn't help but notice the tears streaking her face.

51

Kitto backed into the wall as Crow held the newspaper-wrapped package of gunpowder up to his face, pressing it against his mouth and nose; he breathed in stale port and gin, the dry-tinder stink of the gunpowder.

'Gunpowder?' He spoke with the chilling precision of the practised inebriate. 'What the devil do you mean by it? Did what I said to you mean absolutely nothing? And where the fucking hell have you been?'

Kitto had never seen him so angry, nor for a long time so drunk. He didn't care. The words flew from his lips before he had the sense to keep his mouth shut. 'You're quick to judge for a traitorous bastard fucking his own stepmother.' He was so exhilarated by speaking the truth at last that he didn't care who heard or what the consequences might be. Doubtless the servants all knew anyway: they always did. With a swift back-handed blow, Crow sent him stumbling against an ottoman, and a bowl of tulips carelessly left on it shattered against the floor. The pain was dizzying; he heard one of the servants gasp. He tasted blood and surged to his feet; he could handle himself in a fight, he'd be no coward, but Crow was older with the longer reach, and lightning fast even in such a cup-shot state as this. He wrenched Kitto's arm behind his back, forcing him up the stairs, twisting his shoulder so hard that everything went black. Kitto lost his footing, smashing his shins against the brass stair-treads, but Crow didn't seem to notice or care. By the time they reached the top of the stairs, Kitto wished he'd never started it – that Arkwright had never started it – and the next blow caught him so hard across the face that he crashed across the width of the landing, hitting a chair just within the nearest bedchamber. He felt a small, distinct pop deep in one ear and then such harsh bright pain that he cried out. Fear dulled the pain's edge, and Kitto knew that he must run or he'd not get out of the house alive. The ringing in his ear rose to a maddening whistle. Crow was speaking in French again now, firing questions at him. 'Where did you get the gunpowder? Where did you get it?'

Kitto didn't care any more what Crow thought or even what he might do. Wild anger soared through him. 'Why should I tell you anything?' Another blow landed across his face; he tasted blood but couldn't stop. 'I wish Papa had found you dead and rotting on that fucking battlefield. You've no right to order what I do.'

Gripping Kitto's arms, Crow drove him hard back against the wall. Dull pain shot from the base of Kitto's skull down his spine. Winded by fear and anger, he hadn't drawn breath before Crow knocked him down again with another blow. He stumbled against a chair. It scraped across the floor. The agony in his ear was like nothing he'd ever known. He spat blood on to the carpet; it poured from his nose in hot gobbets, shockingly red.

Crow hauled him to his feet, spitting each word into his face: 'Where did you get that fucking gunpowder? Who sold it to you?'

It was harder still to speak, but Kitto knew he had to try and make this stop, because Crow was drunk enough to keep going. 'No more. You're hurting me.'

Crow shoved him against the wall again, speaking in a harsh whisper. 'Damned fucking right I am. Now tell me.'

52

M aggie had witnessed far worse, but it was still a shock to see blood smeared across a knotted-silk hall carpet. The sight of it turned her stomach. The dark, sticky smear of blood awoke memories she must force away: Martinique, so long ago, sun on her back, the despairing quiet of the slave market punctuated by cries as parents were led from children, brothers from sisters. *Don't think about it,* she told herself. *Don't go there.* The boy had quietened but Maggie knew what happened when people were beaten to death: they did go quiet, you heard nothing but the blows, and then they died. If the master hanged for murder then where would they all be? And well he might. He could have been Earl of the Moon for all the French cared. Being born a lord was no longer enough to save a man from the gallows: it was more the other way up, these days. Who would employ a servant last paid by a killer? Without decent employment, Maggie knew that she would either starve or hang for stealing.

A knot of footmen in braided livery and housemaids with dust-smeared aprons had gathered in the downstairs hall around the mess of tulips, broken china and scattered earth,

all staring anxiously up the stairs; Annie Jones was still holding
a brass coal-scuttle. Maggie could only be relieved Lady Hester
had fled just a bare half moment before his lordship struck the
first blow. Before Maggie knew what she was doing she was up
the stairs herself. No one stopped her: not even Mr Mowbray
dared risk drawing his lordship's attention to her. Heart racing,
Maggie hovered by an ewer of water left on the gilt-inlaid
sideboard between Master Kitto's bedchamber and the Blue
Room. She took the ewer in both hands; it was heavy: good
thick china. She gripped the handle, steadying it, the heft of
water. She stood in the doorway, watching now as his lordship
struck the boy such a blow that he stumbled and fell, striking
his head against the polished teak corner of an upholstered
blanket-chest. He lay on the Turkey rug without moving. His
lordship shouted something at him in a language Maggie didn't
recognise. He snatched a handful of the boy's bloodied shirt,
ready to pull him to his feet. Kitto's head lolled to the side, and
Maggie knew that if she was going to act, she had to do it now.
She wasn't about to become the sort of indigent wretch with no
position just because her employer couldn't stomach his claret
and beat his own brother to death.

She dashed the ewer at his lordship, watching with horrified
fascination as the water splashed full across the side of the
head, half unable to believe what she'd just done. He reached
to where his pistol-holster would have been to reassure himself
of the presence of a weapon he didn't have, thank God.

'A child. I killed a fucking child,' he said to her. 'Fuck this
game. Fuck the lot of it.' His lordship pushed past and he left
Maggie quite alone, still holding the empty jug.

53

'Her grace will see you now.' The Duke of Albemarle's butler was a heavyset man with jowls of thick white flesh, and he spoke without looking at Hester. She heard her name announced in a drawing-room with weighty scarlet curtains half drawn across the light, far from the airy beauty of Lamorna House. How could she go back there after what Kitto had said? He'd spoken in Cornish even she didn't fully understand; he'd chosen words no one had ever before uttered in her presence. Even so, their meaning was clear enough. Louisa and Crow. It had been obvious, really, from the start. The way Louisa had spoken his name. *Jack.* She'd owned him. All that time Hester had thought Crow was falling in love with her, just as she was with him – the last fact quite eviscerating now she saw it in the light of truth. She had begun to love him, and now this: he and Louisa, and him knowing what Louisa had done to her.

Hester's eyes adjusted to the light, and she saw her great-aunt again. The Duchess of Albemarle sat in a winged armchair drawn close to a sullen fire, unsmiling. There was no tea-tray on the table. The walls, papered with a pattern of birds, closed in around her: dull red and faded gold, all beaks and grasping claws. It was so dark, and the walls smelled damp as though no one ever opened the windows to freshen the air. One would feel quite shut in. Maggie had drawn her laces too tight this morning, surely, and the gown choked, buttoned up close to her throat. She'd been a fool to obey this summons, and yet it had not been possible to stay at home a moment longer, knowing what she did. But she'd left Kitto to face Crow alone, and Crow in such a condition.

'Step closer, girl. Draw back the curtain so that I can see you.'

Hester obeyed, her skin crawling with anger. *Girl*. Like a servant. Like a slave.

'Come closer.'

She stood before the older woman's chair, not invited to sit. Hester was repulsed; she wanted to step away, but she would show her aunt that she was not afraid.

'I suppose you want to know why I sent for you?'

'I would not presume to ask, madam,' Hester said.

The duchess smiled, acknowledging the hit. 'I've been rather patient. I'm not entirely sure what sort of game Louisa Helford thinks she's playing, but you may have noticed my son has daughters of his own out this Season. Did it ever cross your mind that your presence in London might injure their chances of contracting suitable alliances?'

Hester felt rage soar through her; she would not show it, she was above this woman. 'I'm afraid I don't see how your granddaughters' come-out relates to me at all. Of course, you know of my marriage, but I'm not out myself; I'm in mourning for my father, your grace.'

'Ah, your father. Did you ever wonder why he kept you so long on that island?' the duchess went on. 'Captain John Harewood appeared to have enough native intelligence to understand that a girl like you has no place whatsoever parading herself in a civilised drawing-room. It's a pity Lord Lamorna and Louisa don't have the wit to see matters how they really are. Now go back home to Cornwall before I find a way to make sure that you are never able to show your face in London again. That husband of yours won't be able to protect you forever, you know. He'll soon see that he's made a mistake – he'll find a way to get rid of you. He's a Lamorna, dear – they soon lose interest in their wives.'

'Just as your husband lost interest in his own brother's child?' Hester asked lightly. 'I must admit, I don't blame Mama for wanting to arrange a marriage by any possible means. It can't have been particularly enjoyable, spending her whole life at a boarding school and knowing she was to be a governess, penniless and quite friendless, with the rest of you all living here in such elegant splendour.' She turned and walked out without waiting for the butler, and without caring what ruin her great-aunt might choose to make of her reputation. Crow had loved Louisa. Perhaps he still did. Perhaps he went from bed to bed, pleasing himself where he saw fit. None of it mattered.

54

Hester leaned back against the brocade upholstery in the carriage, suppressing the need to quietly curse. In Arkwright's place, Jim drove with terrified care, taking each corner so slowly that she wanted to scream, even as she came to the desolate realisation that she had no particular desire to go home. Crow had betrayed her. In his world, she'd become an outsider to be stared and sneered at, shielded only by the force of his presence and what she had begun to wonder might even be his love. And all the time he'd been with Louisa. Tears sprang to her eyes: she longed to go home, to run through the sea-grass on the dunes behind Popplestone Porth and watch the sun set across the Atlantic. She would have given anything to simply walk from Castle Bryher and down through the town on some tedious errand to collect a basket of strawberries or a tea-cloth-wrapped parcel of fresh butter and eggs from the farm. No one she passed would have whispered behind their hands, far less humiliated and betrayed her. But she was Miss Hester of Castle Bryher no longer, and she could never go home. She was the Countess of Lamorna, destined to be an exotic curiosity for the rest of her life, with only a faithless drunk for a husband. She wondered again how Arkwright could have been so stupid as to turn Kitto into Crow's hands with such appalling timing. Surely they knew each other well enough for Arkwright to guess what might happen? Who could have deliberately chosen to unleash a scene like that on a Tuesday morning, in such a public part of the house? When the carriage rolled into Berkeley Square, Hester pushed up the window and leaned out, tapping on the roof to get Jim's attention. He reined in, alarmed.

'Set me down in the mews, if you please, Jim. I should like to speak to Mr Arkwright.'

'But he's gone, milady. He went off first thing – he'd not have let me drive you, otherwise, save he wasn't on an errand for his lordship that couldn't wait, he said.'

Uneasy, Hester thanked him and took her seat, pushing up the window and locking it with the brass catch. She had seen enough of Crow and Arkwright to sense a peculiar bond between them that went beyond that of master and servant. Some deep-down instinct told her that Arkwright was the only man alive to whom Crow might actually listen, if he chose to speak up. And he'd gone. Jim halted the carriage outside the front door; she listened to the wheel-bearings creak as he climbed down from the box to let her out, his forehead beaded with perspiration.

'You did very well,' she said as he handed her out and down the step. 'I'm very sorry to have put you to the trouble, with Mr Arkwright away.' She added casually, 'Have you any notion when he might be back?'

Jim smiled with relief, but he still looked hag-ridden. 'No, milady – I'm sorry. He only said it was an errand for his lordship, and he might be from home till Saturday at the least.'

Mowbray was oddly subdued as he let her in the front door. 'Lady Lamorna sends her compliments,' he said. 'She had the goodness to desire me to pass on her apologies, your ladyship, but Lord Burford could not be brought upon to wait until you had got back, being so desirous of completing a good few stages before nightfall. They are travelling with his elderly mother, you see.'

'Of course,' Hester said lightly. 'Wales is a long way distant, I perceive. They will want to be well on their way, I should think.'

She stood at Mowbray's side in the entrance hall, seeing it as if for the first time: the polished floor, the bright rugs, the deep soft shade of blue on the walls. A pewter dish of early peonies sent as a gift from Lady Sefton's hothouse sat on the hall table, and each pale globe seemed to emit its own light. A strange sense of peace had settled over the house, as though even the walls had let out a long-held breath. What had happened after she ran out to the carriage, her eyesight blurring with tears? Crow had been so very angry. Afraid for Kitto, she ran upstairs and found his bedchamber door wide open. A young maid was on her knees scrubbing the carpet; she gasped and started as Hester came in.

'Annie' – Hester forced herself to sound calm – 'where is Master Kitto?'

Annie tucked a strand of pale brown hair behind her ear. Her lips moved convulsively. 'I don't know, milady. No one does.'

'What did my husband do?' Hester stared at the faded Indian rug, age-dimmed greenish yellow vines and dusk-pink flowers, marred by a streak of dark, reddish brown. 'Is that blood?' Papa had never laid a hand on her, nor commanded anyone else to do so. Boys and even girls were beaten sometimes, she knew, but could Crow really do such a thing? 'Where is my husband, Annie? Tell me where he is, if you please. I would speak to him.'

Annie clutched her cloth. 'He's gone, your ladyship.'

Light-headed, Hester took hold of the bed-post. The covers were still smooth, just as Annie or one of the other maids had left them: the bed had not been slept in. Surely she was going to be sick. 'He left with Master Kitto?'

'No, milady. His lordship gave orders that Master Kitto was to be locked in here, and then he went away with Mr Arkwright—'

'Locked in? How amazingly medieval, after all.' Hester sat on the bed. 'I suppose Master Kitto got out of the window? It only needed that.'

Annie got to her feet, eyeing Hester warily. 'Mr Mowbray himself locked the door. It was an order from his lordship direct, if you take my meaning. But Mrs Halls was ever so afraid about the – the carpet, milady, and when Master Kitto didn't come out for his breakfast, Mr Mowbray opened the door himself, and found the window was open, yes—'

'Where did he go?' Briefly, Hester shut her eyes, acting on a childish hope that she might open them to find Kitto and Crow reconciled downstairs, and Kitto's accusation about Crow and Louisa nothing more than a terrible mistake. It wasn't a mistake, though. She was sure of that: it explained Louisa's hatred, when once she had been merely patronising.

'Faversham, milady. To the master's house there, Oakhurst – it's where I grew up, milady, so I remembered when Mr Mowbray chanced to mention it. If you don't mind me saying, milady, but you don't look well. Ought I fetch Maggie to you?'

With some effort, Hester got to her feet. 'No, thank you. I shall be better directly. I am only a little tired.'

Drawn like a moth to a lamp, she went to the library and found the door unlocked. She stood at the sideboard, running her fingertips over the drift of unopened letters; most were still folded and sealed with nubbins of red wax. Crow's father's steward had died the winter before Waterloo, hadn't he?

The old earl had clearly neither replaced the man before leaving for that feverish, ill-fated season in Brussels himself nor attempted any of his duties; he hadn't known he was going to die within weeks of landing in England again, succumbing to a fever contracted as he searched the battlefield for Crow's body. *A girl like you has no place in a civilised drawing-room.* Hester's aunt's words echoed in her mind, and she couldn't forget a single one. What if she bore Crow a child? What then? Her own child would be condemned to the same unkind jibes and sidelong, expressive glances she'd been shielded from for so long on Bryher.

Hester glanced down at the letters. What was it about this place that was so secret, so forbidden? What else did her husband have to hide? To read Crow's father's correspondence was wrong, quite wrong, despite all that Crow had done to betray her, surely? Hester watched her own hands sorting through the untouched heap of letters, picking them up, setting them down, and realised she did not care that it was wrong. Some of the letters were clearly unread, still sealed. There were missives to Crow's father from old lovers – 'my darling Mark' – unpaid bills from jewellers, milliners and glove-makers, and even a letter from the Dean at Eton, giving notice of Kitto's expulsion, in January 1815, for repeated but unspecified crimes of insubordination. That explained why he'd been with his family in Brussels before Waterloo: she had sometimes wondered. There was nothing, though, to suggest why Crow might lock the room. A quarter of an hour had passed before she spotted another familiar name showing through a still-folded sheet of cheap paper: 'Arkwright'. On the morning she'd brought Crow the narcissi, Arkwright had looked up at the window with that shocking, unguarded hatred, violent as a sudden slap. The letter was still sealed, the red smear of wax intact. Making love to another woman was no worse a turn

than most men served their wives. She'd been a fool not to
expect it, that was all. A fool to be so disappointed, to feel so
ashamed and so stupid. Hester opened the letter and forgot
about Crow entirely. It was written in a fair, well-practised
hand, but evidently in some haste, the last few lines smudged.

My Lord, Forgive my humble station; I am your tenant and write
to beg clemency for a family in my Parish of Scarsdale, a Mother
and Child in such piteous Distress that it could hardly fail to move
one. The Father, one J. Arkwright, being away presently engaged
with our army in the Peninsula, has it seems no knowledge of
the Distressful situation that has befallen his Dependants. The
Mother, falling ill, was dismissed from her position as kitchen-
maid by your tenant Mr Hexham, and in consequence fell into
such a pitiably destitute state – made worse by the appalling
harvest and the inflated price of wheat – that her Child stole
bread. The magistrate, Mr Hexham himself, also your tenant,
in taking a Stand, has sentenced the boy to be hanged, which
seems to me to be quite without mercy, given that the child is
not quite Seven years old, his birth being recorded by myself in
the Parish Register. I have been informed by another servant,
who did not wish to be named, that Mrs Arkwright had refused
Mr Hexham's Advances. The Capital sentence is to be carried
out on Friday, and I beg Your Honour will write to Mr Hexham
and see if this cruel and vindictive course of action might not be
altered by your Influence.

Hester let the folded paper drop to the sideboard. The letter
was dated 1812: it had been read five years too late. Arkwright's
son had surely been hanged by a vengeful magistrate for stealing
a loaf of bread. A little boy of seven. Who, then, could blame
Arkwright for that look of hatred? Crow's father had done
nothing to help. He hadn't even bothered to open or read the

letter, and now Arkwright's child was dead. The hatred made sense, at least, but Arkwright had such a sure touch with horses and even in a Season so thin of company London swarmed with tonnish families who had come for the assemblies and the opera: why must Arkwright remain with Crow after the Lamornas had contributed to the death of his child? Hester traced one finger over the letter, written on such thin paper, and in such desperation. Why was Arkwright still here? Why was he with Crow every day? It made no sense until she considered that it had been Arkwright who brought Kitto to Crow that morning, he'd been in some way responsible for the dreadful scene that erupted. A boy of seven, taken from his mother and hanged: tears gathered in her eyes and she pushed them away with the heel of her hand as a light knock sounded at the door. What exactly had Arkwright intended when he lit up that furious row between Crow and Kitto?

'Come in.' She didn't care if the servants whispered to Crow that she'd been in his library; it was her right to come here.

Maggie closed the door behind her. 'A letter came for you this morning, milady.'

Catlin, at last. It had to be. Who else would write to her? Hester took it, her hands shaking as she looked down at Catlin's careful script. 'Miss H Harewood, Lamorna House'. Catlin was still alive, or had been when the letter was posted. A week ago? Two? She'd know that neat, looping hand any-where, learned at her side in the little island schoolroom set up in the nave of All Saints Church. Hester looked up at the quiet click as Maggie closed the door after her, leaving her alone once more. For a moment, Catlin's letter made no sense: just a list of numbers, written in Cornish. She'd used the cipher. *Eth. Seyth.* And then Hester could smell rotting seaweed at low water, hear the rush of the sea, hundreds of tiny pebbles scuttling in the tide-break. At the back of her mind she saw Catlin running away from her up the gorse-studded dunes behind the beach at Popplestones, red hair streaming in the wind, thick woollen skirts tossing and tangling about her legs. *Keep up, Hester! War hast!* She pulled open the desk drawer, searching for a slate, for paper, but found nothing save an old travellers' waybill for the journey from Bath to London. The writing desk yielded a blunt pen and an inkstand still with a slick of black ink in the bottom. Hester wrote on the back of the waybill, pausing as she sifted through thirteen years of memory – recipes for an acne poultice of strawberry leaves and crushed hard-boiled eggs, Papa's face as he lay dying, Cousin Jane threading a needle, a clutch of white shells at the bottom of a rock pool. By the time Hester had finished, the light had faded and she could barely see the scribbled mess before her. *The Duke of Wellington requests that the Earl of Lamorna frees him from the island of Bryher. The French garrison stationed here will be in no position to present an obstacle.*

Hester sat at the desk in a state of shock. Crow was still a soldier: he had been Wellington's intelligence officer. Clearly, he still was. Possibilities blossomed: if Crow freed his commander, Wellington was three weeks' sail from General Allanby and the rest of the British army stranded in the Americas. The Iron Duke would have his redcoats once more, and when he did, there existed the smallest possibility of victory against the French, nothing more than a breath of hope, but hope of freedom all the same. And yet freedom from the Buonapartes could only come at a price. She remembered Papa's blood spreading in a dark pool across the stillroom floor: if there was to be war again, men, women and children would die so in their homes. Hester became aware of a queer rustling, like leaves shaken in the wind, and looked down to see that she had crumpled Catlin's letter in her hand.

Crow had betrayed her. Like a fool she'd given up her own

freedom to marry him, all for the sake of her honour, all to avoid shame: she wanted nothing but the certainty that she would never need to see him again, that she wouldn't have to look at his face knowing he had been lying with Louisa whenever he was not with her, his hands in her hair, the tip of his finger tracing a line down Louisa's naked back instead of her own. And yet now she had no choice but to find him. To trust him. If Crow was still in the employ of the Duke of Wellington, surely Faversham was the last place he'd have gone to? Surely he would conceal his true whereabouts? Her only chance of finding him rested on what was doubtless a lie.

55

A thick, damp fog had descended, and Catlin could smell the turning of the tide. 'This way, your grace.' Silent, Wellington followed her without so much as a quickened breath even though his boots must be sinking into the sand just as her own shoes were. He was stronger than he looked and, in truth, Wellington didn't look like much at all, just an ordinary man in his plain blue coat. She led him through the dunes, across the heathery sweep of moorland, and up the gorse-studded flank of Watch Hill, sand-grass swaying in the wind.

'The wind's getting up already.' Had he crossed the channel to Trescaw safely, that amber-eyed boy? *By the time he gets to France, or to England, his grace will be long gone.* It couldn't do any harm, surely, to have saved a life? Wellington reached out to steady her, one strong hand a light touch beneath her elbow, as though she were a lady. He raised the captain's spyglass, letting it travel across the misty skyline, across the waters of the New Grimsby Sound, now flooded once more with glossy ocean overhung with low cloud, then turning south-west to look out down the South-Western Approaches, across the hump of Samson Hill and beyond.

'There's very little shipping now, I take it.'

He'd been watching the ocean from Castle Bryher. Watching all the time. 'No, my lord. The French have come down with great severity on the free-traders, more so than even the English, and with the blockade we see no English or Cornish boats out here. We were safe here on Bryher, employed by Captain Harewood, but the rest of Scilly has taken it very difficult. I'm sorry to say that the free trade fed the Scillies, sir. Now they can barely feed themselves on the other islands. There was four families on Samson till last year and two on Tean – they all went to the mainland before Christmas save the Tean-Garretts, and they'll not last much longer, I believe. No, I should be surprised if we saw any ships, my lord.'

Wellington nodded, turning back to face the castle as it guarded New Grimsby Sound from any ocean-going vessels with wicked intent. 'Well then, what is that?'

Catlin turned to follow his line of sight. A ship, emerging from the fog. He was right. She could make out the topmasts of a frigate, the dark bulk of the hull. No English or Cornish craft that size was allowed beyond the blockade.

'It could be Dutch privateers again,' Catlin said. 'If everyone knows the captain's dead, it really could be. We used to have a terrible lot of trouble with them – it was why the navy stationed the captain here, I believe.' But even as she spoke, she knew Ney's final letter had reached its target after all, and the French had sent replacement troops.

'Well,' Wellington said, as if she wasn't there at all, 'so high a price to pay for our success. Don't be afraid, Mrs Rescorla. I'll give myself up to them before any more of your people are harmed.'

'Don't be a fool, sir. If Ney told them what I did, do you really think they'll let any of us live?' Wellington was doubtless not often called a fool, and never by his servants. Catlin caught her breath. 'Your grace,' she went on, 'the French must not even land, they mustn't set foot on island soil. If they do, we're all lost. It'll all have been for nothing.'

Wellington sighed. 'And how do you propose to stop them, Mrs Rescorla? It's a simple matter of sailing up the channel. If food is so short on the other islands, can we even depend on the fact that none will send a pilot out to the French to guide them in?'

Was she really about to say this? It was wicked, but she was already a killer. She was already going to hell. Perhaps those French soldiers on that frigate had earned themselves a drowning. 'No one's done it for years, sir. It's more a story than anything else. But my grandfather used to say that before Captain Harewood fortified Castle Bryher, we used to kindle false lights when things were hard. He said that in lean years when the cattle had no milk a wreck was the difference between living and dying.'

'That much hasn't changed, I dare say,' Wellington said, and Catlin knew he was going to do exactly as she wanted.

56

Maggie adjusted the row of plain buttons that fastened Lady Hester's cloak. 'Milady, you ought not to go by yourself. I'll come with you.' She spoke in a low voice – even in her mistress's bedroom they might be overheard. No one in this house could be trusted.

Lady Hester smoothed the fabric of the breeches over her thighs. It was indecent to Maggie's mind, but dressed as a man, she'd certainly be safer. 'I'm married, Maggie, I don't need a chaperone any more.' There was a queer, hysterical edge to her voice that Maggie didn't like overmuch, not that there was a great deal she could do about it.

'It's not that, milady – there were more riots along Cheapside last night. There's been forty guillotined at Newgate just since last week, and there's a very ugly temper to the streets. London was never a place for a woman alone and now it's even worse. Let me attend you, please.' *You silly girl.* What on earth was she playing at?

It was as if she hadn't even spoken. 'Pass me that bag, Maggie.'

'You ought to leave this house, milady. It's not safe here. But not alone. Not like this.'

Lady Hester looked up then, all swift and sharp. 'What do you mean?'

What harm could it do to tell her the truth now that Mr Arkwright had gone off with his lordship? There would be French soldiers in this house before long, Maggie was certain. 'It's milord's groom,' she said. 'The one that went for a soldier – Mr Arkwright. He's a revolutionary, ma'am – a Spencean. Him and that Mr Castle who come here. They want to bring down the likes of your husband. There's going to be trouble, I'm sure.'

'I might ask how you know all this, but I don't believe there's time. I'm not the only one who must leave.' Lady Hester pushed open the clasp, drawing out a thick roll of banknotes tied with a length of white satin ribbon. The ribbon alone was worth at least a penny and, as for the rest, Maggie had never seen so much money. The sight of it was strangely appalling: it was enough for any decent person to live on with a bit of neat economy for the rest of their life. 'Take it, Maggie. It's yours.'

'What do you mean, ma'am?' Was this some sort of cruel joke?

Lady Hester waited as Maggie bound up her hair in a length of worn-out linen. 'Listen: you can't stay here either. It's too dangerous. I'm going to find my husband, and then I'm going home to Bryher. Take the money and leave London. Take the mail-coach to Norfolk or Lincoln or anywhere a reasonable distance from a French garrison.'

It was clear she meant it, however unbelievable it all seemed. 'But—'

'Set yourself up as a milliner: half the squires' wives in any county from one end of England to the other will want your hats once they learn Lady Louisa wore them. There's a letter of recommendation folded up with the money: no one is to know which Lady Lamorna wrote it, after all. I understand if you're afraid but you must leave, and so should the rest of the staff if they've any sense. Please just take me at my word and go.'

Maggie's fingers closed around the roll of banknotes, soft and yielding to the pressure of her fingers. 'I'm not afraid, milady.'

'Good. Now be careful.'

Maggie stood holding the money, unable to move or to speak, scarcely able to believe what had just happened or to allow herself to fully comprehend the weight of notes she clutched. It wasn't until she heard the quiet click of the bedroom door that Maggie realised that John Harewood's child had gone, and that she would probably never see her again.

PART THREE

57

Just a few hours later Hester rode across Tower Bridge, trying to suppress panic as she breathed in the stink of the Thames at low tide: greenish-brown, pock-marked mudflats had been revealed by the retreating water, and from her vantage point she saw small figures toiling along the shore: mudlarks hunting for glass bottles, old shoe buckles, even buttons – anything that might be teased from the muck and bartered or sold. Watching the ant-like intensity of their labour Hester felt naked and unprotected, a long way from the questionable safety of Lamorna House. With no one to guard her safety and only a roll of banknotes in her saddlebag, she was a single robbery away from being reduced to the same sort of desperation. *Good girl, Mawgan.* She leaned forward and patted the mare's neck. Mawgan seemed to understand that she was not in the hands of a horsewoman and followed her clumsy direction with such kind patience that Hester had to force herself not to think of Crow choosing her. *She'll suit you*, he'd said, making no mention of her lack of expertise. But she must not think of Crow any more. Dressed in the servants' clothes Maggie had taken from the washroom on her orders, she was someone new again. The breeches clung to her thighs: she felt both powerful and horrendously exposed. She was not just a girl cringing in a black gown in an overheated drawing-room, but a person who would demand a price for the death of her father. 'Good girl, Gil.' She clicked her tongue behind her teeth as Kitto, Crow and Arkwright had done on their long journey north, relieved when the Dalmatian came to wait at her side. Gil had followed despite her objections, pacing quietly at Mawgan's side, oblivious to all attempts to shoo her away, even to the missile thrown in her direction on Long Acre. After the undignified business of dismounting, muddying one stocking and retrieving her boot, Hester had admitted defeat and reluctantly accepted the Dalmatian's escort. She was glad of it now.

'Which way now, Gil?' Hester reined in as they clattered from the bridge on to cobbles. 'It's the most ridiculous thing in the world – all I can say is that I know Kent is more or less southeast of London, and Faversham is somewhere on the coast. Hardly the most precise directions.' The streets were eerily empty, but the thought of asking for assistance was almost as terrifying as the prospect of getting lost, never finding Crow, and never delivering Catlin's message. She had to find him: there was no choice in the matter, but how could she risk admitting to a starving local that she was without friends, without help of any kind? 'Gil!' Hester called out as the Dalmatian trotted on ahead, plunging with such unswerving certainty into the tangle of narrow, filth-strewn alleyways that Hester had no choice but to follow, with the slow, delightful realisation that Gil had run alongside the Lamorna carriage so many times that these streets were no mystery to her, at least: she knew the way.

London left behind at last, the village of Blackheath gave way to higher ground: rolling heathland and stunted, wind-tossed trees. Gil curled up on a pale tussock of grass and Mawgan's flanks heaved, damp with sweat. Hester turned to look back at the city, knowing Kitto was lost in the vast tangle of streets and alleyways. And yet what choice did she have but to leave without knowing where he was? Wellington had summoned Crow. She'd come this far, and she must go on. She'd ridden out of London, alone. She'd followed a carriage-dog and reached the south-eastern reaches of the great city, alone. She'd done it all by herself. Crow would answer to her yet. Hester touched Mawgan's flanks with her heels and the mare moved off on the instant. She was acting on the instructions of the Duke of Wellington himself. *Send Lamorna.* She might avenge her father's death, and even if Crow had something to say about his wife riding around the country quite alone, she had plenty for him to hear. Dressed like a down-at-heel undergroom with no livery, she was ten a penny – just someone's servant. Mawgan stirred beneath her, restless. She couldn't stay on the fringes of London forever. She glanced at Gil, half expecting her to run off, but the dog stayed at her side, as if Gil knew she was only waiting. Hester clicked her tongue behind her teeth again, and Gil moved on at Mawgan's side. Hester spoke aloud, hoping that doing so might banish a little of her fear. 'Come on, then. At least one of us knows where she's going.'

58

Kitto sat in the corner of the Carlisle tavern, half an inch of warm ale still in the bottom of a tankard tainted with a tang of raw onion. Whitechapel was quiet at this time. So close to the curfew, no one had any desire to draw the attention of the night-guard. He needed more gunpowder. All he could do was pray Mr Castle would turn up again. He'd worry about the fact he couldn't pay when the time came. A trail of blood ran from one ear. The pain was astonishing – a deep, aching throb. The constant ringing in his head never went away and had cheated him of the few hours' sleep he'd tried to snatch, that and the shameful memory of tears. He'd thought the blows would never stop coming, across his face again and again until that queer popping sensation burst inside his right ear. Even after a day, he needed gin or rum to dull the pain but there was no coin for it. He was never going home. The only way he could feed himself now was to work or steal if that failed. He had nothing. His ear hurt so much that it was hard to think; Crow had taken away the gunpowder, so how could he now take revenge against the French, unless he got more?

He would show Crow that the Helfords of Lamorna were not cowards. He would blow Carlton House and the Empress Joséphine to the sky till it rained broken bodies. He would make them all pay. He'd just have to wait till Castle showed up again.

A hand clamped down on Kitto's shoulder and he jumped, breath seizing in his chest as he turned to face a thin-faced man in a dirty apron: a landlord grown sick of him loitering without spending. He'd heard nothing as the man approached. Were his ears ruined for good? When the landlord spoke, he didn't look unkind, but every word sounded muffled, as if Kitto were listening from another room. 'I've paying customers wanting seats. You've been here long enough, lad.'

Kitto turned to face him. 'Please, I can't go back—' His own voice sounded unrecognisable. Fear lanced through him. He could hardly hear through the agony in his ear.

'Run away from a bad master, is it? You'll solve nothing sitting by my fire. Go back home and get the beating over with is my advice – it'll soon be all forgotten.'

'I can't.'

The landlord sighed, turning to face the woman behind the bar; she was watching them, spooning pickled eggs from a barrel into a dish. 'Poor lad, looks like he's already had a go-about. He's hurt,' she said. 'You know what some of the masters are like – what about that lad killed at the tannery last month? Nothing was even done about it. The last bells will go soon – he'll be picked up by the bloody French. Where do you live, love? Where's your family?'

Kitto swallowed a burst of dizzying nausea. It wasn't safe here. They were asking too many questions. He couldn't be taken home. He couldn't see Crow ever again. He got up, pushing back the bench, but the door to the street swung open just as he was ready to run. Had Crow found him? Kitto felt light-headed and sick. The only thing worse than seeing his brother again would be facing him in a public place.

'I'm quite all right,' he said to the tavern-maid, her face a blur. 'I was waiting for someone. Thank you, but I must go.'

'Listen to him, he's no apprentice. He's Quality,' the landlord said. 'Get that door shut, Bess – there might be coin in this for us.'

Kitto ran for the door but the person who had just come in stepped across his path. Castle. He looked Kitto up and down. 'Well then, just the lad I've been looking for.' He turned to the landlord. 'A half of blue ruin for me and one for the boy – no need to take your time.'

Kitto had nowhere else to go, and gin might make the pain easier to bear. He sat down at the nearest table, staring down at the woodgrain as Castle went off to piss. He looked up only when Bess laid the two tin jugs before him.

'You want to steer clear of his like.' Bess spoke quietly. 'Your kind ought not to be mixed up in Mr Castle's business, understand?'

Kitto ignored her. What did she know? She was just a tavern-maid. Shaking her head, she went off, weaving between the customers jockeying for space at the bar. Castle sat down opposite Kitto and sipped his gin. 'Thought I might be hearing good news by now, lad, about the French. Lost your nerve? Easy enough to do, especially for a rich boy like you.'

'Someone turned me in to my brother. You know who he is, don't you? He took the gunpowder. I've no money for more. Not yet.' In truth, Kitto had no idea where to go now, or what to do. There wasn't a place he could call home, and there was no one he'd still call family save perhaps Hester, and she could do nothing to help him. 'Give me more gunpowder, and I'll finish the job.'

Castle smiled. 'Gunpowder costs, and I'm willing to bet you

can't pay. You seem a bright lad. If you really want to give the lovely Empress Joséphine something to think about, I might be of a mind to help – and it won't cost you a penny.'

Ten minutes later, Kitto stood outside the tavern holding a strike-a-light wrapped in oilcloth.

59

It was safer to work without a lamp, to allow his eyes to get used to the darkness deep in the bowels of Carlton House, just as he'd done in the French garrison at Newlyn. Kitto crouched in the silent passageway, waiting for the footman's steps to fade into silence. Papa used to come here all the time, drinking claret and champagne in the gilded state-rooms where once the regent had entertained at a supper-party with mechanical boats plying a river engineered to flow along the middle of the table. But that was long ago, before the French came. If only he could step out into the state-rooms now occupied by Jérôme Buonaparte and his retinue and find Papa there with the regent and all their friends, just playing billiards in a gilded drawing-room. *What are you doing here, old chap?* Papa would say, but he wouldn't be angry. He never was. Only with Crow.

'What are you doing?'

Kitto froze. A girl's voice. Slow, careful, he stood. She was no older than him, fourteen at the most, dark curls escaping from her white cap, a slow smile as she looked him up and down. Despite everything, his face grew hot. He took a step backwards. She was holding a chamber pot.

'Are you the new boy?' Her southern accent was strong, but he knew enough French to understand her. 'Her upstairs likes all the pretty ones, you know. She'll have you in her bed before long if you don't watch out.'

He nodded.

'Haven't you got your uniform yet? You ought to see Monsieur Denouille as soon as you can. She's awfully particular about that. She'll have you whipped.' The girl leaned closer, her lips curving into a smile, her eyes bright with laughter. 'But you know what they say? She likes that, too.'

Kitto nodded, not daring to step away. 'They sent me for coal.'

The girl wrinkled her nose. She seemed not to notice his own accent, which wasn't much short of a miracle. 'At this time of day? All the scuttles are meant to be filled before anyone rises. Why've you got nothing to carry it in, then?'

He shrugged, as if to ask how he was meant to account for the peculiarities of the upper servants. 'I forgot.'

She sighed. 'Down the hall, on the left. Monsieur Jacques always leaves a few buckets by the door as you go in. Mind how you go, beautiful.'

Breathing hard, he watched her walk off down the dim, candlelit corridor, her hips swaying beneath heavy woollen skirts. Close, very close. He had so little time. No part of Carlton House was deserted for long, the warren of whitewashed servants' passages streamed with footmen and chamber-maids carrying piles of folded sheets, chamber pots, trays of covered pewter dishes. He'd be caught if he wasn't quick. In the back of his mind he saw Roza, and he saw Nessa and Mr Gwyn, the three of them swinging from the chestnut tree at Nansmornow. Led by the scent of the coal-dust, Kitto pushed open the door that led to the coal-cellar. He closed his fingers around the strike-a-light in his pocket, half choked with sulphur-scented black dust. They would burn. They would all burn.

*

Kitto crouched at the foothills of the coal-heap, fighting the urge to cough sulphuric dust from his lungs. He drew the roll of touchpaper from his pocket, unrolled the oilcloth wrapping and tipped the flint into the palm of one hand as he reached for his knife. Pain pulsed in his ear, through his head; all he could hear was an odd, reedy whistling like wind rushing around the casements at Nansmornow when a storm blew in from the Atlantic. His fingers shook as he crumpled the touchpaper. The French had to go. The Helfords of Lamorna were not cowards. If Crow would do nothing, then he must. He couldn't turn back now. Kitto struck the flint against the blade of his knife, spilling a pile of crimson sparks on to the touchpaper. The coal-dust surrounding it began to smoke, to sizzle. He laid kindling over the sparks. The sparks grew into small, licking flames. The flames were hungry; the fire grew. Smoke would plume from windows; the fire would eat everything in its path. Backing towards the door, he pictured the maidservant with that chamber pot and her laughing eyes dark with terror as she ran from a starving blaze. *God forgive me, God forgive me—* And just as Kitto reached the door of the coal-cellar at Carlton House, backing away from the flames he had made, he felt a hand on his shoulder and turned to face three blue-jacketed French soldiers.

'What do you think you're doing?'

'It's bloody clear as day what he's doing. On his way to the coal-cellar, she said. No livery. Your luck's just run out, you murderous little bastard.'

The moment Kitto knew he had to run – that he would die if he didn't run – it was already too late.

60

Catlin wrapped Aunt Evans's old cloak tighter around her shoulders: the darkness felt so final, somehow, on nights when there was no moon on the rise. The wind was always vicious up on Samson Hill and that afternoon it had risen in the south: there would be twenty-foot waves slapping across the scattered rocks needling Samson Flats. Two flashes of light every few moments coming from South Hill on Samson: that's what the French would be looking for, charting safe passage up St Mary's Roads. Thanks to Jacca Garrett, rowing in sweaty haste across the channel before sundown, there would be no light lit on Samson tonight. Everyone on Bryher still left alive had gathered to watch as Uncle Evans passed John Garrett a faggot of oil-soaked rag, blue with young flames as he lit the lantern. Catlin was seized with terror. It was her fault. She was the one who had suggested poison. Her own wickedness and murder had led Ney to write to the mainland for more men. If she'd let well enough alone there wouldn't be a French ship at all. There was simply nowhere to run, only the small islands of Samson and Tean and all the wide Atlantic at their backs – they couldn't all flood to the Tean-Garrett farmhouse and bring the ire of the French down on old Thomas and his family. This must succeed. They could not fail, not now.

'What'll we do if it doesn't work, your grace?' It cost Catlin some effort to keep her voice steady. 'There must be I don't know how many soldiers on a ship that size.'

At her side, Wellington watched across the channel, unmoving. 'It'll work, Mrs Rescorla.'

'But what if it doesn't and the French come anyway? We'll all be killed and it's my fault.'

'Think like a general, not a housekeeper. If the French come to Bryher, we'll fight them, that's all. Your captain commanded a fine fortress, you know.' And the way he spoke made it sound almost as though no more than twenty men and boys and a scattering of women really could hold back an attack of the victorious French army, and for the first time Catlin could see why men had always followed him as they had, even when there seemed no hope at all.

She felt a rush of heat and Uncle Evans stood back from the lantern, drawing back the shutter, and Catlin imagined a French sailor spotting a little point of light across the water, his relief at finding safe guidance, believing this false light to be the guide that should have been burning on Samson. Uncle Evans spat on the windblown grass, laying one hand on Catlin's shoulder. 'Don't look so meek, girl. We've lit these to save the island, from starvation or from French soldiers scrapping with the bloody English. What difference does it make? We go on, that's all that matters.'

The false lights of Bryher burned again, and Catlin could only pray that no more French soldiers would follow.

It was a bad night but Captain Georges Phillippe had seen the *Soigné* and her crew all safely through it. He glanced at the timepiece on his desk, counting the pin-prick-sized flashes of light just visible across the water. Yes, that was it: two flashes. Those were the guiding lights he'd been told to watch for, and with this wind they'd be anchored in less than half an hour and he'd be on the outside of some decent brandy. They'd signal for a pilot in the morning. Georges glanced again at the chart spread out on the table, and then went to the half-doors giving out on to the afterdeck. Shouldn't those lights be further to the north-east? It was cold anyway – a freezing fog – but even so Georges's own skin seemed to freeze as he realised that his trust in a flickering light only just discernible in the fog had been mistaken. He'd been drawn in by another light, drawn far too close to land which his charts told him was knifed through with sharp outcrops of rock notorious for claiming the lives of more seamen than Georges chose to count. The grating thunder of a tarred timber hull as it shattered to matchsticks against unforgiving rock was not entirely unexpected. Captain Georges Philippe had wrecked his last command.

61

Gil stopped at the crossroads, waiting in the mud. Puddles gathered in the cart-ruts, red-gold in the late sunlight. 'No, Gil. It's another ten miles to Faversham.' Hester ached with cold and her belly clenched with hunger, the last of the bread from the bundle Maggie had given her was now long gone. Gil only watched her, one brown eye, one blue, not moving. 'Come on, you silly stubborn oaf.' She had trotted at Hester's side all day – for thirty miles at least – and she had slept last night curled in the nook between Hester's belly and her knees, horse, dog and woman huddled together for warmth as wind shifted the dark branches above, wet from the damp leaf mould sopping her clothes. Gil was loyal, but she was also infuriatingly stubborn.

'This way.' With her knees, Hester steered the mare left. Faversham in ten miles. She dreaded enquiring there for Crow – he was the last person she wanted to see but find him she must. Gil would just have to follow, as she'd done for two days and a night, trusting and unstoppable. She couldn't be delayed now by a dog. 'We're not going into the forest, Gil, that's the wrong way. Come on—' And the red-gold sky broke open, hammered by an explosion that jerked Hester so far forward in the saddle

348

that she snatched at the pommel, breathless. Mawgan reared and screamed, Gil howled, and a column of slate-grey smoke filled the sky. But Gil didn't turn and run away, she hurled herself towards the thickening trees, a mass of black-spotted fury and strength, and Hester followed her. Hoofbeats cracked across the gathering night, iron-shod, and in that moment Hester knew that the riders were behind her, not ahead.

I'm not afraid, I'm not. Hester shivered as the trees closed around her; the air was thick and hot and smoke filled her lungs. Gil stopped and went still, lying down on the forest floor, last autumn's dead leaves dark against her pale, dappled bulk. The thundering of hoofbeats behind her grew louder and, turning, she glimpsed blue jackets in the smoky twilit gloom between the trees. French troops on the hunt. She was trapped: caught between stalkers and their prey. Musket-fire crackled and spat, and the mare stumbled, throwing Hester from the saddle – she jerked her feet from the stirrups, rolled away, and dragged the pistol from its holster. Lying on her side, she heaped powder on to the priming tray. Gasping, she turned, and the vast, glossy bulk of the mare's body heaved spasmodically, her flank streaming with dark blood, her flesh blown open. A vast silence stretched through the woods, and Hester laid her hand on the horse's heaving shoulder. 'That's it,' she whispered, tears streaming down her face. 'Good girl. Good girl.' The great beast shuddered and went still. Hester sobbed and rolled again, on her belly in the leaf mould and muck of the forest floor as four blue-jacketed French militiamen surged towards her on horseback, crashing through the bracken. Mawgan was dead – kind Mawgan, who had carried her with such gentleness. Hester tore a cartridge open with her teeth, gagging on the bitter taste of gunpowder. Her hand shook as she rammed the primed cartridge into the barrel of her pistol, cocked it, aimed and fired, and the first of the soldiers was jerked backwards from his saddle like a puppet on strings.

62

Forge-red light filled the sky and Crow felt the explosion deep in his chest. *Fuck*. There was no way to go but on. He ran, surging away from the light, the heat; then he threw himself to the ground, arms around his head as he hit the mess of leaf-dirt and pine needles. Fucking chaos. It was best not to think about how many men might've been inside the mint, nothing now but scorched meat. All those French banknotes, now nothing more than ash. Gold bars, dripping. Crow smiled into the ground, leaves and Kentish dirt in his teeth. And now it was the usual unanswerable questions: *If I stay here, will they find me? I'll be shot. If I get up and run, will they see me? I'll be shot.*

Musket-fire cracked across the night sky. *Tirailleurs*. What were they doing here? The French guards at the mint had been the first to die, their throats cut, and yet the French night-guard were out now, swarming just like ants if you prodded the nest. How had they known? The nearest garrison was miles away, at Rye. How could French troops have got here this quickly without being forewarned? Hadn't Grant said he wouldn't summon him until immediately after the Occupation patrol had passed Faversham, leaving days until they would be expected here again? Crow waited, listening, uneasy cold creeping through him. He could hear footfalls, voices. The French were making no effort to hide their presence. The arrogance of it. Christ. They were closer now, not further away. Had they spotted him, lying on the floor? He'd told Joséphine nothing of this mission, so who was the traitor this time? Who had given them away? *This is it.* Dying in the mud again. His father's voice: *One day, boy, those nine lives of yours are going to be spent.* Life after life. Run or lie still? If he ran, he was a moving target, even in the dark. If he lay still, he might never be seen, the *tirailleurs* might pass by. But if they didn't he was going to be shot here in the mud. He couldn't breathe. Hoofbeats shook the earth, and Crow was back in the mud at Hougoumont, the horses almost upon him. Lice swarmed beneath his skin, between muscle and bone, and his mouth cracked open in a silent scream. The French guard were close. Gunfire ripped across the night. Crow hitched the musket from the shoulder-strap, tearing the top off a shot-canister, shoving it down into the barrel. He'd be shot in the back again. His father's voice again: *I'll ask you this only once, Jack. Why were you shot in the back?* Just as he should have felt shot slam into his flesh, he heard musket-fire again and the scream of a horse, and the French stopped firing at him. Someone had shot the *tirailleurs*. Arkwright and Grant were both well ahead, so it could not be them. Someone else.

63

His father's ninth child, Bleiz Lozac'h was born on the banks of the River Rance as the women of Dinan rubbed lye-soap into sweat-sticky sheets; he'd slipped into the world and on to the grass on the riverside before his mother even had time to stagger home, held up instead by one of her sisters and an aunt as she squatted in the cow parsley. Bleiz grew up leg-deep in the warm, slow-moving waters of the great river herself; he could swim before ever he spoke a word of French. Thanks to that river, twenty years after his hurtling arrival in the world, Bleiz swam from the holy island of Trescaw to St Mary's and hauled himself up the seaweed-scattered beach, walking alone down the lane to Hugh-town, where at last there were enough people that he had the chance of not being immediately known as a stranger.

His belly ached with hunger; he'd eaten nothing for two days but raw limpets scraped off the rocks with his jack-knife, swallowing them whole like salty lumps of cold phlegm. There was no possibility of eating anything else till he reached the mainland. He couldn't risk being caught stealing, not now. It was a relief to be lost in a crowd as market-traders gathered in the dawn light in the square at Hugh-town. There was an air of expectant excitement, children skittering from doorway to doorway, criss-crossing the cobbled alley before him, women gathered in doorways, leaning in at windows to talk to each other, their long woollen skirts trailing in mud that stank of flyblown seaweed at low tide. He thought of Marie-Claire again, and whispered a prayer that she had grown with child for her full nine months and delivered the baby safe. Here in the Scillies, he was closer to home than he had been in three years. Beyond the blockade, this was the only part of Cornwall where the free-traders still had a chance, dangerous as it was. Everyone knew the islanders were running brandy, gold and information across the Western Approaches at least twice a month. Bleiz could join a boat; he could go home to Dinan.

He stepped across the path of a small girl wearing an ash-smeared apron. 'What's going on?' he said, in Breton. Would she understand?

The little girl stared at him a moment, and Bleiz prayed she thought he was just some mainlander, and that she had understood his Breton, the sister-tongue of her own Cornish. 'A wreck, isn't it? Didn't you know? Some poor lot of Frenchie sailors all drowned. Mother said they'd lit false lights on Bryher, but then they would do that. Bryher folk's all sly and wicked as they come.'

The Duke of Wellington was going to escape. He, Bleiz Lozac'h, was the only man who knew enough to stop him. No matter how much Bleiz wanted to go home, he couldn't rely on news of the wreck reaching De Mornay. He had to reach the mainland.

64

Crow lay curled up on one side. As he woke, his fingers closed around the musket before he'd even opened his eyes. Every sinew in his body throbbed; his clothes were damp with dew. Early morning light shafted between the trees. He wasn't dead. Not yet. He'd just shot down all the men he could see and run through the trees, hardly knowing if he was in Spain in 1810, France in 1813, or England now. Disjointed memories crowded his mind, flickering and confusing. A forest of French beech and ash, long ago. A stranger shooting down Occupation soldiers. He'd killed more than one himself, he was sure. Even though he was quite alone, the urge to run or to fight rose up again with furious force: sometimes it was as though he'd never be able to escape that feeling. Swearing through his teeth, Crow got up and began to walk, passing three dead, white-faced French soldiers still lying where they had fallen, the horses long gone. The nearest dead man had lost his shako, revealing a freckled, bald head now being slowly traversed by a beetle. No point in wondering who'd survived the night. He'd learn, soon enough. You always did, in the end. Arkwright? Grant? He leaned against a tree. *Get a hold on yourself.*

For Christ's sake. He caught the scent of drifting smoke. *Listen.* On instinct, he'd moved in silence, years of practice hammered into him. More smoke: no one had heard him come. He waited, but heard no French – only the low hum of familiar voices. Arkwright and Grant. How was it that even now after all these years part of him still dreaded a withering look from Arkwright? *Took your time, my lord?* There were three people gathered in the clearing: Arkwright, Grant and a third figure – some servant, by the look of it. Crow watched the servant, a lad in faded, mud-coloured clothes, a heavy woollen cloak pulled down over his eyes. Arkwright sprawled out near the fire, blowing a cloud as usual. Grant was on his feet, though, parade-ground straight. The musket ready to fire, Crow broke his own cover, walking towards the light and heat of the fire.

'What the bloody hell,' he said, 'is going on?'

Arkwright only shrugged, trails of smoke drifting from his nostrils as he stared into the fire. It was obvious someone had betrayed their position to the French and this vagrant servant could be anyone. What had he seen? What did he know? Crow recalled he'd only ever seen Grant stand stone-still like that in the presence of Wellington himself, or when ladies were present. And Wellington wasn't here now. There was only one woman in the world who would do this, who would even consider it.

'Put that musket down.' Hester stood her ground, her face tight with fury. What was wrong with her; what was she doing here, wearing those clothes, servants' clothes? A man's clothes. What right had she got to do that?

He lost control, shouting at her. 'What are you doing here on your own?'

'What were you doing in Cornwall, more to the point, when you found me? What are you, some kind of rebel?' Her speech was devastatingly controlled in comparison to his; her gaze travelled between Crow, Arkwright and Grant, hot with disgust. 'Did you think I might be useful? Because of who my father was?' She smiled, but there was no trace of laughter. 'Helping me was nothing to do with whatever debt you felt you owed Papa, was it? You needed me – like a chess piece. I'm no different from the slaves your grandfather bought in the market at Jamestown.'

Crow was stunned for a moment into speechlessness: he had never heard a woman speak to a man in such a way, as though he were no more than a child. How had she known where to find him? How had she learned what he was? 'Holy God,' he said. 'Hester, tell me. What in Christ's name are you doing here?'

'*Shut up.* I'm here only to avenge my father – not to unravel the unholy mess you've made of your own family.'

He was unable to form words. *Shut up.* A woman had told him to shut up: his wife. She looked disgusted, as though she had stepped in shit: his wife. Crow caught hold of a slow-drifting thought, spiralling from the back of his mind like a leaf borne on the wind: save himself and apparently also Hester, Grant and Arkwright were the only other two to know of their position, or the timing of the attack on the mint.

'Indeed I know your little secret, too.' Heedless of the fact that Grant stood stiff as a ladder only paces away, and Arkwright was still by the fire, Hester was still talking, and he hadn't the smallest notion of how to make her stop. 'Doubtless you were too drunk to take notice, but I heard every word of your argument with Kitto, and I know what you did to him afterwards. I saw the blood on the carpet – blood! As though you were a pair of animals. And I know all about Louisa.'

'Hester—'

'I've no interest in anything you might say. And I suggest you might consider the difference between just discipline and thoughtless violence next time you think of brawling with your brother in your own home. And now he's run away, and I can scarcely blame him.'

'What?' Panic shot through him. 'Where is he?'

'I don't know!' Hester spat. 'Thanks to you, he was gone by the time I came home. God only knows where he went, and I doubt very much that he's ever coming home. And if you want to know why I came, read this. I certainly have little desire to see you.' She handed him a folded sheet of paper, covered with an encrypted scrawl in an ill-educated hand he'd never seen before. He stood holding the letter, looking from Grant to Arkwright, trying to fight the growing certainty that one of them had, by accident or design, betrayed their attack on the mint to the French. Arkwright had by now got slowly to his feet, and was standing at Grant's side, watching with apparent disinterest that Crow immediately recognized as acute observation.

At last, Grant spoke. 'She refused to let either of us see the letter, or even deign to explain her presence. She insisted on speaking only to you. What do you mean to do with her now? Can you not keep your own wife under control?'

'Allow me to save you the trouble of decoding the cipher,' Hester said, before anyone else had the chance to speak.

'I thank you, no.' Crow held it out of her reach; if he survived the next ten minutes without having his throat cut by either Arkwright or Grant – whoever the traitor was – he could deal with her another time. He unfolded the paper, scanning the encrypted lines of numbers; after so many long years of practice, the patterns of particular letters leaped out at him instantly; it really was in Cornish. How had Wellington found someone to cipher for him in Cornish?

The Duke of Wellington requests that the Earl of Lamorna frees him from the island of Bryher. The French garrison stationed here will be in no position to present an obstacle.

He looked up, hardly able to comprehend what he had just read. And what the hell was the matter with Arkwright? That tense stillness had spread through him; he was motionless, just like a roe-deer spotted in the moonlight. 'If we can get the Duke off Bryher, we can get him to Allanby,' he said, buying time: this was nothing the other traitor hadn't heard before. 'Allanby's still got sixty thousand men kicking their heels in Newfoundland. It's an army. We've a chance to send the French running by the end of next year if we don't lose our nerve.'

'Thank you, I'm quite aware.' Grant lit a cigarillo of his own, wordlessly passing his flint to Arkwright, who unsheathed his jack-knife and plunged it into the small of Grant's back, straight into the kidney. Grant let out a strangled gasp, and Arkwright jerked out the knife, letting the corpse crash to the ground at their feet, stirring up a wave of dead leaves that had all floated back to the ground before anyone spoke.

65

The walls of Kitto's cell closed in around him. It was so dark, windowless. The stones glistened with damp, and it stank of wet, and of stale urine, and old shit. Crow would come. He always did. Louisa would write to him, perhaps, and he would come home. Oakhurst wasn't so very far away. Just a day's ride, and that would be enough time, surely. Kitto tried not to think about French soldiers reining in outside the house, some lieutenant banging on the front door with a musket-butt, splintering the smooth black paint. He remembered Roza. What would the soldiers do to Louisa? Even she didn't deserve Roza's fate. What would they do to Hester, whose presence made Crow almost the man he used to be? Long ago, Crow had come home from the sea on a night when Papa was entertaining the prince regent at Nansmornow, their friends and their lightskirts all in the drawing-room, and no one much cared where Kitto was or what he might see, and so he sat beneath the polished table with Captain Cook's *Voyage to Otaheite*, reading by lamplight as Papa beat the prince at hazard, and a naked woman they called Cerise poured claret. A young man came in who looked like Papa, only younger, and so Kitto knew that must be his brother Jack, because all the Helfords were cut from the same cloth, everyone said so. His brother bowed before the prince and said, 'Your servant, sir,' to Papa, who looked away and poured himself another glass of wine, unable, it seemed, to wait for Cerise to perform the duty for him.

'Have mercy, Lamorna,' the prince said. 'You're very cold towards the boy. Hot enough for you in the West Indies, was it, young Crowlas?'

'Nearly so, your highness.'

Still Papa said nothing, even though it must have been years since they'd seen one another, and Cerise watched Crow like a man in a desert of Araby looking at a cup of water. 'Now there's handsome,' she said.

And Crow had laughed, turning away from their father, spotting Kitto beneath the table. He pushed one hand into the pocket of his jacket, braided at the epaulettes with silver, which meant that he was no ordinary midshipman now but a lieutenant. A cowrie shell on a knotted leather thong hung from his fingers. 'Here you are, brat,' he said. 'Now show me where they're hiding the best of the larder.' Papa and the prince and their friends went back to their game, and Kitto led Crow out through the servants' door on to the back stairs.

Kitto stared at the walls of his cell. Crow would come, despite it all. Surely he would come. He always did.

66

Arkwright turned to Crow and wiped rain from his face, shoving the mattock into his saddlebag, his hands filthy with blood and grave-mud. 'Bloody bastard must've turned in '14 when they had him prisoner in Paris. Explains why he was always such a useless twat, at least. I did wonder.'

Hester stood staring at Captain Grant's shallow resting place in a state of stunned shock. Crow kicked leaves over the long shadow of newly turned earth and just shook his head, tight-lipped; only once before had she seen him so angry. He refused to meet her eyes. 'Hold the gelding,' he ordered Arkwright. Without another word, Crow advanced upon her and, without ceremony or permission, he lifted her by the waist and tossed her up into the saddle, one hand on her rear as she gasped, snatching at the gelding's mane to steady herself. Without a word, he mounted up behind her. She longed for the dignity of riding alone, but poor, kind Mawgan was dead. Arkwright averted his eyes, handing Crow the reins, and they rode through thinning woodland towards open fields in a mud-splattered, tearing rush. Behind her, Crow was rigid with fury, still hot and sweating with the effort of helping Arkwright to dig the grave, his long, elegant fingers white with tension as he gripped the reins. At a gallop, they turned from a muddy, puddle-rutted lane down a tree-lined avenue that curved around to a black-and-white Tudor manor house with an apple orchard planted at the front, the trees still dusted with thick, pale blossom. This must be Oakhurst, then, not that Crow bothered to appraise her of the fact. By the time he reined in outside an enormous studded oak front door, she herself was rigid with fury, sliding from the saddle as soon as he had dismounted. He passed Arkwright the reins, turning to face her. She hadn't even noticed how heavily it was raining. His hair was soaked, his shirt pasted to his chest. The air between them seemed so hot she couldn't breathe it.

'Don't you ever dare manhandle me again!' Hester snapped, and without knowing where else to go, she fled for the front door of the house, splashing through puddles even as a flurry of servants appeared, staring with open-mouthed shock at her shirt and breeches. Walking straight past them, she was intensely aware of Crow in pursuit, just paces behind. In equal terror and fury, with hardly a thought except to place one foot before the other, she found herself in a long, old-fashioned farmhouse kitchen with an enormous scrubbed table, and an unprepossessing boy of about seven turning a spitting joint of mutton in the fire. A red-faced cook with sweaty hair drawn up into an untidy bun stepped across her path, blessing herself when Crow came in immediately afterwards. He slammed the door behind him with such force that three plates fell from a Welsh dresser and smashed on the flagstones. The cook let out a faint scream, floury hands pressed to her mouth, and the boy turning the spit had frozen, staring.

'How dare you,' Crow shouted at her, as if the whole episode with Grant had never happened, and they were just continuing where they had left off in the woods. 'How dare you speak to me like that before my men? And how dare you come here alone? Have you no idea?' He turned to the cook and the spit-boy. 'Get out – what the bloody hell else are you doing?' They fled in mute alarm, and his gaze travelled up and down her body. 'Jesus Christ.'

She looked down, and saw that her own borrowed shirt was just as soaked as his, plastered to her skin. The wet linen clung to her breasts as they rose from her corset for all his servants to see. Shame collided with her fury and grasping blindly at the table, she picked up the first solid object she could find and hurled it at him with all her strength, wanting only to hurt him.

'Fucking hell!' Crow dodged the pestle, and it smashed into the dresser, destroying innumerable plates with a stunning burst of sound. 'Come here!' he demanded, raking his hair back from his face with his fingers.

She had begun to love him, and all the time he had been with Louisa. 'Why should I?' He had humiliated her in every possible way. 'You're nothing but a thug, a violent drunk—'

'I could have done worse to him!' he shouted. 'You've lived all your life on an island, you were just a girl, protected every hour of the day. Have you no idea what it is like for us at school, or in the navy, or the army? He'd have had the skin flayed from his back, do you not see? In the war, soldiers were hanged for less by their own officers.'

'There is no war! You are his brother, not his commanding officer. How dare you try to make excuses?' He was not the man she thought he had been, he had betrayed her; wanting only to hurt and punish him, Hester reached for another weapon, an earthenware bowl filled with slices of dried apple, and threw it so hard that when he dodged the impact, it struck a row of copper pans hanging on the wall, scattering pale apple slices and shattering into shards.

'I know!' he said. 'I know it was wrong. Do you think I don't know how wrong I was?' Before she could catch her breath, he was upon her, holding her arms at her sides with a curious, savage, gentle strength, as if to prove that he would not hurt her. She tore away and slapped his face with all the force she could muster and he took hold of her wrist, backing her up to the wall until their faces were just inches apart.

'I didn't touch her after we were married,' he said, breathing hard. 'I swear to God, Hester. It ended before I married you.'

'Why should I believe you? Why should I believe anything you say?'

'Because it's true. Because I love you.'

She closed her eyes for a moment and saw spinning coloured shapes in the darkness. 'I hate you,' she said. 'Oh, God, I hate you.'

They reached for one another in the same half-moment. He lifted her on to the kitchen table, scattering bowls and plates that broke into pieces on the floor, and he tasted of blood, of dirt, and as she lay down on the scrubbed oak, he cupped the back of her head in one hand; it made little sense, she knew, but she had at last come home.

Hester woke in near darkness, half choked by the starch-pressed flounces of a nightgown fashionable nearly thirty years before, the linen still rich with the scent of the dried herbs it had been folded with so long ago. Wary of Occupation patrols, Crow had posted guards – loyal servants – but some small touch of fear had awoken her from a deep sleep. No one knew how deeply Grant's betrayal had run. Had he actually named Arkwright and Crow? Even now, troops might be circling the house. She sat up, loosening the ribbons at her throat, reaching out for the guttering stub of candle still flickering in the pewter dish on her bedside table. They had shared a supper of scorched mutton and stewed greens with Arkwright, Hester conscious of the fact that they had somehow slipped from a world where Crow and Arkwright were master and servant to one in which they were bivouacking soldiers eating at the same table. Afterwards, Crow had ignored the flustering of his housekeeper and escorted her up the stairs to this bedchamber himself. He had not joined her, though. He'd gone to guard the lane, but there was so much left unsaid between them. Even after such a union, the fragile bond of trust was unrepaired.

She pushed away a memory of mud and leaf mould spattering Colonel Grant's dead white face as Crow and Arkwright shovelled earth into a grave scraped out of the dirt. If it hadn't been for Arkwright, she and Crow might have been waiting for the guillotine even now. Grant, Crow said, had been the one to betray his mission to the French, and God only knew how much else. What did it matter if Arkwright was involved with the Spenceans? After what had happened to his little boy, was it really so surprising he wanted justice for the poor? Beyond the velvet canopies of her bed, shadows loomed and shuddered, and she heard again what must have woken her – a voice, someone crying out in the night. Crow. So he'd gone to sleep, but not with her. She heard him call out again, caught in some dream, or perhaps a memory: *Run, fucking run. Run now.* Her throat dry, Hester waited. Sleep was hours from her grasp now, she knew, if it even came again at all. The candle shuddered and guttered, the wick sinking into a puddle of wax. The household would never rest: the Oakhurst servants must be out of their beds again in a matter of hours. Hester swung her legs out of bed, frigid air eddying around her ankles. The nightgown hung to the floor: it fitted her. Had it belonged to his mother? His French mother. She took up the pewter dish, shielding the candle with one hand. She and Cat had crept about the secret places of Castle Bryher just like this, such a long time ago, years spinning past like dead leaves on the wind. Cat wouldn't have been scared. *There's no such thing as ghosts, you daftie. Except the Grey Lady of St Mary's of course—*

Shut up, Catlin! Hester could almost hear her laughing.

She closed the bedchamber door, a now-silent hallway lit only by moonlight spilling in through an arched, leaded window at one end. Where was he? She walked across moonlit floorboards, stirring up a strong scent of beeswax and dust with each hesitating footstep. The floors had been polished but not swept, the house not kept aired. Cat would have muttered beneath her breath; she would have sent the maids of Oakhurst scurrying like mice before a barn cat. Hester ran the rest of the way down the corridor. All was quiet. Where was he? A vast gulf of dark empty space fell away to her right: the top of the stairs. The door overlooking it was larger than the rest, a pattern of living, twisting rosebuds carved into the wood, the delight – she imagined – of a medieval baron's daughter, long ago. *Here.* Hester felt for the handle, cold iron at her fingertips. The room was vast, moonlight spilling in through four windows, the curtains not drawn; cold, fresh air bringing with it the faint scent of the Kentish sea. The curtains were not drawn, either, around the bed. Crow lay curled on one side, a black tangle of hair damp against the pillow. The curve of his cheekbone glistened with sweat. He was naked, his lean, tattooed body cast grey in the moonlight, as though he were carved out of stone. Hester clutched at the candle-dish. Hot wax splashed her hands. He was still asleep: he was dreaming. What did he see, when night came? What did he live again? She set down the candle on a heavy wooden kist that served as a bedside table. Gathering up the folds of the nightgown, she climbed into the bed, sheets warm with the heat of his body. At her touch, he awoke, sitting up, breathing hard, running both hands through his hair again in a gesture she knew now meant that he felt helpless.

'*Mon Dieu*,' he said, quietly. '*Je suis désolé*, Hester.'

'What is it? What's the matter?'

He let out a breath, with one hand over his eyes as if longing to push away whatever he saw, whatever had woken him up in the night.

'Tell me,' she said, 'and perhaps it will go away.'

'It will never. I cannot,' he said. 'Oh, God.'

Sitting at his side, she gathered him in her arms. His shoulders heaved spasmodically, and he pulled away. 'Hester, no. If you knew the things I've done...'

'I shot a man.' She pushed the hair back from his face. 'I drowned four more. We do what we must to survive, and we make our peace with God, and you were a soldier. Tell me.'

He sat back, moving away from her, and for a moment she thought he was not going to speak. 'You know I wasn't only Wellington's ADC? I was in the Corps of Guides, too – a spy under Grant's command. On the day before Waterloo,' he said, 'when we knew that Blücher was dead and Gneisenau had retreated with the Prussians, Wellington sent me to find out if the Dutch–Belgians would stay loyal to us, and still be our allies. There was a boy.' He broke off, staring out of the leaded window at the apple trees tossing in the wind in the garden below. 'A Belgian child. He was carrying a coded message. He wouldn't give it to me. He wouldn't tell me what they intended to do. And so I killed him to find out, to get at the cipher. I cut his throat, and he died. He was no older than Kitto, and I killed him. And it was all for nothing, because even when I knew, I didn't reach Wellington in time to tell him. It was my fault, and I killed a child for nothing, for no reason.' He pulled away. 'Hester, I will understand if you want to leave me. If you want to live away from me.'

She took him by the hands. He'd killed a child, trying to save his country. 'Yes,' she said, 'I can see why it keeps you awake.' She pulled him close to her, and he rested his forehead in the hollow beneath her collarbone, and she wrapped her arms around him, and she held him until he fell asleep.

67

Crow woke to dawn light stretching across ancient floor-boards: he had emerged from the darkness of sleep, not a dream. An arm lay draped across his waist: the soft heat of a female body against his. He shifted one hand to rest on the arm, the warmth of her skin. Hester. A sweet, warm flame of delight uncurled within him and was instantly extinguished by a wave of shame. She had come in the night despite all he'd done. *Get to bed, you stupid bugger.* Arkwright had come to relieve him from guard-duty in the hours before dawn, rain-wet leaves dripping into the ridged mud of the lane and on to the shoulders of his coat, a haze of droplets silvered by the light of the moon behind him. *You'll be no use to anyone otherwise.* He ought to do the decent thing, finally. He should take up his musket and walk with it down to the eastern reaches of the garden. He should blow out his brains. He was an abomination. He should not exist. He found that he cared less about Grant and his betrayal than he did for his wife. Even though Hester knew now what he had done, what he was, she still lay beside him. Crow turned to face her; she was asleep, heavy dark lashes resting against her skin, her mass of light, soft curls seeming to float above the pillow. A widow, she would be better off without him, but he still had a part to play. Wellington had summoned him, and he must go – he would have to leave her again. She wore an old-fashioned nightgown of thick, lace-edged linen that Louisa would have burned. It was undone at the throat, age-yellowed satin ribbons hanging loose, revealing the shadowed hollows at her collarbone, white lace against her warm, brown skin. A wave of such strong, vivid emotion flooded through him that he felt an absurd urge to cry for the first time since Maman had died at Nansmornow. And Hester woke, watching him, her eyes like dark amber. He'd told her the truth, and she was still here. He didn't know what to say; he dared not touch her, she was so beautiful.

'I'm sorry,' he said immediately. 'Hester, I'm so sorry.'

And Crow remembered shaking John Harewood's hand on the deck of the *Belle*; he remembered John's face in the lamplight so many years before that day, showing him how to plot a course on a chart. *If there is ever anything I can do, sir, to repay all you've done for me...*

Hester spoke without opening her eyes, her face no more than a hand's breadth from his. 'Good.'

'God knows I'll try to be a better man for you.' Why could he not escape the lingering sense she was hiding something? 'Hester. Is there anything that you want to tell me?'

She leaned on her elbow, watching him now. 'No. Only that I'm coming with you to Bryher.'

He sighed. 'We can't take such a risk – the letter could be a trap.'

'Catlin would never do that.'

'She may have had little choice.' Crow hoped that she couldn't begin to imagine what a man like Marshal Ney was capable of. Hester made no reply, but only reached out with one hand, letting it rest on his side as he lay watching her. And why must he leave her? This time, he would reach Wellington before it was too late. This time, any failure would not be his. At least the mess with Grant had shown where Arkwright's loyalties really lay: Hester would be protected with him, Crow knew, until it was safe for them to follow him to Bryher, and if anyone in London could find Kitto, it was Arkwright.

'Please – Hester, will you go back to London with Arkwright?' he said. 'Join me on Scilly when I can be sure it's safe. Find Kitto, and wait for me in Newlyn. I'll send word to the Star. If anyone can find my brother in all London, it's Arkwright. And if Kitto will consent to go with anyone, it's you. Hester?'

'Yes?' She watched him from beneath lowered lashes, pushing the hair away from his forehead.

'When you find him, tell him I'm sorry.' And he must leave her, and go into battle again, and pray once more that duty would be stronger than fear.

68

The cobbled streets of Faversham were slick with rain. The harbour thronged with fishermen and French soldiers still soused with last night's brandy: Crow remembered the boredom of blockade duty, sitting on some worm-eaten frigate for weeks on end. He walked on, taking care not to catch anyone's eye, French soldiers and Kentish fishermen alike. It was impossible: he needed to be in both London and Scilly. He thought of Kitto in London, alone and with nothing to lose, and then of Wellington waiting for him at Castle Bryher. He had failed at Waterloo, but this was his chance to make amends. He placed his trust in Arkwright. Arkwright would escort Hester to London, where they would find Kitto and bring him to Scilly once the immediate danger on Bryher had passed. The Azores would be a good bet – halfway to America and Allanby's troops, and where what was left of the navy had found safe harbour. The thought of trusting so much responsibility to another – even Arkwright – drove waves of unease through him, but he couldn't see that there was any other choice. Wellington had personally requested his aid. He'd been given a second chance.

After such a catastrophic failure how many men were granted the possibility to make it right?

Crow walked down through the harbour past hollow-eyed men wheeling half-empty barrows of fish – worse even than what anyone was bringing home in Cornwall. There, the blockade ships had to anchor further out to avoid being smashed against the black rocks, but Faversham pool was wide and deep, and the blockade ships loomed close to the harbour's mouth, yawing and heeling as the tide turned. The fleet could catch next to nothing. The blockades were murder to English and Cornish alike. Crow weaved past fishermen with starved faces, soldiers in their blue jackets and ragged children who grasped at his greatcoat. If he gave all the coin he had he'd be surrounded, he'd draw French eyes and for the second time Wellington would wait for him in vain. He couldn't let that happen again.

'I'm sorry, I have nothing.'

'Please, sir, a fine bang-up gentleman like you, of course you've got something to spare, my lord.'

'They say the baby will die without bread, my lord—'

He walked on: one single coin and they were desperate enough to all come running. And too many people here knew his face, his name. By the time Crow reached the quay, sweat ran freely down his back, sticking to his shirt. The boat tied up right at the quay was a little day-schooner, too small. He stepped into her and then swiftly stepped into the yawl tied up alongside. Too small again: he needed something that would withstand what was going to feel like half the Atlantic slamming against the side of her hull. Crow went from boat to boat, deaf to every curse and protest. The tip and sway of a wooden hull beneath his feet felt like coming home. At last, he stepped into a neat little oyster-boat with a mizzen-mast and blood-red sails, and he could tell by the feel of her that she'd draw enough line to hold her course in a cross-wind.

'What do you want?' The fisherman spat a wad of tobacco just shy of Crow's boots; Hoby would have wept to see the state of them. Crow dug one hand into the pocket of his greatcoat and held up the bag of coin.

'What I want is for you to take me to Cornwall.'

69

Hester fretted with the gelding's mane as she held the bridle, coarse rusty hairs twisting around her fingers. The Rose and Crown lay a short distance from Oakhurst on the main post-road to London and the courtyard teemed with men and women conversing in urgent voices, darting anxious looks at each other over the heads of frightened children with tear-streaked faces. With poor Mawgan dead, and the horses in Crow's stable at Oakhurst long since requisitioned by the French, she had ridden to the Rose and Crown in the saddle with Arkwright: he'd left her whilst he went in search of a second mount. How could she be quite sure Arkwright wouldn't stab her just as easily as he'd finished Grant? Crow's absence was an almost unbearable lack, and she even missed Gil – the old Dalmatian now safely resting before the fire at Oakhurst. She'd never heard so many people speaking at once, talking, shouting, crying. Then she spotted Arkwright pushing his way back through the crowd towards her, leading the horse he'd just bought. Hester sensed an uneasy, animal tension in him; he was ready to move in half a moment.

'What did you discover?' she demanded. 'Why are all these

people leaving London?' She fought to steady her voice. 'Where are they going?'

Arkwright shook his head. He glanced across the courtyard at the sound of carriage wheels in the road outside. 'You'd do best not to look.' And the moment he spoke, the mass of humanity in the courtyard surged towards the mail-coach turning into the yard. Hester stared as the driver cracked his whip. A man in his shirtsleeves tugged on the carriage door, gripping a bulging bag in one hand, and the noise rose again, punctuated by the cries of children.

'They'll take our horses.'

Arkwright shook his head, wordless, and took the bridle of the new horse along with that of his own mount. 'Riots again, they're saying. It's got worse. Thirty guillotined at Newgate yesterday for disorder. That's not all.' And he did look at her then.

'Just tell me, Arkwright,' she said. 'Whatever it is, I'm not going to fall into a fit of hysterics.'

'Someone tried to burn Carlton House. There's going to be an execution – a big one, by Whitehall.'

Carlton House. The French wouldn't let this lie: a direct attack. Hester folded her arms, unease blistering into fear she was determined not to show. The mail-coach wheeled out of the courtyard, men and women hanging on behind. A girl with two small children clung to the roof. They were going to fall. It wasn't safe. How desperate must they be to risk the fall, the broken bones? They'd be crushed by the carriage wheels. And she was going into London, where all these terrified people had run from. What had happened to Kitto? Roza Carew hadn't even been a rebel and they'd raped and hanged her.

'Have they caught who did it?'

'That's it, my lady.' Arkwright looked away for a moment. 'They're saying it's the boy.'

Kitto. She couldn't hold on to the secret any longer. Hester stared at him, making him watch her. 'You engineered this, didn't you, Arkwright? You hate them – the Lamornas – and I know why.'

The swift, sudden change in the expression in his eyes told her all she needed to know: shock, followed by a flicker of something else – guilt, shame?

Hester's throat felt dry again; it was hard to expel the words. 'I know what happened to your son, Mr Arkwright.'

'You know nothing. I'll get you out of here alive but that's it. There's nothing I owe the Lamornas.'

Kitto was in prison. Kitto was going to die, and Arkwright had wanted this all along. 'No, of course you don't,' Hester said. 'But I know what you did. You told Crow what Kitto had done – buying all that gunpowder. But you weren't trying to help at all, were you? You knew what Crow would do, and what Kitto would do because of it. And now he's going to hang. Did you really mean it should go this far?'

Arkwright mounted up. 'I've no quarrel with you. Do you want me to get you out of here or not? You might be married to a Lamorna but I don't hold you to blame.' He looked out across the courtyard – the teeming, panicking crowd surged closer.

Hester stood by her horse. The animal's rising panic doubled her own. *Breathe.* 'Crow's father never read the curate's letter,' she said. 'I was the first to open it. Lord Lamorna never knew about your son. It wasn't that Crow's father didn't care, or thought he deserved to hang, because he didn't. And I'm sorry, Mr Arkwright, I'm so, so sorry, because it wasn't right, and it wasn't fair.'

'What do you know about any of it?' Arkwright's voice cracked, the first time she had ever heard him express any real feeling. 'A sea-captain's daughter sitting pretty on your island.'

He twisted the cork from his hip flask, and Hester caught the sharp scent of cheap rum as he drank. 'It's the last thing I wanted. Jérôme was looking for a reason to set the whole country alight and there's Christ knows how many rebels were ready to give it him. I was in Paris when the Revolution blew up. It started well and ended badly, and here it's not even started well.'

'What did you intend then?' Hester demanded, distraught at the idea of Kitto in a prison cell, waiting to hang. Arkwright just shook his head. 'I know all about Mr Castle, Arkwright. I've seen him with you at Lamorna House. I heard you talking.'

Arkwright turned to face her, his face rigid with suppressed emotion. 'Then you've less sense than I thought.'

He'd killed Grant in less than a minute.

'Why won't you just listen?' Despite her fear, Hester could have slapped him. Why must men be so infernally thick-headed, so slow to understand anything occurring beyond the order they had ordained? 'Mr Arkwright, I couldn't care less if you're a Spencean, but I saw your friend Mr Castle at Carlton House. What possible reason could he have to go there? Ask yourself that. What's a revolutionary doing right in the middle of the Occupation court?'

'What a mess,' Arkwright said, as if to himself. 'What a damned, fucking mess.' He turned away, swung himself up into the saddle, and rode away across the courtyard, leaving Hester alone to face the crowd.

'Kitto's death won't solve anything – I hope you're proud of yourself!' she shouted after him, hauling herself up into the saddle, slapping a man's hand away from the bridle. Arkwright wasn't going to listen. He didn't care. Hester twisted the reins around her hands, praying she could control the panicking gelding as the crowd surged closer, hands grabbing and snatching at her cloak, her gown, her leg in the stirrups, anything to unseat her and take the horse for themselves.

70

Arkwright halted his mare outside the courtyard gates flung open to the lane, oblivious to the terrified, weary Londoners surging around him. The yard heaved with people and the noise rose like a thick pall of smoke. A crowd packed that tight never dispersed without blood spilled. In one sentence, Hester had confirmed his worst suspicions about Castle. She was wrong in one respect: there was every reason an English revolutionary might seek to strike a deal with the French, but Wedderburn had given that job to Arkwright, not Castle. Castle was always urging the men on, always stirring. Just as Arkwright had feared, the man was an agent provocateur, trying to scupper the revolution from within. Doubtless Castle had helped that fool of a boy to attack Carlton House itself, and Arkwright had as good as handed him the chance to do it. It'd been so easy to unleash Crow on his brother like a wild dog and make them both suffer for it. Arkwright had thirsted for that moment of revenge for years, but the moment it was done he'd felt no better. Petey had still died in terror, led to the gallows hoping for his dad to save him. Yes, the need to make the Lamornas pay for Petey's death had clouded his mind: sense, reason, the lot. He wanted them to suffer as he had suffered, as Petey had suffered. But now he was as good as a damned agent provocateur himself. He wondered if Castle were in the pay of the French or the aristocracy or both.

He couldn't do it. He couldn't leave the girl to be knocked from her saddle, robbed and abused at the hands of those starving wretches at the Rose and Crown. That was the truth of it. He couldn't. In the back of his mind he saw Jenny standing in the doorway of the tiny cottage rented in the grounds of the manor house at Scarsdale, watching him go with tears in her eyes, smiling in that brave way she had. *What I've always loved about you, Joe, is you're a kind man in a cruel world.* A day's ride to York and then the mail to London, time to join the regiment again, his leave over and done with. He'd run out of the gate, Petey had. Run for a last goodbye, and Arkwright remembered the feel of his son's strong little arms around his neck, and how the smell of baking bread clung in his dusty hair. *You be a good boy for Mam, won't you? I'll be back again before you know it.* It was the last time he'd seen his wife and child, and he tried not to think of a lad of nearly seven led to the gallows crying for his mam, hoping even as he felt the weight of the noose on his shoulders that his dad would come and they would ride away together, and he remembered the heat of the Spanish sun on his back as he'd read the letter from the curate, and how he'd turned away and vomited into the dirt, letting the letter fall into the dust, and how much he'd hated Crow because his father had done fuck all to help. It was not to be thought of. It could not be borne. Arkwright had seen a lot of men hang. It was not a pretty way to die. Arkwright dug his knee into the mare's flank, turning her back into the courtyard. He reached Hester just as the men hauled her from the saddle.

'How dare you!' Hester screamed and grabbed at the reins, but she was outnumbered, and the men surrounding her would have done anything to save their own families. Arkwright could understand that. He loaded his musket in less than half a minute, clearing a space around Hester and her mount in half the time again. 'Get your bloody hands off her.' He'd no intention of firing, but people who had lost everything in a matter of days were easily frightened, and the men scattered. It wasn't her fault. None of it was her fault. 'Get up, you fool!' He held the reins as she hauled herself into the saddle with unladylike speed and precision.

'Thank you.' She met his gaze directly, her tear-streaked face mired with a great smear of sweat-sticky dust. 'Thank you, Mr Arkwright.' He sensed her distrust, even now. 'I'll do what I can for Kitto.'

'What's it to you, anyway? What do you owe them, the Lamornas?'

'I owe them nothing, but Kitto is a child, and he's been used badly. Even if that weren't the case, if he's hanged it'll make things worse for us all, not better. More riots, more fighting. It's the people who can't defend themselves who suffer the most.'

Arkwright watched her. She meant it. 'You're not a bad shot. If you can get near enough, shoot the boy before they hang him. Make it a quick end.'

Nothing had mattered except Nessa since he got the letter about Petey, but she called him Mr Arkwright, and she looked at him with such relief. Let her think she might do something to save the boy. It was too late.

On his way to the garrison, Bleiz followed the winding lane as it led up towards the westering sun, leaving the port of Newlyn and the glittering expanse of Mount's Bay behind him.

A five-bar gate separated a weed-filled carriageway from the lane – leaning on the gate, Bleiz saw the rambling old manor of Borlaze shielded by a barrage of ancient chestnut trees heavy with their blossom shaped like candles half melted down to the quick. He'd hardly pushed open the gate before a couple of gritty-looking bastards from one of the southern divisions rode up on matching chestnuts – doubtless once the pride of some luckless *seigneur*'s stable.

'What do you want?' The nearest soldier spat on the ground from the saddle; the white froth of his spittle clung to the sunburst of a dandelion head.

'Settle down,' Bleiz replied in French. 'You need to take me to the lieutenant. Quick as you like, friend.'

The other soldier sneered. 'And why's that? De Mornay's hard on deserters, you know.'

'I'm no deserter—'

'A Frenchman that stands like a soldier in civilian clothes? Explain that to de Mornay, friend. He's in a shitty mood this morning, so I can't guarantee he'll listen to a word you say before he gets us to hang you from one of those pretty trees.'

Bleiz shrugged; he'd come too far to let this pair of fat-arsed idiots see they'd riled him. He'd come to the mainland with a story, but no proof. The local garrison leader would regret it if he didn't trust him, certainly, but regret would do Bleiz no good once he'd choked to death at the end of a rope. 'Just shut up and take me indoors, would you?'

Ney was dead. If he couldn't talk the garrison into sending more troops out to that hellish collection of islands, the Duke of Wellington was going to walk free.

71

Anywhere else but the Lamorna valley and Crow would have broken an ankle, stumbling across scruffy, gorse-studded moorland on a moonless night. Even after so many years away he remembered the valley, or the valley remembered him, and it was enough, staying as low to the ground as he could get, wet clothes chafing his skin raw. It was better not to think at all, to let his mind wander, his feet and hands remember where the mine-shafts were. He'd gone in up to his waist when the Kentish oyster-boat paddled as close to shore as her captain dared, and even that had cost him far more than they deserved. But he was here, soaked and alone, and he would reach Wellington in time. This time, he would not be too late. Crow could requisition any seaworthy boat on Scilly and sail west with his commander, and by the time the French knew anything about it, searching for Wellington would be like hunting a needle through a hayloft. He could only pray that winning this battle would not be at the cost of losing his wife and his brother. He could only trust Arkwright to bring Hester and Kitto safely to Scilly before he had to set sail with Wellington. The servants, too, must be gone from Lamorna House long before Jérôme sent guards to bring him in. He could do nothing about any of it: he forced himself to stem rising panic and ignore the fact that almost the entire situation was beyond his direct control. In the back of Crow's mind, he saw the white-walled tumble of houses rising up from the bay at Ponta Delgada and the forest-fringed mountains above. Eight hundred nautical miles off the coast of Portugal, and much closer to Allanby and the sixty thousand British troops kicking their heels in the Americas. And Crow smiled in the dark. Yes, the Azores would be a good place to go next.

The Wink looked deserted, not a chink of light seeping through the smallest of cracks in the tavern's front door or shutters. Crow knew better than to believe there was no one inside. He waited outside, his sodden clothes dripping on the limestone stoop worn smooth by countless feet over hundreds of years. He wouldn't hear a thing, not from out here; the walls were old and thick, and the men of Lamorna were used to speaking in whispers on moonless nights, even before the French had come to Cornwall. He slid his knuckles down the old, worn oak, the lightest touch of a knock, leaning close to the door to whisper in Cornish. It swung open just a crack, revealing George Chirk's lamplit face. Crow slid inside, letting Chirk bar the door again behind him. The taproom was thick with tension – all four Chirk brothers, Harry Simmens, two of the Trewarthen boys. Jôwan Coth leaned on the bar, six glasses of brandy lined up before him. To a man, they all bowed their heads when he came in. He never demanded that; he never expected it as a right that was due to him – he had abandoned them for thirteen years, he'd gone to sea, he'd fought in a war – but they honoured him all the same now that he was home again.

'My lord, we had no notion you were coming.' Jôwan Coth poured him a burner, amber liquid slopping in the bottom of the glass.

'I wasn't planning it, Jôwan Coth.' He downed the brandy, watching the familiar faces. They were nervous, eager to be off. 'You're trading tonight, aren't you?'

'Foolish not to, with no moon. And everyone's hungry. The barley's flat with rain, my lord. Even if we get sun now, it'll be full of rot come harvest-home.'

'Where are you going?' It didn't matter. Their destination would be different now, but if they were caught, the fewer people who knew the truth, the better. The Chirks, the Simmenses and the Trewarthens were hard men. Even so, anyone might crack with the correct threat applied. Every man had his own limit, his own weak spot.

'France. Saint-Malo, my lord – or just down the coast, anyway.'

George Chirk and Harry Simmens glanced at one another, and Jôwan Coth looked Crow up and down, and at the seawater running off his boots, and went out of the door behind the bar. They were getting uneasy, restive, like dogs in needs of a run. 'Well enough,' Crow said. 'Before you risk the Channel, I need you to take me to the Scillies.'

A moment of silence, seven men all looking from one to the other as the weight of what he asked settled upon them.

John Chirk nodded. 'There's something dirty going on up there, my lord. A whole stream of kegs and cases and dead men washed up with the tide last week and it keeps coming.'

'What manner of men?'

'Blue-jackets, my lord. They're saying it's the *Soigné* – that French man-o'-war.'

Jôwan Coth came back in, dropping a pile of folded clothes on the bar. 'Not what you're used to, milord, I dare say, but better than freezing before you've done whatever crack-brained thing you mean to do.'

Crow leaned across, digging into the heap, emerging with

a fistful of blue French military serge, the gilded braiding of a drowned man's jacket glittering in the dim lamplight.

He smiled. They had a chance, then – a small one, but a chance all the same.

72

Ocean heaved beneath the keel, dark and shining. The boys were silent; all Crow could hear was the rhythm of their breathing, the creak of the mainsail rigging as he leaned on the tiller, closing on the looming ships of the blockade. He could see the *Belle* herself, and he glanced up at the luff again.

'Go about.' He spoke in French, and John Chirk and Harry Simmens understood what he meant, even if his words made no sense, quick to move in their salvaged blue jackets. Crow leaned on the tiller again and Harry released the mainsheet and John the jibsheet, lines running across their palms. The boat came about, her sails filling again beautifully, and Crow thought, absurdly, of his father, who had been the first to teach him how to tack out of the harbour at Lamorna Cove. A long time ago now.

The *Belle* loomed closer; her coppered hull limed with barnacles. Captain Harewod would have spat fire at the state of her. She needed cleaning, looking after. On the next tack, all being still alive, they would pass directly between her and the next vessel, a thirty-four-gun frigate Crow didn't recognise, once proud, her masts now naked, the sails not even furled but

taken down; she was now imprisoning the country where she
had been built. They wouldn't make it between the two vessels
on this tack. They would have to row.

'What in the name of bloody Christ are you doing down
there?' A voice from the deck, and Crow felt cold fear slide
down his back.

French. They think we're French.

'Acting under orders. Now fuck off, unless you want me to
report that you got in my way?'

'Whose orders?'

Crow glanced back at the silent men, huddled in their
positions, waiting. They were relying on him to get them out of
this: their lives were in his hands.

'Ney's, you idiot.' Did they even know Wellington was on
Bryher? Had that particular piece of news been allowed to
trickle down through the ranks? Crow leaned back, staring
up the side of the ship, watching the shadowy figure leaning
over the taffrail. There were others hovering behind, doubtless
a couple of half-pissed lieutenants arguing the toss. He was
tempted to shoot, but that would've been a fool's game. What
were they going to do? Christ, just decide. And then at last,
at last, the leaning figure spoke again: 'Better hurry up then,
hadn't you?'

'Do us a favour and signal down the lines – I don't want
some idiot with no idea packing this damned fucking wreck
with grapeshot. We're a day late to him as it is. He's going to
have my hide.'

'Understood.'

Crow turned to John Chirk, who had the oars, still speaking
in French. 'Get on with it, you fool. We haven't got all night.'

Chirk waited a moment, not understanding, and Crow
sensed the men on the deck far above still watching them,
wondering why the delay, why they didn't just dip their oars

and get away, if they were so long awaited. Crow leaned across and jerked the oars from Chirk's grasp, taking them himself.

It was going to be a long night.

73

Crouched in the corner of his cell, Kitto heard footsteps. He was trying to think of Nansmornow, of the wide sweep of beach at Lamorna Cove, dipping for shrimps among the rock pools and how he used to take them home for Mrs Gwyn to boil and send up to Papa with bread and butter, of the smell of Papa's tonic combined with the faint scent of starch rising from his cravat. It was hard to forget that tomorrow – or the next day, or the one after that – he was going to die. He supposed they would send a priest to hear his confession, that he might die absolved. This was the worst part, waiting. He might as well already be dead. His life was done. Fourteen years. He would have given anything now for fourteen more.

The key scraped in the lock, a wet, metallic sound, and the guard said, 'Visitor.'

Crow – might it not be Crow? Huddled in his corner, Kitto looked up, and hope ended when he saw the cloaked figure of a woman. He would die after all. The door closed with a slam, and the girl threw back the hood of her cloak: Hester. Without a word, she crouched down before him and held him against her in a way that no one had done since Nessa and Roza died, smoothing the hair away from his eyes. He held on, breathing in her scent of clean muslin.

'What are you doing?' he demanded. 'You need to get away from here, do you understand? Leave London, Hets. It's not safe.'

Hester sighed, giving him a shake. 'You absolute fool, Kitto.' Her face was streaked with tears. 'What have you done?'

For a moment, he couldn't speak. 'What about the servants – they'll be in danger. The French told me they'd hang, too, because of me. That they'd all be accused of sedition, everyone in the house, even Louisa. I wouldn't have had that happen for the world, even to her.'

'Well, the French weren't quick enough. All the servants have left. And Louisa has gone to marry Lord Burford.'

Kitto let out a long, shuddering breath. 'I'm sorry, Hets. You heard what I said to Crow, didn't you? I was so angry. I didn't think.'

'Neither, it seems, did he.'

He looked away from her, unable to contain the overwhelming feeling of dread, and Hester reached out and took his hand.

'He doesn't know you're here – Crow doesn't know you're here.' Then she fell silent.

Kitto nodded. There would be no rescue.

'Listen,' Hester went on. 'I daren't tell you where he is, Kitto. If they tried to make you tell them – it's not worth the price. But I want you to know that he's got no idea you're here, and that he was sorry for what he did. Do you understand? He was so sorry.'

'You should go.' His eyes were burning; he couldn't let her see that.

'I must—' Hester broke off as Kitto's guard hammered on the door with the butt of his musket. 'Listen,' she said, in Cornish. 'I'll be there. If anything happens, Kitto – if you see the slightest chance to escape when they take you from here to Whitehall, there's always hope. Run as if the devil himself is on your heels. The whole of London has been rioting since you were arrested. I'll wait for you at the Royal George – you know, the inn where the mail to Penzance leaves from.'

Kitto looked away. 'Don't be a fool, Hester. It's my time. Nothing's going to happen except that I'm going to die.'

'But just in case,' Hester said, squeezing his hand. 'I'll wait for you at the Royal George.'

'You'll be waiting the devil of a long time. You need to get out of London. It's not safe for you here. Do you want to end in my place?' He couldn't keep the anger from his voice. What did she think she was playing at, raising his hopes when there was no hope to be had?

The door swung open. Their time had run out, and when Hester had gone, Kitto knew that was the last time he would ever see anyone who loved him.

74

Crow waded through the surf, holding the musket and a swag of cartridges above his head, every shred of flesh in his shoulders shrieking with the effort; if the powder got wet he'd pay for it. He couldn't come this far only to fail, unless he was already too late. He could see the lights of a village from here, a cluster of bright points against the gloom of a moonless dawn. That dark bulk pricked with lights up in the hills behind it must be Castle Bryher, and he remembered how he'd sworn that he must visit the captain but never had, and prayed that Arkwright had got Hester safely back to London, and would bring her to him, and Kitto. He thought of Louisa, conveyed from London in Burford's new carriage. She'd always known how to look after herself. It had been a bad turn, allowing her to learn that she wasn't his any more by bringing Hester home as his wife. *Have you ever,* she'd said to him once, *thought of anyone in your entire life other than yourself?* She was probably laughing about it even now. The beach rose up towards the quay, and he knelt for a moment on the cobbles, allowing for just one moment a wave of deep exhaustion to sweep through him; he was cold to the bone, but he was here. He had done it, and someone was coming, one man alone, holding a Davy lamp that shed a globe of warm yellow light.

'You took your time, Lamorna. I suppose I should be grateful that you came at all.' He would know that voice anywhere.

Crow picked up his pace, walking up the quay. It was Wellington, after all this time. After John Harewood, the closest he had to a father: Wellington, the man he had failed, the man he had cheated and lied for, the man for whom he had utterly abandoned all honour. He remembered Wellington standing at his bedside in his father's house on the Rue de la Loi. Even in the grip of fever spreading from his infected wounds, he'd understood what was required of him. *Buonaparte has landed in Folkestone, my boy. I expect they shall come for me soon. It will be necessary to retreat for a short while, I should think, before we can advance again. See what's over the next hill for me, won't you, Jack, when you get home? They'll trust you, the French, with your mother's blood. Let them think you're on their side. Do whatever it takes to learn what they intend. Whatever it takes, do you understand? Even if it means sacrificing your own men.*

They both stopped where they stood, a few feet apart, and Crow saluted, one fist held up to his forehead.

'Well then,' Wellington said, and he reached out to take Crow's hand, but he wasn't smiling, not that he often did. You'd think he would now, though, after all this.

The words stuck in Crow's throat. 'Where are the French? Ney and the others?'

Wellington shook his head, dismissing them. 'Dead and buried. We saw to that. You've come in good time.'

'Ponta Delgada?' Crow said. 'I can send a gig to St Mary's if none of the islanders has a boat with enough belly to reach the Azores. I'll take you across, sir. I beg your leave to wait for Arkwright to bring my wife and brother.'

This was victory, and yet why did Wellington look so ruined? This was their chance to send the French running at last, the beginning of the end for Buonaparte in this corner of Europe, at least. Wellington sighed, releasing his hand. 'Have you seen *The Times*?'

He shook his head. 'No, sir. I've been travelling for days. Arkwright and I destroyed the mint at Faversham, so that ought to give Joséphine something to write about. It'll be a fine distraction, sir, while we get you off the island, I suppose.' The truth about Grant would have to wait.

Wellington took him by the elbow, turning him towards the rough hillside leading up to the bulk of Castle Bryher. He was so exhausted. He had to sleep. Surely he could sleep now, at least for a while? 'We had the mail-boat yesterday,' Wellington went on. 'I'm afraid I've some bad news, Jack. It's about your brother.'

75

So many faces, so many people, even so early, the sky dark away to the west. The cart rolled along, and Kitto held on to the side, gripping the rough planks. He remembered the scraping of a key in the lock of his cell; it had still been dark, then. His last day. Crow hadn't come; he never would. The people were so close, reaching out to him. *My lord, my lord...* He was no one's lord, he was going to die. He was going to climb the steps up to the scaffold; he was going to hang. Perhaps they'd try again with the priest, but maybe not; he'd accepted no sacrament, no absolution. Was he supposed to make a speech, to repent, to beg forgiveness of the people he'd killed? What would be the point in that? He'd done it. He'd killed them. He couldn't change it, and he was going straight to hell. If he were a soldier, it wouldn't be wrong.

Kitto looked down at his bound wrists, and the faces in the crowds blurred and blended together, and his head spun, and the soldiers in the cart with him were silent and tense. He heard men shouting, a woman screaming, but he could make no sense of the words, and the streets heaved with people, and for a moment he breathed in the smell of fresh cakes – that must be the baker's shop on Fleet Street – and he would never eat anything, ever again, and he hoped it would be quick, and that the rope would be long enough that his neck would break straight away, that he wouldn't strangle inch by inch, and surely Crow would come because he always did, and there were hands on the cart, faces he didn't know, they were pulling the cart, tugging it, trying to haul it on one side, roaring and screaming into the faces of the French soldiers. It was another riot, and this time they were all rioting for him. He saw the gallows now, a grim black shape against a blue sky, but the streets around Whitehall were so crammed with shouting, furious Londoners that it was going to take half an hour to reach it, half an hour that would feel like a hundred years until he climbed those wooden steps on to the scaffold, waiting for the weight of the rope.

Heat beat down between Jacques's shoulders as he stood on the gallows, the boards beneath his feet sending up the clean, sharp scent of fresh-cut pine. The sooner this hanging was over with the better, and a mucky business it was going to be. What was wrong with the guillotine? Nice and clean and quick, the way a death should be. Jacques supposed the Bonapartes wanted to make a point with all these barbaric old-fashioned killings, and the rebel deserved it anyway, a fire-starter – he'd tried to burn Carlton House itself, all those innocents burned quite alive. Christ, the crowd were loud, though: they weren't happy – there was no carnival edge to this killing-day, no one selling gingerbread in the throng below the gallows. If this day didn't end in more rioting and more hangings he'd lose that bet with Benoît up at the guardhouse. Nothing but English barbarians, the lot of them. But when Jacques stole a look at the prisoner, standing ready by the noose, he saw only a boy. He couldn't have been more than fifteen, dead white and shaking, too –

he was the same age as Jacques's own lad, and what he wouldn't give to be riding up the old lane towards home where they'd all be waiting for him. A week till he could go home on leave and see them all. A week till it would all be over, and this lad's pain all done with, too.

Not long now, lad, Jacques found himself thinking, in much the same spirit as when his own boy had to have a back tooth drawn. *It'll all be over soon.* The boy stumbled as Benoît led him forward to the noose. His hands were tied behind his back; he could do nothing – what must that feel like, helpless, knowing death was moments away?

76

Hester pushed her way to the tavern's upstairs windows. She hadn't come this far, bivouacking with Arkwright and Jim the stable-lad at Lamorna House, boiling dried peas on the range in the kitchen and living in filthy clothes, only to fail now. She had to at least try. Arkwright had been right about the Golden Hind – from the window, the sky was an incongruous bright blue beyond the grim silhouette of the gallows erected outside Whitehall, swallows stitching their way across the crow-strewn sky. Everyone had come up to get a good view of the hanging, keeping clear of the ugly crowd in the street below.

'Watch out.' A blacksmith in a leather apron spat in the sawdust at her feet, stepping in her path.

'Please. Let me get to the window.' Hester pushed back her cloak, lifting the musket from the shoulder straps. Idiots. The room fell silent as her intention became clear, and a space cleared around her, sawdust scuffed right down to floorboards blackened with generations of spilled ale and London street grime. She reached into her reticule for the cartridge. She had taken a fistful from Arkwright, but there was only one chance to get this right. The silence dissolved into a low rumble of voices that grew louder with every moment, but Hester could make no sense of it. *One chance.* They jostled her from behind: she couldn't take aim; at this rate, she was going to fail.

'Do you want him to die?' Hester turned, shouting at the assembly behind her. 'Or not? It'll start with the aristocrats, and it'll finish with people like you and me, just as it did in France. If we want fairness, we'll have to find a better way. Now be quiet and allow me some space.'

No one even moved. They were all watching her.

'They've led him up the steps, poor boy.' One of the tavern-maids wiped her hands on her apron, pressing closer to the window.

One chance. The musket Arkwright had given her was much heavier than her pistol. She would have to be strong. She would have to be steady. Kitto was such a small figure on the scaffold, hands tied around his back, the hooded executioner beside him; two blue-jacketed soldiers stood by the hanging noose. Hester cocked the musket, leaning it on the window-ledge, and bit off the end of the cartridge. The bitter taste of gunpowder filled her mouth and she held the wad of paper in her cheek, no time to spit it. She lined up one of the soldiers against the sight bead, aiming square between his shoulders. Even if she got this right, there was still another soldier to deal with, and the executioner himself. But there was also a furious, seething crowd intent on doing harm to the French. *One chance.* Hester fired from the open window. Thirty yards away, across the heads of the surging, roaring crowd, a soldier turned, and the bullet slammed into the boards of the scaffold a foot to his left.

Wellington watched Crow turn away; he walked back down the beach towards the sea as though he might walk through it and across the land, all the way to London. The rising sun cast pale gold light upon the waves. Would it have been kinder not to tell him, or to wait till after the hanging had surely been done, rather than giving him this moment when he knew the boy was likely still alive but there was nothing he could do? Perhaps the boy's death would ignite an even greater thirst for revenge amongst the populace. God only knew he and Allanby were going to need all the help they could get. Crow was the only one of the family to have survived Waterloo – his one remaining ADC. Wellington knew he had no one else.

Crow walked into the sea right up to his boots, the waters of the bay foaming about his legs, and he dropped to his knees, there in the water, as if praying. He'd shown promise, young Crow. Quick and clever, he was, Grant's right-hand man and a fine code-breaker – not the first good lad to be cut down in this mess. So many of them, all gone, so many bright, brave, laughing lads. They would have done anything for him, and they'd given everything for him, the family. There was nothing quite like a British soldier, when all was said and done. With the rising sun in his eyes, Wellington walked down the hard-packed wet sand, not yet littered with the casts of lugworms, still lacking those scribbled signatures of piped wet sand. He was still depending on Crow to get him out of here. The boy couldn't fail now, and so Wellington followed him into the sea, the cold a shock even through leather. Where in God's name was he to get another pair of boots? Crow was on his knees with his face to the rising sun, soaked to the skin. He said nothing. He didn't move.

'On your feet, soldier,' Wellington said. 'Let's make it worthwhile.'

Jacques felt the heat of the second shot slam into his chest; the force of the blow sent him spinning like a dancer, like all those times he'd held Adeline close to him when the pipers played on May Day and they'd spun together beneath the night. His face smashed against something hard, and he saw the sky above, so blue and so far away, studded with swift-moving clouds, and in the moment of Jacques's dying he was aware of a single tooth flying away and bouncing across the bare, new-planed boards of the gallows, an insignificant burst of pain, and he hoped that his boy would do well enough without him; he saw him now, standing on the gate and waving as he'd marched away with the regiment all those years ago. There was nothing to be done, not now.

77

Joséphine sat alone in her private sitting-room, convulsively twisting a handkerchief between her fingers with every burst of broken glass. Bonaparte was obviously too busy with his affairs in Russia to consider her future: by the time word of the riots reached him, she'd be dead. She wondered if Jérôme and Catherina had been killed by the mob – those heavy footfalls she'd heard, the gunshots – or whether they'd simply left her to her fate. Either way, she was quite alone, unable to call on the single person she might once have relied on. In all the time Crow had been her envoy, she'd never known him take longer than a day to reply to a summons – a hastily folded sheet in his sprawling handwriting – or to arrive in person. No, he was gone. And now his brother was to be hanged, and, despite all her efforts, London now, they said, was little better than Paris in the Terror.

Joséphine pushed away crawling fear and crossed the room to the desk. Bonaparte had been wrong to order the prince regent's death, wrong to wish such vengeance on the English people, but he no longer listened to anyone, least of all her; buoyed by his victory at Waterloo, he pursued military action at far-flung reaches of the Empire when it was clear he ought to have been consolidating his position closer to home, not leaving such a delicate affair to his incompetent brother. Joséphine pressed her hands against her face, breathing hard. She must calm herself. Long ago, Robespierre's men had come for her at four o'clock in the morning. She'd barely had time to lace her gown before the soldiers took her away, leaving the children with only servants to care for them. After more than twenty years, the terror of that morning had never really gone away; it only ever receded and returned with varying force, just like a wave. She must write to Hortense and Eugène. She must say goodbye. She drew several sheets of her favourite silk-pressed paper from the desk drawer. The sound of footfalls grew louder. Closer. She was not going to be able to finish even the first letter. However would she have posted them, anyway? They were coming for her. Joséphine laid down her pen, pinned to her seat with fear. The door opened, and Joséphine rose to her feet, shaking. Once, she had been an empress in more than just name. She had ruled Paris, and her husband the world. Paris had been enough. She would not let the English drag her away. She would walk like a queen.

'Your grace?'

Joséphine stared at Arkwright, uncomprehending. She had feared death from so many quarters, but never this. He crossed the room towards her; he looked just like an ordinary soldier with his grizzled hair and wide shoulders. He'd drawn no weapon, he raised no pistol or bayonet. She found herself unable to move, trapped behind the desk. Arkwright just walked right up to it, laying his broad, sun-browned hands on the marble before her. 'Are you coming, lass, or not?'

Kitto watched the French soldier crash to the gallow-boards in a spray of blood. Fever pulsed through his body, so that it was impossible to think. The noose swung to his right, but, whirling around to stare at his fallen comrade, the second soldier lunged at Kitto, missing his arm by a bare half-inch. The crowd roared, and Kitto was dimly aware of more soldiers mounting the gallows and surging towards him. Looking down at the mass of faces below, Kitto realised everyone in the crowd was screaming the same word, over and over again in an unstoppable chant. *Run. Run, run, run, run—*

78

For days and days the wind had kept Bleiz and the rest of de Mornay's men ashore, kicking their heels in Newlyn, refusing to blow. Not today. This would be the second sailing – ten men were already cutting across the bay towards the blockade and beyond, out to the islands. In a borrowed regimental jacket, Bleiz watched de Mornay's men board an oyster-boat requisitioned from a fishing family who had assembled outside the garrisoned manor house of Borlaze only that morning. In the end the father had broken down weeping as his wife watched, dry-eyed. Bleiz pitied them, but there was no choice. The streets of the town were empty, the sullen, starving inhabitants keeping well withindoors. If it was true the *Soigné* had been wrecked, de Mornay would do better without a man-o'-war. What good were cannons when you were drowning, the hull stove in by a rock? The islanders would have to wreck every boat that came near before they would suspect a Cornish fisher, and one most likely already known to them.

'Get a move on, private!' De Mornay was red in the face. It was below him to believe the word of a mere private, and a

Breton at that, but even he wasn't stupid enough to risk more letters from high command about the foolishness of his conduct.

Bleiz stepped on to the gangplank, shouldering his resupplied kit – the familiar weight of the rifle, the knapsack. All he wanted to do was go home. He should have taken that chance whilst he still had it, a free man on St Mary's. What business of his was it if the Duke of Wellington escaped to fight again?

In that long-ago time when they were still girls, and still milk-sisters, Catlin and Hester had talked into the night as their candle burned down to stubs. They had spoken of many things, but also about the men they would marry. Together, they had watched Tom Rescorla sail across the channel with the mail-boat, helping his uncle with the mackerel-catch – and the free trade, if the truth were to be told. Tom was gone, joined the army, dead and gone. Tears burned Catlin's eyes as she stood in the drawing-room, breathing in the scent of fresh beeswax. She and Tilly had scrubbed the stone-flagged floor and polished the tables and chairs; they had swept the carpets until their knees were sore and their elbows stiff, scrubbing away all sign of Marshal Ney and the French. Well, Catlin had chosen Tom Rescorla and lost him, too, but this was the husband Hester had taken – not the respectable African tea merchant her father had wanted, but a pretty young man sitting in the winged armchair in the drawing-room, holding himself so still Catlin half wondered if he hadn't died in the middle of his last drunken stupor. *Oh, Het,* she thought. *What have you done?* She'd never even wanted a husband, and now to have such a one as this.

The earl looked up as Catlin approached, and she could see in part why Hester had accepted him. God willing that face would be worthwhile, because it wanted only twenty minutes to ten in the morning and he'd rung for brandy. He smiled at her, but the movement of his face was queer: free of true feeling, like that of a puppet made from a child's stocking. His young brother was dead, after all. Catlin knew how that felt. Hollow, like nothing mattered.

'Thank you, Mrs Rescorla,' he said, in that quiet way he seemed to have, and took the glass of brandy from the green japanned tray she held. Wellington was agitating to sail, she knew. She'd heard them arguing in the library, Crow swearing he wouldn't leave Bryher without his wife and some servant or other, and Wellington insisting they were running out of time.

Come on, Het, she thought. *Don't make him choose between you.*

Catlin realised that for the first time since Tom died something now mattered to her: Bryher, and Hester herself, and victory over the French. She'd done her best to serve all of these other people. When would it ever be time to serve herself? Catlin bobbed her curtsey and turned to go back to the stillroom. She had remedies to brew. Old Mrs Garrett was ailing again and wouldn't last long but at least she could be made comfortable with the goose-grease salve to rub her aching limbs as she lay in her bed, remembering when she had lain there with her babies, long ago. Aunt Evans's headaches were troubling her again, too. It was time to walk around to the herb garden and pick more feverfew. Small wonder poor Aunt Evans's head ached: it would be a matter of astonishment if anyone on Bryher had slept a decent night through for weeks. For now, Catlin had more than enough to do. She heard steps: why should anyone be running in the hallway? Catlin felt the colour rush to her face, ashamed that any servant under her charge should behave with such a lack of restraint when there were guests in the house. Hester's husband just sat as though nothing had happened at all, staring out of the window at the sea, turning that glass of brandy as if watching it catch the light gave him the only pleasure he could still know, and Catlin turned to face Jacca Garrett, who ran into the room at full tilt.

'Mistress!' He gasped for breath – built for comfort, not speed, Jacca was. He went on in panicked, disjointed Cornish. 'Mistress, where is the Englishman? Wellington!' he shouted. 'There's French all over Town Beach. They've killed my dad!'

Catlin swallowed the rebuke she had lined up for him and ran to the door, but Lord Lamorna was faster.

'Get everyone inside; get everyone into the house,' he said to Catlin. 'We'll fight them.'

79

Kitto lay in the dark, jolting and dreaming. The cries of the vast crowd around the gallows rose and fell with relentless power, like waves crashing against a beach... *Run, run, run, run—* In his dream, he leaped from the gallows and fell, tumbling for what seemed like an eternity before one of the soldiers snatched at his arm, taking a firm hold. *There's still time, you little English bastard—* His shoulder had dislocated in a burst of agony, and he was dragged from below, hands reaching up to haul him free. Even as musket-fire peppered the crowd, he'd run along slippery cobblestones, borne along by the mob.

He'd lost any real sense of where he was. His head swam; he burned one moment and froze the next, and the agony in his ear was relentless. He shouldn't be alive but he was, and he thought he could hear Hester talking to him, saying they'd crossed the Tamar, that they were in Cornwall. Faces appeared before him and swam away; people spoke but he could make no sense of what they said. He remembered being ushered down back alleys and through stinking hovels, and warren after warren of slum streets so crowded with overhanging buildings that it was dark as night. He heard snatches of panicked conversation. *Not in my house, I want no French soldiers here. Get him away, get him out of here: we'll show the bastards. Come on, my friend, you can do it. Nearly there. Nearly.* Kitto lost count of the times he'd dropped to his knees and was hauled back to his feet, dragged along. At last, they let him lie down. Dimly aware that he had collapsed with his face pressed into straw and horseshit in a courtyard that seemed familiar, Kitto had turned his head to see Hester running towards him in a cloak with a muddy hem. The next moment, she'd knelt beside him, just as she was now, clutching his arm as she spoke in a fierce, hard whisper. 'We're going home, do you hear me, Kitto Helford?' Going home? Did she mean Nansmornow? Kitto would have liked very much to go home, but as he drifted headlong into another faint, Kitto had the vague, unhappy sense that there would be no one there to greet him, and that it would be just like those dreams he used to have on his first night at school, when he got all the way back home only to find Nansmornow ruined and in darkness, lamps unlit, the windows broken and gone, and no Papa, no Nessa, no Roza, no servants even, and no candle in the dark.

After five days spent jolting in the London to Penzance mail-coach, fighting a constant terror that they would be apprehended by French troops, or that Kitto would succumb to the fever racking his body, Hester was exhausted. *Just let them come at us,* the coachman had said, stroking his blunderbuss as his lip curled with hatred, *I'll give the French a taste of their own.* It had been little consolation, and she'd hardly slept more than half an hour at a time since Kitto had been borne into the courtyard at the Royal George in London, helped along by a sweat-soaked and filthy gang of well-wishers they would likely never see again to thank.

Newlyn was deserted: moonlight cast a silver trail across the dark, glittering waters of Mount's Bay. At Hester's side, Kitto sat down on the cobbles on the town quay. He was in the grip of a vicious fever and could move no further: she had forced him as far as he could go. Crow had told her to wait in Newlyn till he sent word that it was safe on Scilly, but he'd no idea that half the Occupation army would be searching for them. Kitto's only hope, surely, was to get beyond the blockade and leave both England and Cornwall far behind. She was going to have to steal a boat, take him with her and pray they were not sailing into a trap on Scilly: she could see no other reasonable choice. She walked along the harbour, restlessly examining the moored-up vessels. They needed something small enough to reasonably cheat the watchmen on the blockade, who would surely be even more vigilant than they had been before. A boat she could handle herself. Kitto knew how to sail, but Kitto was deep in his fever. Doubts crowded her mind again: had she saved the boy from the gallows only to kill him by cajoling him from some bed that might be safe for now, at least, to come with her on a precarious voyage in the dark? Kneeling at Kitto's side, she shook him gently.

'Come on, you've got to stand up. I'll help you. See, we'll just climb down like this, and I'll cast off, and we'll be on Bryher before you know it.'

The little yacht tipped horribly as Kitto crumpled, lying curled up in the bows, water soaking through his clothes. He was so ill, and it was going to take all night to sail home, if they even made it past the blockade without being shot. Hester tugged the cloak around her shoulders and took up the mooring line, leaning across to the harbour wall to cast off. If she'd done wrong, it was too late now to turn back.

80

The air in Captain Harewood's study was thicker than egg custard: with Frenchmen all over the island again, nobody dared even to open a window. Little Abey Elliot let out a cry, stilled by his mother. Everyone on Bryher save Wellington and Lord Lamorna was crammed in any which way, sitting on the floor in silent horror, even Lord Lamorna's men. Jacca had one arm around his auntie, her face streaked with tears, although Jacca was doing his brave best not to cry himself. Old Mr Garrett was dead – there were at least three others not accounted for since the soldiers had come. Ten of them, Wellington had said, and it was her fault, although he did not know that and never would if she could help it. Either the French on the mainland had sent reinforcements after the wreck or this was because she had let that boy go, with his golden-brown hair and his white, freckle-dappled arms that had reminded her with such hurtful force of Tom's. What if he'd got back to the mainland somehow, and spread word of what she'd done? They might have wrecked the *Soigné* but it hadn't been enough. Now all she could do was trust in an Englishman and a drink-addled Cornish lord to preserve every last life left on Bryher.

At Catlin's side, Tilly began to sob. Catlin held her tighter. 'Don't you worry, you silly girl. It'll all be well, you'll see.'

Tilly looked up at her, tearstained and afraid. Catlin could tell that this time, even Tilly didn't believe her.

Hester gripped the tiller with numb fingers, nudging the yacht into or away from the wind whenever a wrinkle crept into the luff of the mainsail. She was so cold that tears spilled from her eyes and spittle ran from one corner of her mouth, and she was too exhausted to wipe it away. The blockade fell away to the north. She had sailed right beneath the nose of the Occupation, but it was a hollow victory. Kitto lay beneath her cloak, unmoving. He was still breathing, but for how long she had no way of knowing. If he died, it would be her fault, hers and Crow's together, a marriage of blame. The fever had set in Kitto's ear: it leaked thick yellow pus. What was worse, marrying a man who thought that deafening his young brother was a reasonable punishment, or marrying a man unable to control his anger? Either way, she had done it.

Away to the east, the sky was beginning to lighten, and Hester could see the dark hump of St Martin's on the horizon, the day-mark bright white on the hillside. She was nearly home. But why did she think she could hear voices, away to the west? She had been awake all night. She was tired. She needed to rest. She was becoming hysterical. Who could be out here? No one on Scilly would be sailing for the mainland at a time such as this. But as the sky lightened, Hester saw that she was not alone on the water. Another boat lay in her sight-line, away to the south-west, nothing more than a scrap of white sail at this distance. It was too small, surely, to be heading anywhere but the Scillies. For the longest while, she heard nothing but the shallow, uneven rhythm of Kitto's breathing, and the soft lapping of a racing tide against the hull; her sails were trimmed so neatly that they filled with wind, silent, carrying her fast across the water towards what she now realised was the sound of men speaking in French.

Hester glanced at her sails again, and then down at Kitto. His face was very white, his eyes closed. He was soaked; even the cloak covering him was damp to the touch. She had as good as killed him anyway, and now she had sailed directly into a trap of her own making. She reached across the oilcloth-wrapped musket. She was going to have to kill again.

Crow was at the top of the tower with nothing but blue, cloud-scudded sky above him, the musket cold against his cheek and the wind in his hair. There were eight Frenchmen left alive, crouching between the serried ranks of lavender and rosemary bushes in the sand-fringed herb garden. Two had died inside, the first in the hallway after Mrs Rescorla sent a kitchen knife skidding across the polished floor towards Crow, and he could still feel the resistance of flesh against the knifepoint, the look of horrified terror in the man's eyes as Crow held him up against the wall by the throat. Wellington had shot the other with cool, calm precision – Crow had never seen him fire a musket before. Wellington stood beside him now, Old Douro they used to call him, Old Hooky. The men had never loved him, but they'd trusted him. Crow didn't trust him now: he'd just eviscerated a man on his command. Who had that man left behind? A wife? A mother?

'Lamorna, what are you waiting for? Take out their right flank before they reach the servants' door or we'll have them swarming through the house.'

Crow's finger froze half an inch from the flintlock. 'I can't, your grace.' *I can't kill anyone. I see their faces before I sleep, when I wake.* 'I don't think I can do it any more.' He rested his forehead on the crenellated tower-wall. Kitto was dead because of him. First his father, then his brother.

'Don't be bloody idiotic, Jack. This is hardly the time to lose your nerve. Get on with it.' Wellington fired a shot himself, then another. Down in the garden, two more men fell. They hadn't a chance, really: this was a fortress, the navy had sent Harewood here to frighten away privateers, and it had worked. What could six French soldiers do? 'There are women and children in the tower below us. If we don't pick off every last one of those soldiers, they'll die like pigs in the slaughter-yard. Now get to work: I never thought you were a coward.' Wellington punctuated his speech with a swift, expert performance of firing and reloading; with every shot, another man dropped like a marionette with the strings cut. Killing was easier from a distance. Crow could only see one Frenchman now, and Wellington's powder wouldn't light. Crow watched the blue-jacketed figure far below skid across the rocks in a crazed series of zigzags, heading towards the back kitchen at the base of the tower. A coward. In half a moment, the soldier would be too close to the tower to fire on; he'd have to run down seven flights of stairs and meet him at a disadvantage. Crow lined up the fleeing soldier's blue jacket against the sight-bead on the barrel of his musket and fired. The man fell.

For one long, silent moment Wellington and Crow just stood and watched one another, the wide ocean spreading out towards each and every point of the compass, littered with a scattering of green and rock-edged islets. 'No, sir,' Crow said, breathing hard. 'You're right. I'm not a coward. I'm a killer.'

'I should damn well think so. Come on, let's get the plebeians out of my library and back to their work. Harewood had some rather decent claret, you know.'

81

Bleiz felt the shock of the shot before he understood that someone was firing at the boat. Chaos broke out, all the men unshouldering their rifles, looking wildly about for the threat. They were wrong, of course, about the source of their most immediate danger.

'Over there – another boat! Fire!'

'Hold fire!' It took Bleiz some moments to realise that he was the one who had spoken out in the presence of all these superior officers, issuing a counter-order. He was sure that even this was some sort of court-martialling offence. Much good would their superior manner do any of them at the bottom of the Atlantic. 'The boat, sir,' Bleiz went on. 'It's sinking. Whoever it is, they've not shot at us, but the boat.'

In all the chaos, no one but Bleiz had noticed that. They were at least five nautical miles from land and the little oyster-boat that had carried them so bravely from Newlyn was significantly lower in the water than she had been not five minutes before. Bleiz had seen boats sink before. Always slow at first, fast at the end.

'What in the devil's name are we meant to do?' someone

cried out. One of the corporals began to pray aloud. Bleiz only thought of his Marie-Claire, and the mimosa tree outside his father's house on the harbour front in Dinan, and the sweet, buttery, nutty taste of his mother's buckwheat crêpes. These were soldiers and – unlike Bleiz – not sailors. Papa had first shown him how to caulk a stove-in hull the summer he was eight years old. He could do it now. He was going home if these fools would let him.

'Don't worry, sir. I can make this all right.'

The corporal stopped praying. 'You know what to do?'

Bleiz saluted. 'My father's a fisherman – I was brought up to the trade, sir, and I know how to manage this as best we can. But I don't think that putting in at the Scillies will serve us well, sir, if I might make so bold. Not with all the locals so unfriendly. I venture to suggest we ought to nip straight across to Roscoff. I think perhaps it's time we all went home, don't you?'

Bleiz knew he had just talked himself before a firing-squad if he'd judged these men incorrectly.

'I do see precisely what you mean, Private Lozac'h. Do what you need to do, and plot a course for Roscoff. It's by far the most sensible option.'

Bleiz nodded, joy spreading through every fibre of his being. 'Of course, sir. Of course.'

He was going home. At last. He was going home.

82

Crow stood on the quay by the church, watching sunlight glance off the water. Mrs Rescorla's Uncle Evans had been right after all: the wind was picking up at last. Once out of the Western Approaches they'd be putting alongside in Ponta Delgada inside the fortnight, with any luck. He must row to St Mary's and pick up the neat little cutter moored at Hugh-town; the *Sophie*, Evans said her name was. No guns, but tidy enough to get Wellington halfway across the Atlantic to the Azores. Crow shut his eyes, thinking of the last time he had been there, seven years ago, after that long tour of the West Indies and all the trouble at St Martin's Bay. There had been a letter waiting for him when the mail-bag was brought on board in Ponta Delgada, the scent of crushed orange peel on the air, mingling with pipe-smoke, rotting sardines and all the stink of a city. The direction was inscribed in a careful, unpractised hand.

> Captain Viscount Crowlas,
> Ponta Delgada,
> Azores.

DEAR JACK,
This is my first term. The food is very bad. If you are anywhere near in the way of dates, may I have some please? The other boys

have a box of things from home & I should think their mothers give them it but I don't think Papa knew.

Maman had been dead seven years by the time Kitto went to Eton: he must have gone with little other than the clothes he stood up in, his absence, Crow was sure, barely noticed by their father. Where was he now? Rotting in the unmarked grave of a criminal as rain fell on a rioting London, failed first by his father and then his brother.

'My lord?' Crow looked up; there was a note of panic in John Chirk's voice, and it wasn't like him. Chirk was steady as they came. He was looking out to sea – what they could see of it, anyway, for a thick white fog had settled on the sound between Bryher and the next largest island, Trescaw. 'There's someone out there, I'm sure, sir.'

Crow waited, listening. Chirk was right. Not more French, surely? He could hear the soft splash of oars in the water, the ragged breathing of an exhausted rower. There was no wind yet, despite Evans's predictions. Whoever this was, they had rowed a long way. Crow couldn't summon the will to speak. If it was the French again then let them come. He'd take as many to hell as he could gather. Hester was not going to come. He'd get Wellington off Bryher but, frankly, nothing particularly mattered now. Everyone he held dear was dead or lost to him: he'd abandoned his own helpless wife in a country boiling with riot and unrest. He'd failed to reach Wellington at Waterloo; the battle had been lost because of him. Every time he tried to put right a wrong, he wronged again. What was the sense in trying to do right, when every act injured someone new? Crow lifted the flask to his lips and drank, the brandy burning a fiery path down his throat. Crow was aware of Chirk and Harry watching him, waiting for him to act. Now there was no possible way he could ever return to Nansmornow, all he wanted was to walk through the rose garden his great-grandmother had planted when King James was on the throne; he wanted to run out of the park and through the Lamorna valley down to the turquoise Cornish sea. He wanted to sleep in the bed he had been born in, with Hester curled around his body, so warm against him, and he wanted to stay there all day and show her everything he knew, her breath hot against his skin. Please God Arkwright would keep her safe.

'It's a woman.' Harry turned away, smiling with relief.

'Might still be French soldiers, though, with the *Soigné* wrecked.' Chirk's voice was tight with tension. 'Wouldn't be the first time they've sailed under false colours. We need more men. We can't meet them like this, whoever it is – not again.'

A little yacht loomed out of the fog. He could see enough now to make out the strong outline of the woman's form as she hauled at the oars, no doubt doing her best to guess whether she was coming alongside the town quay or about to go aground on the rocks now concealed by the high tide. He heard himself call out to her. 'Throw a line. You're nearly in.'

She stopped rowing, the splash of dipping oars stopped and all he could hear now were waves lapping at the quay wall and the broken arrhythmic breathing of someone at the limit of their endurance. A line came curling out of the fog and he hauled in the yacht, Chirk and Harry on their knees, ready to grab the guardrail so the hull didn't scrape against the quay. The wind had come around enough to blow the yacht beam-on to the quay wall; the rower reached out to fend off with an oar, and Crow crouched down to take hold of it, guiding her in, and saw that it was Hester. She looked at him only for a moment, then leaned forwards over the oars, exhausted, her shoulders heaving.

'I'm sorry,' she said, and he couldn't make sense of it. He heard himself speaking, incoherent, joy and gratitude flooding through him because she was here, she was alive. He went to grasp her hands, but her palms were red raw and bleeding – how far had she come, rowing all the way, and without Arkwright?

'Hester,' he said, 'my Het,' and he helped her ashore, unable to believe that she was really here, standing before him, and that he hadn't lost everyone, that he still had Hester. She stood shaking, trying to breathe; her eyes were shadowed and her face shiny with sweat as she looked up at him.

'I'm sorry,' she said again. 'I thought it was for the best. I should have stayed in Newlyn. I'm sorry.'

'My lord,' Chirk said. He was already in the boat, looking up with a bewildered, horrified expression on his face. Crow felt a rush of nameless emotion and climbed over the rail and into the yacht. He found Kitto lying cold in the bilges, wrapped in a sodden cloak. Crow crouched at his side, unable to comprehend that Hester had brought his brother back to him, that he had not been hanged in London after all, that God had seen fit to offer them both another chance. He felt for a pulse. It was there, but weak.

'I should have stayed in Newlyn.' Hester's voice shook as she shivered on the quay, looking at him with such dread that he felt cold inside, horrified that he had the power to make anyone so afraid. 'We got him out of London. I can't even begin to tell you how... He was alive in Newlyn. I don't think he's going to live.'

'It's my fault, not yours,' Crow said, 'the whole of it, Hester. John' – he spoke to Chirk – 'help me.' And with Hester at his side, Crow walked up to Castle Bryher carrying his brother, and praying to a God who could only really be malevolent that Kitto would survive.

83

'Thank God for a calm,' Hester said. 'If the fever breaks today, the *Sophie* might sail at the end of the week without it being murder. Not that I'm in any place to judge a murderer.'

'Me neither, miss. Keep still.' Their eyes met for a moment, and Catlin unwrapped the bandages from around Hester's oar-burned palms. They were healing well with no scent of decay, and no red, hot swelling. That she and Hester were both still alive was nothing short of a miracle. Catlin stirred the pot of honey and lavender poultice she had kept warm by the fire, dripping the warm liquid on to the wounds, binding them again in clean linen. The scent of honey and feverfew filled the stillroom, and Catlin pushed back her stool, going to the fireplace where she had the tisane resting to keep warm in the cup-holder on the firedog.

Hester waited until her back was turned before she spoke. 'I don't know what I'll do if Kitto dies, Cat. It'll be my fault – I ought never to have left the mainland with him.'

'With French soldiers everywhere? Nonsense. Sometimes there's no right choice.' Catlin turned, dipping her ladle into the copper pot, tipping the sweet-smelling draught into a tall flask she had always kept for the purpose of carrying medicines up and down the winding tower stairs. 'You take it. Can you manage with the bandages, do you think? Take the warm water and some fresh compresses, too. Wait – you need a basket or I'll be cleaning up the steps after you.'

Hester stood up, accepting the basket Catlin took from the pile she kept near the door, ready for picking herbs. Always a pretty girl, Hester was beautiful today, with one of Mrs Garrick's neat-woven shawls around her shoulders and her hair all loose: it floated around her like a halo. Catlin couldn't help smiling just to look at her, at the fact that they were both still breathing.

'I don't know how to carry on, Cat,' she said. Hester, who had endured so much; Hester who was victorious, a heroine. 'With him – with my husband. I find that I'm still so angry with him.' She looked down. 'I'm sorry. I haven't forgotten, you know, about Tom. At least Crow is here.'

Catlin didn't say that she'd seen in his lordship's eyes the look of a man who wished he were dead. She didn't say that poor Adam Evans had looked like that, years ago, and jumped off the Malledgan rock on a sunlit morning. He had been washed up on Tean, bloated and bleached by sun and sea, and they'd had to tell that new clergyman he'd slipped scraping limpets into a cook-pot for his mother, or Adam would have been buried beyond the churchyard. Despair, in the end, was the greatest sin. 'Aunt Evans said that he never touched the wine on his tray last night.' It was something. Perhaps it was crueller to give Hester hope.

Hester sighed. 'Probably because he's got a flask of brandy. I'd not be surprised if he had. It's my fault, Cat. I married him.'

'I don't see that you had much choice at the time,' Catlin told her. 'And to be fair, who wouldn't be taken in by a face like that? Listen to me: all you can do is keep going. One day at a time. Time heals, not all that thinking and moping. Time and doing, miss.'

84

Kitto had been put in the tower bedroom Hester had slept in as a child, with those blue velvet curtains drawn across a window that looked out towards the Atlantic. She remembered lying among her pillows as a little girl, listening to the whisper and rush of the ocean. She paused outside the door before going in, afraid of what she would find. Crow was sitting by the bed, leaning back in the armchair Uncle Evans and Jacca had moved upstairs. He wore no cravat and his shirt was unlaced, and even glimpsing the tattoos on his chest made her want to follow them with her fingertips, tracing their dark pattern all the way down his belly. He hadn't shaved, his jaw shadowed with black hair. He was asleep: he hadn't come to her bed at all since the day she'd rowed ashore, almost a week ago now, at the start of the flat calm, spending every moment at his brother's bedside. No one questioned his need to be there. Kitto lay with his face turned away from the window. The fevered flush had faded.

'Well?' She laid a hand on Kitto's forehead, cool at last, and looked up at Crow. She dared not hope.

'The fever broke at dawn.' Crow's voice cracked as he spoke

and she knew at once he'd thought Kitto was going to die at the height of the fever as their father had done – a sickness not dealt out by God's will alone but by an injury he had caused. Kitto was asleep and when she eased the old compress from beneath his ear it was clean for the first time, with no sign of the infected yellow pus. Catlin would skin her if she didn't prepare another, though: Catlin was convinced that some filthy miasma at Newgate prison had crept inside Kitto's ear, inflaming the injury Crow had done him. Everything must be kept clean. Hester folded a starched muslin cloth, wetting it from the can. The water was laced with lavender oil, filling the room with a warm, sleepy scent. Lifting Kitto's head, she slid the clout beneath his ear, straightening the folded cloth beneath it that kept his pillow dry. She dropped the old dressings into her basket and looked up to see Crow watching her from his armchair, the skin beneath his eyes bruised purple. He deserved to suffer for what he'd done. There was so much unsaid. She didn't know where to begin or what to do.

Crow leaned against the back of the chair; she watched the heavy rise and fall of his chest. 'Can't you let him rest?'

'Catlin says he must have this draught. You were lucky.' Hester's voice shook; she didn't know whether she was speaking to Kitto or to Crow. Crow watched her, unflinching. Even now the fever had broken, Kitto was not yet out of danger.

'I don't want any damned draught.' Kitto spoke without opening his eyes.

Crow leaned further back in the armchair, smiling a little. 'If Mrs Rescorla says you must, then you will. Believe me, you don't want to cross her, *boya*.'

Kitto woke fully at the sound of his brother's voice, turning to look at him. 'What are you doing here, Jack?'

Hester passed the warm flask to Crow. 'He's making sure you drink all of this, that's all.'

'Rather you than me, Kitto,' Crow said, and for a moment he looked so young. 'Get it over with is my advice.'

They both had to help him sit up and lean back against the pillow. Hester glanced at Crow and for a moment saw past his mask of assured authority; he was grief-stricken. Saying nothing, he reached out and laid a hand on Kitto's shoulder, and for a moment they simply looked at one another.

'Jack, I've done the most awful thing,' Kitto said, in Cornish. 'I put Hester in danger—'

'I know what she did.' Crow passed him the cup of tisane. He spoke with such a hard edge to his voice that Kitto flinched, and Crow reached for his lighting-flint. 'Don't look like that. The fault is all mine, every bit of it, and I can never repay Hester for what she did.'

She looked away. Was this the closest they would get to reconciliation?

'Be fair, it's not all your fault,' Kitto said. 'But when Allanby gets to the Azores with all the troops you'll buy me a commission into your regiment, won't you? I want to be in the Coldstreams.'

Crow laughed, lighting his cigarillo. 'Opportunistic wretch. My God, Kitto – no. Over my dead body will you live as I've done.'

Hester went out before Kitto could reply, leaving them alone. As she left, she heard Crow saying, '*Drog ew genam.*' *I'm sorry.* Half despairing and half amused, she wondered if it were possible for them to pass a day in each other's company without arguing. Even when each was attempting a heartfelt apology they couldn't help it. *Keep on doing,* Catlin had said, *be useful,* but she felt quite drained with exhaustion, unable to turn her mind to anything. The *Sophie* would be putting out from New Grimsby Sound before the end of the week, sailing on this rising breeze. She was a wife. She ought to be telling little Tilly what to pack for Crow, but somehow she couldn't bring herself to think of leaving Bryher for what might be the last time. Once they reached the Azores, Crow would go on to America with Wellington, and she would be left without him. She walked to the arched window, looking out at the gardens Papa had planted all those years ago, rows of lavender, rosemary and wild roses, and the bulk of Watch Hill rising up beyond, and a blue sky scudded with small white clouds that foretold a coming wind. In London, Louisa had said that granting Papa lordship over these islands had been an insult, but he'd loved Bryher and her people all the same; he'd made a mockery of the injury intended.

She had no notion of how long she'd been watching the garden and the sea before Crow came to stand behind her, resting his hands on the windowsill on either side of her own; she felt the heat of his body, the hard strength of his chest. She sensed a release of pressure somewhere deep within, and turned her head to the side, leaning on his arm. He held her to him, lifting her hair away from her neck, running his fingers through it so that her back arched, and she felt his lips brush the skin there.

'I don't know what to do,' he said. 'I was brought up always to know, and to make a good show of it if I didn't. But the longer I know you, the more I realise that you're so much wiser than me.'

'Indeed I am.' She turned to face him. 'For instance, I know what you must do now.'

He leaned down to kiss her forehead, and then her lips. 'And what is that?'

'Go to bed,' Hester said. 'Come to bed.'

85

High hawthorn hedges hemmed the lane, leaves silvered with beads of dew that shone like the paste pearls Arkwright had given Jenny on their wedding day. They rode only at night, passing burned-out villages and the rotting remains of hanged or bayoneted so-called rebels people were too afraid to bury. French troops swept through the countryside, destroying crops, pillaging whatever they chose and leaving those left behind to starve by the end of winter. It was as bad as the autumn and winter of '15, just after the invasion. It would never end, and Arkwright was weary of fear and killing.

'Wait here and keep out of the way.' He brought the carriage to a halt in the lane, laying one hand on young Jim's shoulder. He'd found the stable-lad alone in the stables at Lamorna House, left behind when all the mealy-mouthed indoor servants had run to save their own hides. He wasn't expecting Joséphine to move from the carriage. She was too afraid, as well she might be. What had he done, bringing her along? He was a bloody feckless fool, only he'd not been able to forget Jenny telling him so long ago that she loved him because he was a kind man in a cruel world. When Nessa took those snowdrops from him like he'd given her a dish of pearls, just for a moment he'd been glad to be alive, even half grateful to Crow, the bloody young fool, for saving his life at Vitoria. And who knew? Perhaps he'd a hand of cards to play yet. Joe Arkwright and Napoleon Bonaparte.

Through the mist, Arkwright saw a wooden gate. Twenty years before, he'd walked beneath that carved archway with Jenny on his arm, and the whole of Scarsdale waiting outside for the pair of them, willing to raise a glass to a young soldier with no family and no friends if he wed the Scarsdale lass on his arm. Just a rootless military man with an unmemorable face and a gift for foreign tongues, that's all. The churchyard was ringed with a low stone wall that bulged oddly in the corner furthest from the lych-gate, cradling what looked to be an unmarked grave, nothing but a pair of low, green mounds with no headstone.

'Do you want me to hold her for you, mister?' Jim was quick enough: he'd sensed what Arkwright had in mind, although he'd no idea of why. Without a word, Arkwright slid down from the saddle, handing Jim the reins, grateful that the boy looked away across the lane as he walked to the lych-gate. Arkwright went with a slow, heavy tread across the graveyard until he stood by the two small green mounds beside Jenny's parents' headstones. He'd not been able to afford one for his wife and son, had been away too long to arrange the particulars. What he wouldn't give to lie between them beneath that quiet earth. If only he could still be abed early one morning, with the fire's embers glowing like yellow cat's eyes in the dark and Jenny asleep on his arm and Petey between them, his dark head round as a cannonball, the three of them safe and together. He should never have left this place; he should have starved with his wife and child. Better that than marching away to fight a war that would only be lost, leaving them alone. With so many dead, how could there ever be a winner? There never would be.

86

Out of long habit, Maggie woke early. Young Ellen Barber had kindled her bedroom fire already; she was a good girl, not lazy, and the child had already thrown open one of the shutters to admit the morning light. It had been raining again, but the smell of wet earth and damp leaves was enough to overpower that of the open sewer in the street outside as it ran free, engorged and freshened with rainwater. The little attic bedchamber above the shop, though small, was neat and snug, with a green counterpane from the marketplace and a woollen rug by the hearth that Maggie had chosen herself in the draper's. Ellen had already made her own truckle bed, the thick linen sheet carefully folded back over a checked blanket. Between them, Maggie and Ellen kept the entire shop scrubbed with lye-soap, chasing away the dirt and filth left by a debt-ridden candlemaker. Stretching out in bed, Maggie allowed herself a small smile as she remembered the morning of her arrival in Lichfield, weeks before. Blinking owlishly, she had stepped down from the darkness of the overnight stagecoach on to the rain-soaked cobbles and into the courtyard of the Hare and Hounds. She'd come to Lichfield with little more than the money and the clothes she stood up in and – thanks to the gossip in St Giles – the knowledge that there was at least one prominent black family in town who she prayed might stand her friends in this new place where she was all alone. With soldiers all over London, there had been little enough time to consider anything else. The Barbers had indeed been kind: listening to her story with mingled astonishment and horror, they had insisted that she lodge with them until suitable premises could be found, and she had repaid their kindness by employing Ellen, the eldest daughter. It was satisfying, too, how quickly that sluttish Mrs Palmer had changed her tune. Maggie's red-faced landlady had swept from incredulous fury – *We do not commonly rent, madam, to persons of your order* – to staring in greedy disbelief at the thin roll of banknotes Maggie had held before her. Rent for a year paid in advance, a receipt carefully folded in the strongbox beneath her bed, and the roll of notes still too thick to curl her fingers around.

Maggie folded her nightgown, placing it neatly beneath her pillow, and stepped into her chemise and corset, lacing it with the practised ease of one who had always done so for herself. Dressed for the day, she went downstairs and found Ellen taking delivery of two rolls of striped muslin. Stacking them with the other bolts of bright fabric behind the counter, Maggie went to the worktop, surveying the selection of bonnets and hats still to be finished and set out on display. Mrs Winter would be calling for her daughter's this morning.

Maggie reached for the basket of wax cherries and silk rosettes. 'Set the kettle to boil, Ellen, there's a good girl, and we'll have some tea.' Grasping a silver pin between her lips, she threaded a needle, carefully stitching a cluster of red cherries to the straw poke bonnet, just where they would most precisely set off Miss Winter's dark curls.

87

Catlin went up on to the deck of the *Sophie*, her sails white as gull's wings in the light of a waxing moon. The crew were all island men and, knowing their mothers or grandmothers, she'd likely come to no harm among them. She couldn't sleep, not even rocked by the steady motion in the little cabin they'd found for her. Lord Lamorna was taking a watch for Captain Hicks, talking quietly to Wellington as he stood at the wheel. And so now Hester must be the one to watch as her husband marched away with the army. They were only resting in the Azores a fortnight or so before Wellington would set sail for America. Poor Het: anyone could tell that she'd come to love him, and he her, and now they must be parted. Catlin leaned on the guardrail, looking up at all those stars spread across the sky, so cold and so far away. They'd been at sea for a week now, with no sign yet of French ships in pursuit, but she couldn't really be at rest, and wondered if she ever would.

'You will be getting cold up here, Mrs Rescorla.'

She jumped a little. 'I'm perfectly comfortable, your grace.' It was funny to think he cared, especially when she thought back to their first meeting in Captain Harewood's study. He'd been on the verge of sending her to the Penzance poorhouse, and now here they both were. Fixing her gaze on the ocean heaving at the *Sophie*'s keel, Catlin held her breath as she listened to the hush of cloth as the Duke of Wellington stripped off his blue jacket, feeling the sudden warmth as he let it fall around her shoulders. For what seemed a long while, she had nothing to say and neither did he, standing a little apart from her as they both looked out to sea.

'I couldn't sleep, your grace.' Her voice sounded dry and cracked. 'When I think of what I've done, and all those who died.' On the day before they sailed, she had sat in a pew at All Saints for a whole afternoon, but God, it seemed, would be silent on this matter.

'You did what was necessary, Mrs Rescorla, as must we all. There come times when individual lives no longer matter, and one must think in larger terms.'

'Well, I'm not sorry we beat them in the end, your grace. I just hope that one morning I might wake up and not think of it.' She turned to look at him then, standing on the deck in his shirtsleeves. Wellington's expression didn't change.

'I don't doubt it, Mrs Rescorla.' And Catlin knew then that she'd never forget, just as he would not.

88

Early evening sunlight pooled on the dining-room table at the governor's mansion in Ponta Delgada, and Kitto looked down at the battery of cutlery spread out before him, unsure if he'd reach for the pear-knife at the end of supper without having made a fool of himself. It was the first time he'd ever led a woman in to dine: Governor Hallsworthy's widowed sister now sat at his right-hand side – her insignificance equal to his own, her black gown of heavy bombazine twill redolent of dusty lavender-bags. At his left, Hallsworthy's debutante daughter made little attempt to hide her disgust at being seated beside an earl's younger brother instead of the earl himself. Across the table, Crow gave Kitto a warning look. Crow might have scandalised half London before the war, but he was even more of a stickler for form than Papa had been. Magnificent in his scarlet coat, one might even feel proud of him again. No, Kitto's duties hadn't ended when he pulled out Mrs Boyd's gilded chair: he was meant to be conversing with her, too.

'Lady Hallsworthy tells me you're quite the amateur naturalist,' Mrs Boyd said. 'Will you have some of the omelette, dear? There is some wonderful birdlife in the mountains,

I'm told, although I believe it to be very cold, even at this time of year.'

Kitto replied as best he could, just grateful that he managed to drink the soup without spilling it down his jacket or choke on a bone from the dish of cod cheeks in cream sauce. Did they all know what a fool he'd been, that he'd allowed himself to be captured by the French and then rescued by a woman? He should have been protecting Hester, not the other way around.

'Isn't it an extraordinary story, Kitto?' Mrs Boyd persisted, spreading potted shrimp on to a slice of brown bread, and Kitto realised the topic of conversation had veered towards Hester and Catlin. Crow sat back and watched and Kitto wondered if he alone could see the anger in his brother's expression: Hester was not to be a subject for discussion.

'But do tell us how it happened, Duke,' Lady Hallsworthy said to Wellington. 'How did Lord Lamorna know where you had been imprisoned when the French were so secretive about it? We all fell for the story that you had been sent up to the Hebrides or the Orkneys or some such place, and I dare say even if there were some among us who questioned the story it would have been anyone's guess where you'd really been sent.'

Kitto's eyes watered as he sipped his wine: a heavy Spanish red that sent his head spinning.

'Oh, Harewood's housekeeper was a rather quick young woman, for a servant,' Wellington said. 'It was easy enough to explain the concept of a simple French numeric cipher to her, and her husband had died at Quatre Bras, so she was only too happy to thicken up the code by giving me a few lessons in Cornish.'

'How impossibly romantic!' Lady Hallsworthy gazed at Wellington with open admiration. 'I thought Cornish had died out as a language years ago.'

Crow had been watching his commander, half smiling. 'Oh no, my lady,' he said. 'Cornish is still quite widely spoken by servants. It was all,' he went on, 'a lot more simple than it might first appear.'

'We were lucky, of course, that the Occupation garrison on Bryher got the rough end of a fever,' Wellington remarked, allowing the footman to fill his glass. 'Once Lamorna arrived, we were quite easily able to overpower the few remaining French. A happy combination of circumstances – I should still be languishing in Captain Harewood's study, otherwise.'

Kitto looked down at his wine glass. No one would ever know what had really happened, and Wellington was no more than a liar, happy to take the credit for the bravery of Hester and Mrs Rescorla. Across the table Crow shook his head, and so Kitto said nothing, quite sure now that if there were any heroes left in the world, they were not those who would sit in the House of Lords every spring, if God willing the French were ever expelled from England.

'Well then, Lamorna, and what do you mean to do with this young gentleman? I take it you've some sort of plan for his advancement.'

Kitto looked up at the sound of Hallsworthy's booming voice to find everyone watching him save Crow, who merely toyed with the stem of his wine glass.

'University, Sir George, I should think,' Crow said idly. 'Florence, or perhaps the Low Countries. You remind me I must write.'

Wellington, helping himself to beef tapenade at the head of the table, speared an olive on his fork with savage precision. 'A damned waste if you ask me, Jack.'

Wellington might be a bloody liar but if he chose to take such a stand now, Kitto knew he'd never get another chance like it. 'I'd as lief join the army, your grace,' he said, and couldn't tell if

Crow was more annoyed about him speaking across the table than about the public challenge. Judging by the expression on his face, likely both in equal measure.

'We could do worse than to have the boy if he can learn to listen to orders,' Wellington remarked, sipping his wine.

'A remote possibility, your grace.' Crow pushed back his chair and stood up. 'Forgive me,' he said, 'I must attend my wife. It's extremely unlike her to be unwell.'

Kitto watched him go, quite unable to swallow, his mouth full of beef in congealing gravy. If Crow worried enough about Hester to leave the table, she must be in danger after all. Mrs Rescorla had insisted with devastating sarcasm that she was sure Wellington would survive an evening not sitting next to a lady: she had not seemed concerned, and surely Mrs Rescorla knew enough of sickness to be certain? And yet Papa's fever had started with a simple headache, just the night after he rode back into Brussels with Crow's battered, crushed body in a carriage. *I'm afraid he's not likely to live, old chap,* Papa had said. *In these times, we must all be courageous.* But in the end, it had been Crow who lived and Papa who died. Kitto drained his glass of wine when Lord Hallsworthy's butler closed the door after Crow, and an unsettling silence rippled throughout the room. Mrs Boyd ended it by turning to him and asking in her kindly way had he tried any of the pineapples from her brother-in-law's hothouses.

Sitting at his other side, Miss Hallsworthy gave him a sly smile. 'Perhaps a taste for the exotic is a Helford trait?'

Kitto felt the blood rush to his cheeks. Miss Hallsworthy had spoken in the sort of confiding tone that implied complicity on his part, as though he would agree, and make some equally tasteless remark in response. 'You must never have encountered my brother before we came to your father's house,' he said. 'He has a taste for quality only.'

89

Crow had set up the easel for her on the balcony overlooking the great bay; a breeze blew inland from the ocean, and a stray curl teased Hester's cheek as she set down her paintbrush, adding a touch of shadow to Papa's cheekbone, breathing in the scent of linseed oil and paint. She had captured the rich dark brown of his skin, so beautiful against the pale muslin cravat at his throat. Papa had always favoured a simple knot. He stared back at her from the painting with that calm, humorous expression she remembered so well, and it made her want to cry. She remembered the heat of his heart's blood puddling in her lap, holding him as he lay dying, in those moments before Marshal Ney's French soldiers had torn her away, dragging her to her feet. She remembered those last words Papa had spoken, in a language she did not understand: *Nne m o!* It could have meant anything, anything at all. Perhaps it had been the language he was born with, but he'd been enslaved, separated from his family, too deeply distressed ever to speak of the terrible loss, and she had no way of knowing, and no one to ask. Their own history had been stolen – and a crime of almost incomprehensible magnitude perpetrated against her father's people by those who had looked like her mother and, now, her husband. Where did she fit into it all? If she only understood the meaning of those words, perhaps she might know herself a little better.

She sat before the portrait of her father and spoke to him, still holding the brush. 'Hello, Papa. *Nne m o.*' He stared back at her, the expression in his deep brown eyes kindly as it had been in life, but unchanging. She would never hear his voice again. There was so much she wanted to ask him, and so much she wanted to tell him, but he was gone forever. Rising from her chair, Hester set down the brush and went to the balcony, looking up at the seagulls tossed on the wind like blossom shaken from a tree, and at the vast cloud-streaked dome of the sky. Was there a heaven above it? Would Papa know her again, when she died? Would God forgive her for the lives she had taken, even if only to preserve her own? She drank in the sea-air, almost dizzy with joy at being able to wake up every day to see the ocean. It was like being an eagle in a nest up here; beyond the stacks of red-tiled rooftops, green cliffs tumbled down to the vast sweep of the Atlantic, a bright, shocking blue that made her heart ache for the clear waters at home, for the silver carpet of sand running along Rushy Bay, for the green pools tucked in between the rocks by Church Quay. The sails of the fleet were like so many seabirds from this height, flashes of white against the blue, just like gulls resting on the waves. More than forty ships of the line, with more to come. Buonaparte would learn what it was to face the British navy again, and a gathered British army fresh from the Americas with two years of rest and relentless drilling behind it.

'Hester.'

She turned to find Crow standing in the doorway that led to the cool, shuttered darkness of their bedchamber; he was in full uniform, holding his shako, wearing the white breeches and scarlet jacket, the black cravat and the sash around his waist, the silver-gilt gorget glittering on his chest.

Hester smiled, getting to her feet. 'You do look very well, dressed like that.' She could not bear to think of him leaving, but he would be sailing with Wellington for America: there was an invasion to plan, a revolution, a rebellion – whatever one chose to call it, men would die. It had been decided between them that it was too dangerous for her to follow him to Charlestown. There were slave markets dotted up and down the coast. She might be safer in the Azores, but the absence would be longer. She might never see him again.

He took her hand in his, raising it to his lips. 'And you? Are you better this morning? I didn't want to wake you.'

'I'm well. I suppose I must have eaten something that didn't agree with me – perhaps it was the stewed octopus. A pretty poor show for an island girl.'

'Well, don't exert yourself. I shan't be long today.' He ran a hand through his hair in that now-familiar gesture of helplessness. 'Kitto won't be persuaded. He could be reading natural philosophy in Florence, but no, he must go and get shot in the mud instead. And now we meet the commissioning sergeant in less than half an hour.'

'He is your brother. Why should you expect Kitto to be any more persuadable than you are? And with me employing all the arts I know.' She stepped forwards, touching his face – he had been shaved that morning by his Spanish valet, and he took her hand again, kissing her fingertips. Why would he not see that he had paid his dues, done his duty, that he might walk away from this endless war and not be thought a coward? He looked at her with half-closed eyes, smiling. 'Stupid men,' she said, tracing a line along the arched wing of his cheekbone, 'stupid men with your stupid honour, and your duty.'

'We'll be back before supper. We dine with the governor

again, you know, if you're well enough.' He smiled at her again, his eyes dark with unspoken emotion; then he ducked his head in a bow, turned and went out.

Moments later, she heard voices and leaned over the balcony a little; Crow and Kitto had just emerged from the house into the winding, cobbled street below, their dark heads side by side, partially obscured by those constellations of blue-pink flowers she could only ever recall the Portuguese name for – *hortênsia* – Papa would have liked those; he would have remembered the name in English and Latin. They were arguing about something, she couldn't quite make out what, and they walked off down the street together, Kitto crying out in protest at some remark of his brother's and carelessly shoving Crow's arm; she smiled, watching them go. It wouldn't be many days now until the fleet left for Charlestown, where Admiral Gunning was busy overseeing the construction of new ships of the line. The navy was rising again just like the army: Papa would have liked that. He would have liked those little sweet-scented oranges, too, that were piled up in the marketplaces, still wearing their waxy green leaves. She sat down again and poured coffee from the silver pot on the marble-topped table, adding milk from a rose-patterned jug. She leaned back on the chair, sun-warmed wood heating her skin through the thin muslin of her gown, the coffee-cup warm in her hands, paper-thin bone china and rich thick coffee swimming with good milk.

'Did you want the oranges now?'

Hester turned, smiling. Catlin held a bowl, her hair combed back beneath a new white cap. 'Oh, sit down, Cat, do.' It'd never be the same again; they would never run together up the dunes beyond the sands at Popplestones or paddle ankle-deep in the shallows, watching out across New Grimsby Sound for sight of the mail-boat. They were more than mistress and servant, though. And this time, Catlin sat in the chair beside her, letting out a sigh, and what had led to this unravelling within her, as if Catlin Rescorla were in love again?

'Just for a moment, then.' Catlin sighed, watching the sails in the harbour, too. 'I hope there are no French spies here, that's all.'

'There are certain to be some, but Allanby has so many men.'

'If he'd had them at Waterloo, we wouldn't have lost. Drink your coffee before it gets cold.'

There was no arguing with that. Hester lifted the cup to her lips, but the coffee was bitter and nausea rushed up her throat. The little wrought-iron table slipped away as she reached for it, her cup teetering on the edge, and the world spun as though she were falling from a great height: ocean, sky, rooftops, balcony, oranges, all a whirl. Crow. She wanted Crow, and he was going away. Once they sailed, she wouldn't see him again, not for years. Catlin reached out to catch the cup.

'That was quick.' Hester breathed with slow, deliberate care. 'The milk has gone over. It's so hot here, isn't it?' She didn't want Catlin to think she blamed her: God alone knows how they contrived to keep anything fresh in this heat, which of course was why the thought of her bread and butter waiting on the green plate on the shaded kitchen windowsill sent her stomach heaving.

'It's fresh today; I had it in my tea. Good fresh milk.' Catlin watched as though she knew something Hester didn't, and she was smiling, but there was the sadness, too, and what could it mean?

'Tell me the truth, Cat. Is it as it was with Cousin Jane, when you knew she had the black jaundice? Am I going to die?'

And Catlin picked up her bowl of oranges. 'It's life, not death, that we're dealing with, Het.'

Hester stared at her, pressing one hand to her mouth. Her fingers smelled of coffee, and she gagged again, leaning back in the chair with her eyes closed.

'Had you not guessed, you mazey-headed girl?' Catlin said, matter-of-fact. 'Sick as a cat on and off for days. We've been here six weeks and you haven't bled. When was the last time?'

Hester stared out at the glittering ocean, at the pale sails of the fleet. 'I can't remember. I've – I've been rather busy.'

Catlin gave her a no-nonsense look. 'Well, give it a few months and you'll be more so.'

And Hester looked up at the sky, holding one hand now to the soft warmth of her belly. By the time she bore Crow's child, he would be long gone.

90

Light lanced in through one of the high, narrow windows in the small garrison overlooking the wide sweep of the harbour; Crow stood with Kitto before the commissioning sergeant's desk.

'Ready to sign, your honour?' The sergeant looked up with a smile.

At Crow's side, Kitto said nothing but only took up the pen and wrote his name, his handwriting always a surprise, so cautiously tidy.

'Let me be the first to congratulate you.'

Kitto smiled and shook the sergeant's hand, too absurdly happy to speak, and the sergeant turned to Crow. 'A fine day for your family, my lord.' Kitto turned to look at him then, with a need for approval that was so flagrant and so richly undeserved that Crow reached for his cigarillo-case and lit one from the candle guttering on the sergeant's desk.

'A fine day indeed, sergeant.' He blew out a thin stream of smoke; if he could control the velocity of the smoke he could control his own life and the lives of those he loved. He must just keep going, one step after another. 'If you can get him to listen to a word you say.'

'I should think he will listen very well to Colonel Bannister. Will you be rejoining the regiment, your honour, or do you remain with the Duke?'

'He has a use for me yet, it seems.' Crow turned to Kitto. 'Come on, then. We must visit the quartermaster and get your kit. And the rest of mine, for that matter.' He walked out side by side with his brother, but when Kitto turned to ask him about reporting at the parade ground near the orange grove in the hills behind the town, all Crow saw was a young Belgian soldier with his throat cut, black blood staining the front of his shirt.

'Jack?' Kitto said, and the Belgian soldier disappeared, flickering out of existence as if he had never been – only he had; he had lived, he had been born to a mother and died at Crow's hands. 'What did I do wrong?' Kitto said. Crow did not know what he dreaded more, hearing of Kitto's death – musket-ball, cannonball, his flesh laid open by a sabre – or how profoundly it might unravel the boy to be made into a killer himself. Perhaps he would be like Arkwright, able to live with it. He felt Arkwright's absence so acutely that it was almost a presence, just as men said they longed to scratch between the toes of a long-amputated foot, the ghost of what had once been.

'Nothing,' Crow told him, finishing the cigarillo. 'You did very well. Come, we should drink to this.' Taking his brother by the elbow, he led him down a winding side-alley to the row of wholly disreputable taverns that looked out across the glittering bay, taking care not to look too closely at the shadows. Frequented by the usual fishermen as well as a gathering force of jack tars and shabby, dishevelled Englishmen flocking to Wellington's side so that they might call themselves soldiers again, the taverns were full even so early in the morning, the air thick with the scent of rum, and the smell of it swept thirteen years from Crow's life, and he closed his eyes for a moment, sure that when he opened them again he would be on the deck of the *Belle* with John Harewood at his side, showing him how to use a sextant. Mechanically, Crow greeted those men who apparently knew him; among them, he seemed to see the faces of those he knew were long gone – friends lost at Waterloo and in the bloody years running up to it; Harewood himself; Grant. Without Arkwright, he felt so curiously vulnerable and unprotected despite what Arkwright and Castle had done between them to send Kitto to the gallows. He himself was more to blame than anyone else, Arkwright included. Outside once more, he raised the glass to his lips, but after one burning sip of rum, he drank no more. Kitto's eyes were watering at the taste, and Crow found himself smiling.

'Good thing you've just joined the army, not the navy.'

Kitto laughed and Crow remembered when he had drunk all night, looking for him all over London, and how the following morning it had seemed only reasonable that he should knock his own brother to the ground before a house full of servants. Arkwright had known him only too well. That sort of oblivion offered temptation he knew he must resist, and he set down his own glass on the low wall separating the front yard of the tavern from the street.

'*Lowr*,' he said. *Enough*. 'Do you know what? I find I've little enough taste for rum this morning myself. Come, there are plenty of birds up in the mountains. We'd do better to practise your aim with a musket.'

'It's not so bad already, you know.'

'It needs to be better.'

Kitto turned to him then, now quite serious as they passed a street-trader selling oranges. 'Jack,' he said. 'How will

I not run away, in battle? I'm not such a fool as to think it won't be terrifying.'

Jesus Christ. 'You know, we face it as women must face childbed. Some live through it, some won't. Each time, it's a reckoning. It's in God's hands.'

'Like Mama didn't live after I was born.'

She'd bled to death. When they'd taken him in to bid her farewell, the basket of sodden sheets left outside the bedchamber door had crawled with glossy, blue-black flies. 'Yes,' Crow said. 'Like that, I suppose.'

Kitto shook his head. 'But it's God's will alone for women when a baby comes. They don't have to choose how it will end. They can only wait. On the battlefield, we have to decide – to choose whether to run away or to charge and fight. And I think that if I ran away, it would be worse than death, but I'm not sure I'll be able to stop myself.'

Crow slung one arm across his shoulder; he remembered when Kitto had been a red-faced scrap of humanity no longer than his own forearm, and how much he'd wanted to hate him, but had not been able to. 'Well, women have so little choice about anything else, it would be unfair if they had to choose whether to face death or not. As men, we are masters of our own fate – is it not fair that we must sometimes be forced to choose how we die?'

'That's true. Women should be protected from such a choice. I don't know how I'll make it. What if I do run away, Jack?'

'Listen, you won't. It's like teaching a dog to put up pheasants instead of chasing them. The teaching takes over. It's hard to explain, but when there are men on either side of you, and you're in formation, it's easier to run into whatever you're facing, or to keep firing.' Crow prayed to God that he was right, and that Kitto would not be one of those who rushed to retreat. 'You're a bloody heedless young fool, anyway. Colonel

Bannister will have a battle on his hands to stop you going in headlong. Now come on, it's a long walk up into those mountains, and we must be back before nightfall.'

'All right,' Kitto said, with complete and utter trust, and Crow was half appalled that his own words inspired such airy confidence.

'Can you not force a smile?' Hester whispered into Crow's ear as they stood together at Governor Hallsworthy's reception. At least she was better today: it worried him so much when she looked so haggard, and it was hard to believe Catlin when she said there was nothing at all the matter with her.

'Is it so obvious?' Crow watched his brother across the room; Kitto was laughing with Hallsworthy and a fair-haired young girl whose mother watched him with an over-eager smile. God, he was almost at the age where he'd have to be warned about matchmaking mothers. Crow felt so old. Over the years, Crow had noticed that some young recruits looked even more youthful in uniform, but it wasn't so with Kitto. Dressed in the scarlet jacket of the Coldstream Regiment, with the black cravat at his throat, he was no longer a child. From the back, the boy might have been any other Coldstreamer going to join his battalion. When he turned, though, it was impossible to ignore the fact that it was Kitto now in uniform with a glass of champagne in his hand, gladly going off to fight in another war, just as Crow himself had gladly gone more than ten years before.

Hester took his hand. 'Yes, it's amazingly obvious that you're devastated. I don't know how you ever won at cards.'

'He's alive. We're all alive. It should feel like a victory,' Crow said; even Hester couldn't tease him out of this. 'Why does it not?'

Hester only shook her head; sensing his need to drink, she raised his hand to her lips. There was no victory: there never could be.

'It's nothing but play.' He repeated what Arkwright had once told him, long ago, watching his brother talking to Wellington and so impossibly proud that Crow wanted to shake him. 'It's a game of chance for high stakes, and none of the players takes any of the risk. We're nothing but chess pieces, Het.'

Kitto turned and smiled across the room at them both, and it was all Crow could do to stand still, to restrain himself from demanding before all these people that Kitto immediately took off that regimental jacket and applied himself to study, to gaming or whoring – to anything other than war. But the boy had forgiven him one unforgivable act already. All he could do was watch him go. Crow raised Hester's fingers to his own lips. Together, they walked out of the wide doors flung open on to the balcony overlooking a small orchard thick with lemon-blossom, and then the ocean.

'So war is nothing but chess pieces and futility?' Hester said. 'Is that why you choose to go?' Anger lent such irresistible animation to her.

'No, I go because it's still my duty.'

'It is not! You have other duties. You have Nansmornow. When the French are gone, they'll need you more than ever. There is a whole country to rebuild.'

She was right, of course – she always was – but what she did not understand was that he couldn't turn back now.

'Listen,' Hester said, fierce as she turned to face him. He couldn't help resting one hand on the soft curve of her shoulder, letting his thumb graze her neck. He didn't know how he would bear leaving her. 'Listen,' she went on. 'If you stay here, no one will think you were afraid to go.' She reached up, cupping the back of his head in one hand, and her touch sent a blaze of heat through him. 'Don't you see? Sometimes, it is more courageous to walk away. Jack, listen to me—' She broke off. It was the first time she had ever called him by his Christian name, and he saw in her eyes that it made her think of Louisa, too. 'Really listen. You don't need to prove to anyone that you're not afraid to go, Jack Helford.'

She had touched with such sure precision on the truth that he flinched. How dared she? 'It is not your business to order my life.' He regretted the words the instant he spoke them.

'It's yours, you hard-headed fool! Jack—' She broke off. 'If you go to war again, it will never get better, don't you understand? Those things you see and the dreams you have will consume you. Even if you never drink another drop you'll do it again, what you did to Kitto. You'll do it to him, to me. Or to our child.'

Our child. He opened his mouth to speak but could not.

Hester nodded. 'Yes, Crow,' she said, 'we'll have battles enough of our own to fight. Now, will you still go to war?'

'No.' He smiled, despite the terror, joy and grief. 'No, Het. I'll stay with you.' He leaned down so that their foreheads rested together, her hands in his. Wherever she went, he would go too.

AN AHISTORICAL NOTE

False Lights is a novel about what might have been, and Castle Bryher exists only in the form of odd, scattered mentions in historical records. It may well never have existed at all. But if you leave mainland Cornwall and cross thirty miles of open water, take a boat from St Mary's to Bryher and walk through the scattering of houses, boatsheds and farm buildings known as the town, and climb all the way up to the high ground, you will see Cromwell's Tower on the island of Tresco. From a certain angle, this fortification looks as if it might actually sit on top of Hangman's Island, a rocky outcrop accessible from Kitchen Porth beach on Bryher at low tide. And, of course, there is Waterloo itself, and the outcome of the battle. Wellington himself said, 'It has been a damned nice thing. The nearest run thing you ever saw in your life', and you don't have to read much about the battle before it becomes extremely clear that he was right. It all could have been so different. I hope that serious historians will excuse me for resurrecting Joséphine Bonaparte, who in actual fact had died in 1814. It is sometimes said that Napoleon believed she was his lucky star, so perhaps she had to live in order for history to be different, despite their divorce.

The Cornish language, if not entirely dead by this time, was doubtless in very deep decline with no fluent speakers that we know of. This is a trend that has now, thankfully, been reversed, and there are many fluent Cornish speakers today. Most of the characters in this book are, of course, entirely fictional, but some – though still figments of my imagination – were inspired by real historical figures: Hester by Dido Elizabeth Belle, her father by Captain John Perkins, and Crow by various personalities who lived through the Peninsular War and Waterloo itself.

ACKNOWLEDGEMENTS

I am indebted to my agent, Catherine Clarke, without whom *False Lights* would never have existed, and to my editor Rosie de Courcy, who brought this story into the light of day, and to my father-in-law, Sam Llewellyn, who for many years listened patiently to my ramblings about writing a Regency novel with a difference. It takes a team to make a book and lead it out into the world, and I am so grateful to everyone at Head of Zeus who has lent their expertise to this story – Amanda Ridout, Sophie Robinson, Richenda Todd, Clémence Jacquinet, Suzanne Sangster and the designer, Anna Morrison, are all part of a highly skilled operation.

I owe a great debt to those who helped to make this story better by reading it and offering painstaking, thoughtful suggestions, and to those who spoke to me about their experiences. Any errors are entirely my fault, and I hope to learn from mistakes that I have made. Heartfelt thanks are due to all at Waterloo Uncovered for the unparalleled insight into warfare and the battlefield itself, particularly Dr Stuart Eve (to whom I owe many drinks), Mark Evans, David Ulke, Dr Tony Pollard and Alasdair White. I am sincerely grateful to Justina Ireland

and Stephenjohn Holgate for their thoughtful reading and comments on race and identity, to Joanne Penn for her valuable contribution at an early stage, to Yvonne Chioma Mbanefo for her assistance with the Igbo language, to the Cornish language team at Cornwall County Council – Dan Prohaska and Mark Trevethan – and to Andrew Roberts for his expert input about the progress of battle at Waterloo. My sincere thanks are also due to Sarah and Sheridan Swinson for all their support. And, last but not least, thank you to my friends Rhian Ivory and Liz Hyder for reading the book as a work in progress – you made me feel it was all going to be possible.